TOXIC

MAFIA WARS NEW YORK - BOOK ONE

MAGGIE COLE

PULSE PRESS INC

PROLOGUE

Bridget O'Connor

24 Years Ago

"Let's play spin the bottle!" my best friend Cara exclaims, beaming at me like it's the best idea in the world, then clinking her tumbler of whiskey against mine.

It's my sweet sixteen party. My father finally agreed to let me scoot out of the main event with the rest of my friends and promised me he'd leave us alone. It wasn't hard to convince him once our clan and the Marinos showed up. He has so many powerful men around him, along with single women fighting for his attention, that he won't lack anything in the entertainment department all night.

My mother left us years ago. She decided she couldn't handle the mafia life and tried to take my brothers and me with her,

1

but my father stopped her. He told her if she wanted to go, she could, but we were staying with him where we belonged. She chose her freedom.

Apparently, my four brothers and I aren't that important to her. Since then, all we get is a phone call every Christmas. My older brothers, Aidan and Brody, are like me. We barely speak to my mother for more than a minute. My youngest brothers, Devin and Tynan, used to talk to her longer. It pained me, watching them. Hope would light in their eyes, and her promise to come see us soon always fell flat. Now, no one puts any stock in her word. She makes no effort to travel from California to see us. And ever since my father divorced my mother, he's become the top bachelor to snag.

Cara smirks. "Bridget?"

A butterfly spreads its wings so large in my gut, I grab the bar counter to hold myself up. My father had his staff remove all the liquor before the party started, but it was pointless. I attend the most expensive private high school in New York City. Most of my friends—both girls and guys— have Bailey's Irish Cream in their morning coffee and vodka for lunch. It's not a drink of choice, but it doesn't smell like whiskey or other alcohol. And the teachers might know what's going on, but they act like they don't. I suppose it's easier for them since most of my friends' parents take their word over any authority figure.

So even though my father had the alcohol removed and replaced with soda and other drinks he deemed safe, the bar is now covered in everything you can imagine.

Cara's eyes dart to the Marino twins, and my cheeks instantly flush. I've known Dante and Gianni forever. I'm a sophomore, and they're seniors. Their brother, Massimo, is a freshman, and he's across the room, but I barely notice him.

Dante and Gianni are a different story. They're identical twins and the epitome of tall, dark, and handsome. Their sculpted cheekbones are every girl's fantasy. Their intense, brooding eyes can pin you wherever you are and make it feel like time is standing still. They tower over me, and both are boxers. Dante is more serious about it than Gianni, but their muscles are just as identical as their faces.

Sometimes, I can't tell who's who until they speak. But I've had so many long conversations with Dante, it doesn't take more than a few words before I know if it's him or Gianni.

One day, Dante gave me a cell phone. My father didn't see the need for me to have one and I didn't care. But Dante did. He surprised me with it and showed me how to text. That night, and every night after, we spent hours sending messages until one of us fell asleep.

The twins are the most popular guys in our school, and it's not a secret they change places at times, whether it's for a test or even with girls. The unsuspecting victim should be upset, but it's almost become a rite of passage at our school. If you've made out or gone all the way with the Marino twins, versus just one of them, it's an instant spot in the cool girls' club. And some of the girls are the ones spreading the gossip before Dante or Gianni even have a chance.

One look at them creates flutters in my stomach that make me dizzy. If I find out it's Gianni I'm looking at, then the flutters die. But never with Dante. With him, they only burn hotter.

It wasn't always this way though. It only started happening this past year. I've known them my entire life. Almost every holiday or special event is at their house or ours. We've always hung out, but I never thought about it until one day, the way Dante looked at me made my heart stammer. After that, I've been crushing hard. I thought it was all one-sided, and his extra attention was me wishing for more, until about a month ago.

It was a typical monthly party at his father, Angelo's, house. Dante and Gianni had turned eighteen, and Angelo gave them their own wings at the Marino compound. All of us kids went into Gianni's side of the house, which also had a brand-new theater screen.

Instead of fancy theater seating, Gianni chose couches and ottomans. Angelo somehow snagged a copy of the latest action movie that was still in the theater, and we all got comfy with popcorn, alcohol, and blankets.

Dante sat next to me, and Gianni was on the other side. It wasn't out of the ordinary. Dante and I have always had a closer friendship, and the twins are never far from the other. It wasn't the first time I sat between them, but when Dante tossed a blanket over the two of us, my skin buzzed as if it knew something was going to happen. Then he stretched his long legs on the ottoman.

"Put your feet up and get comfy, Bridge," he ordered.

I did it, and he handed me a beer.

The movie had just gotten past the first scene when his knuckles slid down the side of my leg. I was wearing shorts, and his touch on my bare skin made me hold my breath.

4

I froze, wondering if it was a mistake, staring at the screen and not comprehending one word. Then he slid his hand between my thighs, and my insides liquefied. I swallowed hard. Then, keeping my head still, I used my peripheral vision to peek at him.

He tossed popcorn in his mouth and took a swig of beer, like nothing was going on. At the same time, the tips of his long fingers slid under my cut-off denim.

No boy had ever gotten so close to my most intimate region, and the way my pussy ached for him to touch it surprised me.

Then he did it.

He slid his hand through my panties, a finger up my entrance, and rubbed my clit with this thumb.

I shuddered on the spot. Heat overwhelmed me so intensely, I knew my face had to be the color of a tomato.

Gianni leaned close to me and scanned my face, smirking. "You all right?"

It was another reminder of the sixth sense he and Dante had. It made the fire in my cheeks burn hotter. I elbowed him and hissed, "Shut up. I'm watching the movie."

"Sure you are." He put his hand under the blanket and touched my thigh, but I slapped it off me.

"Stop it," I whispered.

More arrogance flashed on his face until Dante leaned over my breasts while shoving his finger deeper in me and curling it. He quietly muttered, "Don't touch her."

The twins exchanged a look. I don't know what it meant, but they did. They could always have silent conversations. That one look made Gianni slide his arm around Cara and say something that made her giggle.

"Shut up," my brother Aidan barked, throwing popcorn at us before returning his attention to the movie.

Dante's thumb moved quicker, and his hot breath slid across my chest, thanks to my tank top. Tingles assaulted me everywhere, and he murmured in my ear, "Have a drink."

I turned toward him, my mouth an inch from his lips, adrenaline pooling in my cells, and my heart beating so fast, I was sure everyone in the room could hear it.

His mouth curved into so much arrogance, it caught me off guard. He pinned his dark gaze on me, and I couldn't look away. Then, everything exploded around me, as if he knew what was about to happen. My eyes rolled and I whimpered. As much as I tried not to make a sound, I couldn't help it. Thankfully, besides Dante, I think only Gianni and Cara heard it, because my brothers, their girlfriends, and the rest of the Marino kids never bothered to look our way.

Fire sparked in those dark eyes. He removed his hand from my body then shoved his fingers in his mouth, arching his eyebrows in a smirk, before returning to the movie.

I was hardly breathing again before his fingers were crawling back up my thigh, and he was starting all over.

I lost track of how many times he made me come. When the movie was over, he went to play pool with the others and ignored me the rest of the night.

That was a month ago. Since then, he's acted like nothing happened, having conversations with me like we always have.

Not once has he touched me or looked at me the way he did that night.

All I think about is him.

His eyes.

His cheekbones.

His cocky lips I want on mine, as well as places no other boy has ever touched.

And something about the way his body towers over me, as if he could make me his and protect me from the world, makes my insides throb. Not that I have anyone to worry about. My father is the head of the Irish clan in New York, and even I'm not naive enough not to know what that means.

No one will ever get close enough to hurt me. My father would kill anyone, and everyone knows it. But still, I like thinking about being Dante's and him protecting me.

Cara is the only person who knows what happened, unless Dante told anyone. Well, I'm sure Gianni knows something went on. And Cara slept with Gianni that night. Ever since, she's been trying to play it cool but is dying for a replay.

All day leading up to my party, I wondered if tonight would be the night Dante would pay attention to me again. Cara's game suggestion makes me nervous. What are the chances Dante will end up with me and not someone else? When I don't answer her, she shouts, "Who wants to play spin the bottle?"

The room turns silent, and I refrain from looking at Dante, yet I feel his eyes on me.

It's Gianni who answers, "I'm down."

"Siblings are off-limits. I'm not touching my sister," Aidan says.

"Eww. Yuck," I state, horrified at the thought.

"Hey, you know what happened at Matt's party," he replies.

My stomach flips. This is how fucked up the kids at my school are. Matt and his sister Lana had a party last weekend. Matt spun the bottle, and when it stopped, Lana was in front of it. No one trusted them to do anything in the closet, so they pressured them to kiss in front of everyone, and instead of saying no, they gave in to the pressure and played tongue tag for the entire fifteen minutes.

"Agreed. I'll go first," Dante states and grabs an unopened bottle of wine he snagged from his father's party. He sits on the floor, and everyone follows.

Flutters fill my gut, and when he spins the bottle, I pray it stops on me.

Around and around it goes, first fast, then slower and slower. I don't take my eyes off it, and the room is entirely silent, with the only sound being the glass on the carpet.

When it stops, my heart does, too. My mouth turns dry, and I slowly lift my eyes to Dante.

He smirks. "Well, what are you waiting for, Bridge? Get your ass in the closet."

"Shit. Not my sister," Aidan mutters.

8

Gianni scoffs and challenges, "Rules are rules. You want to break them? If so, we can eliminate the sibling one, too."

Aidan rises. "Whatever. I need another drink." He storms off to the bar.

Dante's expression stays neutral. He rises and holds his hand out to help me off the floor.

My pulse shoots through the ceiling. I take his hand and he tugs me up then leads me to the closet. The thick, eight-foot, mahogany door clicks shut, and everything turns dark.

His body heat penetrates my skin. I feel it before his hands slide over my cheeks and he tilts my head up. His hot breath merges with mine, and every atom in my body lights up.

"Have you missed me?" he softly asks, his thumbs caressing my cheeks.

Dropping my guard, I close my eyes and admit, "Yes."

He steps closer until I'm against the wall, and his hard flesh is against mine. "Did you think about my hands on you again?"

I swallow hard. "Yes."

"Maybe we should stop pretending this is something it's not then." He kisses my forehead then under my eyes and my nose.

I gasp and manage to ask, "What do you mean?"

"I like you. I always have. And I think you like me. So maybe I should take you on a date, away from all these cocksuckers. Just you and me. What do you say, Bridge?"

His thumb brushes my bottom lip, and I shiver. "Okay."

"Happy birthday, Bridge," he murmurs. Then his hot breath is all over me. His tongue is in my mouth, flicking against mine like there's no tomorrow, as if I'm his everything—the only thing he could ever want.

My knees buckle, and he presses closer, pinning me between himself and the wall.

I was so wrong about what it would be like to kiss Dante Marino. I thought it would be good. I assumed he would know what he was doing, and that I would like it.

I never imagined my body would hum against his, or the rest of the world would disappear, or every single touch he gave me would make me feel things I never felt before.

I didn't know I would melt into him as if my body belonged with his—as if it *were* his.

Before I know it, there's a knock on the door and it flies open, reminding me we aren't alone. My eyes adjust to catch Dante's wink then he steps back and strolls out of the closet.

My brother's voice calls out, "Don't fucking say a word about whatever you just did with my sister."

The room erupts in heckles, and I catch my breath.

He's going to take me out.

Dante Marino is finally going to take me out.

When I step out of the closet, blood drains from my head to my toes. My heart drops to my stomach.

What is she doing here? This is my party. I didn't invite her.

Lisa, the head of the cheerleading squad and homecoming queen, is drunk and throws her arms around Dante. It's a known fact she slept with Gianni last week.

My stomach flips. I want to yell at her to get off him. I want to scream at him to push her aside.

But he doesn't.

She grabs his crotch and slurs something about a blowjob.

Gianni grunts. "Your turn, bro." He nods to the side room, and I suddenly feel sick.

Don't do it. Don't go, I silently plead.

There's a brief moment of hesitation, and I think Dante isn't going to go. My hope explodes all around me, but then my heart does.

Gianni steps forward so Lisa's squished between him and his brother. He tugs Lisa's hair back, causing her chest to press into Dante, and her mouth gasps in an O. He scans her face and says, "Be a good girl and make sure you swallow for him, all right?"

Her face flushes and she giggles. I want to die on the spot.

No, no, no! This can't be happening.

He won't do it. He won't after he just confessed he likes me and wants to take me out.

Gianni pats her ass and points toward the door. "You got ten minutes. Then Cara and I get the room."

Dante's shoulders flex, and he hesitates again.

Gianni releases Lisa and asks, "What's wrong? Why aren't you going?"

Dante glances at Lisa. "Don't waste my time if you're going to spit all over me."

She giggles again and tugs on his hand, leading him to the other room.

I think I might die. I want to crawl in a hole and never come out. When they come back into the room after ten minutes, Dante ignores me.

Still, I hold on to hope that he'll still call me. It makes me hate myself even more. Every night, I wait for his text messages like an idiot. Not once does he ever message me.

Then I get a boyfriend.

The first time I bring him to a party at his parents', Dante is suddenly on top of me like a fly in honey, ignoring his girlfriend, who gets pissed along with my boyfriend. That night he texts me.

Dante: *What are you doing with that loser?*

Me: *What are you talking about? He's not a loser.*

Dante: *You can do a lot better.*

Me: *Not really your business.*

Dante: *Why did you stop coming to my fights?*

My chest tightens.

Me: *Why did you let Lisa suck you off after telling me you wanted to take me out?*

Dante: *I'm a dude. We do stupid shit. Are you going to hold it against me forever?*

My heart races faster.

Dante: *If it makes you feel better, I was only hard because I couldn't stop thinking about you.*

I take several large breaths, not knowing how to respond and reprimanding myself that his statement gives me a twinge of happiness.

Dante: *Break up with him. Come to my fight this weekend. We'll hang out after.*

Several minutes pass as I contemplate whether I should do it or not.

Dante: *Bridge, I miss you. I'm sorry.*

Me: *Okay. I'll come.*

Dante: *Make sure you break up with him. I mean it. He's not good enough for you.*

I don't sleep at all that night. I do what he says, unable to stop myself from wanting him. When the weekend comes, I go to his fight.

He wins. His brothers, along with an entourage of girls, are waiting for him when he comes out of the locker room. They rush up to him, and his eyes meet mine.

"Give me a minute," he says.

My heart drops as he approaches me. I see it in his expression before he leans down and hugs me. "Thanks for coming."

I force myself to reply, "Sure. Congrats."

He smiles, and guilt is all over his face.

"We aren't hanging out, are we?" I ask.

"Something has come up. Can I take a rain check?"

I glance at the girls with his brothers, trying not to cry. I straighten my shoulders. "Sure. No problem."

"Thanks." He gives me another hug, and I feel sick.

For the next few years, I hang on to every twisted part of me that still wants him as mine. Even though he graduates, I still see him at least once a month at parties.

Nothing ever changes. He, Gianni, and Massimo always have girls hanging on them anytime I see them. From time to time, Dante will catch me gazing at him. There are always these moments, a brief encounter where he'll stare at me, giving me his smoldering look, reminding me how we used to be friends and about his broken promises.

When my father insists I get a business degree, I decide the only way I'll escape Dante is to leave town. There's only one place my father will let me go, and that's Chicago because he has an alliance with the O'Malleys. He claims they'll watch over me.

I don't even care where it is as long as it's out of New York and somewhere far away from Dante.

There's nothing I will ever get from him. Holding on to any notion we'll ever be together is setting myself up for a lifetime of unhappiness. I need to forget everything about Dante Marino, except one thing.

He's toxic.

$\mathcal{MC}$

Dante

Four Months Later

"BRIDGET'S IN TOWN?" I ASK MY PAPÀ, SURPRISED. I SHOULDN'T be. It's a few days before Christmas, but she didn't come home for Thanksgiving. Tully claimed she wanted to study for her upcoming exams, but I wasn't buying it.

She hates me.

The moment I found out she was going to Chicago, I texted her, but she didn't reply. I called her, but she didn't answer or return my calls.

Then she left New York without a goodbye or even a "fuck you."

In the last four months, I've drunk dialed her in the middle of the night too many times to count. I've texted her stupid shit I cringe about the next day. Not once has she responded. It's like I no longer exist.

"Yes. Tully said she arrived yesterday," Papà informs me.

Gianni groans. "Jesus. Tell me you aren't going to drool over Bridget all night."

"Shut the fuck up," I bark. "We're friends. You know this."

"Friends?" His arrogant expression makes my gut twist. Gianni's as big of a dick as I am, maybe bigger. But one thing he knows is how to be is a friend, and there's no denying I didn't treat Bridget like a friend.

"If you two don't have any questions for me, take your conversation out of here," my father orders, but his dark eyes sear into mine, warning me without saying anything further. It's not the first time Bridget has come into the conversation, and he only had to warn me once. I denied my feelings toward her, but Papà isn't stupid. He saw it before Gianni said anything. It was the night before I fingered her in the movie theater. He heard Gianni warning me not to mess with Bridget, and it was all it took for my father to give me a stern lecture about showing Bridget respect.

Something about that conversation made me push the limit. I was already trying to figure out how to cross the line from the friend zone. My papà's words should have stopped me, but all they did was make me want to prove to myself I could have her.

Watching Bridget's eyes roll and listening to her tiny whimper fascinated me. Everyone around us, and who we were, disappeared. All it did was kick my desire for her into overdrive.

Then the lights turned on, and our brothers came into view. Tully and Papà came into the wing and said they were ready to show us how to play pool. I ignored Bridget the rest of the night then returned to our nightly text conversations, acting like we were still only friends.

The night of her sweet sixteen, I was praying the bottle stopped at her feet. When it did, I couldn't believe my luck. The moment I stepped inside the closet, I told myself I wouldn't hide from her—from us—anymore. I meant what I said about taking her out. And her kisses... Jesus. They were more than I bargained for, more than I imagined, and more real than any girl I had ever kissed.

She wanted me. *Really* wanted me.

But then reality hit when we stepped outside, and I fucked it all up again, succumbing to the pressure of what my brother and I had created.

We were kings of the school with reputations we constructed when we were freshmen to pass the time. It all started with one girl who wanted us both. She slept with me then kept asking about Gianni. At first, it upset me. I liked her. She was my first. But then I got angry and told Gianni to pretend he was me.

He had no problem getting in her pants, solidifying his role in our game. Between the two of us, I often wonder whose morals are more screwed up. Often, I think it's Gianni, but then I do something unethical and it makes me rethink my conclusion.

I told him to fuck her to piss her off, thinking she would be horrified, but she wasn't. And that was the beginning of

Gianni and me passing girls to each other and making them do all sorts of crazy, lewd things.

Now, I don't give a shit about any of that. High school seems long and gone. Those snobs and pricks we spent four years with are all at Ivy League schools or snorting themselves to death on cocaine on their daddies' yachts. And the night of Bridget's sweet sixteen party, I was already over it. But everyone was looking at me, including Gianni. He had that warning in his eyes, and he didn't need to speak. He knew I wanted Bridget and would have kissed her in the closet. Hell, I had been dying to kiss her.

Challenging me in front of all the other kids was Gianni's way of protecting me. It may seem like he was just being a dick, but in his way, he was looking out for me... looking out for our family.

I've regretted that moment and standing Bridget up after my boxing match ever since. And no matter how much I try to escape her or attempt to find another woman to take her place, the itch for her never dies.

It's driving me nuts that she's ignoring me. So, tonight, I'm going to stop being a coward. Fuck my papà's orders and all of Gianni's warnings. I'm going to correct all these wrongs I've done and convince her to move back to New York.

I ignore my papà's stern gaze, and we leave. Gianni stops me as soon as we move several feet past the office. "I don't get it, bro."

My hands turn to fists at my sides, knowing it's about Bridget. "What's that?"

"She's in Chicago. She's Tully's daughter. Let it go. There's plenty of ass to get beside hers, and we've been through this," Gianni states.

My rage grows. She's the only girl I've ever talked to who seemed to get me. She didn't care I was a Marino, how much money I had, or what it would do for her popularity to be with me. Bridget liked me for me. And all the stupid shit I did to her, I regret. Instead of having the balls to tell her how I felt and take her out, I listened to Gianni's warnings.

I was an idiot, and now I'm paying the price.

She's gone.

I miss everything about her—the way her face lights up when she laughs, the text conversations I cut off to try and stop my attraction toward her, and both of us secretly watching the other during our family events.

Not having her at my parents' monthly parties makes me feel off. I'm constantly looking for her, even though I know she's hundreds of miles away.

Every girl I fuck, I pretend she's her. I close my eyes and try to drown them out, attempting to hear her voice and see her face.

So, Gianni and my father may be right about her being Tully's daughter and not a good idea, but I'm past all the bullshit. I'm going to make her mine, and wherever the cards fall, they fall. But I'm not going to continue to be a coward. I can't stop obsessing over her, and if that isn't a sign we should be together, then what is?

"Just shut the hell up," I bark at Gianni, and one of our house-keepers jumps then scurries by.

He pushes me to the corner. "She's not a girl to play with or fall for. She's not Italian and she's Tully's daughter. It can't go anywhere. You know this," he tells me for the hundredth time.

I hate that he's right. Bridget is supposed to marry an Irish guy, and I'm supposed to have an Italian bride. It's the way things work in our families. My brothers and I can sleep with any girl we want of any ethnicity, but we can't have one for a serious girlfriend. Papà warned us plenty of times, telling us to get all our itches out of us until we found our Italian brides because there was no other expectation.

Especially for me. My birthright, being born two minutes before Gianni, makes me the future head of the Marinos. The bloodline needs to be pure to ensure our family's reign.

Those two minutes are why I kept listening to Gianni. He wasn't telling me this to be a dick. He was trying to stop me from starting something with Bridget that has zero chance of ending well.

My father would kill me if I ever hurt our alliance with the O'Connors. He and Tully have been friends for as long as I can remember, but they also have our backs. And while my father let my brother and I have our fun in high school, we were immersed in the business as soon as we graduated. I'm fully aware of the dangers of severing our alliance. If Tully ever found out I hurt Bridget, there would be blood to pay.

My blood.

We're no different from any other crime family regarding our activities. We don't just murder our enemies. We have a dungeon below our house. Extortion, corruption of public officials, loan sharking, tax fraud, and stock manipulation are all part of our wheelhouse. Add in labor racketeering with the unions and the infiltration of legitimate businesses, and we're the textbook definition of the Italian mob.

Our orders come directly from Giuseppe Berlusconi, the true godfather of all Italians. Everyone except for the Abruzzo and Rossi pricks abide by his law. They splintered off once they got on American soil and tried to take over our territory. But here in New York, Tully is king of the Irish, and my father is king of the Italians. I'm the prince next in line, so I don't have the leeway Gianni, Massimo, or even my youngest brother Tristano has.

Still, I push past Gianni. "Drop it," I order, making my way to the gym. I'm ready to have my training session and wish I could plant a few right hooks on his face.

Gianni mutters, "You're asking for a death wish."

I storm past my trainer and pick up the jump rope, ignoring him. All I see is Bridget's face. Her green eyes glow with happiness, then confusion, then sadness. I've seen all those emotions from her, and I know I caused them. It only makes me angrier.

My trainer yells for me to move to the speed bag. I do it without adding my wraps or gloves, ignoring his orders to put them on. But no matter how hard I hit, nothing calms the fury or makes Bridget's face leave my mind.

All day I'm anxious, a jumbled mess trying to figure out the right thing to say when I see her. When it comes time for the party, I put on my black pants, a form-fitting red T-shirt, and a black sport coat. I'm the first one downstairs, which isn't normal. I usually appear an hour or so after the party starts.

My mamma smiles when she sees me. She loves parties, especially at Christmas time. Our house is decorated everywhere, with trees in every room. And she always has fun activities for the children.

"Need any help?" I ask.

She shakes her head. "Everything is done. You look nice."

"So do you," I reply, scanning her maroon velvet cocktail dress as my seven-year-old sister, Arianna, runs into the room, followed by my papà, who is chasing her. She's wearing an identical dress to my mamma and is the spitting image of her.

"Dante! Save me!" Arianna squeals, jumping in my arms.

For a moment, my nerves over seeing Bridget fall to the wayside. I love my little sister. I swing her around and move her in front of my papà.

He tickles her stomach.

"Papà! Dante!" she says on a giggle.

I kiss her cheek and set her down. She runs behind my mamma.

Papà kisses Mamma on the lips. "You look stunning, amore mio."

Mamma's cheeks slightly heat, and her eyes twinkle like they always do whenever Papà compliments her. She runs her hand over his shoulder. "And you."

Papà raises his eyebrows. "Dante. You're down here early."

I shrug. "I'm ready for a drink." It's not a lie. I go to the bar and pour myself three fingers of Macallan scotch then take a large swig. It's a smooth burn coating my throat, down to my stomach, but it doesn't help my nerves.

One of my father's advisors comes into the house with his wife and two young daughters. Arianna runs over to them, and within minutes, more guests arrive.

My hands turn clammy, watching the entrance for Bridget. It's well into the hour before she, her father, and brothers arrive.

The moment she walks in, my breath gets caught in my lungs. Everything about her looks the same but different. The only way to describe her is that she's glowing. Her eyes have always morphed from green to blue. Right now, they seem bright blue. Her cheeks have a radiance about them, more intense than before. The red sequin dress she's wearing hugs her body in perfection, and she looks curvier than I remember. Her blonde hair hangs in curls, with one side pinned back in a blingy clip, showcasing her high cheek-bones and red lips.

My dick turns so hard, I don't move for several minutes, grateful I'm in a boring conversation with the men and no one's looking at my lower body.

For over an hour, I pretend to engage in the conversation, nodding at times yet barely hearing a word. Too many times to count, I force myself to tear my eyes off her, only to pin them back on her. And then she catches me.

My heart almost stops beating. She's mid-laugh when she sees me. My stomach drops when her face falls. She clenches her jaw then turns back to her conversation.

Fuck this. I'm wasting time.

I excuse myself and approach her. She's talking to two of my mamma's friends. I reach for her elbow, and she freezes. Turning on the charm, I grin. "If you'll excuse us, all our old high school friends are waiting to see Bridget."

"Oh, yes. Of course," one of the ladies replies.

The other one nods.

Bridget says, "No, I'm—"

"They're going to come in here and ruin my parents' party if you don't go," I lie, then lead Bridget out of the room before she can say anything else. I don't hang out with anyone from high school. There's not one person I find interesting, and my life has responsibilities. I highly doubt any of them could ever understand.

Those responsibilities are exactly why I shouldn't be doing this, I reprimand myself but then push it away.

I'm not going to be a coward anymore.

As soon as we step out of the ballroom, Bridget spins and shirks out of my grasp, firing darts so sharp, it's like I can feel them. "What. Do. You. Want. Dante?"

My stomach dives. I knew she hated me. But it's not the reaction I was looking for. What did I expect though? Did I really believe she would just forget I was a complete jackass all these years? I reply, "I'll tell you in a minute," then return to leading her away.

"Dante, let me go," she seethes.

I steer her into the den and lock the door.

"What are you doing?" she snaps.

"How are you?"

"I'm good. No, I'm great. Now get out of my way." She tries to shove me off the door, but I spin her against it.

She gapes, and an angry fire explodes in her expression.

I press as close to her as possible. "I've missed you. I'm sorry for what I did—for everything."

She laughs. It's a sarcastic, hurt-filled laugh that makes me cringe. "Sorry? I've heard that before. Now get out of my way."

I don't. I can't. No matter how mad at me she is, I have to make this right. I slide my hands over her cheeks. I order, "Come home. I'll right every wrong I've ever done to you. There will be no more girls, no more shit, just you and me."

She huffs, her lips quivering. "Sure, Dante. And the moment I break up with my boyfriend, you'll take a rain check. I know your game. I'm not interested, and I'm not breaking up with Sean."

The hairs on my arms rise. I didn't know she had a boyfriend, but of course she does. She's the catch of a life-time. I'm sure she has numerous guys on campus chasing her.

Is he why she didn't come home for Thanksgiving?

My chest tightens so much I can't breathe. I grit my teeth. "I don't know who Sean is, but he's not good enough for you."

Her eyes turn to slits. "He's more of a man than you'll ever be."

Her words knock into me like a right hook to my face. My stomach dives, and my insides quiver like an upset baby. "Listen to me, Bridge. Whoever this college boy is—"

"He's not in college. And don't call me Bridge. Don't act like we're friends. You lost the right to call me anything but Bridget."

Everything about this conversation is worse than I thought it would be. I angrily ask, "So some rich businessman is over there taking advantage of you?"

Her eyes turn to slits. "You would think that."

"What's that mean?"

"It means, I don't care about any of the superficial crap all those people in our high school do. You know, those people who you had to impress." More anger radiates off her, but I can't deny her statement, which only makes me loathe my previous actions further.

"I didn't mean it like that. If he's not a rich businessman, then who is he?" I pry.

"It's not your business, but he's an O'Malley."

Pain fills my chest, squeezing my heart. This is worse than I thought if she's dating an Irish guy in a crime family. It's too close to home—too close to who Tully would expect her to marry. And they have an alliance. I snarl, "An O'Malley?"

Her eyes glisten. "Yeah. And unlike you, he loves me. *I love him.*"

The world around me collapses. I insist, "You don't."

"I do," she replies, and I die a bit more.

Then I see it. The look in her eyes and everything about her happy glow now makes sense. Still, I'm a fighter. I'm not going down until she's mine. So I dip closer to her face and press my lips to hers, trying to slide my tongue in her mouth, but she doesn't open it. She tries to turn her head, but I'm holding it firmly.

The moment I retreat an inch, she slaps me. It's hard and echoes through the room. I step back and hold my cheek.

Her chest rises and falls faster. Hatred fills her expression. "Don't ever touch me again. I just told you I love someone else."

Unable to keep burying myself deeper, I admit, "I love you, Bridge. I always have. Let him go, come home, and I'll never disappoint you again. I promise you."

Her eyes fill with tears, but they never fall. She squares her shoulders. "No. For the first time in my life, I have someone who loves me for me."

"I love you for you."

"No, you don't."

"I do," I maintain.

"Too late, Dante. I don't have feelings for you anymore. My heart belongs to Sean."

The words are a knife slicing me, yet I can't concede the win to her. "If you come home—"

"I'm never coming home!" she yells.

I step back as if she slapped me again.

She lowers her voice. "I'm in love. *With him.* Everything about Sean, I can't get enough of, including his family. I will *never* leave him. I will *never* return to New York except to visit."

"You just met him."

"It doesn't matter. He's the one. And unlike you, he doesn't play games. There's no toxic shit swirling around me all day long. He wants me. Every day, he shows me how much he wants me. Not a moment goes by where he isn't clear on how much he wants me."

"I promise you, no matter how much you think he wants you, I want you more. If you come home—"

She throws her hands in the air, shaking them in front of my face. "I don't have any feelings left for you! What about this don't you get? Sean is my life. That's who I want to spend my time with, not you, Dante."

I momentarily close my eyes, grinding my molars. "I know I fucked things up between us. I know you're pissed at me."

"It's not even about that. I don't care anymore. I love Sean. There's nothing you could ever do to make me love you again."

My heart disintegrates into tiny pieces until there is nothing left. Hearing her admit she used to love me but no longer does is more painful than I ever thought possible.

"Bridget," I plead one last time, but my mouth is dry, and I can't seem to find words.

"Goodbye, Dante. It was never meant to be between us. Stop calling and texting me. Move on. I have." She walks out of the room, and it's like watching my life leave my body.

I've officially lost everything, and I don't know how to get it back.

2

Bridget

A Week Later

No matter how nice it's been to see my father and brothers, I miss Sean. I'm ready to go back to Chicago and wonder why I let my father pressure me into spending the holidays in New York.

Plus, I'm still pissed that Dante kissed me.

It's the same bullshit as usual. The minute I have some chance of happiness, he tries to destroy it. And I don't believe for one minute he would mean a word he said past last night. All he would do is use me like always, destroy my relationship with Sean, then throw me back again.

All our encounter did was make me hate Dante more. It makes me feel like I cheated on Sean, even though I didn't return Dante's affection. I've gone back and forth all week, debating whether I should tell Sean or not. I'm still undecided when my phone rings from an undisclosed number.

"Hello?" I answer.

"Hey, baby." Sean's voice comes through the line, and I can feel his smile. It's loud wherever he's at, and it's only noon, but I wonder if the pub is full for the holiday.

My flutters take off. "Hi! Why isn't your number popping up?"

He chuckles. "Why don't you tell me your address, and I'll tell you in person?"

My heart stammers. "Are you serious?"

"Yep. Now tell me your address before I have to put more money into this phone."

I rattle it off then say, "I'll have my father's driver come get you."

"No, it'll take longer to see you. I'll grab a cab."

"Are you sure?"

"Yeah, baby. I'll see you soon."

"Bye!" I hang up, filled with excitement. I leave the living room and make my way toward my bedroom to fix myself up.

My father stops me in the hallway. "Why do you look so happy?"

"Sean's here!"

He arches his eyebrows, glancing behind me. "Oh?"

"He's at the airport and grabbing a cab."

"I see." My father clenches his jaw. He's met Sean during his trips to Chicago, but it's the same expression he always has whenever I have a boyfriend.

"Daddy, can you be nice when he gets here?"

"I'm always nice."

I put my hand on my hip and tilt my head. "Why don't you like Sean?"

My father shifts on his feet. "I never said I don't like him."

"Then what is it?"

My father studies me. "He's not good enough for you."

"That's not true!" I protest, remembering how Dante said the same thing, which only angers me further.

"It is. No one will be," my father adds.

I soften my tone. "He is. And I love him."

He nods. "I know. I see it." He takes a deep breath. "Is he staying here?"

"Can he?"

"Yes, but if I catch him in your room, he's leaving in a body bag."

I roll my eyes but pat my father's arm. "Okay. I won't let him in my room."

You didn't say I can't go in his...

I practically skip to my suite, throw my hair in a bun, take another shower, then put on fresh makeup. I'm finishing when the doorbell rings.

I run downstairs, but my father already has the door open. Sean steps inside with an overnight bag over his shoulder and shakes my father's hand.

I squeal and jump into his arms. "I can't believe you're here!"

Sean lifts me off the ground, his green eyes lighting up. The smile I'll never get enough of fills his face. He kisses me, not like his usual all-consuming ones, but I know it's because my father is standing next to us. He says, "Couldn't handle not spending New Year's Eve with you."

I hug him tighter. "I missed you so much!"

He murmurs in my ear, "I missed you, too, Bridge. Chicago sucks without you."

My father clears his throat. "Sean, have you eaten?"

Sean spins me, but his hand dips over my ass. "Nope."

Dad nods. "I have a meeting, so I can't join you, but our chefs can make you something. I'll be back before our party tonight."

"Or I can make him something," I say, not wanting Sean to feel intimidated by my father's wealth. My time in Chicago taught me that ordinary people don't live how my father raised my brothers and me. The O'Malleys are down to earth, even though Darragh has money. He doesn't flaunt it the way the crime families in New York do, but I'm not stupid. I know he has it. Yet, I love how Sean and his family work for a living, not trying to impress anyone. It's the exact opposite of my entire upbringing.

My father gives me one of his exasperated looks. He doesn't understand why I don't seem to care about all the luxuries we have.

"See you later," I say and lead Sean through the house.

As soon as we turn the corner, he tugs me into him and kisses me. This time, it's not the sweet boy-next-door kiss he planted on my lips in front of my father.

My butterflies go nuts, and when he pulls back, he grins. "Fuck, I've missed you."

I glide my fingers through his strawberry-blond hair. "You have no idea how much I missed you."

His dimple pops out. "Are you glad I surprised you?"

"Yes!"

He kisses me again. "So, I have a date for New Years?"

I beam. "Of course." His stomach growls, and I laugh. "Come on."

We go into the kitchen, and our chef, Patrick, looks perplexed when I tell him he doesn't need to make anything for us, that I'll do it.

His eyes widen. "Ms. O'Connor, please, it's my job."

"No. I'll—"

Sean puts his finger on my lips. "Let the man do his job."

"Thank you," Patrick says, looking relieved. "What would you like?"

Sean shrugs. "Whatever's easy for you. Surprise me. I'm not picky."

"And for you?" Patrick asks me.

"The same," I reply, and my stomach flips.

Sean pulls me into the next room then sits. He tugs me onto his lap then tucks my hair behind my ear. "Why do you look nervous?"

I scrunch my forehead, trying to figure out what to say. I finally blurt out, "I don't want you to be uncomfortable."

His face falls. "Why would I be?"

I wince, staying silent.

"Ah. I see. Because of your father's money?"

"That sounds really bad," I admit.

"But it's true?"

I momentarily squeeze my eyes shut then nod. "Yeah."

His lips twitch. "Are you uncomfortable at my nana's pub?"

"What? No! Of course not!"

"What about the house I share with my brothers?"

"I love your house. But you're there, and that's all I care about," I confess.

He gives me a chaste kiss on my lips. "That's all I care about, too, Bridge. So chill out and let me see how the other half live." He wiggles his eyebrows.

I laugh, and my nerves die. That's the thing about Sean. He always makes me laugh, no matter what the situation. "Okay."

His hand slides up my shirt, stroking my spine. "Your dad isn't letting me stay in your room, though, is he?"

I lean closer. "He said you couldn't go in my room. He didn't say anything about me sneaking into yours."

Sean chuckles. "Dirty girl."

"I still can't believe you're here," I acknowledge.

"Couldn't have you kissing someone else at midnight, could I?"

My stomach flips, and I look away. Guilt fills me about Dante having his lips on mine.

Sean's voice turns serious. "Bridget?"

I swallow the lump in my throat. My insides quiver, and when I lock eyes with Sean, I feel so sick, I get dizzy.

His eyes widen, and his hand stops moving on my back. The color drains from his cheeks. "Did you—" He sniffs hard. "Did you kiss someone else?"

I shake my head, whispering, "Yes. No. I-I didn't want it."

Anger flares in Sean's tone. "What the fuck does that mean, Bridget? Did you, or did you not, kiss someone?"

"No! I didn't kiss anyone. But he...he kissed me."

Sean rises, putting me on my feet.

"Sean!"

He paces, pulling at his hair. Tears fall down my cheeks. He spins, his green eyes flaring with rage. "It was him, wasn't it?"

"Yes," I admit, wishing I never told Sean about Dante.

I met Sean on the first day I got to Chicago. My father and I went to the pub so I could meet Darragh and the other O'Malleys. The moment Sean's and my eyes locked, the earth shifted. It freaked me out. I was still running from Dante's shadow.

Sean immediately asked me out. At first, I told him no, too scared to get my heart broken again. But he wouldn't take no for an answer and showed up at my dorm room the following day, asking me out again. When I told him no, he wouldn't leave until I told him why. I spilled everything and told him I wasn't ready to date anyone, even though he insisted Dante was an idiot who didn't deserve any more of my time.

The next day was my first day of classes. Sean brought me coffee and a doughnut then walked me to class. He waited until it was over then walked me across campus to the next one. All day, he was there, making me laugh about stupid things. By the time the last class was over, my flutters were in full effect, and I was praying he was going to be outside.

He was. And I couldn't resist him when he asked me to go to a Cubs game that night. I knew nothing about baseball, but I went and enjoyed every moment of it because I was with him.

All Sean's ever shown me is that he's everything Dante isn't. When I told Dante I didn't love him anymore, I meant it. My heart belongs to Sean and only him.

Hurt fills Sean's face. I cup his cheeks. "Please believe me. He kissed me, and I didn't kiss him back. I even slapped him. I told him I love you and not him."

Sean's hardened expression never falters. The fear and pain in his eyes make me feel like I betrayed him. "Let me guess. He realizes what an ass he is and wants you back."

More tears drip off my cheeks. "It doesn't matter."

"He put his lips on yours. Of course it matters!" Sean snarls.

My hands shake against his cheeks. "I meant he doesn't matter to me. You're all that matters."

His jaw clenches.

"Sean, it wasn't my fault. I swear!"

Death explodes in his orbs. "Oh, I know it wasn't your fault. I know all about what guys like him do. But why were you even with him?"

"I saw him at the Christmas party."

"And you didn't tell me?"

"I-I didn't want to do it over the phone."

Sean tilts his head toward the ceiling, his cheeks turning redder every second that passes.

"Sean, please," I whisper, putting my hand over his racing heart.

Tense silence fills the air, making my fear burst all around us.

"Please. Don't break up with me. I love you," I beg through tears.

His eyes meet mine. "Tell me it's over with him, Bridget. Tell me that you have zero feelings left for him."

I grab his cheeks again. "The only feelings I have are for you. I love you, not him."

His nostrils flare, but he tugs me into him. "I shouldn't have let you come here without me. I should have known he'd try to mess with you again."

I glance up. "He won't. I won't let him."

Sean squeezes his eyes shut. "He kissed you."

"I didn't kiss him back," I repeat.

"He had no right."

"I know. I'm-I'm sorry. Maybe I shouldn't have told you," I blurt out without thinking.

Green fire burns in Sean's eyes. "We said no secrets."

"I know. But I feel like I've ruined us now."

Sean shakes his head. "Jesus, you don't get it, do you, Bridge?"

"Get what?" I ask as my fear grows.

"You're it for me. There is no ruining us."

I sniffle. "So you aren't going to break up with me?"

He drags his knuckles down my cheek. "No. But if that bastard comes near you again, I'm taking him out."

"He won't. I told him to stay away."

Patrick walks in with a tray of sandwiches. "Sorry to interrupt." He sets down the platter and leaves.

"Come eat," I say and pull Sean toward the table.

He sits then pulls me on his lap, ordering, "Kiss me first and remind me you're mine."

"I am yours. Only yours," I vow. Then I put everything into our kiss.

Sean's my future. I'm not letting anyone come between us, especially not Dante Marino.

$\mathcal{MC}$

Dante

Three Years Later

"SO YOU'LL PICK ME UP LATER TONIGHT?" GIORGIA ASKS, sliding her heel on.

Shit. Why did I agree to go?

I was drunk.

I stretch my arms, barely awake. "Yeah, sure."

She lunges on top of me, pinning her brown eyes to mine. Her chestnut hair falls against my cheek. "Don't be late, okay? I don't want to hear about it from my father."

I pat her ass. "Noted."

She kisses me and then shimmies off my body. As soon as she leaves, I roll over and groan into the pillow. The last thing I want to do is go with her to the country club Valentine's Day Ball. It's a prestigious event filled with a bunch of pricks I went to school with, and I have no time for it. Nor do I have any desire to celebrate Valentine's Day.

Thoughts of last year at this time make me grip the sheets. Giorgia and I had been dating for a month. When I didn't shower her with gifts and make a big deal about the hallmark holiday, she cried all night.

I broke up with her, but somehow, she managed to find her way back into my bed.

In theory, Giorgia's the perfect woman for me. She's Italian, her father is one of my father's top advisors, and she's beautiful. But something is missing. I don't know what it is, yet every time she tries to bring up the topic of us taking the next step, I feel nauseous. It almost pushes me to break up with her, but then she rides my cock. It always convinces me she's worth keeping around.

Then she mumbles she loves me, and the cycle starts all over again.

So this holiday of shouting to the world who you love isn't my cup of tea.

It would be if Bridget were here.

I groan again, cursing myself for even thinking about her. I've only seen her once or twice a year since I professed my love for her. Her boyfriend is always with her, scowling at me. The New Year's Eve party I went to the week after I kissed her proved to be even more disastrous. I had a renewed energy to convince her we were meant to be together. I didn't know Sean had surprised her and was in

New York. She avoided me most of the night, but I cornered her outside the restroom. Sean saw it and was quickly in my face.

He claimed she was his. My stupid-ass demanded she was mine and then ordered Bridget to leave him. If Gianni hadn't pulled me out of Tully's house before he or our father knew what happened, blood would have been everywhere.

Since then, she's always with him, glowing with happiness, and both of them are all over each other. They're worse than the stereotypical couple. They don't just seem to be a happy couple.

They *are* one.

Anytime I think about it, I morph between the jealous bastard I am and the side of me that wants Bridget to be happy. It only takes a few seconds until I remind myself it's with him, and my noble thoughts get shut up quickly.

What makes it worse is everyone loves him, including my brothers. They state he's funny, laid-back, and charming.

He's all the things I'm not.

For self-preservation, I always make sure I bring a date with me whenever they'll be at an event. I try to put on a public display as much as they do. It's all in vain though. It doesn't even seem to bug Bridget.

Over the years, things have gotten cordial between the three of us. It's like he's so confident in his and Bridget's relationship, I'm not even a threat.

It pisses me off.

She should have been mine.

Adding to the sting is that the lucky bastard genuinely makes me laugh. I loathe myself after each incident. I'll peek over at Bridget, and she's not only laughing, but she's looking at him with her *I'm so in love with you* expression in her eyes. My heart stops beating whenever it happens.

If I force myself to think about it, I'd actually like him if he hadn't stolen my girl.

Okay, that's a lie. I pushed her to him, and I know it.

That realization only makes me detest myself further.

My alarm rings, and I toss on my workout gear, then head downstairs. I go into the dining room. My family is already there eating.

I grab a plate and fill it with bacon and eggs then toss a croissant on it. I plop in the seat between Arianna and Tristano.

"Happy Valentine's Day!" Arianna chirps, and her smile lights up the room.

I refrain from groaning then tug her into me, giving her a noogie. She's only ten, so who am I to rain on her parade? "Happy Valentine's Day." I kiss the top of her head.

"Such a stupid holiday," Tristano mutters.

I elbow him. "Keep it to yourself."

He arches his eyebrows. "Okay, what did you get for Giorgia?"

I shove eggs in my mouth then wash them down with coffee. "I'll grab some flowers or something."

Tristano snorts. "Exactly my point."

"I love Valentine's Day," Arianna chirps.

"You would," Tristano replies.

"Enough. Don't spoil it for your sister," Papà orders.

"I ran into Giorgia on the way out. She said you're going to the ball at the club tonight?" Mamma asks.

Massimo snickers.

I toss a croissant at him. "Shut up."

"You're whipped," Gianni teases.

I toss a piece of bread at him as well.

"Stop throwing food," Papà orders.

"Then tell them to shut up," I mumble and eat a bite of my croissant.

"I think it's nice," Mamma says.

I ignore it and keep piling the food inside my mouth so I don't have to talk, cursing myself again for ever agreeing to go to this stupid event.

"Tully's coming over at three. We've got some issues that have popped up. I want the three of you in my office before he arrives," Papà states.

"I have my meeting with Rubio," I reply.

"Change it."

I cross my arms. "It's to go through the new shipments."

"Enough. I said, change it," Papà reiterates.

"We already scheduled distribution to start right after. The pickup is at four," I remind him, pissed he's telling me to change my meeting, which is going to screw up my entire day. Plus, this is my first significant project I secured on my own.

"Meet with Rubio before. End of conversation."

I take a sip of water then rise, angry that it's Tully who's making me rearrange my schedule. Tully makes me think of Bridget, and I've already thought enough about her today. I sarcastically respond, "Yeah, I'll just tell everyone to stop what they're doing and bend over since Tully's coming over."

Papà slams his hand on the table. "Watch your mouth."

Arianna jumps next to me, and her eyes widen.

Mamma wraps her arm around Arianna then glares at Papà.

But he doesn't break his gaze off mine.

Gianni rises. "Dante, let's go before we're late." He walks around the table and kisses Arianna on her head. "Have fun at your party today."

"Wait! I didn't give you your valentine!" She picks up a red envelope and hands it to him then gives the rest of us one.

I immediately feel guilty. I know how excited she's been, and I didn't get her anything. I open the envelope and pull out a red heart that says *"Hope your day is filled with lots of love. Be my Valentine. Arianna."*

Love. Fat chance.

Gianni hands her a card with a small box of chocolates. Massimo pulls a teddy bear and card out from underneath

48

the table. I silently groan. Of course, I'm the only one who forgot to pick something up, and she's been bouncing off the walls all week about this stupid day.

I lean down over her. "Guess what?"

Her excited brown eyes make me smile. She barely gets out, "What?"

"I have a super cool gift for you, but I can't give it to you until tonight."

She beams. "What is it?"

"You'll have to wait and see. Have fun at your party." I kiss her forehead and leave with Gianni and Massimo for the gym.

"You forgot, didn't you?" Massimo asks when we're out of earshot.

"Yep."

"So, what are you going to get her?" Gianni asks.

I groan. "No clue."

"Better be something amazing after promising her that," Massimo warns.

I ignore him and open the door to the gym then go to the mat and stretch.

My brothers follow.

"What do you think Tully wants?" Gianni asks.

"Don't give a shit, but I'm sick of changing my life every time Tully comes over," I fume.

"So dramatic," Massimo teases.

"Shut up," I bark.

"You do sound dramatic," Gianni adds.

"Both of you can fuck off," I snarl, pissed with how everyone keeps making me think of Bridget and especially on today of all days.

Massimo leans over his body and pulls on his toes. "Hope your attitude is better tonight for Giorgia's sake."

"Jesus. Shut up," I roar and jump off the mat. I go to the treadmill and jump on, turning the speed up higher than I usually do at the start.

I run, jump rope, and punch the bag so many times, my hands begin to hurt. I do push-ups and sit-ups until my muscles shake. I battle the ropes, pounding them into the ground so hard and for so long, I can barely grip them anymore.

When Massimo and Gianni leave the gym, I step back on the treadmill and run some more.

Nothing makes Bridget's face or the sound of her laughter disappear.

Nothing lessens the dread of going to the event tonight with Giorgia.

Nothing dulls the nagging feeling I have that I'm never finding anyone like Bridget. That no matter who I meet, they're never going to come close. And that makes me hate myself more because, at one point in time, I could have had her as mine.

When my alarm rings, I finally stop, full of sweat. I go to my suite, shower, then double-check my Glock is loaded. I call Rubio and reschedule my meeting with him.

The only brief moment of calm I feel is when I get in my matte black Gemballa Porsche Carrera GT. It's a rare car. They only made twenty-five, and I snagged one the moment I saw it, eagerly forking over the four-hundred-thousand-plus price tag.

I don't typically drive it during the winter months. The snow gets bad in New York, and it's easier to let my father's drivers take us all over the place. But today, I need some sense of something right in my life. And the roads are clear from the last storm we had.

I weave in and out of traffic then walkie-talkie my assistant on my Nextel. It's a newer phone that has both a walkie-talkie feature and the ability to call or text. My father likes it because he thinks the Feds have less chance of recording us over the walkie-talkie.

I'm not discussing anything the Feds would be interested in, but it's a more convenient feature in my opinion.

"Pina, order a dozen roses for Giorgia."

"Well, good morning to you, too, Dante," she chirps.

"Not in the mood."

She huffs. "Fine, Mr. Grumps. Where do you want them delivered?"

I ignore her smart remark. She's the only assistant I've been able to keep over the last three years. It's her nickname for me and not the first time I've heard it. The other eight women I hired didn't even last a month. I snap, "Her house. Where else?" Giorgia doesn't work or do anything besides spend her days at the country club and spa. It's something else that irritates me about her, but it's normal for many women whose fathers are in the mafia.

"Just asking. No need to bite my head off," Pina states. And that right there is why it works between us. She doesn't cry or back down when I say whatever the hell is on my mind. I don't have to worry about hurting her feelings because she calls me out on my mood swings. I don't have them all the time, but whenever I wake up thinking about Bridget, it seems to come out.

There's another beep on my phone. She asks, "What color? I assume red?"

I press the button, replying, "Why do I give a fuck about the color?" I turn right and step on the accelerator.

She huffs. "Red means love. Since it's Valentine's Day—"

I press the button cutting her off then press it again so she can hear me. "Do not send red! What other choices do I have?"

"Pink roses symbolize gratitude, grace, and joy."

"Next," I demand.

"White is pretty."

"What's the meaning?" I ask, not believing I'm getting a lesson on the freaking color of flowers.

"Purity, innocence, and in some cases, chastity."

I snort. "Yeah, definitely not Giorgia. What else?"

"Purple roses are harder to find, but they indicate a fascination or adoration. What about that?" Pina inquires.

My gut flips. "Definitely not." I cross the state line into New Jersey. I veer away from the rich residential part and drive toward the side where the run-down factories and increased crime reign.

Pina's voice turns to irritation. "We're running out of colors. You have been seeing her for over a year."

"What's left?" I ask in irritation, not wanting a reminder of the time, since it only makes Giorgia's clock tick faster.

"Orange roses indicate enthusiasm and passion. That could work for today," Pina suggests.

I have passion when she's fucking me.

I sigh, not liking the clawing in my gut. *This should be simple, for crying out loud.* I question, "Are there any other choices?"

"Yeah, but I don't think you want it for Valentine's Day."

"Why?"

"Well, yellow means friendship and caring."

"Send yellow."

"Seriously?"

"Yeah. Stop asking questions," I demand.

"Glad you aren't my boyfriend," she adds.

"Did I ask for your opinion on this matter?"

"No, but you love it when I add it," she gushes then adds, "What do you want the card to say?"

My chest tightens further, and I scrub my face, then I turn down a street with factories looming on both sides. "Happy Valentine's Day. Dante."

The inside of the car is quiet for several moments, but my Nextel finally beeps. "Nothing else?"

"No. That's it.

"All right. Consider it done."

I toss my phone in the cupholder and pull into the factory. The legitimate side is Rubio's father's detergent company. The non-legit side is the place we import jewels from all over the world. It's not a new venture for my father, but this is the first time I found another illegal supplier of gemstones. And these aren't imported. They're straight from Dry Cottonwood Creek in Montana, so it substantially cuts our cost in half, skyrocketing our profits.

The Montana sapphires tend to be small and flat. When cut in pieces, less than ten percent are more than one carat. Anything above half a carat has a sharp price increase, and the new supplier guaranteed the container would have all different sizes.

I walkie-talkie Rubio I'm here, and the garage door on the back of the building opens. As soon as I pull in, the door closes.

Rubio's stocky frame comes into view. His slicked-back hair is so stiff it doesn't move. He motions for the other workers to vacate the area and slaps my hand when I get out of the car. "Dante. You're going to like this shipment."

For the first time today, I feel a surge of excitement. "Yeah?"

His dark eyes meet mine. "They're good. Really good."

"Stop talking then, and show me what we're dealing with," I order.

He leads me to a side office and unlocks the door. As soon as I step in, the buzzing in my veins grows. Another man, my father's appraiser, is sitting at the desk with his magnifying glass and other tools.

"Ettore," I say.

He lifts his gray hair-filled head, smiling. Crinkles pop out around his blue eyes. "Dante. These are good."

"So I hear." I sit down across from him.

He points to a large container. "Those are all done. All good, less than five percent are under half a carat. The rest is all above. These are the last ones and your most valuable."

I study the Montana sapphires and hold my breath. The largest one, I pick up. The crystal has flecks of blues and greens throughout it. Mesmerized, I immediately think of Bridget's eyes.

"That's over five carats—definitely your most valuable piece," Ettore claims.

I wrap my fist around it. "How many pieces do you have left?"

"Only three. These are all flawless. You did good, Dante," he says, and pride sweeps through me.

Rubio slides a box at me. "Present from our suppliers."

"What is it?"

"Open it."

I lift the lid on the red velvet box. A gold necklace with a deep-red garnet shimmers in the light. I glance at Rubio.

"They said they have access if we're interested."

"Same quality. These guys you found are the real deal," Ettore declares.

"What's the demand for these?" I ask, holding the red gem up toward the light.

"Decent, but they might move slower than the sapphires," Ettore answers.

"Tell them to send another container of Montana sapphires, and I'll take a half container of these garnets." I rise, grab a velvet bag, and slide the five-carat sapphire in it. I put that and the garnet box in my pocket. "Offload them and let me know when the money is transferred," I instruct Rubio then get in my car and leave.

I'm feeling pretty good when I get back to the house for my meeting with my father. I'm even not bothered Tully is there.

Until he drops a bomb on me.

"Bridget and Sean just got engaged," Tully announces and holds his tumbler of whiskey in the air. The room erupts in congratulations.

Stunned, the hairs on my arms rise, and my stomach flips so fast, I have to choke down the bile rising in my throat. My lungs constrict, but I somehow manage to put on a smile and hold up my scotch for my father's quick toast.

I barely hear the conversation, and as soon as I can get out of the room, I go straight to my wing and into my office. I pour another glass of Macallan, filling it to the top.

What the fuck?

She's getting married.

It's official. She's never going to be mine.

I pull the velvet pouch out of my pocket and stare at the gem for hours, trying to settle my quivering insides, not even tasting the alcohol. My phone pulls me out of my trance. I glance at the screen, and all the rage and other feelings I don't know how to deal with consume me.

"What?" I snap.

"Is that any way to talk to me?" Giorgia asks then giggles.

And I'm suddenly over it. I'm over pretending that someday this will go anywhere. I'm through with stupid events I hate and being Giorgia's arm candy. I'm no longer going to stay with her because she's the type of woman I'm expected to settle down and marry.

"We're over," I state.

The line turns silent. I run my thumb over the sapphire. She finally clears her throat. "Is this a joke?"

"No. Don't call me again." I hang up and stay a few more hours in my office until Arianna comes flying into the room.

"Guess what?" she sings.

I force myself to put on a smile. "What's that?"

She puts a pink bag on my desk and pulls a ton of envelopes out, beaming. "I got fifty-two valentines!"

I get up and sit next to her, picking up some of them and reading all the corny messages.

Bridget's gone. She's never coming back.

"When are you leaving tonight? Do you want to go in the kitchen and try the cookies Mamma just made?" Arianna asks.

I take a deep breath then reach for the velvet box. "I thought I'd give you your Valentine's gift."

Arianna's eyes widen. She tilts her head and bites her lip. "Is that for me?"

"Yeah. Here." I place the box in front of her.

She gingerly opens it and gasps.

"Do you like it?"

She jumps up and puts her arms around me, and it takes everything I have to keep my shit together. "I love it!"

I sniff hard then clasp the necklace around her thin neck. It hangs lower than it should, so I tell her, "I'll get the chain adjusted."

"No, I love it like this!"

I smile, feeling a tiny bit better, then state, "I'm glad you have on such a pretty dress."

"Why?"

"I thought you'd want to be my Valentine and go to dinner tonight?"

Her eyes light up. "Really? What about the ball with Giorgia?"

"I'll tell you a secret if you want?"

She nods and her face turns serious.

I admit, "I don't think Giorgia is the one."

"No?"

"Nope."

She scrunches her face. "Are you sad?"

I force a smile. "Nope. And I'm glad I know now, because I want you to be my Valentine."

Arianna hugs me again and I kiss her forehead.

"Go tell Mamma I'm taking you out, sweetheart. We'll leave in thirty minutes."

"Okay!" She runs out of the room.

I take the Montana sapphire and lock it in my safe. What I'm doing with it, I'm not sure. All it's going to do is torture me.

The only thing I can think is that it's meant to be Bridget's, but that's never happening.

4

Bridget

Five Years Later

SEAN JR.'S WAIL FILLS THE RESTAURANT. I RUB HIS BACK, TRYING to calm him and ignoring the rude stares.

Nasty bitches. He's only two.

Why did I convince myself a piece of apple pie was worth taking him out?

I'm in New York, visiting my father. I'm thirty weeks pregnant, and Sean and I decided to take one final trip. He and my father had something to do with clan business, so I braved this little adventure that I'm now regretting. The restaurant I'm in is pretty exclusive, so I usually don't come here, but they have the best pie. Yet, all I've done is exhaust myself coming here.

"Sweetie, what's wrong?" I coo.

His face is bright red, and tears stain his cheeks. Drool slides down his chin, and I wipe it.

"Oh, sweetie. Are your molars coming in?" I slide my finger in his cheek, and there's no doubt. His gums are bright red.

He screams, beating his tiny fists on my chest, and one woman states in an intentionally loud voice, "Kids who can't stay quiet should stay home."

"Actually, bitchy women shouldn't leave their house," a deep, familiar voice replies behind me.

The woman gasps.

I spin and freeze.

Dante looms over me in his black suit and tie. His dark eyes fix on mine. Before I know what's happening, he pulls out the chair next to me and sits. "Bridge, good to see you."

Sean Jr. pounds a fist into my cheek, and I wince.

"Whoa! Easy there, killer!" Dante says then grabs Sean.

"What—"

"Hey, you can't hit your mommy like that," he says in a calm voice, holding Sean's face near his.

To my surprise, Sean's cries get softer. He sniffles and tilts his head.

"That's it, buddy. Now, what's wrong?"

"His molars are coming in," I blurt out, unsure why Dante's able to calm my son when I'm not, but I'm grateful.

Dante arches his eyebrows. "What do you do for that?"

I shake my head, suddenly feeling super overwhelmed and like a bad mom. I admit, "Give him something cool for him to chew on, but I don't have anything." Tears bust out everywhere.

Dante's eyes widen. He scoots closer then repositions Sean so he's bouncing on his knee. "Okay. Don't worry. We'll figure it out."

"What are you doing here?" I ask.

"Lunch appointment. I should ask you that." He glances at my stomach.

I shrug. "I wanted apple pie."

He scans the table. "Did you already eat?"

I sniffle. "No. They haven't come back to take my order. I should go. This was a bad idea." I start to rise, and he puts his hand on my shoulder.

"Sit down, Bridge. Hold on." He stands with Sean and motions for a server to come over.

A barely eighteen-year-old redhead eyes him over. "Hey. You need something?"

"A slice of apple pie."

"Ice cream, whip cream, or both?"

"Both and heated, right, Bridge?" he asks me.

I nod, surprised he remembers.

Dante gives her his million-dollar smile. "Make it two, and I need a glass of ice water right away."

She bats her eyes at him and leaves. Sean sniffles and whines, but it's lower than before.

Dante stares at me. "It's been a while since I've seen you. I didn't know you were in New York."

"I wanted to take one last trip before I had the baby."

He glances at my huge stomach. "When is she... he... due?"

I smile. "She's due in a few months. I'm seven months today."

Concern fills his face. "And you're feeling okay?"

"Yeah. Just super hormonal right now. Sorry about crying."

He chuckles. "No worries." He drags his finger down Sean's cheek, which stops his whines for a moment. "Did you come to New York on your own?"

I shake my head. "My dad and Sean are doing something work related."

"Ah. I see. And you braved this excursion all by yourself?"

"Stupid, wasn't it?" I confess.

"Depends how good the pie is," he replies.

A tiny laugh escapes me.

The server sets a glass of ice water down and says, "The pie will just be another minute."

"Thanks," Dante and I say at the same time.

She leaves, and Dante picks up the tiny baby spoon and plunges it in water.

"What are you doing?"

"My mamma did this when Arianna was teething. It usually calmed her down. Well, that or whiskey on her gums."

"Now you're just trying to be Irish," I taunt.

He grunts then removes the spoon and slides it in Sean's mouth against his gums, but so he can't bite on it.

Sean calms and rests his head against Dante's torso then turns his cheek against him.

"Wow. I'm impressed with your skills," I admit and wince. "But I think your suit is going to have tear stains."

"No biggie. So how's Chicago?"

I smile. "It's good."

He nods, studying me for a brief moment. He quietly says, "I'm happy for you, Bridge."

An emotion lodges in my throat. I curse my pregnancy hormones again then choke out, "Thanks. So what's new with you?"

He shakes his head. "Nothing exciting. Same life as always."

Something about the way he says it makes me feel sad. Maybe I'm just super pregnant and emotional, but I put my hand on his forearm. "Are you okay?"

He smiles, but it seems forced. "Yep."

The server puts two plates of pie down. "Need anything else?"

"We're good. Thanks," Dante replies. She leaves, and he points to the apple pie. "Dig in, mamma."

I laugh again, not used to seeing his funny side like I used to when we were younger. He hands me a spoon, and I cut through the whipped cream, ice cream, and pie and put it in my mouth.

"Well?" he asks, his eyes twinkling.

I chew and swallow. "It's good. Try it."

He takes a bite of his then agrees, "It's good. Can Sean have ice cream?"

"Sure."

He releases the spoon in Sean's mouth and he cries again. Dante replaces it with ice cream. As soon as it passes Sean's lips, the tears stop and he wants more.

Dante laughs and gives him some more. "Easily pleased."

"Don't you have to go to your meeting?" I ask.

"Not anymore. This is way more interesting," he states and shoves a huge bite of food in his mouth.

I smile, put another spoonful of apple pie in my mouth, and suddenly am grateful I'm not alone. It's something I never thought I would feel with Dante next to me, but over the years, Sean, Dante, and I have all been fine. I guess you can say we're more than acquaintances but not super-close friends.

"How long are you in town?" he asks.

"Just until tomorrow. We've been here for two weeks."

He hesitates, the darkness in his eyes swirling as he assesses me. He states, "Well, I'm glad I got to see you."

Without having to think about it, I reply, "Me, too. How's Eva?"

His face hardens, and he shifts in his seat. "Not sure. We broke up a few months ago."

"Oh. I'm sorry."

"It's okay. I think I'm resolved to the fact I'm going to be single for the rest of my life. It's easier."

I tilt my head.

"Why are you looking at me like that?" he questions.

"I think that would be a shame."

His gaze locks onto mine. "Why's that?"

I watch Sean happily lying against his suit coat. "You'd make a good dad."

He glances at Sean. "Nah. I just think your little guy likes my ice cream." He feeds him some more.

"Hmm. Well, I—" A popping sensation erupts in my lower body. It feels like I'm peeing myself. I jerk my head down and panic. "Oh God!"

"What's wrong?"

"I... oh God!" I cry out.

He tosses his spoon on the table. "Bridge, what's happening?"

"I think my water just broke. I'm-I'm only seven months. It's too early!"

He sends a text on his phone, tosses cash on the table, then rises with Sean. He slings the diaper bag over his shoulder. "Can you walk?"

"Yeah," I state, freaking out.

Dante holds his hand out. "Okay, stay calm. My driver's outside. Let's get you to the hospital."

"My baby—"

"Bridge, I need you to get up if you can," he sternly orders.

"Right." I swing my legs out then take his hand and put my other on the table. I rise, and liquid floods the floor. I stare at it in horror.

Dante pulls me out of my trance. "Are you sure you're okay to walk?"

"Yes."

He puts his arm around my waist, Sean on his hip, and leads me outside. His driver pulls up, and he helps me get in the car.

Sean screams, and Dante bounces him on his hip. "It's okay, buddy."

I grip Dante's suit coat. "I need Sean to be there. I can't have the baby without him!"

"Try to stay calm, Bridge," Dante repeats then pulls out his phone and tries Sean, but he doesn't answer. He tries my father and gets the same response.

"Oh God!" I fret, as the panic grows bigger.

Dante puts the phone to his ear and grasps my hand, rubbing his thumb over it. "Papà, I ran into Bridget, and her water broke. We can't get a hold of Sean or Tully. Find out where they are and tell them to meet us at Mt. Sinai." He hangs up, and the smell of poop fills the car.

"Oh shit. Sorry... Sean... I need to change him."

"I'll do it. Aren't you supposed to breathe or something?" Dante asks, digging into the diaper bag.

"Probably. But... this is too soon!" I restate then more tears fall.

He pulls a diaper out and tugs my chin toward him. "I need you to stay calm. Can you do that for me?"

I cry harder. "Yes. No. I don't know."

His orbs seer into mine. They're calm and firm, as if he's right and there's no question. "You can. You're Bridget O'Connor."

"O'Malley, you mean!"

"Sorry. Yes. Bridget O'Malley. Now do your fancy breathing. I'm moving to the other seat to change Sean, okay?"

I take a few deep breaths then nod.

"Good." He tucks my hair behind my ear. "Keep breathing."

I obey. He moves to the other seat to change Sean. When he snaps his onesie, we pull up to the emergency room. He gets out with Sean and the bag then helps me out. As soon as we get inside, they make me sit in a wheelchair and rush us to the labor and delivery floor.

"Sir, we need you to fill out your wife's paperwork," a nurse says.

"That would be me," Sean calls out behind me.

A moment of short-lived relief appears. I turn. "Thank God you're here. It's—it's too soon."

His face is full of worry, and he crouches down in front of me, placing his hand on my cheek. Sean gives me a chaste kiss, but it doesn't relieve my anxiety. And I see his fear mirroring mine, even though he's trying to hide it.

"Ma'am, we need to move you. Whoever is the father can come," the nurse states.

Sean rises. "That's me." He glances at Sean Jr.

"Don't worry. I've got him," Dante informs us.

Sean releases a nervous breath then pats Dante's back. "Thanks."

The nurse wheels me away with Sean at my side.

My labor is quick and painful. The moment Fiona comes into the world, they take her out of the room and into the neonatal intensive care unit. I demand, "Sean, go with them."

"You can't right now. We'll come get you when the baby is stable," a nurse states, leaving the room.

"Stable? What does that mean?" I cry out.

Sean shakes his head. "I'm not sure."

"Is she going to be okay?" I ask, not sure if I want to know the answer.

Sean sniffs hard, sliding his hand on my forehead. "Yeah. She's an O'Malley. She'll fight if needed."

I cry harder, and he tugs me into him. His heart thumps into my ear.

"You did good, Bridge," he murmurs, kissing the top of my head.

"I didn't. She came too early!" I sob.

He holds me tighter. "Nonsense."

"Will you go get Sean Jr.?" I ask, suddenly needing to hold my son.

"Sure." He steps back and leaves the room. I try to pull myself together so I don't scare my son, but it's hard. I feel like I'm barely hanging on.

Both Sean, Dante, and Sean Jr. come into the room. Sean Jr. cries when he sees me, and I hold out my arms. He curls into me and sniffles for a few minutes.

"Thanks for watching him," I tell Dante.

"Anytime. We were checking out the nurses. He likes blondes." He winks.

Both Sean and I let out a laugh, which I didn't think was possible at this moment.

"I owe you," Sean says, patting his back again.

Dante opens his mouth to speak, but a nurse steps into the room.

"Good news! Your little girl is stable. She weighs more than we expected, so we think your doctor might have been off on his estimate about how far along you were. She's four and a half pounds. Mr. O'Malley, you can come to the neonatal intensive care unit now if you wish." She motions for Sean to follow.

Tears of relief fall down my cheeks. "Can I go, too?"

"I'm sorry, ma'am, but the doctor needs to check you over one more time. He should be here in the next half hour or so."

Sean looks at me, debating whether to stay or go.

"Go see our daughter," I order.

He nods and asks Dante, "Can you stay with Bridge and Sean?"

"Of course."

Sean leaves.

Dante hovers over me, shifting on his feet. "How are you feeling, Bridge?"

"Like I just pushed a bowling ball out of my lower body," I admit.

His lips twitch. "Can I get you anything?"

"Sit. You're making me nervous."

He grins. "All right." He pulls up a chair. "Your dad's on his way."

"Why wasn't he with Sean?"

"Don't know."

A moment of silence passes.

"Thank you. For... for everything," I state.

"At least you got a few bites of your apple pie," he teases.

I grab his hand. "Dante."

His eyes meet mine. For the first time in years, I see the boy who was my friend before I ever developed a crush on him or he broke my heart. I see the good person I knew him as all the years I grew up alongside him.

"I mean it. Thank you," I repeat.

He studies me, hesitating for a long time, then he cautiously responds, "No reason to thank me. We're friends, right?"

I smile, feeling emotional again, then blink harder as fresh tears fall. "Yeah. We're friends."

5

Dante

4 Years Later

MAMMA PUTS HER HAND OVER HER CHEST, PAUSING MID-sentence. Her cheeks turn red.

"Mamma, what's wrong?" I ask.

Gianni steps closer, putting his hand on her back, appearing as worried as I feel. He exchanges a glance with me.

She smiles. "I'm okay. I think I have some acid reflux."

"This is the fourth time this week," Gianni points out.

"You need to see the doctor," I add.

She squares her shoulders. "I'm fine. Now, which women are gracing us with their presence tonight?" She narrows her eyes on us.

I groan. "Don't start." My mother is constantly nagging us about the steady stream of women we date and telling us to settle down to give her grandbabies. Yet neither Gianni nor I are close to walking down the aisle.

"We're flying solo, and let's skip the lecture," Gianni states.

"You aren't getting any younger," she says, as if we aren't aware, or she hasn't already said it a thousand times.

"What do you need help with?" I inquire, hoping to change the subject.

She sighs then rubs her neck. "Do me a favor and check on Arianna. Make sure she doesn't have that short hot-pink dress on, or your papà is going to have a heart attack."

Gianni grumbles, "You go. I don't want to deal with her whiny attitude tonight."

"Gee, thanks," I reply but head for the stairs. Arianna isn't a brat, but lately, she's giving all of us a run for our money. She's too beautiful for her own good, and my brothers and I are sick of threatening all the idiots she dates. She's pressing my parents' buttons with her short dresses and low-cut shirts.

She and Tristano share a wing. I pass him on the way to her room, making out with his girlfriend of the month. It's another thing upsetting my mamma. He and Massimo seem to have the same revolving door Gianni and I have regarding women.

Tristano has his newest conquest against the doorframe. His body looms over hers. I don't even stop. He introduced me last night, but I gave up trying to remember the names of my brothers' ass of the week. Hell, sometimes I have a hard enough time remembering my own.

I knock on Arianna's door.

"Come in," she shouts.

I step inside her suite, and my gut drops. She's wearing the exact dress my mamma was worried about. "You can't wear that."

She huffs. "Watch me."

"Don't get snotty with me."

Golden fire erupts in her orbs, shooting flames my way. She puts her hand on her hip and points at me. "You aren't my father."

"Nope. But he's going to tell you the same thing I am."

She snorts. "Whatever. And don't talk to my boyfriend tonight."

The hairs on my arms rise. "Boyfriend? When did you get a new boyfriend?"

"Not your concern," she chirps then sits on the couch and slides her foot into a four-inch black stiletto.

"What's his name?"

Her eyes drift to mine. "Bee Rad."

"Bee Rad? What kind of a fucking name is Bee Rad? How do you even spell it?" I ask.

"Ugh. Don't be so naive! It's b-r-a-d."

"You mean his name is Brad."

She shakes her head. "No. It's Bee Rad."

"You just spelled Brad."

"B-rad. He hyphenates, okay? Jeez. Get with the program, Dante. How old are you that you're this out of touch with the world?"

My blood boils at the thought of this loser talking to my sister, much less putting his hands on her. "Only a moron would call himself Bee Rad."

She fastens her shoe and rises. "He's not a moron, and don't be rude, or I won't introduce you."

I ignore her threat and cross my arms. "Change your dress before Papà has a heart attack."

"No. It's not even that short," she claims.

"Are you serious? I can practically see your ass cheeks," I bellow.

She spins in front of her full-length mirror and glances behind her. "You're such an exaggerator."

"No, I'm not. Get changed."

"No."

"I said to change," I state, getting fed up with this entire conversation. I can only imagine Bee Rad staring at my sister's ass and licking his greedy chops.

"I'm not."

"If you don't change—"

"What? Are you going to throw me in Papà's dungeon? Oh, wait." She puts her index finger on her cheek and glances at the ceiling then innocently widens her eyes. "It's everyone's dungeon, isn't it?"

My chest tightens. A few weeks ago, Massimo wasn't as careful as he should have been when he went to torture an Abruzzo we had taken down there. Arianna was already copping an attitude with us. Numerous times, she had asked my father to join the family business, even though he and my mamma have repeatedly told her she isn't ever getting involved in it. When Massimo saw her downstairs, he took her straight to our father, who told her to forget what she saw and stay out of our business. Her discovery of the dungeon seems to have made her even more pissed off at us. And now she's dating even bigger losers.

Her comment about the dungeon is enough to make me want to go into it and kill someone. "That's enough. Change your dress or stay in your suite all night. I'm not telling you again." I storm out of her room and go down to the ballroom.

The guests have started arriving. I say hi to several in the hallway, and the moment I step inside the ballroom, I hear, "Dante!"

Sean Jr. runs over to me. I crouch down, and he leaps into my arms.

"Hey, buddy!" I mess up his strawberry-blond hair. It's the same color as his father's, and he's the spitting image of him. I tickle him under his ribs.

"Stop!" he yells several times while screeching with laughter.

I finally set him down, and he runs off toward the other children. I rise, and Bridget appears. My heart squeezes like it always does. We've come a long way. I'm happy I at least have her in my life, but I can't seem to get past my attraction to her.

Regardless, I'll never act on it. She's happy, and over the years, Sean and I have genuinely become friends. I would never hurt either of them.

"He's been looking for you since we got here," she states.

I kiss her on the cheek and hug her, forcing myself not to linger too long. "You look beautiful."

Her face lights up, and I reprimand myself when my cock twitches. She takes a sip of her whiskey and glances past me. "Thanks. Who's your date tonight?"

"Solo," I admit.

"Don't tell me you broke up with Costanza?"

"Guilty," I confess.

She scrunches her face. "I liked her. What happened?"

She isn't you.

I curse myself again. Costanza is a nice woman, probably nicer than all the others I've dated. But she wanted more, and as much as I tried to make myself give it to her, I couldn't. I didn't love her. I shrug. "Not meant to be."

Sean steps up beside her with Fiona in his arms. I push her blonde hair off her cheek, kiss it, and he releases her. She runs off to find the other kids.

I shake Sean's hand. "How long are you in town?"

Sean replies, "A few days. I've got a fight mid-week."

"Who's it with?" I ask.

"A Polish guy named Darek. I barely took him out last time. He's a beast."

"How did he finally go down?"

"Left hook."

I hold my fist out, and Sean bumps it. "Nice."

"It was. But I heard he's been doing three-a-days."

"Jesus. He's either Superman or looking to kill himself," I state, knowing how hard two workouts a day are when you're training for a fight.

"Like I said. He's a beast."

The lights flicker, and we all turn. My father hands my mother a flute of champagne and puts his arm around her right as Arianna walks into the ballroom with whom I assume is Bee Rad.

"Fuck's sake," I mutter. He's got tattoos all over his neck, including his face. A hoop glints in his nose, and the gauges in his ears are at least an inch in diameter. He has bad-boy attitude written all over him, and my insides fume. Besides the fact I just don't like how he looks, I think he has to be in his twenties. His palm on my sister's ass only infuriates me more.

"Want me to toss him out of here, or are you going to?" Sean snarls.

"Easy," Bridget states.

Papà glances at Arianna and clenches his jaw. She's wearing the dress I told her not to. Gianni shakes his head at me from across the room. Arianna smirks at all of us.

Papà clears his throat and tightens his arm around Mamma's waist. He holds his champagne in the air and says, "Thank you all for coming tonight. Like always—"

Mamma gasps for breath, clutches her chest, and her eyes roll. She drops her champagne. My father also releases his. The glass bursts all over the parquet floor as he catches her right as her knees give out.

The room becomes loud and chaotic. Within seconds, my brothers, Arianna, and I are at the front of the room, watching as our family doctor, Silvio, gives Mamma chest compressions.

It's like a slow-motion horror movie. Everyone is screaming or crying. At some point, the ambulance arrives, but the paramedics' efforts are just as useless as Silvio's.

Mamma is dead. Her fifty-five-year-old corpse gets zipped into a black bag. Arianna sobs, and her body shakes in my arms as they wheel Mamma past us.

At some point, the guests leave, until no one remains, except Tully, Bridget, Sean, and the kids.

My papà returns to the ballroom, his eyes appearing as empty as I feel. Arianna runs to him, wailing, and I'm unable to look at everyone's faces anymore.

I take off, weaving through the house until I'm in my mother's library. I grab one of the books from the shelf and toss it as hard as possible against the wall. One by one, I throw all of them until there's nothing left, and I'm breathing hard, still holding back my tears.

It's then I feel her hand on my shoulders. Bridget's voice, full of anguish, softly says, "Dante."

I close my eyes, fighting demons rising so furious in me, I'm scared to turn around.

She cautiously steps in front of me, with her eyes glistening a brilliant green. Her lips quiver, and I hate myself more than I ever have.

All I want to do is kiss her. My mother just keeled over from a fucking heart attack, and all I can think about is how Bridget is supposed to be mine.

"Dante." She reaches for my cheek, and her tears spill.

I close my eyes. "You need to go, Bridget."

"I don't think you should be by yourself right now."

I squeeze my lids tighter, my insides trembling so hard, I feel like I'm going to explode. I grind my molars then seethe, "Go away, Bridget."

She doesn't move. Her hand stays on my cheek, and for a moment, I lean into it. But then I remember who she belongs to.

It's not me.

My eyelids fling open. I bark, "Get out of here!"

"But—"

"Leave before I do something I'll regret, Bridget!"

Her eyes widen, and she gasps while removing her hand.

And I feel lost from that action. So fucking lost, the world collapses around me, and I don't think it'll ever return to normal.

I try to swallow the golf ball of emotion in my throat, but my mouth is so dry it hurts. Staring at Bridget as she hesitates about what to do, full of concern for me, only makes the pain of losing my mother mix with the ache I thought I buried long ago.

There are only three women I've ever loved—my mother, Arianna, and Bridget. And having her look me in the face while knowing I can't have her seems extra cruel right now. I'll never see my mamma again, yet Bridget is right in front of me, and I still can't love her how I want to. It's another punch to the gut, knocking the wind out of me.

"Leave," I repeat then turn away from her.

"I'm here if you need anything," she softly says then walks away. Her heels click on the tile in the hallway. It's only when I can't hear them anymore that I lose my shit.

6

Bridget

Five Years Later

"Ashes to ashes, dust to dust," Father Antonio says.

The wind whips so hard, it almost knocks me backward into my dad's large frame. I internally wince from the bruises on the back of my body, which haven't healed. It's something I've learned to deal with the last few days.

Fiona and Sean Jr. are in front of me, sobbing. I'm shaking, full of grief and fear. It never seems to stop. The last week, while all my worst fears played out in front of me, it's like I've been on the edge of a cliff, waiting to fall and crash onto rocks. I'm trying my hardest to be strong for my kids, but there's nothing left to hang on to.

One wrong move, and any chance they have of a normal life will be gone.

Lightning streaks across the sky and thunder booms loud as the coffin is lowered into the ground. There's only one body part in it.

Sean's hand.

Rain suddenly pours out of the sky, hitting my face. I close my eyes, wishing the pain would go away, praying for some miracle that this is a nightmare and I'm going to wake up in Sean's arms.

But it's not. I won't ever feel them around me again. I'll never hear his laugh or see his smile. My children will grow up without the best father they could have ever had.

Every time I glance across the cemetery lot, two of the five men who killed him are there, staring at me, passing unspoken threats across Sean's coffin.

They're two of the five men who raped me in an abandoned parking lot at night while they tied Sean to the hood of a car and laughed as he screamed, begging for them to stop. Between their laughter, the other three thugs kept asking me if I liked Bailey or Rossi dick better.

They're the two men who married Sean's older sisters and called themselves his brothers, our family, yet it was all lies.

They're the same two men who sat on my back deck the day after, drinking beer as if it were normal, while my battered body ached and my heart bled. Like now, I can still smell everything about the men from that night—their sweat, the garlic and alcohol on their breath, the faint hint of lavender on their clothes from one of their detergents.

My children played in the backyard as my brothers-in-law, Niall and Shamus, told me the new rules of my life—rules that take any part of my heart that's left and turn it into the same ashes as Sean's only body part that will disintegrate in the ground.

If I don't follow their orders, they will throw me into one of their whorehouses. But that isn't what I'm terrified of the most. It's the threat to auction my children to the highest bidder that makes me follow their demands, hiding the truth from everyone.

Well, that and I don't know who to trust, including some of my father's top clansmen who arrived in Chicago for the funeral. They seem a little too close to Niall and Shamus, who warned me there were more Baileys and Rossis in the O'Malley clan, as well as my father's, and they would know if I told anyone.

I've never been involved in my father's affairs, yet I understand how he reacts. He would tell me he knows his men and no one will hurt the kids or me ever again. He would order his men to hunt for Lorenzo Rossi and the other three unnamed men I didn't recognize. Until Niall, Shamus, and all four were dead, he wouldn't rest.

So I can't take the risk. I have to protect my children. Sean Jr.'s only 11, Fiona only 9, and every decision I make has to be to keep them safe.

Sean's siblings, who are like my own, I can barely look at or speak to. They think I'm taking the kids to stay with my father for a while. All of them, including my father, have no idea of the other rules. As soon as the wake is over, I'm to leave Chicago, change the kids' and my names from

O'Malley to O'Connor, and never contact any O'Malleys again. The first time I do, the Baileys and Rossis will come after me—after the kids.

The priest ends the ceremony, and my father guides us to his car. I lead my children through the rain, cursing myself too many times for my ignorance. I always thought no one would ever hurt me. I was Tully O'Connor's daughter and Sean O'Malley's wife.

Yet, I was wrong. So very wrong and ignorant.

I never thought about anyone being a traitor. When Sean ordered me to drop him off and told me if anything happened to him to take the kids to my father's in New York, I should never have driven away.

It's why I turned around and came back.

It was too late.

Sean might have told me to take the kids to New York for our safety, but he would never have wanted me to cut off his family.

My kids love every one of the O'Malley family members.

I love them.

They love us.

It's cruel, especially right now. It'll only multiply the pain for everyone. But I don't know what else to do.

Fiona and Sean Jr. sob harder when we get into the car. My father and I do our best to comfort them, but I'm lost.

How do you make a child feel better when their entire world is crumbling around them?

Plus, the guilt of what's to come makes me feel like I can't breathe.

The ride to O'Malley's pub is quick. When we walk in, I can't stop the tears. This pub has been my home since I left New York. It's where I met Sean. It holds a lifetime of memories, yet not enough.

It's the last time I'll ever step foot in it.

The entire wake, I spend with the O'Malleys I love around me. Declan, Nolan, Killian, and Nora are just as spaced out as I feel. I'm thankful they aren't close to their twin sisters, who married Niall and Shamus. It keeps them away from me until my father announces we need to leave for our flight.

He argued with me about returning to New York tonight, but I wasn't about to break a rule. My brother, Brody, finally stepped in and told Dad whatever I wanted to do was best.

Sean's brothers and Nora hug the kids and me. I've never held them so tight. They're going to hate me. They won't ever understand what I'm going to do. And it takes everything I have to remain standing.

I get through it, but then Niall and Shamus step in front of the door, embracing the kids and me.

The scent of their skin flares in my nostrils, mixed with whiskey, just like that night. My skin crawls, and my stomach dives so deep I get nauseous. My tears turn to full-blown sobs, and Shamus tightens his arms around me, making it last longer.

When Niall picks up Fiona, and Shamus hugs Sean, I force myself not to pull them away, but all I want is for them to get their hands off my children.

It feels like time stands still until I shuffle my kids through the door. The rain once again pounds down on us. We travel in silence to the private airport. It's not far, and it's dark by the time we board my father's plane. When we take off, I stare out the window in the direction of the home Sean and I shared. It's the only home my children have ever known. It's the one Sean and his brothers remodeled and surprised me with when I was pregnant with Sean Jr. It's the one my kids spent all their birthdays and holidays inside. But it's also the one Niall and Shamus demanded I put on the market to sell tomorrow.

The lights of Chicago blink below us. Even through the rain, it's beautiful. I've seen it a lot due to all the trips Sean and I took to New York.

The first time I ever flew into Chicago, I felt the life and hope that this was my destiny. I was only eighteen years old, but something about the first moment I saw it made me feel like I was where I was supposed to be, as if I had found a new home.

Now, only agony spreads through my veins. Sean is gone, but taking his family and Chicago away make it seem rawer, somehow more permanent.

Fiona curls up in my lap and falls asleep. Sean Jr. is on my brother, Aidan's, lap, staring at me. He's a replication of his father, minus the twinkle in his eyes or silly grin on his lips. Tonight, emptiness resides in his eyes, and it resonates with how I feel.

When we get to New York, the kids share my bed. Once they're asleep, I can no longer hold everything in. I allow my silent tears to fall again, drenching my pillowcase.

The following day, I shut the door to my father's office, pushing through the disgust swirling around me. "I need you to get my house on the market today."

His eyes widen. "Why would you—"

"It's not safe in Chicago anymore for the kids or me. I need the house on the market today. Are you going to help me or not?"

Dad tilts his head, and my insides quiver harder. He's not used to me talking to him in such a harsh manner. He asks, "What do you know about what happened, Bridget?"

The lump grows in my throat, cutting off my airway. I square my shoulders. "Nothing. Sean kept his business away from me, but he said if anything ever happened to him to come to New York with the kids to be under your protection."

My father shifts on his feet. "When did he say this?"

"The night he went missing. Forget I said anything. I'll figure it out myself." I turn to leave.

"Bridget, stop."

I freeze but don't turn around.

"Of course I'll help you."

"Today. I need it on the market today. Promise me," I order.

"You're sure?"

"Yes." I leave the room, wanting to tell him everything and not to sell my home.

But I can't. These are the new rules.

Later that night, my father's butler comes into the main room. "Mr. Marino is in the den, requesting to see Ms. O'Connor. He said his plane just landed from Italy."

"Which one?" my father asks.

"Dante."

"Dante's here?" Sean Jr. asks, his lips trembling.

I close my eyes, not wanting to see anyone but unsure how to get around this when Sean is already running toward the door. Fiona follows him as well as my father.

When I get within eyesight of the den, Sean and Fiona are both sobbing in Dante's arms.

I stare at them through blurry tears. When Dante looks up and pins his dark gaze on mine, I only cry harder.

The thought to spill everything to Dante that happened is so powerful, it scares me.

So, I walk away and hide out in the sitting room, trying to drink whiskey, but my hand won't stop shaking. At some point, he finds me. I'm in a trance, staring out the window, trying to feel Sean's arms around me.

Dante's hand makes circles on my back, and his deep voice cuts through the air. "Bridge. I'm so sorry. We all came home as soon as we heard."

The whiskey glass slips from my hand, shattering on the floor. He pulls me into his chest. I don't look at him as I wail into it. When I finally can speak, I meet his eyes.

There's pity in them. It's something I've never seen in Dante Marino. I hate everything about his stare. It makes me think once again about telling him everything. So I push away from him, booking it toward the door.

"Leave me alone, Dante. I don't need you around my children or me. Don't come back."

"Bridget, what are you talking about?" he questions.

I speed up and move up the staircase, not looking at him. "I meant what I said. We aren't friends. We were never friends. Don't come back."

"Bridget!" he roars.

I run faster, locking myself in my suite, taking deep breaths. No matter what, I need to stay away from Dante. He's the one person I might not be able to hide the truth from. And I won't risk my children's lives.

7

Bridget

5 Years Later

"Whatever, Bridget," Sean sneers.

"Stop calling me Bridget! I'm your mother!" I cry out for the hundredth time.

He scowls. "Don't you mean a liar?"

My insides shake so hard, I grip the doorframe for support. "Sean—"

"Oh, you're just in time, Fiona. Bridget is going to give us another lecture on—"

"Enough!" Dad's voice booms.

I momentarily close my eyes only to catch Sean refocusing his glare on my father. Ever since he overheard us arguing about the O'Malleys and found out I lied about them not wanting to be in our lives anymore, the love my children have for me seems to have vanished.

They hate me.

I hate me.

Over the last five years, I've spun a massive untruth about the O'Malleys to keep my children safe, but it was that or have the Baileys and Rossis come after them. Then my father made some deal with Sean's brother, Killian. Dad came home, insisting that enough was enough and that he wasn't going along with this anymore. He demanded I tell him why I've lied about the O'Malleys not wanting to see the kids. For weeks, we've gone around and around. I've always held my ground that the kids aren't seeing them. That it's not safe.

Dad kept pushing, just like my brothers. A year ago, my brothers went to Ireland to handle family business. While I missed them, a part of me was happy. I only had to deal with Dad. Whenever I ended our conversations, we'd spend days not talking, but I always kept my kids safe.

Until everything came crashing down around me. One day, my father said he wasn't backing down anymore, and that's when we really got into it. Our voices got louder, and the door flew open.

I'll never escape the betrayal on Fiona's expression or forget the look on Sean's face when he said, "Uncle Killian wants to see us? You lied to us?"

And now, my kids are stepping into the lair. Pandora's box is open, and everything is unraveling around me. I no longer know how to protect them. Sean is insisting on changing his last name back to O'Malley and claiming he's moving to Chicago. He tries to convince Fiona to do the same every chance he gets. My fourteen-year-old baby girl is just confused. I see her indecision on whether to follow her brother or forgive me. All of it breaks my heart on a daily basis.

Sean jerks his head toward my father. His anger radiates all around him. He challenges, "You aren't any better than *her*, are you?"

"Sean, stop," I beg.

Dad steps next to me. I put my arm out to stop him from getting any closer. The situation only gets more volatile, and I lose control of the ability to hold my tears.

Dad points his long finger at Sean, his face red, seething, "I'm two seconds away from canceling your evening."

Sean sarcastically laughs. "You think you're going to keep me from my family? My blood? Go ahead. Try it."

"Sean, stop!" Fiona cries out.

He spins toward her. "They aren't stopping us from seeing our blood any longer!"

"You're making it worse. Killian and Arianna will be here in a few hours. Don't ruin it," she begs.

"Ruin it? They've tried to destroy our relationship with our family. They don't get to make choices for us anymore."

"You talk about things you have no knowledge of," Dad states. He may not know the truth, but he always had my back, until he made that deal with Killian. He still tries to maintain it. He knows how much I love my kids. I don't understand why he did what he did. He had no right. So for the first time in forty-two years, I'm at odds with my father, too. The loving home I've tried to create for my children no longer exists. It's a daily battlefield. Dad continues, "And while you're in my home—"

"You think I want to be here?" Sean roars.

Dad lowers his voice, but there's a threat to it. "You're pushing it, Sean."

"You're such a hypocrite," Sean snarls.

"Sean! Stop!" I plead. Before this happened, my son was never disrespectful. He was just like his father and always tried to protect Fiona and me, even though he's only sixteen. He loved my father. Now, his hurt controls his actions, and I'm not sure what to do.

I'm afraid my children will never forgive me, but most of all, I'm petrified of who might come after them. My father agreed to put extra security on them, but even that makes me nervous.

Since we moved here, I've insisted their guards are blood only. My first cousins, Zayden and Kian, are assigned to Sean. Dallan and Nevan watch over Fiona. All four of their security details have reasons to hate the Baileys and Rossis. It helps me sleep better at night, but I still watch them closely. The kids are angry about that as well, but I'm not budging. I'm *never* letting my guard down again. I curse myself too many times a day for being so naive while in Chicago.

Over the years, my father has found traitors in his clan. It always happens when I feel weak. The longing for my dead husband never goes away. Every time I have to lie about his family, I feel sick. I know he would hate what I'm doing. Family was everything to him—to us.

Then the flashbacks of that night will hit me out of the blue. Someone will walk by with lavender scent on their clothes, or I'll hear the name Bailey or Rossi, or we'll be in the car and headlights will shine at us. All I can see is Sean tied to the hood. It pushes me closer to breaking down and telling my father the truth. My moment of weakness always appears when another traitor in his clan pops up. It makes me keep my secrets in the vault I created.

"If you do anything to fuck up our night with Killian and Arianna, you'll pay," Sean warns, his green eyes darkening.

"Are you threatening me?" Dad huffs.

"Stop! Both of you, stop! Dad, go," I order.

Now my father is pissed at me, too. His leer turns toward me. "He will not continue to disrespect us in this house."

"Please, go," I implore through clenched teeth.

"Yeah, return to ordering your thugs around," Sean taunts.

"Sean! Stop it!" Fiona shouts.

I push my father out of the room, just wanting this to end. I slam the door shut behind me.

"This needs to end, Bridget," Dad states.

I wipe my face and accuse, "This is your fault. You made a deal you had no right to make."

His face hardens, and he glances at the ceiling. In a cold voice, he replies, "They'll be here in under two hours. It's time to face the music and put this behind us, Bridget."

A new panic sweeps through me. I need to get out of here. There's no way I can face Killian or Arianna.

She and I had lunch a few weeks before she got married. The charity I work for wanted her on the committee. I've stayed away from the Marinos and their parties since Sean died, not wanting to see Dante. I was too afraid the same urge to tell him everything would pop up like the last time I saw him after Sean died. And I'm embarrassed by what I said to him. He was a good friend to me—to Sean and the kids. The more time that passed, the harder it became to show my face.

The minute I learned Arianna was marrying Killian, I felt the thread start to unravel. There was no way Killian and the kids' paths weren't going to intersect. It was only a matter of time, and I didn't know what to do.

My father insisted Sean and Fiona went with him to the Christmas parties and were here when he hosted them. But I always leave the night events are at our house.

It's been five years since I saw Dante or any other Marino. So when Susan on the committee said, "Bridget, you know Arianna, correct?" I had to face it and reach out to her.

All our lunch did was remind me how much I missed her and the Marinos. But something about them feels too much like the O'Malleys. They have a close-knit family, and I don't think I can handle the reminder of all I've lost. I realized after my lunch with Arianna, it's another reason I stayed away.

I step away from Dad and move toward the staircase. "You invited the O'Malleys. This is your event, not mine."

His voice turns sharper. "You aren't doing this tonight. Running isn't going to help, Bridget."

I spin on the landing and point at him. "You made this deal. I disagree with it, and you have no idea what you did. Make sure the kids don't leave the house." I turn and rush up the stairs then lock myself in my room.

I assume I'll do exactly what I always do during these times. I'll get dressed up and have my driver take me all over New York. I never get out of the car. I just stare out the window at the city lights, talking to Sean in my head and asking him to forgive me for all the extra pain I've caused his family and our children. And I usually drink too much whiskey while crying and feeling lonelier than ever.

I don't have friends, except for Cara, who just arrived back in the city. She was in Europe for years and had no idea Sean died. After I had the kids, we drifted apart, each busy with our own lives. I ran into her at a coffee shop a month ago.

She keeps asking me to go out, but I've only had lunch with her. Besides the charity events I've immersed myself in, I'm active at the kids' school. My father insisted they attend the same one I did, stating it's the best education in New York, possibly the country. But I remember all too well what goes on in that place, so I'm always there, always watching, always making sure my children don't get wrapped up in toxic shit with their classmates.

I have enough toxic chaos in my veins to last a lifetime.

Until they heard Dad and me arguing over the O'Malleys, Sean and Fiona liked me being at their school. Maybe it was because their father died, but they never were embarrassed or complained. Now, they both avoid me like the plague.

I take a cold shower, trying to freeze all the sadness, grief, and hatred for myself out of me, but I can't. I throw on a little black dress, slide into my heels, then toss my phone, ID, and credit card in an evening bag. I'm unsure why I always do this. Maybe it's to fool everyone into thinking I have a life. Perhaps it's to make me feel like I have one. Regardless, the life I used to know, the person I used to be, no longer exists.

And now my kids, who I've worked so hard to protect and keep safe, have a bigger target on their backs. The only control I felt I had is shattering around me. I don't know how to hold it all together.

I manage to sneak out of the house a few minutes before Killian and Arianna arrive. As my driver veers the car onto the main road, my stomach flips. A black SUV passes us, similar to my father's, and I know it's them. I duck, even though no one can see past the blacked-out windows.

It's not that late, barely dinner time, still a bit light out. I pick up the canister and tumbler then pour some whiskey. Loneliness immediately expands within me. It's always there, constantly nagging me, but it somehow feels worse tonight.

My phone vibrates, and I glance at it, then wish I didn't.

Sean: *You left. Figures. You're such a coward.*

I cringe then let a large mouthful of whiskey burn down to my stomach. He's right. I am a coward. There's no way I can face Killian or even Arianna now that she knows what I've done.

Hours pass, and I keep drinking, trying to dull the pain. For some reason, my tears don't drop. Maybe I already cried enough today. Everything feels hollow, except for the loneliness that won't go away.

It's dark when my phone rings, pulling me out of my trance. I usually let everything go to voicemail, but I answer it, wondering if something is wrong with the kids.

"Hello."

"Bridget! Where are you?" Cara chirps.

"In the car." I take another large swig, feeling a bit dizzy.

"Doing what?"

I laugh humorlessly. "Drinking. Trying to forget my kids hate me."

Concern fills her voice. "What are you talking about?"

"Nothing."

"So you're alone?"

"Yeah, why?"

"Great, you can be my ride or die tonight."

I bark a genuine laugh. I don't know why I allow myself the simple pleasure, but it's the first time in a long time something strikes me as funny. "Do people still say that?"

"Don't know, but I just did. Pick me up. There's a new underground club, and I'll have them add you to the list."

"Underground club? What does that mean?"

"It means no one will know you're there and you can forget about all your problems. Now tell your hottie driver to swing by and pick me up."

Forget about my problems.

Something in me snaps. "Fine. What's your address?"

I roll the divider down and she tells me, then I give my driver instructions.

It takes ten minutes to get to her place, and I finish my drink before we arrive. When he pulls the SUV up to the curb, Cara comes flying out of her building. She slides next to me and hugs me.

I hug her back, wondering when the last time I had human contact was, now that my kids no longer want anything to do with me and I'm at odds with my father. It feels good. I'm suddenly craving anything that makes me feel human again.

She tilts her head. Her blue eyes pin mine. "Are you okay?"

I shrug then hand her a glass. "Normal day in paradise. Whiskey?"

"I'll take the vodka with some tonic."

"Is that what you drink now?"

She shrugs. "Sometimes."

I mix her drink. She tells the driver where to go. We engage in small talk until we pull up to the building. There's no line or other vehicles.

"Is this the wrong address?" I ask.

"No. We have five minutes to go in, or we won't be allowed inside. It's how they keep it hidden."

"Why do they need it hidden?" I ask.

Cara's lips twitch. "Let's just say things aren't totally kosher."

"What does that mean?"

"It's the elite doing what they want. You know how they roll."

Nervous tension builds in my stomach. "Meaning?"

She opens the door. "Come on. We have an invite into a VIP suite. It'll be fun, and nothing is off-limits."

"Off-limits?"

"Yeah. No one judging you or making you feel bad. Let's go." She reaches in for me.

No one will make me feel bad.

I finish the last sip of my drink then take her hand and get out.

"Tell your driver to go. We won't get in if he doesn't leave," she instructs.

"Seriously?"

"Yes. He can park a few blocks up."

I relay the message to my driver and he argues with me. I never go anywhere without my father's men, but since everything feels like it's spiraling out of control, what do I have left to lose? I demand he leaves and tell him if he doesn't, he's fired.

When the SUV is out of sight, Cara leads me into a building. Several beefy bouncers stand behind a petite woman who checks our names off a list. She opens a door, and one of the bouncers nods for us to go through.

The hallway is dark, with dim lights on the walls. The music gets louder as we take more steps. When we step out into the main area, I freeze.

Where the hell did Cara bring me?

Several floors overlook where we stand. There are tables scattered around oversized beds. Restraints hang from the ceiling over the mattresses. Everywhere I look, people are having sex.

"You brought me to a sex club?" I blurt out.

Cara laughs. "You don't have to do anything you don't want to. Come on. The VIP suites aren't like this." She pulls on my arm. We step aside as a server in nothing but a blingy thong passes us, carrying a tray lined with what I assume is cocaine and champagne.

"I'm a mom! I can't be here!" I claim, sobering up a bit.

Cara tilts her head. "You're more than a mom. You don't have to do anything you don't want to," she reiterates. "Let's have fun and forget about life. You need a good night out." She tugs me toward an elevator.

I should stop following her and call my driver to get me, but I don't. I get in the elevator with her, my stomach flipping faster as we approach the top level. When we step out, she tugs me into a suite.

A tall, dark-haired man steps forward. He greets her in Italian then kisses her cheek.

She replies in Italian, which surprises me. I wasn't aware she knew it, but I sometimes forget that she's been all over Europe. I only know a little from growing up around the Marinos. Cara tugs me closer to her. "Uberto, this is my friend Bridget."

He drags his eyes over my body then meets my gaze. His smile grows, and he leans forward, kissing my cheek. "Nice to meet you."

"Are you going to introduce me to your friend, Cara?" another man asks from behind me.

I spin, my stomach in knots. I'm not used to men looking at me or even talking to them. Since Sean died, I stay far away unless it's my father. This man is eyeing me up like he's a dog who hasn't eaten in days.

"Michelotto." Cara rises on her tiptoes. He plants a kiss on her cheek. She beams. "This is my bestie, Bridget."

He says something in Italian I don't understand while pinning his blue eyes on mine, then leans forward and kisses my cheek. "You're stunning."

I take a deep breath and smile, wishing I knew how to act around male attention. It's been so long, and it all feels uncomfortable. The only thing I focus on is my children. I've shot down offers from single dads at the school or men who talk to me at charity events, but I feel completely out of place in this social setting.

"What can I get you to drink, Bridget?" Michelotto asks.

I clear my throat. "Whiskey, please."

"Straight?"

I nod.

He licks his lips as if in approval. Cara grabs my hand and weaves me through the people to a set of couches. We sit, and Uberto slides his arm around her shoulder. "How have you been?"

She smiles. "Good."

"It's been a long time." His eyes dip to her chest, then he leans in and says something in her ear while gliding his hand between her thighs.

She giggles, murmuring something in his ear.

I shift in my seat, looking the other way.

Michelotto beelines toward us with two drinks in his hand. He sits next to me.

The hairs on my arms rise. I take the tumbler and down two large mouthfuls, but I've already drunk so much, it doesn't even burn.

Michelotto scoots closer. "You live in New York?"

I take a deep breath and turn to him. "Yeah. What about you?"

He smiles. "I roam between Italy and here. I'll be in New York for the next year at least."

I take a few more sips, trying to calm my nerves. He's good-looking and seems nice, but I didn't prepare myself to be in this situation. The VIP room doesn't have people screwing everywhere like downstairs, but people are making out. Women sit on men's laps. One woman has her dress off and is in her lingerie. It reminds me how I haven't had anyone touch me since...

Since that night.

I swallow the lump crawling up my throat then finish the rest of my drink. I get up and grab Michelotto's shoulder when my balance falters. He rises. "Whoa. You okay?"

"Yeah." I straighten up and smile. "Just need another drink."

"Follow me." He escorts me to the bar, and the entire time, I can't stop the voice in my head.

I need to get past that night.

Michelotto motions to the bartender then leans into the bar. "So, what do you do for fun?"

A tiny laugh escapes me. "Nothing."

He traces my jawline.

I attempt to ignore the way my skin crawls.

Get past it, get past it, get past it.

My heart races, and he chuckles, stating, "I find that hard to believe."

The bartender sets the whiskey down. I pick it up, drink some, then turn so my back is against the bar. I survey the room, which is a bad idea. There only seems to be more sexual energy in the room. I stiffen and down half my glass, feeling dizzier. I'm no more comfortable in this place now than when I got here.

Michelotto wraps his arm around my waist and leans into my ear. "You want to get out of here?"

I glance at him in question. "I'm not leaving without Cara."

"I meant to go to another room. Maybe dance a little. Somewhere things aren't so"—he glances at the woman who's only in her bra and panties then arches his eyebrows at me —"risque."

I breathe in relief. "Yes. Sounds good."

His face lights up. He guides me out of the room, down the hall, and into another suite. This one feels more comfortable. There's a small dance floor along with couches, but everyone is fully dressed. No one is doing anything sexual.

"Finish your drink," he instructs.

I do it, downing the whiskey in a few swallows. He grabs my tumbler, sets it down then pulls me out to the dance floor. Within minutes, I'm swaying to the music, which hasn't happened since before Sean's murder.

Since Michelotto doesn't drag me close to him, I start to relax with him.

As the night progresses, we drink more. I forget about all my problems. We naturally move closer, and I don't resist. It feels good to be dancing with a man, and not worrying about protecting my kids or having them fight with me. At some point, Michelotto pulls me over to a couch. He tugs me onto his lap.

Then he kisses me. At first, I don't think about it. It feels good to have someone want me again. I kiss him back until I feel his hand on my thigh. It gives me a flashback of Shamus's hand on my thigh the night of Sean's murder.

I try to push his hand off me, but he keeps it there. He kisses me deeper and holds my head so tight I can't move, inching his hand higher on my leg.

"Stop," I say between his lips, but it's garbled.

"Don't be a tease, Bridget," he replies then shoves his tongue down my throat and yanks me closer.

I swat his hand, trying to get it off me, but he's too strong. So I keep slapping, and pushing, but he spins me on my ass and cages his body over mine.

I try to stand, but I'm too drunk to find my balance. He pins my hands in the air. When his eyes meet mine, everything from the past flashes before me.

All I want to do is die. I scream, but his lips and tongue choke me.

And then, suddenly, he's being yanked off me. Things become blurrier. Punches are thrown and guns are drawn. I hide my head in my hands, cowering on the couch, unable to move. The scents of sweat, garlic, stale alcohol, and lavender flare in my nostrils. No one is touching me, but I feel like I'm being choked.

Someone pulls me off the couch. I'm still in a trance, not sure who it is. I get thrown over a man's shoulder.

Every emotion I have lodges in my throat. I kick him, but it doesn't seem to matter. It's not until I'm tossed into an SUV that I know who has taken me.

The car starts moving as soon as the door slams. I turn, shuddering, as Dante's dark, cold eyes sear into mine.

8

Dante

An Hour Earlier

"MAYBE I SHOULD SUCK YOUR COCK RIGHT NOW," SHILO, A woman I guess you can say I've been dating for the last few months, suggests in my ear. Her nails drag up my erection.

"You know better than to be a tease," I warn.

She giggles, but truth be told, I'm bored. She's way too young for me, barely out of college, but she hasn't asked to get married or said she loves me yet. In my book, that makes her a keeper—for now.

She slurs, "What are you going to—"

My phone vibrates, and I don't hear the rest. I glance at the message. My gut rolls like it's on a never-ending hill.

Rubio: *Bridget O'Connor is in my suite, drunk, with some Italian guy who roams between ours and the Abruzzo suites.*

The hairs on my arms rise. *What the hell is Bridget doing in this club?*

I shove Shilo off my lap, rise, and zip my pants.

"What are you doing?" she cries out.

"We're through. Find someone else." I turn to my brother. "Gianni."

Shilo grabs my arm, her eyes widening. "Dante! What are you talking about?"

I shrug out of her grasp. "You heard me." I bark again, "Gianni!"

He isn't any more of a saint than I am in this place. He tears his lips off a woman he selected when he walked through the club doors. He already has her dress bunched to her waist, and she's grinding on him.

"Now," I bellow.

"Fuck, Dante. Stay here," he orders the woman and then grumbles as we make our way down the hall.

"Bridget's in Rubio's suite with some thug," I inform him.

He pushes me against the wall. "Not our business. Not *your* business."

I refrain from telling him anything to do with Bridget is my business. Instead, I go for the only fact that will get him to stop arguing with me. "He's got Abruzzo ties."

Gianni's face darkens. "Shit."

"Yeah." We continue down the hall, weaving our way through drunk women, ignoring the other crime families.

The club is the one place in the city that all the crime families agreed was a safe-zone location. There's an understanding that no business or violence takes place in the club.

Besides the need to have debauchery in our lives, that's where commonalities end. Families stay in their suites or ignore the others in hallways. And business happens. Plus, all of us are hoping to find some piece of information on the others to use in the future.

When we step into Rubio's room, my heart stammers. My blood pounds like a sledgehammer against my skull.

For the last five years, Bridget's ignored all my attempts to see her, along with my text messages and phone calls. It was like going back twenty years all over again, except this time, it was worse. I wasn't the asshole who created her pain trying to make up for it. Sean was dead, and there was nothing I could do. And every time I saw the kids or Tully, I looked for her, hoping she'd show up, but she never did.

This time, I wasn't messaging her to get in her pants or beg her to be mine. I was worried about her. I wanted to help her, but no matter what I did or how much time passed, I couldn't figure out how to reach her.

So I've only seen her from a distance, watching her from my car as she dropped the kids off at school or disappeared inside the building. Sometimes, I'd text or call her just to see her reaction. Did she really hate me? Was today the day she would finally talk to me?

I'd only succeeded in torturing myself more. She'd throw my calls into voicemail or stare at my text then squeeze her eyes shut. Every now and then, she'd stare at my SUV as if she knew I was only a few hundred feet away from her. *It's how I knew.*

She was still in so much pain. Even from far away, I could see the light was gone in her eyes. Emptiness replaced it, and her greenish-blue orbs seemed almost dull.

Now, she's in front of me, drunk, on the dance floor, and with a man I know nothing about, but I know enough.

If he has any relationship with the Abruzzos, he's bad news.

I step to move toward her, and Gianni pulls me back. "We wait. You know the rules."

I cringe inside, ready to throw every rule to the curb.

"She could get hurt," Gianni states.

Those four words make my fists at the sides of my body hurt. They keep my feet planted where they are.

Every family has to follow the club's rules. Going against them would start a war. So I have to wait until this prick makes a wrong move. Since Bridget's the Irish mafia princess, the club and families will overlook any violence that may occur if he steps out of line. My gut says there's no way this isn't going to get physical. This club demands consent at all times, and there's no way Bridget's letting this thug fuck her here.

Every moment I watch her dance with her body pressed to his makes me angrier. She's drunk, stumbling often. Her eyes are bloodshot, and he keeps handing her more whiskey.

Gianni and I watch, waiting for what I can feel is about to happen. My stomach curls and my fists tighten. I'm utilizing every ounce of restraint I have to hold myself back from tearing him off her.

Then the dickhead makes his move. He takes her to the couch. The moment he kisses her, bile creeps up my throat. Over the years, I got used to Sean's lips on hers. I couldn't even hate him for it. He made her happy and treated her well. As much as I wanted her, if I couldn't have her, I learned to appreciate that she was Sean's. But this thug is never getting my approval.

It doesn't take long before she's slapping his hand. He doesn't stop and gets more aggressive.

Gianni and I practically fly across the room. I'm thankful we're in Rubio's suite. If it were anyone else's, who knows how this will end.

I tear him off her and land a punch on his cheek. He tries to fight back, but I hit him again. Gianni pulls out his gun, and the prick freezes.

Bridget cowers on the sofa, hiding her face. I sling her over my shoulder, storming out of the room. She screams and kicks me, but it only makes me hold her thighs tighter.

Gianni and I say nothing, getting in the elevator. We go straight to the parking garage. Bridget continues to try and fight me, but she's too weak from her intoxicated state for me to even feel it.

It makes me angrier. She has no right to be in this club or this drunk here. It's not safe for her.

Our SUV pulls up the moment we step outside. I put Bridget in the backseat. Gianni and I hop in next to her. The driver takes off, and she slowly turns toward me.

Her glistening, sad eyes are about to overflow. My heart squeezes so damn hard, I can barely breathe.

Gianni knocks on the divider window and calls out, "Tully's."

Bridget glances at Gianni as if just realizing he's here. Her eyes widen, and the tears drop. She grabs my arm. "No. I can't go home. Dante, please."

There are so many things I want to ask her. Too many overdue things I've been dying to know. But I say nothing, not knowing where to start, wondering how she got into that club and how to make sure she never goes there again.

"Our place," Gianni directs the driver.

"No! I-Killian and Arianna are there. I-I can't go there," Bridget frets.

"Bridget—"

"Please. Anywhere but those two places. I-I can't do it right now," she admits and breaks down.

I pull her onto my lap and hold her head to my chest. "Ritz," I tell the driver.

She sobs harder. Somewhere in there are sorries that get caught in her throat and make her chest heave.

Gianni gives me his look. It's a warning that I'm making a mistake. That the last place I should be going is to a hotel with Bridget. And I shouldn't be getting involved in her life again. My brother says all this to me just through his eyes.

I ignore him, tightening my arms around her, then motioning for him to secure the room and get the key when we pull up to the front doors.

He shakes his head but gets out. When the door shuts, I kiss Bridget's blonde hair and mumble, "I need you to pull it together to get past reception."

She tilts her head and slowly meets my gaze, the blues peeking out under her lashes. "Why are you acting nice toward me right now?"

My stomach quivers. I want to tell her if she searches deep enough, she knows why. No matter what's gone on between us, my obsession with her, no matter how hard I've tried, has never wavered. And even though she's never wanted me since before she left for Chicago,I'd step in front of a bullet before I let anything happen to her. But all I say is, "We're friends."

My statement only makes her cry harder. Her expression becomes more painful.

I sigh and hold her head against my chest again. "Bridge, are you going to be able to get through reception? If not, I need to take you to your place or mine."

She nods, sniffling hard. By the time Gianni comes back with the key, she's calmed enough for me to get her out of the car. Still, I take my sport coat off and instruct, "Hold on to my waist." She obeys, and I wrap it around her, so her face is covered.

Gianni gives me a *this is a bad idea* look, but I ignore him and order, "Text me when you find out."

He grinds his molars then gets in the car. It's all I have to say. In all reality, I don't even need to speak it. Whoever that asshole who was on Bridget is, he's getting picked up tonight. As soon as she's okay, I'll be dealing with him in the dungeon.

I swiftly move Bridget past reception, into the elevator, and down the hall. I knew she drank too much, but she stumbles so much, I debate about picking her up. When we get into the suite, I remove the jacket and guide her to the bathroom. I turn on the cold shower and unzip her dress.

"What are you doing?" she asks.

"Sobering you up."

"I'm fine."

I unclasp her bra and pull it off before she can stop me. "You aren't."

She covers her chest with her arms. She demands, "Stop! This isn't appropriate."

Years of anger hit me. "You think going to that club is?"

Her eyes turn to slits. "Don't you dare judge me!"

I slide my hands on her hips, under the thin string of her panties, and in a quick move, tug my hands away so they rip.

"Dante!"

I move her into the shower.

"Jesus! It's freezing," she shouts.

"Yep."

She steps forward, out of the way of the cold stream.

"Get under the water," I order.

She looks at me, breaks down again, then crouches on the tile. Sobbing, she states, "I hate you."

I strip and step in the shower then pull her up. She's right, the water is cold as fuck. Any alcohol I drank that's still in my system seems to disappear. "Well, I don't hate you," I reply and hold her tight to my frame. I pump the wall container of shampoo and lather her hair.

She just cries while I wash her hair and body. When I finally turn off the water, her teeth chatter and her lips are purple.

I wrap a fluffy towel around her, another around her hair, and then one around me. I pick her up and set her on the counter. She stares at me, her eyes more green than blue but bloodshot.

I put paste on the hotel toothbrush. "Open."

She shakes her head. "I don't need your help."

"Open, or I'll make you, Bridge," I softly warn, refraining from saying anything else, trying to erase the thought of that thug's hands and lips on her.

She reluctantly obeys. I carefully brush her teeth. Then I hold a cup of water to her mouth. "Swish."

She sniffles and does it. I comb her hair then carry her to the bed. I slide her under the covers then go back to the bathroom and brush my teeth. When I turn off the lights, I put my phone on the table and get in bed next to her.

"My kids hate me," she whispers.

"No, they don't. They're just upset," I insist near her ear. I tug her into my arms, cocooning my body around hers.

"They do." She turns to me. "You don't know what I've done."

"Regarding the kids?" I question.

She squeezes her eyes shut and nods.

"Yeah, I do. Killian and Arianna told us their side of the story."

More tears fall. "Then you know I'm a horrible mother."

I wipe her cheek. "No, you aren't. What I know is that the O'Malleys want to see the kids. I also know the kids want to see the O'Malleys. What I don't know is why you made this choice. But not a bone in my body thinks you wouldn't have if you didn't have your reasons."

"Well, you're the only one in the entire world, then."

I tuck her wet hair behind her ear. "Then I guess you have one person on your side."

She closes her eyes, and her lips quiver.

I trace her jaw, trying to ignore my cock that's growing harder by the minute. "Why were you in the club, Bridget?"

Darts fly at me from her eyes. Her tone turns ugly. "Why were you there?"

"Do you really want an answer to that?"

She turns away so her ass is against my cock, seething, "Of course, same old Dante. Are you and Gianni still swapping?"

"Why would you care if we were?" I ask, pissed she's bringing that shit up after all these years. I told her so many times how sorry I was for all the sordid crap I put her through in high school before I knew she was dating Sean.

"Guess some things never change," she mutters.

I flip her over so fast, she gasps. I cage my body over hers. "We haven't done that since we graduated high school. But I'm not a saint and won't pretend to be one. You, on the other hand..." I lick my lips, trying to regulate my heartbeat, refraining from dipping an inch lower and taking what I've always wanted to be mine. "You have no business in that club."

More tears and pain fill her orbs. Her voice cracks. "Why? Because I'm a widow? Because I'm a mom? Or is it because Sean would hate me touching anyone else?"

My chest tightens. "Jesus, Bridge. No. You're too good for anyone in that club."

Her forehead scrunches. "I didn't know. Cara told me to pick her up. I-I was already drinking in the car and... I don't know why I didn't leave. But—" She takes a few shaky breaths. "It felt nice not to think for a few hours. Not to be hated."

"No one hates you."

"Everyone does."

I drag my knuckles over her cheek. "I don't hate you."

"You don't know me anymore."

"Yes, I do."

The self-loathing that fills her eyes takes the air out of my lungs. She quietly states, "No. You don't. If you did, you wouldn't be here."

"There's nothing you could ever do that would make me feel that way."

"Why? How can you lie here and say that?"

I finally just blurt it out. "You know why."

The truth hangs between us, filling the air with tension, making my pulse increase.

"I loved Sean. I still do," she whispers through her tears.

I sniff hard, and my chest pushes against her stiff nipples. And everything is so ironic. I'm here, naked, with the only woman I've ever wanted, yet she still doesn't want me. She'll *never* want me. I can't even blame her for it. She had a man who, from day one, cherished her instead of fucking with her head the way I did. So I confess, "I know you do. And as much as I tried to hate him, I didn't. He was a good man. Much better than me."

She places a shaking hand on my cheek, gazing at me with eyes that no longer have light in them. She chokes, "I miss him. So much."

A lump grows in my throat, suffocating me. I tell myself to roll off of her and just be her friend.

But I can't move. I stay frozen, except for my heart that beats so violently it wants to escape my chest.

More tears fall down her cheeks. "I'm so tired of feeling dead."

It makes everything explode exponentially around us. The pain in her expression tugs at every emotion I have. The desire I have for her, that I can't seem to escape, burns hotter, mixing with the electric air around us.

My lips brush against hers as I say, "You aren't dead, dolcezza."

Her warm breath hits mine, and it's like breathing tingles into every cell in my body. Her fingers slide through the back of my hair.

I attempt to ignore the part of me that's trying to be a stand-up guy.

But that's the thing. I've never been a stand-up guy. I take what I want, and for too long, I've only wanted her.

Eyes locked, hearts beating, and skin growing warmer by the second, I lose my ability to hold back.

Our mouths are already touching. I slide my tongue along her lips, slowly tasting her. Warm whiskey mixes with a cool sensation from the mint, intoxicating me further.

She inhales sharply. Her body trembles beneath mine in small shudders, but her hand grips my hair tighter. Then she opens her mouth. Her tongue explores mine, cautiously, until the man that I am, the one who dominates and demands, takes over.

My arms slide under her. I wrap her hair around my fist, and her eyes widen. A hurricane whirls around us, drenching us in an ocean of the past, present, and future.

Everything I remember about kissing Bridget O'Connor becomes a reality once more.

Except this time, we aren't kids. I'm not going to create false promises or walk out of this room and choose another woman, to save face. And I'm not foolish enough to think I might ever get this chance again.

So, unlike with all the women I've had over the last twenty-four years, I fully give in to our kisses, putting everything I have into it instead of holding back and going through the motions to get what I think I need in the moment.

For the first time ever, it's not about me.

It's about her.

My tongue darts in and out of her mouth, hungry. So fucking hungry for everything I've not had since that day in the closet. And desperate to somehow fix all of her problems through my body, which isn't logical, but I've never had common sense around her.

She whimpers into my mouth. One of her hands grabs my ass, and zings run up my spine. Her legs widen and hips lift, but I do the opposite of what I usually would.

Instead of sliding into her and taking what I need, I tug her head back and suck on her neck, then murmur in her ear, "You aren't dead, Bridge. Your light's still in there. If I have to spend every second of the rest of my life finding it and bringing it back to the surface, I will."

She freezes and takes a shaky breath.

I drag my teeth down her neck and suck on her pulse then slide my tongue down her chest until my mouth is covering as much of her breast as possible. I dip my other hand lower and glide a finger through her wet heat.

She moans. Her legs widen more, and she grinds into my palm.

"Fuck, you're beautiful," I mumble, taking her other breast in my mouth and teasing her clit with my thumb.

"Oh God!" she cries out, writhing, digging her nails into my skull and ass.

I shimmy over her, kissing her through her orgasm, muffling all the sounds I've dreamed of for so many years. But they're barely like the sounds I only got a glimpse of in Gianni's movie room all those years ago.

These are desperate, mixed with grief and longing, with no attempt to stay quiet. They aren't an innocent, untouched girl's. They're from a woman who's trying to feel, trying to find life again.

"Dante," she barely gets out, her eyes glistening.

"Shh. It's okay. Everything is okay," I murmur. Then I'm in her pussy, tasting her, teasing her, taking everything I've ever wanted, and not thinking a goddamn moment about myself or the growing ache in my cock. I don't rush it or do anything half-assed. Every second is one more moment I want to repeat.

"Dante...oh God!" her raspy voice cries out. She pulls my hair so hard, I think it might rip from my scalp. Her hot, dewy thighs tremble, squeezing my cheeks.

I switch my fingers to her clit and inch my tongue in and out of her channel, going as deep as I can and swirling it against her walls. Then I rub her clit faster until she's clenching my tongue and cursing.

I lunge over her, shoving her thigh in the air and pressing my forehead to hers. And since I'm a greedy man, I thrust into her in one move, eyes pinned on hers, studying the little bit of light that sparked, trying to burn brighter.

She moans, her mouth in an O, her arms tightening around me. It all gives me the illusion she's mine, and there's no way this could ever be anything different.

Bliss swaddles me as my cock slides against her walls. It's pure fucking heaven, a thousand times better than I imagined it would be, so I hold myself back from going any faster.

But it's like Bridget knows what the primal urge in me is dying to do. Her cheeks heat and her voice cracks. "Fuck me harder."

I groan, flipping her over, and she inhales sharply. I push her head on the pillow and pull her waist up then plunge back into her.

"Jesus!" she breathes.

I lean over her, resting my forearm on the mattress and tugging on her hair, claiming her how I've always wanted to. "You're mine, Bridge. Every part of you is mine."

She closes her eyes and presses her hips into me. "Hard, Dante."

I pound into her, suck on the curve of her neck, and grunt in her ear. "Open your eyes," I demand.

She does, then she comes, the blue in her eyes overtaking the green, still empty and sad but with a hint of her light flickering through.

I thrust through her orgasm as her cunt milks my cock for everything it has, everything it can give. I shoot all of it deep inside her, finally marking her as mine after all these years.

When I can focus again, I lie on my back, tugging her into me, but she spins so she isn't facing me. I'm not sure if it's intentional or not. Several minutes pass until my heart feels normal again.

I stroke her stomach and kiss the back of her head. "You all right, dolcezza?"

She puts her hand over mine, her thumb caressing me, but says nothing. I don't push or say anything else. When she falls asleep, she's in my arms.

But when I wake up the next day, she's gone.

9

Bridget

COLD WIND SLAPS MY FACE WHEN I STEP OUTSIDE THE RITZ. Morning light is trying to crack the darkness, creating a blue hue everywhere. My driver pulls up to the valet area, jumps out of the car, and opens the back door. I hold my head high, avoiding his gaze. I'm aware I look a mess.

As soon as I get in the car, I lean back into the headrest, closing my eyes. My stomach is a quivering mess of anxiety. The scent of Dante's skin still flares in my nostrils, which makes me curse him. It's an aphrodisiac, making every sense in my body wish I hadn't left.

What did I do?

Why did I like it so much?

Dante's voice fills my mind. *"You're mine, Bridge. Every part of you is mine."*

I shudder.

I'm not his.

I can't be.

I'm Sean's and only his.

A tear slips down my cheek, and I wipe it away. The last thing I need is to get involved with Dante Marino. I worked hard to get him out of my system years ago. There's nothing good that can come from what happened last night.

Why do I want to feel his arms around me again?

Why did I ever let Cara take me to that club?

The entire way out of the city and to my father's house, I beat myself up. I'm not in high school anymore. I'm raising teenagers. I don't have time for Dante's twisted games. The only matter I should be concentrating on is how to help my children stop hurting and love me again.

It didn't feel like he was playing a game.

That's what he does though. He uses women then throws them away when he's bored, I remind myself when my driver pulls through my father's gates.

I pull my phone out of my purse, glance at myself in the camera, then wince.

Smudged makeup from the previous night lines my eyes. My air-dried hair is a mess. My dress is wrinkled. I smell like pure, raw sex.

Please don't let me run into anyone, I repeatedly pray as I get out of the car and go into the house. I take off my shoes to eliminate the noise on the marble as I creep through the house. I make my way up the stairs and almost get to my bedroom when my father's voice hits my ears.

"Bridget."

I cringe, take a deep breath, and spin, all while cursing Dante Marino. I shouldn't feel like a teenager caught sneaking into her parents' house, but I do. I might remember asking him not to take me home, but everything about what we did is making me feel like I'm sixteen again.

I hate it.

Nothing good happened when I was sixteen. I spent too many seconds thinking about Dante. Now, I'm almost a forty-one-year-old woman, but somehow, he's made me feel like I'm in the Twilight Zone.

My father's eyes darken into shallow slits as he assesses me. Whiskey sloshes in his tumbler from the tiny circles he makes. He lowers his voice, stepping in front of me. "Where have you been?"

"It's not your concern."

His jaw twitches and he releases a deep breath. "You can't hide from this."

"I don't need a lecture right now. Save it," I order and open my suite door.

He follows me inside and shuts the door.

"Dad, get out," I demand, tossing my shoes in the corner.

He paces while finishing his whiskey then sets the glass on the dresser.

"Leave. I'm going to sleep." I go into my closet and put on Sean's T-shirt I always sleep in. I step back out.

My father is still there. "You're a grown woman. I don't expect you to be alone the rest of your life, but that club— that's not a place for you."

My knees almost give out. I put my hand on the top of the armchair and turn toward the wall, wishing this would all go away.

How does he know?

My driver. Jesus, I'm stupid.

I blurt out, "John's fired. I'll hire and pay for my own driver going forward."

Dad snorts. "John didn't tell me anything until I called him to confirm where he dropped you off. It was after I got summoned into an emergency meeting with the head of all the crime families in New York City last night."

Bile crawls up my throat. I don't know what he's talking about, but I'm about to find out. I'm sure I'm not going to like it one bit.

I'm going to kill Cara for taking me there.

"What are you talking about?" I blink hard, willing my tears not to fall.

He crosses his arms. "How do you know about the club?"

My voice trembles. "Cara asked me to go out. I didn't know where we were going. How do you know about it?"

He glances at his empty tumbler as if needing more whiskey. He pins his focus on me. I want to crawl into a hole. He answers, "It's the only place in the city every crime family has agreed to co-exist peacefully. It's off-limits for violence."

Dizziness hits me. I plop down in the chair. I don't get involved in my father's business, but I'm not naive. While things were blurry, I know Dante and Gianni broke those rules because of me. Panic slaps me, and I cry out, "It wasn't their fault."

"So I hear."

"Wh-what do you mean?"

My father sits on the couch next to my chair. "Tell me you didn't know that man you were with has Abruzzo connections."

My mouth turns dry. Since I was a child, my father warned my brothers and me to stay away from the Abruzzos. They're the only family I'm scared of as much as the Baileys and Rossis. I shake my head hard, not wanting it to be true. I manage to get out a, "No, you know I wouldn't ever associate with them."

Dad's expression softens. "Are you okay?"

Shame forces the hard exterior I've created since Sean died to replace my shock. I square my shoulders. "I'm fine."

Dad shifts in his seat. Anger laces his tone, and I know it too well. It's the one I hear when he's trying to stay in control. "Gianni told me he had you pinned down."

A flashback occurs, but it isn't of last night. It's five years ago when all those men held me down, and Sean was screaming for them to stop. I fight the tears, sadness, and rage. I repeat, "I'm fine."

Relief fills my father's expression. He states, "Don't go back to that club, Bridget. It's not a place for you."

I don't care to go back to the club. But all the years of feeling pissed off over Sean's death flies out of me. "But it's a place for you?"

My father is no saint. Since my mother left, he's gotten more ass than Hugh Hefner in his glory years. But I have a feeling, all the things I saw at the club last night are only the tip of the iceberg. Something about it being okay for my father to spend time in the club but not me adds another layer of anger to my well of never-ending fury.

"I'm the head of the O'Connors," he states.

I sarcastically laugh. "So that allows you to fuck your women in public?"

"There are things that go on in that club—"

"That are okay for you, and I'm assuming my brothers, but not me? God, you're a hypocrite."

He grinds his molars and stares at the ceiling.

I rise. "Time to end this lovely chat."

He snarls, "You will not step foot in that club again. Do you hear me?"

I shrug. "Maybe we should create a schedule."

"Bridget," he bellows.

I jump, not used to my father shouting at me.

He closes his eyes and breathes a few times. His green globes are like two flames dancing in the pit of Hell. "Do not step foot in that club ever again."

I open my door. "Fine. Please leave."

He steps into the doorway then turns. "This issue with the O'Malleys isn't going to go away. You need to face it."

"And whose fault is that?"

He sighs. "I—"

"Made a deal that involved my children. *My children!* Not yours! What did you get out of it, Dad? Hmm?"

He stays quiet.

"I'll never forgive you for this," I seethe then shut the door on him and lock it. I crawl under the covers and hug my pillow when my phone buzzes.

I squeeze my eyes tighter, knowing there is only one person who would be calling me right now.

Don't answer it.

Against my better judgement, I grab my purse off the night-stand, dig out my phone, and stare at the screen.

Dante flashes on it.

I send it to voicemail, just like I have every time over the last five years whenever he attempted to call me. A text pops up.

Dante: *I'm calling again. If you don't answer, I'm coming over to your house.*

My gut sinks. The last thing I need is Dante showing up at my door, so when he calls again, I answer but don't say anything.

His deep voice sends flutters through my stomach. I loathe how after all these years, it's like he flipped a switch to make my body react just like it used to. He demands, "Why did you leave?"

I stay quiet, not sure how to answer.

"Bridge, talk to me, or I'm coming over."

"Jesus. Stop threatening me," I whisper.

He softly chuckles.

"Why are you laughing?" I demand.

"If you weren't so stubborn, I wouldn't have to."

I roll my eyes, but my lips twitch. "What do you want, Dante? It's five in the morning. I have to get up with the kids soon."

"Are you in your bed?" he asks.

I bury my face into the pillow. My heart races, and I answer, "Yes."

He lowers his voice, but it's full of the same arrogance he's always possessed. "Maybe I should come over and give my tongue a workout."

Heat flares in my cheeks, and zings fly to my core. It's something I haven't felt in years. But then again, *everything* about last night was an igniting of memories, twisting the ghost of Dante in high school and the one of Sean, who I spent seventeen years of my life loving...who spent seventeen years loving me.

Thinking about any of those sensations scares me to death—especially when it's Dante Marino creating those reactions.

"It was a mistake. Let's forget it ever happened," I say, grimacing as it comes out.

"You're getting too predictable, dolcezza," he replies, as if he really did assume I would say that, it's not a big deal, and he's slightly bored. "But I've got a secret for you. Want to know what it is?"

I don't answer him, not wanting to give him the satisfaction but also curious about what he will reveal next.

"I'm over playing your game," he states.

"My game? I've never—"

"Five years, Bridge. Five fucking long-ass, painful years. One thousand, eight hundred, thirty-nine days, to be exact, since you last let me see you. And I'll be damned if you shut me out again," he declares.

My lungs stop accepting air. I swallow the golf-ball-sized lump in my throat. "Is that why you told my father?"

"Told your father what?"

"Don't act like I'm stupid, Dante."

"What are you talking about?"

"Are you really going to play dumb?"

"I'm not playing anything. Why don't you fill me in on what you're accusing me of doing?"

I huff. "Fine. You told my father I was at the club."

The line turns silent for a moment until he sternly replies, "No. I didn't. The moment I ripped that thug off you was the moment the heads of the families would have been notified. I haven't talked to anyone since you left me while I was sleeping."

I cringe, hating how that sounds.

"What did your father say?"

"Doesn't matter."

"It does to me."

I sigh. "I'm tired. I need to sleep. I have a full day ahead of me."

The sound of a car door slamming fills the line. "Home," Dante orders in a muffled tone then comes back on the line. "Okay. I'll pick you up at eleven when you finish at school."

I roll over and sit up. "How do you know I'll be at school?"

He grunts. "Don't try to avoid me, or I'll pick you up and carry you out of there."

"What?"

"You heard me. Get some sleep, dolcezza." He hangs up before I can say anything.

I stare at my phone then text him.

Me: *Save the trip. I'm not going anywhere with you.*

Dante: *Sure you are. By the way, you're no longer in charge.*

Me: *Excuse me?*

Dante: *I meant it, Bridget. The only way you're not getting in my car is if your father's guard takes me out. So be very clear about your actions today. Get some sleep.*

I stare at his message, hoping he's joking but knowing he's not.

When the tiny spark of excitement pops through my anger, I wrap Sean's T-shirt around my fist, hating how Dante Marino once again fills me with confusion. Only this time, I'm not a teenage girl. I don't have the luxury of letting him set his hooks in me, only to destroy me. My heart's already on its last leg.

I don't sleep. When my alarm rings, I shower, get ready, and put on a long dress with a high neck. It's the only thing I can think of that doesn't scream too sexy. If I didn't have to deal with the other moms at the school, I wouldn't even wear makeup, so I'm not sending him any signals.

I make my way down the stairs, but my problems with Dante fade. Reality hits me when I get to the bottom.

Sean and Fiona step out the door, and I follow.

"Good morning," I try when we're in the car.

Fiona stares out the window, ignoring me. Sean pins his angry scowl on me and crosses his arms. "Are you not going to ask us how Killian or Arianna are?"

My gut flips, and my voice cracks. "How are they?"

"Jesus. You're pathetic," Sean seethes.

"Do *not* speak to me like that," I warn.

"Whatever." He puts on his headphones and turns toward the window.

The moment the car stops outside of their school, they jump out and bolt through the campus. Their bodyguards, who were in a car behind us, follow them. John keeps the door open. I force myself to get out since the last place I want to be is at school, dealing with the other moms today. I don't look at John, embarrassed he knows where I was last night. I can only imagine his and my father's conversation last night.

I spend the morning going through the motions, sneaking glances at my kids when I see them in the hallway. Just like every day lately, I wonder how they're ever going to forgive me or still stay safe.

I curse my father again for what he's done. When eleven o'clock hits, I leave the school and freeze.

I had forgotten about Dante. His matte black Porsche, which I used to tease him reminds me of the Batmobile, is behind my driver's car. He's talking to John. As if he can sense me, he turns in my direction, and my heart stammers.

Years have only added to Dante's sexiness. His black hair has little pieces of silver streaking through it. It's the same as his short-trimmed beard, which only seems to accentuate his defined cheekbones even more than when we were in high school. But his dark, brooding stare, that I thought I had gotten out of my system years ago, now liquifies my insides.

That's before I assess him in his designer suit, which stretches over his perfectly sculpted body, reminding me just how good his flesh felt against mine. Looking at him should be a sin. It turns me into a quivering mess, which makes me loathe myself more.

His lips twitch like he knows the effect he's having on me.

Maybe he is Batman.

What the hell is wrong with me?

I square my shoulders, forcing my legs to move, giving my knees an imaginary point for not buckling. For a moment, I wonder how I could've been so attracted to Sean, who was as Irish as they come, and still so utterly dazed by Dante, who is the epitome of tall, dark, and Italian. Besides the rock-hard bodies they developed from boxing, there's nothing else similar about their appearance.

"Bridget and I have a charity committee meeting to go to in the city. Make sure the kids go directly home," Dante instructs John. He opens the passenger door of his car then cocks an eyebrow, challenging me.

"I assume you're armed?" John asks.

"Of course," Dante assures him, not taking his orbs off mine.

I grit my teeth and force myself to smile at John. "The kids are out an hour earlier today."

"Yes, ma'am. I'm aware."

I nod and get into Dante's car, refraining from smacking the dirty expression off his face as his eyes linger a little too long on my chest.

He shuts the door, and I inhale his sandalwood and amber scent, wishing my insides would stop throbbing. I cross my legs as he slides in the seat next to me, ambushing me further with his delicious scent. He says nothing, shifts into gear, and floors it out of the parking lot.

"Easy! We're in a school zone."

He shifts again and increases his speed. "It's a high school in the middle of the day. Chill out, Bridge."

"Chill out? I'm a mom with children at that school," I say, trying to ignore the adrenaline soaring through my veins. Once upon a time, I wouldn't have said anything. I would have squealed in delight and wanted him to go as fast as possible. But I'm not that carefree woman anymore.

He cockily glances at me. "Your children are in class. Sit back and relax."

"You're irritating."

He grunts then puts on a pair of mirrored sunglasses. It only makes him look hotter, which adds to my annoyance.

"Why are you so feisty today, dolcezza? I thought I was the moody one," he casually asks then veers onto the expressway, whipping past a slew of cars.

"Ugh!" I grumble.

His hand slides onto my thigh, which might be a safe zone for lots of women, but I know Dante. Nothing about him is without risk. You're always putting yourself in a compromising position. I forgot what that was like when Sean was alive and we moved back into the friend zone. Now that we crossed that line again, I don't trust him touching me.

After last night, I don't trust myself. Still, I can't seem to tell him to remove his hand from my body.

His words make me squirm. "Do I have to pull over and eat your pussy while traffic zooms past us?"

My breath catches, heart races, and blood pounds in my cheeks. I tilt my head. "Stop talking like that."

"Why?"

I take a deep breath, staring out the windshield.

"Guess you made your decision." He zips across all six lanes and onto the shoulder then glides to a complete stop, shifting the gear into park.

Before I can say anything, he has my dress at my waist, my panties to the side. His mouth devours my clit like a dehydrated dog who just got in front of a bowl full of water.

"Dante! What the...oh fuck!" I scream, clutching the dashboard as a volt of endorphins crashes into my cells.

The car shakes violently when a semi passes. He commands, "Again!" then sucks me so hard, I cry out his name.

When I come down, I'm still slightly shaking when he pulls my panties over my sex, drags my dress over my knees, then sits back. The car vibrates from another truck. Dante wipes his mouth then licks his fingers and lips, expertly cleaning my arousal off himself.

I breathe hard, gaping at him, trying to catch my breath and regain my focus.

He smirks. "Feeling better now, dolcezza?"

Flames scorch my cheeks. I turn my head away from him.

His deep, sexy chuckle fills the car. He shifts the gear and pulls out, weaving in and out of traffic like a race car driver, once again.

This time, I don't tell him to slow down. For some reason, I sit back, feeling a bit of calm amid all the chaos and danger, trying to figure out how to get Dante Marino out of my system while cursing myself for wishing his hands were still on my body.

Dante

BRIDGET'S BEEN QUIET FOR THE LAST TEN MINUTES, STARING out the window with the corners of her mouth barely curved up. I lick my lips again, trying to savor the taste of her pussy and not remind her with words she's mine. I've known Bridget my entire life. She can't hide how freaked out I'm making her feel right now. But it's not going to stop me from pushing every boundary she has until she quits worrying and accepts us.

Us.

Finally, after all these years, I have a real chance. No matter what, I'm not fucking this up again. Yet, I'm not dumb enough to believe it's going to be a piece of cake to get her to admit it's finally time for us to be together.

"Where are we going?" Bridget asks about ten minutes later.

"Lunch at my new restaurant."

She arches her eyebrows. "Which one?"

I momentarily lock eyes with hers. "Dolcezza."

A faint blush creeps into her cheeks. "Sweetness?"

"Yeah, but when I call you that, the meaning changes slightly."

"To what?"

"Sweetheart," I admit then dart my eyes back to the road, speeding up and zooming past another car.

"I'm not your sweetheart," she quietly states.

I chuckle. "Keep fighting me, Bridge. I'll punish you all night until you confess your pent-up love for me."

"Jesus. Are you ever not arrogant?"

I ignore her question. "Yeah, that's what you need. Hours upon hours of being punished."

She huffs. "I'm not your child, Dante."

I veer off the expressway, heading into the city. I glance over her body again, and my dick twitches. "No. You're not. Which is why you'll take my punishment and submit." I slow down and stop at a red light then turn toward her.

Blue flames practically jump from her orbs, searing into me. "The last thing I'll ever do is submit to you."

I reach for her chin and hold it firmly in my palm. Her eyes widen, and my pulse increases. "This denial you want to indulge in isn't going to last, dolcezza. If I have to fuck you into submission every day, I will."

Her hot breath hits my forearm and tingles race up it. A horn beeps, tearing me away from her nervous stare. I release her then return to maneuvering through traffic.

"You're the only woman who's sat in that seat and not freaked out over my driving. Minus the school zone issue," I add.

She shifts in her seat, turning toward me. "You drive like Finn. Sean, too, but especially Finn."

"Sean's cousin?"

"Yeah. He's in prison."

"No. He got out," I inform her.

"He did?"

"Yeah. Killian mentioned it."

"Oh. Well...yeah, I guess his sentence would have been up," she comments.

I almost ask her what's going on between her and the O'Malleys and why she made the decisions she did, but I decide to hold off. Instead, I declare, "I'm glad you don't scream while I drive."

A laugh escapes her lips. It's music to my ears. I've always loved her laugh, but I haven't heard it in years.

I question, "What's so funny?"

"I don't know why, but I just imagined Eva sitting here, screaming at you in Italian with her hands flailing all over the place."

I groan. "You nailed that scenario down. Annoyed the fuck out of me."

Bridget laughs some more. "Do you remember when she dropped a little bit of your mom's tiramisu on her dress? She freaked out and had to change. You could barely even see it. Her dress was black."

"Don't remind me. She was so high maintenance."

"She looked perfect, even with chocolate on her. I was the one who was a mess. My boobs were leaking from breast-feeding Sean. All I could think was that she would hate having kids."

"You weren't a mess. You were beautiful as always," I state.

Silence fills the car. I pull up to the entrance as close as possible, get out, and toss the keys to the valet. I've been here enough that he knows my protocol. My Porsche is to stay in their sight at all times. The only reason they would drive it is if an emergency vehicle needed to park in my spot. No one is to touch it.

I open the door for Bridget, help her out, then slide my arm around her waist.

"What are you doing?" she frets, trying to move out of my grasp.

I tighten my hold on her and lean into her ear. "Relax, Bridge."

Two cute wrinkles form on her forehead. "People are going to get the wrong idea."

I murmur, "What would that be? That we're fucking? That we're together? Sounds like the truth to me." I guide us inside and nod to the hostess. She picks up two menus and motions for me to follow her.

Bridget takes a deep breath. "We aren't together."

I grunt. "The sooner you come to terms with this, the better."

"I'm not one of your girls, Dante," she snarls.

I don't respond, steer her into the private room with a circle booth, and motion for the hostess to leave. She obeys, shutting the door. I slide closer to Bridget and put my arm around her shoulders. Her body stiffens while she gives me a death glare.

I state, "Let's get something straight, dolcezza. I'm fully aware you aren't one of my 'girls'. Now, if you need me to keep this between us right now until you get used to our situation, then fine. But there's no more hiding from me or us."

"I'm not looking to get into a relationship with you," she asserts, holding her head higher.

My insides cringe, but I ignore her statement, opening her menu. "The food is good here. I made them put apple pie on the menu, too."

Her body stiffens. She tilts her head. "Apple pie isn't Italian."

"Yeah, but you like it." I push a lock of hair behind her ear.

She lets out a long breath and stares at the table, shifting in her seat. A nervousness I haven't seen since we were kids fills her expression. She meets my eyes. "I haven't talked to you in five years. Why would you do that?"

My pulse races. "You know why."

"What exactly does that mean? You said it last night. Just answer my question and stop toying with me."

The flipping in my stomach increases. I hold down my anger that always pops up when she refers to our past. The mistakes I made while we were teenagers doesn't seem to be something she has forgotten. Time didn't heal all wounds, but I should know that, since I haven't gotten her off my mind for over twenty years. I keep my cool and calmly reply, "I'm not toying with you, Bridge."

Her expression tells me she doesn't believe me. She takes a sip of water then crosses her legs.

I take a few deep breaths then admit, "There's only one thing in my life I regret."

She arches an eyebrow. "What would that be?"

My heart races faster. "Losing you."

A moment passes. She still doesn't look at me and replies, "You never had me to lose."

"Sure I did."

She shakes her head, making eye contact. "No. You didn't."

"Bridge—"

"This is too much for me right now, Dante. I don't want to get into a conversation about the past," she blurts out.

I freeze, contemplating my next move, but decide to give her some space. I release my arm from around her and scoot an inch away. "Okay. Tell me what's going on with the kids."

Her face falls, and she sighs. "They hate me."

"So you keep saying."

"Killian and Arianna already told you the situation."

The server comes into the room, carrying a tray of bruschetta and two aperitivos. She smiles while setting the items down. "Mr. Marino. It's good to see you."

"You, too, Olivia."

"Are there any changes to what you ordered earlier this morning?" she asks.

"No. We're not in a rush, either, so tell the chef."

She nods. "Very well." She spins and leaves the room, shutting the door.

I turn back to Bridget. "Like I stated last night, I heard Killian and Arianna's version of the story. I haven't heard yours."

She shifts and closes her eyes briefly, once again avoiding me. "I'm sure everything Killian said is accurate."

I slide my hand on her thigh and soften my voice. "Why did you keep the kids away from the O'Malleys?"

She blinks hard and her lips twitch. "It's not safe."

"What isn't?"

She squeezes her eyes closed and her voice catches. "I can't talk about this. I will never discuss this with anyone."

The hairs on my arms rise. I move closer, wrapping my arm around her again. "Bridge, if someone is after you, tell me. I'll protect you."

She huffs then wipes her face. "No one can."

"I can."

She tries to scoot out of the booth. "I need to go. I shouldn't have come here."

I tug her back to me then cup her cheek, forcing her to look at me. "Don't run from me. Whatever is going on, let me help."

She shakes her head. The blue and green swirl together in her orbs, full of worry and pain. She whispers, "I'm not talking about this. Now, let me go."

I tighten my arm around her, ignoring her orders. Her demand is weak, and I don't believe she wants to run from me. But she also appears as if she's about to break down at any moment, so I back off from pushing her further. "I'll stop asking you about it for now. Talk to me about Sean and Fiona. Why do you think they hate you?"

"Because they do."

"I don't believe that. But tell me why."

"Sean's threatening to quit school and move to Chicago. Fiona won't talk to me. Anytime Sean does speak to me, he's lashing out. I'm afraid he's going to run away," she admits.

"They're angry. It's still new. Give it some time, and Sean will calm down. Fiona will come around, too," I assert.

She sniffles, and so much pain and fear fill her expression, along with tears. "I don't think so. I-I'm afraid they're going to do something stupid. Sean, especially."

I push a lock of her hair behind her ear. "Let me talk to the kids."

"It won't help."

"You don't know that. Let me try," I insist.

She scrunches her forehead. "I don't want you involved."

I ignore the stabbing sensation in my chest. "I've always been close to the kids, especially Sean. Let me help, Bridge."

Minutes pass full of tense silence.

I soften my tone and repeat, "Let me help. No matter what's happened between us, you know I'd never hurt your kids."

"I don't want it to make things worse."

"I'll be careful. I promise."

The uncertainty in her expression lessens but doesn't entirely disappear.

I cup her cheek, stroking her jawline with my thumb. "I got your back, Bridge. You can trust me. I don't know why you did what you did, but I know you. You wouldn't have done this without your reasons. If the rest of the world wants to judge you and not give you the benefit of the doubt, that's on them. I'll always have your back."

Tears fall down her cheeks, and her lips tremble. "Why? I'm not the same person I used to be, Dante. You don't know me anymore."

I swipe at her tears and move closer to her face. "Your heart hasn't changed, dolcezza. Whatever happened that you're scared about, it doesn't alter the person you are. Nothing you say will make me believe that."

She stays quiet, as if still struggling to trust I'm not making false claims.

I give her a chaste kiss, sit back, then pick up a piece of bruschetta and hold it to her lips. "Eat. Forget about life for a few moments."

She releases a stress-filled breath then takes a bite. I watch her chew then pop the rest into my mouth. I push her drink closer to her, and she takes a sip, swallows, and confesses, "I appreciate you talking to the kids, but I don't think anyone can help the situation."

"We won't know unless I try, right? Besides, I already have it in my head, so you know I'm going to do it regardless."

Her lips twitch. "And you've returned to your arrogance."

"You used to like my arrogance."

Her face falls. "That was a long time ago. Neither of us are those kids anymore."

"Thank God for that. I'll make sure I don't fuck it up this time."

She tilts her head. "I'm not looking to get involved with anyone, Dante. My kids are the only thing that matter to me."

My stomach nosedives, but it only makes me firmly attest, "I'm not just anyone."

"Yeah. That makes this even more dangerous for me."

Her statement hangs in the air like dynamite waiting to explode, yet I still state, "I think we were pretty good together last night, don't you?"

Pink flushes her cheeks. "We shouldn't have done it. We can't again."

I grunt and slide my hand between her legs. She inhales sharply and doesn't move. I lean into her ear. "You're wrong, Bridge. Whether you want to admit it now or not, you need me. No matter what you say, I'm not backing down this time. This thing between us, now that we crossed the line, isn't going to go away. So my suggestion is for you to embrace it."

"I can't handle this right now. Can't we go back to the friend zone?" she asks but squirms when I stroke my thumb over her slit.

"I'll always be your friend, but no, we can't go back to where we were. It's a misconception to think you can ever forget last night happened."

"And how long will it be before you get bored with me? Hmm?" She arches her eyebrows.

"I won't."

"I don't believe you."

Her truth hurts, but I deserve it. I remove my hand and slide my hand through her hair. "I'll prove it to you."

"Dante, I can't—"

"After everything that's gone on, do you really believe I would play with you?"

She closes her eyes briefly. "You always get bored. It doesn't matter what woman you date. It's just who you are."

"And why do you think I get bored?" I angrily sling.

She shrugs. "Commitment issues? I don't know."

"They aren't you. I keep looking for someone to shock me and replace you, but they never do. I'm not a stupid teenager anymore. I'm not losing you again. And this time, I'm going to be everything you need. So all I need to hear from you right now is that you'll give me a chance."

She pins her eyebrows together. "I'm not ready for this. I-I need time to think. I don't want this pressure right now. My entire life is falling apart again. The only thing I need to focus on is protecting my kids."

It's not what I wanted to hear, but at least she didn't tell me no. "Tell me who you're protecting them from."

"I can't. Stop asking me."

"I'll protect you and the kids."

She shakes her head. "Drop it. I'll never put my children in harm's way. Stop asking me about it."

I sigh and lean back, debating about pushing her some more and decide against it. She doesn't trust me right now. "I'll drop it for now, but someday you're going to tell me. And just like that thug who was on you last night, I'm going after whoever it is that is scaring you."

Her eyes widen. "Last night? What are you talking about?"

I pull out my phone and show her photos of Michelotto naked and chained up in our dungeon. "He's never leaving this place. What I did to him this morning is only the start. I'm stretching his life out as long as I can."

She gapes at me then swallows hard.

I tug her closer to me and lock my gaze on hers. "Let me be very clear. No one, and I mean *no one*, will ever hurt you again. So when you're ready, you're going to tell me whoever it is who's scaring you. I'm going to take care of them. You're mine, Bridge. From now on, any man who lays a finger on you or threatens you is creating their own death sentence. And I won't show mercy."

Bridget

MY CHEST SQUEEZES TIGHTER WHEN WE APPROACH THE GATES to my father's house. I remove Dante's hand from my thigh and turn toward him. "Thanks for lunch. I'll see you later."

He grunts. "You're killing me, dolcezza." He idles the car and rolls his window down then nods to the guard. The gates open, Dante drives through, parks in front of the steps, and turns the engine off.

"What are you doing?" I panic.

"Going inside to talk to Sean and Fiona."

"Dante—"

"You aren't changing my mind." He opens the door and gets out.

I close my eyes, attempting to regulate my breathing and

reduce the heart palpitations I'm suddenly having. The sound of my door opening snaps me out of my trance. Dante reaches in for me with his self-assured expression.

I sigh, realizing there is no point in arguing, then take his hand. The moment I'm on my feet, I let go. He puts his hand on the small of my back and guides me into the house.

My father meets us in the entryway, eyeing us over. "Dante, since when are you on charity committees?"

My stomach flips fast. Of course my driver would have filled my dad in on where I went. I shouldn't have assumed anything else.

Dante chuckles. "Sometimes it's in a man's best interest to get involved in things that are unexpected, don't you think?"

Dad's gaze darts between us again then lands on Dante. "Does this have anything to do with last night's events?"

My face heats, embarrassed my father knows I was at the club and with Dante. And I suddenly hate the fact that my fear of my children's safety has allowed him to keep such tight tabs on me. The last thing I need is for my father to know I slept with Dante. I blurt out, "Did the kids get home okay?"

My father hesitates before removing his focus from Dante. "Sean's working out. Fiona's in her room."

Before I can speak, Dante starts walking toward the gym and claims, "Great. I wanted to talk with Sean. See you later, Bridget."

I'm relieved the situation is diffused but slightly uneasy about him talking with Sean. Plus, I want to avoid my father inquiring about anything else where Dante is concerned, so I nod and hightail it to Fiona's room. Taking a deep breath, I knock on her door.

"Come in," she calls out.

I open the door, step inside, and shut it.

Books and papers cover Fiona's bed. She glances up. Her face falls, turning to stone.

My heart stammers, hating every part of that look. Until my father made a deal with Killian and dismantled the situation I carefully crafted over the years, Fiona always beamed at me.

"What do you want?" she asks.

I swallow the lump in my throat, walk across the room, and carefully sit on the bed. "How are you doing?"

She tilts her head, her eyes throwing blueish-green daggers so sharp, my insides quiver. "Fine. Can you leave now?"

"We need to talk."

"Are you going to tell me why you lied to us all these years?" she snaps.

I reach for her hand.

She tugs it back, ordering, "Don't touch me."

I freeze, my hand mid-air, blinking hard to control my emotions. I slowly retreat and softly say, "I understand you're mad at me. I'm sorry I had to do what I did, but it was the right thing to do."

Her eyes widen, and her voice gets louder. "Stop claiming that unless you're going to tell me why you did it."

I stare at the ceiling, breathing deeply several times, then finally refocus on her. "I'll never tell you. It's for your safety. But everything I've ever done is out of love."

She huffs. "Then I have nothing to say. Are you going to leave, or do I need to?" Defiance like I've never seen on her fills her expression.

Every bit of that look radiates hate, anger, and confusion. Her struggle with what I've done is my fault. I created all of it. The cyclone of pain I've caused, and continue to, eats at me further.

She jumps off the bed and picks up her books. "Guess I'm leaving."

Accepting defeat, I rise. "No. I'll go."

She crosses her arms, holding her books tight to her chest. She gives me another hardened stare.

I resist reaching out and hugging her. I've never gone so long not embracing my children. The last few weeks, agony's clawed at my gut until it's raw. All I want to do is stop the onslaught of suffering I'm causing my children. But I can never tell them my reasons for what I've done. I'll go to my grave with the horror of what happened to their father and me the night of his death. And I'll never disclose what Niall and Shamus instructed me to do before I left Chicago.

"I love you. You may never understand why I did what I did, but nothing will ever change how much I love you," I assert.

She doesn't flinch and continues glaring at me.

I quietly leave her room then go into my suite. The events of last night, my current battle with my children, and my lack of sleep suddenly feel exhausting. I throw on Sean's T-shirt and slip under the covers. I shut my eyes, but I can't help wondering what Dante is saying to my son or if my kids will ever forgive me.

I can't blame them. My lack of disclosure would infuriate me if I were them.

And now I have Dante Marino trying to diffuse the situation.

That thought gives me too many mixed feelings. He seemed sincere, like he really wasn't out to harm me, but I know him too well. All the feelings I had for him as a teenager seemed to have resurfaced in the last day, making my head spin faster. Plus, Dante's history of having an attention span the size of a toddler's when it comes to women doesn't bring me any comfort.

I've been a challenge for him in the past. Everything about my time with him in the last twenty-four hours makes me nervous.

I'd love to trust him, but I'm not sure how. And part of me feels guilty I let Dante touch me. Sean's probably looking down on me, pissed off. While I know in my heart Sean would want me happy, he would remind me I'm walking right into Dante's clutches.

And how could being with Dante be so different from Sean, yet I loved every moment of it? Is it possible to enjoy two different men equally?

That thought creates another panic inside me. I shouldn't be comparing anything Sean and I had to Dante's and my night.

Sean and I were real. Dante will disappear soon enough. I know too well how he is.

I mentally and emotionally beat myself up until I fall into a deep sleep. When I wake, I glance at my phone. It's past midnight. I also have a slew of text messages.

Dante: *I spoke with Sean. I'm taking him to a boxing match.*

Dante: *Fiona is coming, too.*

Dante: *Stopped in your room to have you come with us, but I didn't have the heart to wake you. Sweet dreams, dolcezza.*

Cara: *We need to talk about last night. CALL ME.*

There are several missed calls from her, including one a few minutes ago.

I text her back.

Me: *I just got your message. I'll call you in a few minutes.*

I slowly get up and check Sean's and Fiona's rooms. Both of them are sleeping. I return to my suite and dial Cara.

She answers, "Are you okay? I just heard what happened. I'm sorry I left you."

"You left me? When? I thought you were in the other room?"

She lowers her voice. "No. Uberto and I left. I-I'm sorry, Bridget. I didn't know Michelotto would get handsy like that."

I shake off the panicky feeling of him holding me down. "I'm fine, but you shouldn't go to that club anymore, Cara. And Uberto isn't anyone you should hang out with, either."

She snorts sarcastically. "Yeah, so I'm told."

The hairs on my arms rise. "What do you mean?"

She dryly states, "Gianni paid me a visit."

I stay quiet for a moment. Gianni and Cara's relationship in high school ended about as badly as Dante's and mine. Cara was head over heels for him. He used her like every other girl he ever laid eyes on, tossing her aside too many times to count before she wised up and cut him loose. Her demons surrounding him might be deeper than mine with Dante.

I finally ask, "Is this the first time you've seen Gianni since you got back into town?"

"Yes. You can only imagine my surprise when he showed up on my doorstep this evening. Wish I could say age turned him into a despicable, fat slob, but that's wishful thinking."

I tread cautiously. "Why did he visit you?"

A tiny laugh fills the line. "To warn me to stay away from Uberto and the club. As if I'm going to do anything Gianni wants."

"You should stay away from Uberto. He's bad news," I warn again.

She groans. "Not you, too."

"Cara—"

"Look, I don't know what kind of beef your two families have with Uberto, but it has nothing to do with me."

I squeeze my eyes shut. Cara comes from a well-to-do family on the upper east side. We met through school, but her family isn't a crime family like the Marinos or mine. I reiterate, "He's bad news, Cara."

"He's harmless. I'm sorry about what Michelotto did to you last night. He must have drunk way too much. I've never seen him get like that before. Either way, it's unacceptable, but I can assure you it doesn't represent Uberto," she claims.

Deciding it's pointless right now to try and convince her, and only imagining what went down when Gianni visited her, I try to shift the topic. "Don't go to the club anymore. It's not safe."

She huffs. "You and Gianni sound like you got together to lecture and make demands on me."

"Cara—"

"I've been going to the underground clubs for years. I know how to protect myself. You don't have to worry about me. But you're okay, right?"

I sigh, deciding not to push this issue right now, either. I'm sure Gianni got under her skin, and she hasn't shaken him yet. It's best to attempt this conversation at another time. I reply, "Yeah. I'm fine."

"Good. I'm sorry again it happened. Lunch this week?"

"Sure."

"Okay. I need to get some sleep. I'll message you later."

"Night." I hang up, and a text comes in.

Dante: *Are you awake?*

Me: *Yes.*

My phone rings, and I answer. "Hey."

Dante's deep voice makes my butterflies spread their wings. "Did you dream about me?"

"You wish," I say, but my smile grows against my will. After so many years of not letting Dante affect me, he suddenly can ask one question and get my panties in a twist.

My phone buzzes with a FaceTime request. I tap the green button.

A shirtless, sweaty Dante appears. My heart pounds faster, and I tear my eyes off his chiseled pecs only to see his lips twitch. I ask, "Why are you sweaty?"

His eyes twinkle. "Just worked out. I had to get memories of last night and my sexual tension out of me."

My face heats as visuals of Dante's body and lips all over me consume my thoughts.

"Now that you're all rested up, you want me to come over?" He wiggles his eyebrows.

A laugh escapes me. "I thought you said you worked out your sexual tension."

"My dick's getting hard again from looking at you. What do you say, Bridge? I could sneak in and sneak out."

I roll my eyes. "Sure. Sneak in through my father's guards then tiptoe through the house so he doesn't see you. Fat chance."

He suggests, "You could come to mine. My wing has a private entrance."

For a brief moment, I imagine doing just that. It's something I would have done in the past. Then I snap back into reality. That was the old me. Now I'm a forty-one-year-old mother. So, despite the lure of Dante's soaked torso and the memory of his hands and tongue all over me, I reply, "Not happening."

He chuckles. "You mean not happening tonight."

"Or ever."

"We'll see about that. Anyways, I missed you with us. Remember when you used to come to my fights?"

I shift on the bed and hug my knees to my chest. The memory of the last time I went to see him when he ditched me resurfaces. Then all the times I cheered Sean on while he was in the ring in Chicago mixes with those emotions. I stay quiet, holding in the feelings that threaten to take hold and spill over.

Dante's face falls. His voice turns serious. "Why won't you let Sean fight anymore? His father was training him. He misses it."

I shake my head. "I don't want him to get hurt. The last thing he needs is a concussion. You of all people should understand that," I add since Dante no longer competes due to a concussion he got in the ring.

He says nothing for a few moments. His dark eyes study me, creating more flutters in my gut.

"Why aren't you talking? You're making me nervous," I admit.

"I understand your worry, but Sean's got a lot of anger inside him. He needs an outlet for it."

"He's angry because of what I've done. I'm fully aware," I state.

Dante shakes his head. "It's not just that. I think he's bottled up a lot of things."

"What do you mean?"

"I'd rather tell you this in person."

"Too bad. I'm not leaving, and you aren't allowed here. Now spill it," I order.

"What are you scared of, Bridge? Afraid I'll make you scream so loud everyone will hear?" He smirks.

My insides clench. I groan into my hand. "Don't talk like that when we're discussing my children."

He chuckles again. "Fair enough." His face turns serious. "I think this has brought out a lot of emotions he might have held in regarding his father's death."

Guilt hits me. "I tried to find the kids the best therapists when we moved to New York, but Sean never took to it the way Fiona did."

"Boxing would help him," Dante insists.

I shut my eyes, wanting to do whatever will help Sean but also trying to protect him from the realities of the ring. For years, he's argued with me about training. I've always held my ground. Something about him not having his father to guide him in the ring makes it scarier for me.

"You don't have to decide this minute, but think about it," Dante insists.

Torn, I open my eyes and nod. "Okay. I'll think about it, but I don't want you pressuring me about this."

He licks his lips. "I'd rather pressure you about other things."

I try to stop my smile but can't.

His dark eyes brighten. "If I were there right now, I'd strip you out of that oversized shirt."

I glance at the faded T-shirt and grip my hand around the material, blurting out, "It's Sean's."

The light leaves Dante's face. His jaw clenches, and the blackness deepens in his eyes.

Heat overpowers my cheeks. I don't know why I had to say that. It's another realization about how unprepared I am to do this with him. "I'm sorry. I'm not trying to hurt you."

He hesitates for a moment then says, "I know. Get some sleep, Bridge. I'll call you tomorrow. Goodnight."

Before I can put together a coherent reply, he hangs up. I lie back on my pillow, but it takes forever to fall asleep. I think of Sean and how happy he made me—how much he loved me, and I loved him.

Then the feeling of Dante's arms around me and his body pressed against mine consume me. For the first time since meeting Sean all those years ago, I fall asleep thinking about Dante and wishing he were next to me.

Dante

A Week Later

PAPÀ'S PIERCING GAZE DARTS BETWEEN GIANNI AND ME WHILE he announces, "The Abruzzos aren't taking your little stunt at the club lightly."

"Fuck the Abruzzos. Since when are we scared of their actions?" Tristano interjects.

"I don't have a problem taking a few more of them out," Massimo snarls.

"I'll join you," Tristano adds.

Gianni and I exchange a knowing look. While we all have a unified hatred for the Abruzzo's, my youngest brothers don't seem to know when to stay quiet lately. And pushing my father's buttons isn't wise.

Papà's menacing scowl refocuses on my brothers. He points at them, growling, "You don't go looking for trouble. How many times do I have to drill this into your thick heads?"

Tristano's face hardens further. "Did you forget so soon they kidnapped Arianna?"

"Watch your mouth," Papà warns.

"Let's forget the kids in the room and return to the details. What are those pieces of shit up to now?" I ask.

"Fuck off," Massimo curses.

Gianni shifts on his feet, looking bored with the entire scenario. "I've got shit to do today, so if we can move this along."

Papà walks around his desk and unrolls a map, putting his paperweights on the corners. The four of us step closer and watch him point then drag his finger along Newark Bay. "They just increased their men at Port Newark Container Terminal, here and here."

"And why aren't we taking them out?" Massimo fumes.

I don't blame him. The port is one of the busiest container ports in the world. All the goods coming in and out of New York are through there. Over the years, we've created an agreement with the Abruzzos and other crime families in order to co-exist. We all have our specific locations, and crossing over is asking for war. The spot my father is pointing to is a gray zone. It's an area where neither Abruzzos nor Marinos go, so we can both do our business without the threat of each other looming over the other. A family entering a gray zone is an aggressive move and one you don't embark upon unless you're ready to battle.

"I'm with Massimo. Take the bastards out at night and send a message to get back on their own turf, or we're ready for war," I state, still reeling over Arianna's abduction as well as the vision of Bridget pinned to the couch by Michelotto.

"Agreed. I'll do it tonight if you want," Gianni adds.

"Count me in," Tristano mutters.

Papà's face turns red. He shakes his head hard, seething, "Have I not taught you anything?"

"It's better to be on the offensive than defensive," I claim.

My father's voice rises. "We are down dozens of men from the last encounter we had with the Abruzzos. Have you all forgotten?"

Tense silence fills the office. Nine months ago, we had an altercation that took out a few of our toughest men, all blood relations.

Gianni sniffs hard, his disgust digging deeper into his expression. "And did you forget they took us by surprise? That we weren't prepared, and that's why we have several widows in our family now?"

"Of course I didn't. But we can't risk another street battle right now," Papà states.

I cross my arms. "Where are the men Giuseppe promised to send? It's been almost a year. When we were in Italy last, he gave us his word he would help us rebuild."

"He's having issues. The Abruzzos have gotten stronger in Italy as well. He's trying to stabilize, and it's more complicated than he anticipated. Until we get reinforcements, we can't risk a war."

"Which is exactly why we need to take those thugs out now. The four of us can do it tonight. We'll keep it quiet," I declare.

My father slams his hand on his desk, roaring, "Like you kidnapped Michelotto? Because you sure as hell didn't think before you picked him up!"

"I was discreet," Gianni asserts.

Papà's face flushes maroon. "You picked him up hours after your altercation. I was still meeting with the heads of the crime families. Do you have any idea what your actions have done?"

"Made the prick sorry he was ever born," Massimo snickers.

Papà's rage grows. He points to Massimo and Tristano. "You and you. Out. Now!"

"And once again, we miss all the fun," Tristano comments.

"One more word—"

"Easy, or even the diet Arianna has you on isn't going to stop you from having a heart attack," Massimo states, patting Tristano on the back and steering him out of the room.

When the door shuts, my father pins his steely eyes back on Gianni and me. "I expect more from you two. You both know we're vulnerable right now."

"Which is why we need to handle this," I maintain.

"No. We keep our eyes open and stay ready at all times. Hopefully, it's just the Abruzzos testing our patience, and they'll back off soon."

"Jesus, Papà. Do you hear yourself? They aren't going to back off," Gianni claims.

"You don't know that. They have before. And until Giuseppe sends more men—"

"At what point do we find our own men? Hmm? Relying on Giuseppe is putting us at greater risk. We need to revamp our recruiting," I insist.

"Agreed. We can't afford not to. Put Massimo and Tristano on it," Gianna orders.

Papà scrubs his face. "You know the risk we take if we vet anyone incorrectly."

"Then we triple check them, put our guys on them for several months, and watch their every move before letting them in. But we can't keep relying on Giuseppe every time something happens. And the future of the Marinos is in our hands. At some point, you have to let us make some calls," I remind my father.

Tense silence fills the air as his eyes lock on mine. It's a fight we're constantly having. How much leeway he turns over to us.

He finally nods. "All right. I'll allow you to step up the recruiting efforts. But I'm holding both of you responsible. If either of your brothers screw up, it's on your shoulders."

Gianni and I leave the room, exchange a glance, and go to my wing. Once we're in my office and the door's closed, he says,

"Papà is wrong. We need to take out those bastards stepping into the gray zone. If we lose our power in the port, we can kiss everything goodbye."

I pour a glass of scotch and hand it to Gianni then take one myself. The liquor slides down my throat in a welcome burn. Disobeying my father's orders isn't something I thought I would ever do, but I can't disagree with Gianni. While the crime families of New York have an agreement, there have been instances of territories stolen in the past. Within a year, the losing family no longer existed. Without the port, you can't easily make money.

When the alcohol hits my stomach, I glance at the shut door and lower my voice. "Papà will have a fit."

Gianni arches his eyebrows. "We pin it on the Rossis."

I sit back in my chair. "Cause the Abruzzos to rethink their alliance?"

Gianni takes a large swallow of his drink then his lips curl. "I think Papà is wrong about it being the wrong time to start a war, don't you?"

"Only if it's between the right families."

He grunts. "Now you're getting the picture."

I lean closer. "In theory, it sounds smart. But implementation is a different story."

He shrugs. "I'll figure it out. Give me a few days."

I study him then say, "We should discuss this with Papà."

"So he can shut us down?"

I sigh, frustrated from my father's inability to see things how Gianni and I often do. Crossing him isn't something I would have considered years ago, but lately, we disagree on how to handle things. In some ways, I think he's stuck in an old-school mentality, just like Giuseppe Berlusconi, who holds even more power than my father.

Gianni adds, "It's the same thing the O'Malleys and Ivanovs have done. I'll fly to Chicago and speak with Killian and Liam. The Rossis are stronger in New York right now, but they have nowhere to pull from due to the war in Chicago. We could create a serious rift and decrease the overall threat of the Abruzzos and Rossis."

My chest tightens at the thought of going behind Papà's back, but what Gianni is proposing could secure my family's future for decades to come. I finish my scotch and stare at my brother.

His dark grin grows. He rises. "I'll tell Arianna I'm coming for a visit. Stay tuned."

I nod and watch him leave. When the doors shut, I take my phone out of my pocket and glance at the time. Then I text Bridget.

Me: *Put on some jeans. I'm picking you up in an hour.*

Bridget: *What are you talking about?*

Me: *Just do what I say. Tell the kids we're volunteering at a homeless shelter for the night.*

Bridget: *What? I doubt anyone will believe you'd do that.*

I chuckle. It's probably the truth.

Me: *Tell them I'm turning over a new leaf.*

Bridget: *And this conversation gets more comical.*

Me: *Do you want me to tell them? One way or another, I'm picking you up.*

Bridget: *You seem to think you can just order me around.*

Me: *It's been a week since I've seen you. I've given you space. Now put your jeans on your sexy ass, or I'll come over and do it for you.*

Bridget: *Why do I need to wear jeans?*

Me: *You'll see.*

Bridget: *That comment makes me want to wear a long skirt and turtleneck.*

Me: *Do women still own turtlenecks?*

Bridget: *I'm sure I can find one somewhere in my closet.*

Me: *Fine. Wear your turtleneck. But if you don't wear jeans, you're going to regret it.*

Bridget: *Still waiting for you to tell me where you think you're taking me.*

Me: *You now have fifty-five minutes until I pick you up.*

Bridget: *Sorry. Washing my hair tonight.*

Me: *Okay. Scratch my idea, and I'll come help you in the shower.*

Bridget: *You wish.*

Me: *Want to test me?*

Bridget: *You're annoying.*

Me: *You're wasting time. What's it going to be? You and me going out, or you and me in the shower? I'm good with either scenario.*

Several moments pass. The dots appear then disappear several times.

Me: *Okay. Shower it is!*

Bridget: *No! I'll tell your lie no one will believe.*

Me: *Tell them you converted me into a good person.*

Bridget: *Ha! That's another funny concept.*

Me: *Fifty minutes now. See you soon!*

I stick my phone in my pocket, go to my room, then shower and toss on a pair of jeans and a black T-shirt. I text my driver then leave the house and get into the back of the car.

It's autumn, and the leaves have changed colors into brilliant orange, red, and yellow. The daytime light is almost gone, and in a few minutes, it'll be dark.

My phone vibrates, and I look at the text.

Rubio: *My girlfriend arrived, and she's looking better than ever.*

I pump my fist in the air. His "girlfriend" is code for the new gems that were just delivered. Our dealer promised this batch was exceptional, and I've been holding my breath to have Rubio confirm it.

Me: *Have fun tonight. I'll stop by tomorrow.*

The car veers and stops at the gate. The guard lets us through, and I'm soon standing outside Bridget's front door. For the first time in a long time, my stomach flips with nerves. I've been biding my time, waiting to see Bridget again, and giving her some space.

She opens the door, and my heart almost stops. Her long, blonde hair hangs in curls. A faint floral scent wafts into my nostrils. The blue in her eyes blazes with no green anywhere in them. She has her coat in her arms and steps outside, shutting the door quickly.

I chuckle. "What's the rush, dolcezza? Afraid someone is going to see us?"

She beams. "Nope. No one is home."

I put my hand on the small of her back and lead her to the car. "Where are they?"

"The kids are at a school basketball game, and who knows where my father is."

"Guess I picked the right night to take you out, then." I hold the door open and motion for her to get in.

She slides across the seat, and I follow. As soon as the door shuts, I tug her onto my lap and kiss her, holding her face close to mine until she begins to relax and return my affection. I murmur, "That's better. I missed you."

She holds her breath and stares at me.

"You can admit you missed me," I tease, running my hand up under her shirt and stroking her spine.

She continues to stay silent, giving me her laser gaze of uncertainty.

I hate that she isn't sure about us. There are layers of reasons why, stemming from Sean to our past, and I'm not ignorant to it. So I pull her in tighter, kiss her some more, then say, "I'll keep my lips on yours until you confess."

She softly laughs, and it's a glimpse of the old Bridget. The carefree, wild, confident girl I fell in love with so many years ago. She finally admits, "Okay. I missed you a little bit."

I grin. "Just a little."

"Yep. Just a little."

"Hmm. I guess I'll have to work harder tonight, so you miss me more." I slide my tongue back in her mouth until she's out of breath.

When I retreat, I tug her hips so she's sitting closer to my torso. "You look nice."

"Are you going to tell me why I'm wearing jeans?"

"We're going to a bar."

She tilts her head and arches an eyebrow. "A bar?"

"Yep."

"They only wear jeans in this bar?"

I shrug. "Probably not, but for what you're going to be doing, it's best."

Her lips twitch. "What am I going to be doing?"

"You'll see."

"Why do I get the feeling I'm not going to be on board with this?"

I grunt and tug her head back. She gasps, and my dick twitches. "You should trust me a bit more."

"Trust is earned."

I grind my molars then question, "Have I harmed you in any way over the last twenty years? After you got with Sean...?"

She stiffens then slowly shakes her head. "No."

"Okay. Then at some point, you're going to have to rely on that instead of the dickhead version of who I was to you when we were in school."

She releases an anxious breath as guilt fills her expression.

I slide my hands to her cheeks. "Why don't you try giving me your trust tonight. Let's start there."

Her eyes turn to slits. "When you have something planned for me that I know nothing about?"

I chuckle. "Yep. Be the carefree, spontaneous Bridget you used to be. Forget about everything else for the next few hours."

"But what are you going to make me do?" she asks, but her tone has turned playful instead of worried like before.

I press my lips to hers again then answer, "If I told you, it wouldn't be a good test of your new trust in me, now would it?"

She hesitates but then nods. "Okay. You get my full trust for a few hours."

"Great." I wrap my arm around her and push her head to my chest then kiss the top of her hair. "Has anything gotten better with the kids?"

"No. Same hostility as usual."

"Give them some time. They'll come around."

She glances up at me. "You keep saying that as if there's no chance they won't."

"Because I know your kids. And I know you, Bridge. You're a good mom, and they love you. Just give it some time."

"My father is insisting I go to your father's Christmas party this year."

I smile. "Good. It's about time you returned to the festivities."

Fear fills her eyes. "The O'Malleys are all going to be there."

"You have to face them at some point."

"I know," she quietly says.

I tighten my arms around her. "Don't worry. I'll protect you."

She straightens. "That's all I need—the O'Malleys to see me with you."

My chest tightens, and my heart beats harder. "Do you think you're supposed to be alone forever, dolcezza?"

She scrunches her face and looks toward the window, not answering my question.

I lower my voice. "It's been five years. You deserve to be happy."

Her glistening eyes meet mine. "Then why does it feel so wrong?"

I tuck a lock of her hair behind her ear. "I don't know. But eventually, it'll fade and feel right."

The driver's door slams shut. I glance outside then turn back to Bridget. "You ready?"

Her eyes widen. "You're taking me to a country bar?"

I grin. "Yep."

"But you hate country."

"That I do. But tonight, I'm going to love it."

She raises her eyebrows. "Why is that?"

I open the door and step out. Reaching in, I reply, "You'll see."

I lead her into the noisy bar, where a live band is playing on stage. I order two shots of whiskey.

"Kind of early for that, don't you think?" she asks.

"Nope!" I hold a shot out. "Take it."

She does so, and I clink her glass with mine. "Salute."

"Sláinte," she replies, and we down the whiskey.

I grab her glass from her then spin her, so her back is against my torso. I wrap my arms around her and murmur in her ear, "It's time to get that light back in your eyes, and we're going to start tonight."

She turns her head, gazes at me, and gives me a questioning stare.

I peck her on the lips then put my cheek on hers and point to the other side of the bar. A gold mechanical bull gleams as if waiting just for her. "Saddle up, dolcezza. You're going to show me how you used to ride that thing."

13

M C

Bridget

COUNTRY MUSIC BLARES THROUGH THE BAR. RICH MAHOGANY wall panels shine next to the brick. Black booths line the wall, and four-top tables adorn the middle of the room. A guitarist, a drummer, and one singer line the stage.

I shake my head at Dante and claim, "No way!" while assessing the gold mechanical bull. My stomach flips a few times. The last time I rode one was over a decade ago. Sean and I came to New York for my birthday. After several drinks, we made a bet. He only stayed on a few seconds, but I lasted past the eight-second requirement. Sean told everyone who would listen about my "skills."

Dante chuckles. "Do you need another shot?"

"Nice try. Should we grab a table?" I reply.

His grin widens. "Sure. We can do that. But we aren't leaving until you get on that bull. I've had this image in my head for too many years, and it's time I see the real thing."

I cover my face with my hands, groaning. Dante has that look in his eye that tells me we really aren't going anywhere until he gets his way.

His deep chuckle hits my ear at the same time his breath does, sending tingles straight to my core. "Come on, Bridge. Show me your riding skills, so I have some visuals for later on." His tongue swipes the back of my lobe.

I shudder, turning to him and meeting his dark smirk. His arms sweep across my back and tighten, pressing our bodies together. My lower body throbs while I ask, "Do you really want to see me ride it?"

"Yes."

"Fine. I'll ride it under one condition."

"What's that?"

"You go first."

He arches his eyebrows. "I'm not the one with the bull skills."

"Scared?"

He snorts. "Nope."

I bat my eyelashes and smile. "Then get your ass on it."

He drags two fingers across my forehead and tucks my hair behind my ear. "Okay. Let's place a bet."

"A bet?"

"Yeah."

I tilt my head. "What kind of bet?"

Arrogance fills his expression. "If I win, I decide where we're staying tonight. And you don't get to run out while I'm sleeping."

I freeze as the air in my lungs becomes thicker. Staying the night with Dante is trouble. Waking up and dealing with the aftermath is even riskier. It somehow makes it feel like what-ever this thing is between us is somehow real. I'm still trying to trust he's not going to squash me like he did in the past. And the thought of being in a relationship intensifies the guilt I feel about Sean. I had everything with him, so how could it be possible to ever really love someone else?

Dante's challenging stare intensifies. He taunts, "You scared I'll win, dolcezza?"

One thing I've never been good at is backing away from a challenge, and he knows it. I glance at the bull, remembering how it felt all those years ago. It also threw Sean off within seconds. My guess is Dante won't last any longer. I turn back to him and square my shoulders. "Fine. You first."

Satisfaction registers on his face. He maneuvers me to an empty booth. I slide in, and he sits next to me. Then he motions to the server.

"Aren't you supposed to be on the bull?" I ask.

"Later." He places both hands on my cheeks and kisses me, sliding his tongue in my mouth the moment my lips part. A buzz travels down my spine, intensifying as he deepens our kiss.

"Sir, did you want to order?" a woman's voice interrupts.

"Yep," he replies, swipes his tongue back into my mouth, then winks and pulls away. He says, "Two Macallans, neat."

"Did you need menus?"

Dante glances at me. "Hungry?"

"No."

He shakes his head at the server. "Just the drinks."

She nods and leaves.

Dante sits back and wraps his arm around my shoulder. "When I win, you're staying at my place."

Panic fills me. "No way."

"Chill, Bridge. You know I have my own entrance."

"Not happening."

He positions his face so it's in front of mine. "A deal is a deal. Besides, no one will see you. I'll always protect you. Deep down, you already know this."

I adamantly state, "I'm not staying at your house."

He snorts. "Then you better win."

The server comes back and sets our drinks down. "Can I get you anything else?"

"We're good, thanks," Dante replies, without taking his gaze off mine. "Where are we staying if you win?"

My butterflies spread their wings. The mere notion of another night with Dante sends my blood rushing through my veins. Yet, I also know it's a dangerous path to take. There are too many ways he can hurt me, and I can't handle any more pain right now. I take a sip of my drink, letting the burn of the alcohol slide down my throat until it's mixed with my flutters. "We aren't. You're dropping me off at my place then going home."

He grunts. "Not happening. Nor is it the deal."

"It's my side of the deal."

He smirks. "Sorry. Already agreed."

"Well, I'm stating my side of the deal."

He leans into my ear while sliding his hand between my thighs. My face heats as he declares, "I've already claimed you, Bridge. And no matter who wins, we're staying the night together. In fact, I already have the key to the room at the Ritz." He squeezes my pussy, and I squirm into his hand.

I roll my eyes. "You're so arrogant."

"Yep."

"What makes you think I'd pick the Ritz?"

His lips hit my neck under my ear, inflaming the heat filling my cheeks. "You got away with it last time."

I pull back. "What?"

His jaw clenches. "You don't want anyone to know about us. We went there, and no one knew."

"Except my driver, which pretty much means my father knows," I blurt out.

Dante nods. "Which is why you shouldn't have left. I would have taken you home."

I huff. "That's not a better idea."

"Sure it is."

"No, it's not."

He fists my hair and tugs on my head. His face hovers over mine, and I inhale sharply. "I'm going to repeat this, and you need to listen closely. I know how to protect you. I will always protect you. And tomorrow, I'm dropping you off at your house. Do you understand?"

"And you don't think my children and father are going to know what we were doing? You've really lost the plot, now." I snicker then take another drink.

"Tell your father about us."

"No way."

Dante sniffs hard. "Why? What are you worried about?"

I focus on my whiskey and swirl it in the glass, admitting, "The last thing I need is to give my father ideas about us when I'm not even sure what we're doing."

Dante grabs my chin and forces me to look at him. Darkness swirls in his eyes, creating more flutters in my belly. In a confident voice, he says, "We're finally starting our life together. That's what we're doing."

I freeze, not breathing, as a mix of emotions bombard me. This past week, no matter how hard I tried, I've not been able to forget about Dante and what it felt like to be with him. I've almost convinced myself that it's okay if we have a sexual relationship. But a life with him isn't something I've allowed myself to contemplate, nor is it something I would ever expect him to say or want. After all, he's the unattainable bachelor every woman in New York wants to tame. And I know too well he'll eventually get bored.

There is no taming Dante Marino. Plus, I'm not a stupid girl anymore who believes in fairy tales.

"Why are you looking at me like that, dolcezza?" he asks.

"Don't say things to me that don't bear truths."

He slowly licks his lips, studying me. "I thought I've been clear about my feelings for you."

"Sexual feelings are one thing. A life is something else."

"You think this is just about sex?"

"Of course it is."

He shifts in his seat and takes a swig of his whiskey then taps his fingers on the glass for several moments. He finally turns back toward me. "When are you going to get over the past, Bridge? I was an idiot in high school."

My chest tightens at the mention of years ago. A clawing in my gut starts, but it's not about Dante. It's about the life I used to have where I was happy and carefree. It's about the security I felt being an O'Conner then O'Malley, which was false. It's about the unquenchable love I had with Sean that I don't think can happen to a person twice in one lifetime. And if it did, how would I ever survive losing it again?

I ignore Dante's hurt expression and finish the remainder of my drink. I elbow him. "Let's go."

He sighs. "So now you want to leave?"

I finally meet his eyes. "No. We made a bet, remember?"

His lips curve, and the cocky competitor in him surfaces. It's an expression I've always loved, but it also makes me want to beat him.

He slides out of the booth then pulls me up. "When I win, we're going straight to my house."

I smirk. "If you think you're going to win, why'd you check into the Ritz?"

"Either way, I win." He winks. Before I can say anything, he leads me across the bar.

A man flies off the bull and lands on the mat. The crowd cheers, and Dante tugs me closer to him.

I glance up. "That's going to be you."

His hand drops to my ass. "Don't get cocky. I'm very athletic."

I point at the bull. "Well, don't make me wait any longer. Show me your athleticism."

Dante guides me closer and hands cash to a man in a cowboy hat and boots. He eyes us over and asks, "I'm Gus. Want the easy or real version?"

"Real," I blurt out then pat Dante's back. "Give him all you got so he can show us his skills."

"She's going after me. Same speed."

"No mercy," I state, but excitement courses through me, taking me by surprise. I'm not a twenty-year-old anymore. The carefree woman I used to be no longer exists. Yet, something about being with Dante makes me want to be reckless. Even more shocking is it feels good to feel wild again, even if it's just due to a shiny bull in a crowded country bar.

Gus hands clipboards to us. "Sign the waiver, and we'll get going."

Dante and I fill out the forms then hand them back to Gus.

"Have you done this before?" Gus asks.

Dante shakes his head. "Nope."

Gus pats the bull. "Sit as high as you can, near the head. Are you right or left-handed?"

"Left," Dante says, focusing on the bull. It reminds me of when he used to box and would size up his opponent before a match. I bite on my smile from the nostalgia.

Gus grips the rope. "Hold on to this using your dominant hand, and keep your right arm out away from you to maintain your balance. Grip the sides of the bull with your inner thighs as tight as you can. Any questions?"

"Nope."

"Okay, hop on," Gus instructs.

"Let's see what you got," I taunt.

"Watch and learn, Bridge." Dante pats my ass and jumps on the bull.

"Ma'am, step back behind that line," Gus orders.

I obey. When I spin, Gus turns on the bull. It slowly begins to move up, down, then rotates.

Dante holds his form as Gus instructed, boasting, "Piece of cake."

"Got the hang of it?" Gus shouts.

"Yep."

Gus winks at me and hits a button. The bull moves faster, jerking side to side. Dante clenches his jaw and holds tighter, but Gus hits another button. The bull whips in a circle, and Dante flies off. He falls on his stomach on the mat.

The crowd roars, and I run over to Dante, laughing. "Seven seconds."

He turns over and pushes himself off the ground. A smug expression erupts. "You're next."

My stomach flips, and I glance at the gold machine.

Dante puts his hand on my back and leans down. "Come on. I'll help you up. Unless you want to forfeit, leave now, and stay at my place?"

I turn so I'm right in his face. "Nope. I can beat your measly seven seconds."

"Then show me what you've got, dolcezza," he says and kisses my forehead.

Gus puts the step next to the bull. I jump up on it and take a deep breath. He repeats the instructions he gave Dante.

I grip the rope, hold out my left hand, and squeeze my thighs as tight as possible against the metal.

"Ready?" Gus yells out.

Dante crosses his arms. Amusement fills his face.

"Ready," I reply, determined to win.

The bull begins to move. I fall in rhythm with the up and down pattern. When it turns, I brace myself and keep my balance.

"Doing good," Gus shouts.

"Faster," I yell, not wanting to give Dante any reason to say I had it easy.

Gus hits the button. The bull bucks harder then spins. I almost lose my balance but catch it. The crowd cheers, and I squeeze my thighs tighter.

Right when I think I have it figured out, the speed increases. Adrenaline courses through my veins. The bar becomes blurry and louder as I put all my concentration on not falling. The bull spins sharply. I go flying through the air, shrieking, and fall onto the mat.

Applause and whistles erupt all around me.

"Bridge, you okay?" Dante asks, turning me onto my back. His face is full of worry.

For some reason, I find it funny. I laugh until tears come to my eyes.

Dante pulls me to my feet, assessing me. "You're okay?"

I wipe my face and nod, still laughing. "That was fun."

Dante studies me for a moment then grabs my hand and leads me through the bar.

"Where are we going?" I ask.

He says nothing, guiding me through the crowd, down the hallway, and out into the alley. His SUV is parked nearby, his driver standing near the passenger door. He nods then goes into the bar.

"What's going on?" I ask.

"Get in," Dante instructs, opening the back door.

I obey, and he slides next to me. The moment the door shuts, he pins his body over mine, sliding his tongue in my mouth, mumbling, "That was hot, dolcezza. And now you're going to ride me like you rode that bull." His fingers unbutton my jeans. He shoves my pants past my knees then takes care of his own before flipping onto his ass. He pulls me over him so the tip of his cock is against my entrance. His arms circle me, and his hand grasps my hair as he murmurs into my lips, "Take me."

I shudder as I sink on him, gasping into his mouth.

He firmly holds my head in front of his face. His dark orbs drill into mine. In a stern voice, he orders, "Now, ride me. I want to inhale your breath as you come, Bridge."

More flutters erupt. I clutch my arms around him, obeying his commands, taking him as deep as I can.

He groans and moves one hand to my ass cheek, squeezing it and tugging my head back. His teeth graze my lobe. He mumbles, "All week, I've thought about your pussy clenching my cock. I imagined you working me, just like this, and feeling you tremble in my arms. How much did you think about it, dolcezza? Hmm?" His face moves in front of mine.

I lean closer to his lips, but he cuts off my kiss, holding my head and hip firmly so I can't move, while pinning his steely gaze on mine. He orders, "Tell me."

"Every day," I admit.

He studies me for a brief moment then nods before resuming the speed of my hips and flicking his tongue in my mouth.

Grasping him tighter, I sink my knees into the leather, taking him deeper, whimpering from the sweet friction I've been craving since our last encounter.

Fire explodes in his eyes. "You're testing my patience, dolcezza. All these years of wanting you, and you're still not fully mine, are you? You're still testing my patience. And I'm not a patient man."

I roll my hips faster, trying to ignore his statement but having to push down the automatic response that jumps into my mind. It would be easy to tell Dante I'm his while I'm in his arms. But that would have consequences. Once I proclaimed I was his, history shows he'd take off running. I close my eyes, no longer able to take his stare down, and lean into his ear, whispering, "Just fuck me. Take all your words away and just fuck me."

His chest heaves with a sigh, but he pulls me tighter to him, then grips my hip, shimmying my body over his at a new, almost frantic pace.

"Oh God," I breathe. Adrenaline fills up my cells. My walls begin trying to hold on to any part of him I can. The tip of his cock becomes his weapon, thrusting into me over and over, tormenting me until sweat pops out on my skin.

"Fuck," he growls then flips me off him and over so I'm facing the back of the SUV. He pushes me over the seat and presses his body against mine. His hot breath hits the back of my neck as he penetrates me even deeper than before.

Shuddering, I blink several times, trying to regain my focus.

"You want me to fuck you?" he demands.

"Yes!"

"Like this? My cock drenched in you, hard, pulsing, fucking desperate to drown in you?"

"Yes," I admit.

He tugs on my hair and puts his lips on my cheek. "Then confess you want to drown in me, too—that it's not just me, Bridge. Say it."

No analysis is possible. Dante's body in and on mine is sweet relief from every part of reality. I blurt out, "I do. Let me drown."

"I got you, my dolcezza. But right before you sink, I'm pulling you up. Then I'm going to bring you right back there. Before the morning comes, I'm taking everything you have to give me, whether you know you want to or not. Every disillusion you have about us, I'm going to rip apart until you see me... I mean, really see me."

My walls spasm around him. I'm about to spiral, but he stops, pressing his pelvis against my ass. I turn toward his face, desperate for my release. "Don't stop."

His lips curl into an almost-sinister expression. Smoldering, intense flames leap from his eyes. "Tell me you want me."

I try to move my hips but can't. He's got me locked against the seat.

In a stern tone, he demands, "Tell me now, Bridget."

"I want you," I admit.

His jaw clenches, and he sniffs hard. "All of me."

"I want all of you."

The corners of his lips turn up, but he's not satisfied. His hot breath hits my ear, ordering, "Say please."

"Please," I choke out.

"Please, what?"

"Please fuck me."

He shakes his head. "Wrong answer." His hand slides between me and the leather then circles my clit.

"I-I...oh God!"

"Say it, Bridge."

Closing my eyes, I ask, "What do you want me to say?"

He pecks my cheek and lowers his voice. "Keep your eyes shut and say your truth." His other hand moves to my breast, and he pinches my nipple hard.

"Oh!" Heat floods my body, and tremors take hold.

"What do you want, baby? Hmm?"

White and black dots flash in my eyes. "Please. Make me come."

"I'm going to make you come, but not until you're honest with me about what you want."

"Dante, please!" I cry out, craving the high like never before.

"What do you need, dolcezza?"

"You! I need you!" I confess.

His hands and cock manipulate me so quickly, an earthquake rumbles through me. He grunts, burying his face in the curve of my neck. His cock swells, stretching me farther, creating a tidal wave of endorphins that crashes into every fiber of my being.

Our heavy breaths are the only sound in the vehicle. Several minutes go by before he pulls out of me and commands, "Stay still."

I don't move, continue to catch my breath. I try not to worry about what I just blurted out to Dante. I stare at the blackness of the night as my heart begins to regulate.

Dante takes a tissue and cleans his cum off my thighs then flips me over. He tugs my pants up then kisses me on the lips. "Last chance to go to my place."

Reality hits me. I shake my head. "No."

Disappointment drips off his expression. His nostrils flare. He sits back in the seat, texts his driver, and slides his arm around my shoulders.

We say nothing. The driver's door opens and closes. The SUV begins to move. Dante looks at me, but something I haven't seen on his face before has taken over his features. I realize it's challenging and laced with fear. "You lasted fifteen seconds. What's it going to be? Your father's or the Ritz with me?"

Being vulnerable is something Dante Marino doesn't do.

That alone makes my decision for me. My flutters reignite. Unable to choose anything else, I straighten my shoulders and meet his gaze. "The Ritz."

14

Dante

Several Weeks Later

"WHERE ARE WE AT?" PAPÀ ASKS.

"Four of the ten look promising. Nothing has shown up other than their disdain for the Abruzzos and Rossis," Massimo states, dropping four 8x10 photos on the desk.

Papà studies each one then glances at Gianni and me. "You've approved these men?"

"Jesus. Give us some credit. We're not looking to have any cocksuckers join us," Tristano gripes.

My father arches his eyebrows at Gianni and me, ignoring Tristano's outburst.

"All good," Gianni replies.

"Why are we even in the room?" Massimo asks Tristano.

"Enough. Take your ego and check it at the door. You know the pecking order," I reply.

"Too bad your dicks don't match the pecking order," Tristano asserts.

"Have you looked at yours lately?" Gianni taunts.

"Pretty sure ours are bigger than your old, worn-out ones," Massimo interjects.

"Enough!" Papà orders, slamming his hand on the desk.

One of the photos goes flying. I grab it in the air, step forward, and put it back on the desk. Then I point to the pictures. "These four men are our guys. They have personal vendettas against the Abruzzos and Rossis. They fit the profile. They're violent when needed, discreet, and their backgrounds checked out. Let's bring them in and get them acclimated."

Papà assesses the photos then scratches his head. He shifts on his feet and finally nods. His gaze drills into mine, and warning laces his voice. He points to Gianni and me. "Fine. I'll approve it. But these are your guys. If anything goes wrong, I'm holding you two accountable."

Gianni turns to our brothers. "See? Being lower on the totem pole has its advantages."

"Shut up, you dick," Massimo hurls.

Tristano scrubs his face. "Is there anything else? Otherwise, I'm through listening to this shit."

"Go." Papà motions to him and Massimo. "Gianni, Dante, you stay back."

My brothers toss us some more annoyed glances then leave. Gianni and I wait for Papà to speak. Several minutes pass before he says, "Abruzzo men breached the line at the container terminal again."

"Which is why we need to do something about it," I state. Gianni shifts next to me, but I don't look at him. I don't need to. We have a sixth sense and have been putting a plan together behind Papà's back, even though I don't like it. Yet, I haven't fully agreed to Gianni's demands, since making a move like this will have major consequences if my father ever finds out.

"If we're smart about it, we can take them out, and it'll go in our favor," Gianni insists.

My father sighs then sits in his chair. He motions for us to take a seat, too. Once settled, he leans back and crosses his arms. "Do you think I don't know what you've been planning?"

My chest tightens. I once again force myself not to glance at Gianni while keeping a stony expression. I have no idea how my father knew, but I shouldn't be surprised. He always seems to be aware of everything regarding the business.

Tense silence lingers for several moments while Papà's cold stare darts between us.

"If we lose the port to the Abruzzos, there won't be any coming back from it," Gianni warns.

Papà's eyes turn to slits. "And you believe disobeying my order is the solution?"

"I believe taking out those who infringe on our territory or pose a threat is vital for our survival," Gianni asserts.

Calm takes over my father's expression, but it doesn't slow my racing heart. He sits back and presses the tips of his fingers together, assessing us before reminding us, "We take out threats on my orders, not yours."

"At what point are you going to authorize us to move forward on the threat? If we lose the port, I'll be the one dealing with it in the future, not you," I vocalize.

Papà takes several calculated breaths then opens his desk drawer. He removes the map of the port, unrolls it, then sets paperweights in each corner. "Show me what you've been planning."

Gianni and I scoot forward in our chairs. I point to the edge of the gray zone. "We plant our men here. The cameras won't catch it if we move them under the dock."

"Then what? How are you taking them out without it creating a war for us?" Papà asks.

"We pin it on the Rossis," Gianni says.

My father's eyes darken. "How are you pulling that off?"

Gianni and I exchange a glance, and my stomach flips. Papà isn't going to be happy when he learns we've already started putting things in motion, but at this point, it's best just to come clean.

"Delfino and Gilberto Rossi are already in the dungeon."

Red fills my father's cheeks. A long time ago, he stopped going into the dungeon. He leaves it to my brothers and me to handle. However, it's a clear rule he's supposed to be updated about who is down there. He seethes, "You bring Rossis into my house and don't disclose it? Are my own sons betraying me?"

"Don't get dramatic," Gianni snaps, and I want to punch him. Saying that to my father isn't the right response.

I quickly interject. "We're keeping our options open, that's all."

"For something I never approved," Papà roars.

"We were hoping you'd come to your senses and let us execute," I fib, knowing that Gianni convinced me a week ago not to give my father the option to shoot our plan down.

"And now you lie to me," Papà barks.

I grind my molars.

Gianni taps his finger on the map. "This is an issue. You've not given us any reason to believe you're going to handle it. The port needs to be secure. You were too pissed we picked up Michelotto as soon as we did to think rationally. You know what happened to the Sardonis. I'll be damned if I let the Marinos be next, with or without your approval."

My father jumps off his seat, slams his hands on the desk, and leans over. His face turns purple. "Your ignorance is going to be your downfall. What you seem to forget is every action has a consequence."

I scrub my face and blurt out, "We have bullets and guns with Rossi fingerprints on them. It's not like we've not thought this through."

Papà's head jerks toward me. "You're not ready to lead if you can't follow my orders. There's a chain of command for a reason. And while I expect hotheaded moves from your brother, I thought you had more control than him."

"Gee, thanks," Gianni mutters, but I don't have to look at him to know he's bored with this conversation and not taking Papà's warning as seriously as he should.

I sigh. "I do have control. That's why I haven't authorized anything yet."

"Authorized?" my father booms. "You don't authorize unless I do."

Gianni rises, and his chair scrapes against the wood floor. "Your ego will be the downfall of our family. Is it because it was my idea and not yours? What exactly is the problem with our plan?"

My father sarcastically laughs. "You don't listen, do you?"

Gianni sniffs hard. "It gets pretty hard to hear the same thing over and over when all you see are people coming after your family. And I never thought I'd see the day where you'd be a coward and back down."

"Gianni!" I snap.

His dark slits focus on me. "What? Now you're going to return to his side on this issue?"

"No. I didn't say—"

"Get out. Both of you get out. And if you execute any portion of this idea of yours without my approval, you'll be answering to me," Papà warns.

"What are you going to do? Kick us out of the family? Put us in the dungeon?" Gianni taunts.

"Jesus, Gianni!" I scold.

Papà flies around the desk and grabs Gianni by the shirt. "You do not disrespect me in my house."

Gianni glares at him, clenching his jaw.

"Gianni, let's go," I order, wanting to end this confrontation before it escalates any higher. My heart beats harder as time seems to stand still.

My father finally releases Gianni and gives us a final warning. "Do not do anything without my permission."

"Let's go," I repeat.

"No. You stay here, Dante," Papà demands.

My stomach dives. The last thing I want to do is extend this conversation. Gianni gives me a final glance and stomps out of the room.

When the door shuts, my father states, "Tully paid me a visit yesterday."

A new sense of dread fills me. I straighten my shoulders. "And this is my business because...?"

Papà crosses his arms. "He informed me that you seem to be spending a lot of time with Bridget."

I shrug. "So? We've always been friends. What's your point?"

He shakes his head. "No. Since she returned to New York several years ago, you haven't. Based on how you acted in the club, and now this information, I'm intelligent enough to put two and two together."

Anger spirals quickly at the thought of what could have happened to Bridget and the memory of that thug on top of her. "And we're back to the night of the club. Interesting how you and Tully seem to glaze over the fact Bridget was in the middle of being assaulted."

My father lowers his voice. "Of course we aren't."

"Yeah? Then why do you keep holding it over Gianni's and my head that we took out that thug?"

"You're missing the point."

I huff. "There are only two points from where I'm standing. There's one less Abruzzo on this earth to worry about, and Bridget is okay. Other than that, you shouldn't be reprimanding Gianni or me, yet you are."

"Because there are consequences. We only have this problem at the port because of your knee-jerk reaction."

I shift on my feet as more rage ignites. I've been holding it at bay during this entire conversation, but adding Bridget to the scenario only makes me lose my patience. "No. You don't know for sure why the Abruzzos went into the gray zone. It's all speculation. And you know what I don't get?"

"What?"

"Why are you so hell-bent on not even considering our plan? Is Gianni right and it's because you didn't think about it?"

"Watch your mouth."

I snort. "Is there something you want to ask me? This conversation is getting stale. I have shit to do."

Papà shifts on his feet. His voice softens. "What's going on with you and Bridget?"

While I'd love to shout to the world Bridget is mine, I know she doesn't want that. So until she does, I'm not risking anything where she's concerned. "We're friends. Always have been. You and Tully can think whatever you want, but it isn't your business. We're adults, so stick your noses into something else."

My father briefly shuts his eyes and then opens them. The hardness has evaporated, but I much prefer it to the current scenario. "Getting romantically involved with Bridget isn't a good idea."

"Thanks for the pep talk. Is there anything else you need, or am I free to go?"

"Don't lie to me about this. She's been staying out all night with you."

"Are you keeping tabs on me?" I hurl at him.

"Tully said you pick her up and she doesn't return home until before the kids wake up for school."

I take several deep breaths to attempt to calm myself. Leaning closer to my father, I proclaim, "Like I said, my business with Bridget is my business. Stay out of it."

"Dante, she's not one of your girls."

"Jesus! Keep your assumptions to yourself." I turn and leave the room, slamming the door on the way out. I head straight to the gym. When I get there, my brothers are already working out. Massimo is spotting Tristano on the bench press. Gianni is punching the free bag.

I grab some gloves, step in front of the other bag, and begin punching in sync with Gianni.

"I'm not going to allow anyone to threaten our port," he says.

I continue slamming my fists into the bag. "Give Papà some time to process our conversation."

Gianni stops, turns, and wipes the sweat off his brow. "And if he doesn't agree?"

I keep punching, hoping it doesn't come to that. At this point, my father will know we went behind his back, and it's not something I welcome into our lives.

"Don't tell me you're taking his side now," Gianni states.

I spin to him and lower my voice so my other brothers can't hear. If Gianni and I are doing this, I'm not putting their relationship with my father at risk. "You know how I feel about this issue." I tap Gianni's head. "Think, brother. Deep down, you know it's better to get Papà on our side."

He moves his head out of the way and sneers at me. "We're running out of time. Every day we don't act is another day we risk losing the port." He waves his hands between us. "Our future."

I step closer so our faces are an inch apart. "You don't do anything without me, do you understand?"

His face turns to stone.

I put my hand on his shoulder. "Gianni—"

"Hearing you loud and clear." He shrugs out of my hold, tears his boxing gloves off, then picks up a rope and starts jumping.

My phone rings. It's the tone I set for Bridget, so I leave the gym and catch it before it goes to voicemail. "Hey."

"Did I interrupt you?" she asks.

"No, dolcezza. Did you miss me?"

There's a brief pause before she quietly admits, "Yeah."

I grin. "Good. Do I get to see you tonight?"

The line turns silent.

My smile falls. "Bridge, what's going on?"

"I think we need to cool it. My father is asking a lot of questions."

"Yeah, he talked to mine, too. Let's just come clean."

"No."

"Why? What's the big deal? We don't have to tell the kids if you aren't ready."

"We definitely are *not* telling the kids."

I run my hand through my hair, pushing down the frustration that's been growing the last few weeks. No matter what I say to Bridget, she still doesn't fully trust me. Every time I broach the subject about telling our families, she squashes it.

She still sees me as the same guy who didn't grab my chance with her when I could have in high school. I reply, "There's no reason to hide it from our fathers."

"Says you."

I ask her for the hundredth time, "What exactly are you scared will happen?"

Her voice turns stern. "I'm not getting into this."

"So you're going to blow me off like we don't exist just because your father is asking questions?"

"Don't be so dramatic, Dante."

I snort. "I'm the furthest thing from dramatic, and you know it."

"Well, you aren't very convincing right now."

I stare at the wall, shaking my head, reminding myself to be patient with Bridget. After all, it's my fault she doesn't trust me. But I'm not a patient man. Any patience I do have is already wearing thin.

"I have to go. I'll talk to you later," she says.

"Sure." I hang up and go back into the gym. Between the issues at the port, Papà's unwillingness to let Gianni and me handle it, and Bridget's inability to let the past go, no amount of working out will let me escape from my thoughts.

All I keep circling back to is that everything in my life should be moving in the right direction now that Bridget is in it again. Yet, I can't shake the feeling that I'm further away from making her mine than the night I took her out of the club.

The worst part of that feeling is I'm unsure what I can do about it.

15

Bridget

Several Weeks Later

COWARDICE IS SOMETHING I DIDN'T USED TO KNOW. NOW that the O'Malleys are back in my children's lives, I'm officially the biggest coward on Earth. It's not something I'm proud of, and it mixes with my fears. I'm afraid I'll blurt something out about Sean's murder, or why I told my kids lies about the O'Malleys and kept them from them. I straighten my shoulders and look my father in the eyes, insisting, "I'm not going to the Marinos' party."

Dad's eyes turn to dark-green slits. His voice is firm. "This isn't negotiable, Bridget."

"I'm in my forties. You can't order me around," I state, but I'm aware my time is up. Things with Sean and Fiona are still tense and haven't returned to normal. Sean made comments under his breath about me not having the guts to come to the party. Every time he says something, I die a little more inside, partly because I don't know how I will ever look his father's siblings and cousins in the face again. The shame of what I've done has only seemed to intensify since the truth came out. But deep down, I realize that the longer I don't face the music with the O'Malleys, the worse it will get with Sean and Fiona.

My father shakes his head and lowers his voice. "It's Thanksgiving. I should never have allowed you to avoid the Marino parties. Now that the O'Malleys are in town and the kids see them again, your presence is required. If you don't attend, things with Sean are going to get worse, and you know it."

"Thanks to you," I snap, still unable to forgive my dad for making decisions on my children's behalf without my permission. I've contained the kids' visits with the O'Malleys to our house or the Marinos', yet that's coming to an end. Sean and Fiona informed me they made plans to spend time in the city with the O'Malleys over the holiday weekend, and I don't know how to stop it.

Time isn't making my fear of the Baileys or Rossis coming after my kids any less. Every day, I feel like I'm about to spin out. Keeping it together is getting harder the more my children avoid me or video chat or speak with the O'Malleys. This upcoming weekend is a dark cloud hanging over my head. I've had several panic attacks. The only thing I'm grateful for is that they've been in private.

"You're going to need to get over this," Dad asserts.

I cross my arms and stare out the window, taking in the last of the autumn colors. Most of the leaves have blown off the trees, and snow will soon arrive. Everything looks cold and bare, amplifying how I feel.

Dad says, "It's time to return to normal life. Our life involves parties at the Marinos'. And now that you're spending time with Dante, I would think you would want to attend."

My insides flip. I blurt out, "Dante has nothing to do with this issue. Besides, we're just friends, and you know this."

Dad snorts. "Sure."

I hate his sarcasm and the fact he seems to know I'm lying. The last thing I want is anyone to know I'm doing anything with Dante. I've even cooled it way off. I've only seen him twice the last few weeks, even though he's tried to see me more, and I felt tempted to give in to his requests.

"You aren't supposed to live alone, Bridget. I don't believe Sean would have wanted that," Dad claims.

I blink hard, swallowing the emotions that crawl up every time I think about if Sean would be okay with me being with Dante. The truth is, I'm unsure what he would think. Would he be okay with it, knowing our history? Or would it anger him? In Sean's eyes, would it somehow stain the love we had? Would he think I never got over Dante and truly loved him?

Answers never appear to the constant guilt and questions that plague me. It's like I'm trapped, and I can't find the door to get out. And every time Dante proclaims he's changed and he wants a life with me, I feel that trap squeezing me tighter.

"I think we're finished here," I reply then avoid my father's gaze. I leave his office and catch Fiona at the top of the stairs with her boyfriend, Jeremy. He's a senior, the captain of the football team, and does well in school. He's always been polite and seems like a good kid. Fiona is crazy about him. But everything about seeing them at the top of the landing, moving toward her room, creates another panic in me.

I race up the stairs, fling open her door, and catch him kissing her. "Time to go downstairs."

Fiona spins, glaring at me with heated cheeks. "Mom!"

"Jeremy, you're welcome to come to our home anytime, but Fiona's bedroom and the upstairs are off-limits."

"Mom! Don't be so old school."

I point at the door. "Both of you. Out."

Fiona's glare intensifies, but I stand my ground.

Jeremy nods. "Okay, Ms. O'Connor. Sorry to upset you."

I force myself to smile. "It's okay. I just need you to adhere to the rules when you're at our house."

"Yes, ma'am." Jeremy grabs Fiona's hand. "Come on."

Fiona doesn't move. She has the same eyes as me, and they turn a dark blue. She lifts her chin, defiantly pinning them on me. "This is my room. Jeremy, you can stay. Just ignore her."

Anger sweeps through me. This isn't the polite, respectful daughter I raised. "Excuse me?"

"You heard me."

I take a deep breath and focus on Jeremy. "I'm sorry, but you need to leave now."

He shifts on his feet, runs his hand through his dirty blond hair, and his gaze darts between us.

"Out. Time to go home," I reiterate.

Fiona grits her teeth and straightens her shoulders. "No, you can stay."

Jeremy releases her hand and kisses her on the cheek. "I'm going to go. Call me later."

Fiona continues to throw me daggers with her eyes. They intensify as Jeremy slides past me.

As soon as he's out the door, I shut it, then step toward Fiona. "There are very clear rules in this house. You were in the kitchen when Sean and I had this discussion about his girlfriend. No matter how upset with me you are, you still have to obey my rules."

"You're such a hypocrite."

I jerk my head backward. "And why is that?"

She sarcastically laughs. "You're a liar. You act all high and mighty, but you're no better than anyone else."

I swallow the hurt her words cause. "I'm sorry you feel that way. You're grounded until it's time to leave for the Marinos' tomorrow night."

"What! You can't do that!" she cries out.

Fresh oxygen feels stale as I take a deep breath. I've never grounded either of my children. Before our rift, they never disobeyed me. I lower my voice. "I can and just did. Give me your phone."

Her eyes widen. "No."

"Yes." I hold out my hand.

She shakes her head and puts her hand over her pocket. "You have no right to take my phone."

I step closer and keep my hand out. "I'm your mother. I pay the bill. Now, give me your phone, or I'll ground you through the holiday weekend."

She scowls. "You would. Then I would have more time away from my family. That would make you happy, wouldn't it?"

It's another sting, but I ignore it. "What would make me happy is for you to return to the respectful daughter I raised. Now, this is your last warning. Give me your phone, or I'm extending your punishment."

She clenches her jaw, stares me down a moment, but finally pulls her phone out of her pocket. "Fine. Take it." She spins and walks into her bathroom and slams the door.

For several moments, I close my eyes and try to calm my racing heartbeat. I leave her room, go into mine, and put her phone on my desk. My phone vibrates, and I glance at the text.

Dante: *I heard you're attending the party tomorrow night.*

My stomach dives, thinking about facing the O'Malleys and all the memories of previous Marino parties. Once upon a time, I loved them. Hell, even Sean loved them once Dante and he became friends. There was always something magical about holiday parties with the Marinos, and Sean fit right in. Going to a party without him and having fun somehow seems unfair.

The vision of Sean tied to a car, screaming for those men to let me go, pops into my mind. I squeeze my eyes, grasp the edge of the desk, and fight the clawing in my gut. Garlic, stale alcohol, and lavender flare in my nostrils. I hold my stomach as it spins.

My phone rings, but I can't answer. I sit in the chair and do what I've done for the last five years. I put my head between my knees, fight the pain in my heart, and focus on getting fresh oxygen in my lungs.

From time to time, my phone rings again. When I can finally manage, I answer. "What's so urgent, Dante?"

His deep voice hits my ear. The tingles that always erupt whenever I hear it ignite. I wonder how I can go from one state to another so fast. "I'm calling to make sure you're okay."

Okay? Does he know?

No, he can't.

But does he somehow have this sixth sense about what just happened?

"Bridge?"

"Why wouldn't I be okay?"

"I assume you're stressing about seeing the O'Malleys again."

"Well, that and my daughter thinks she can break the rules and have boys in her room."

"What boy?" Dante growls.

For some reason, his protective nature over Fiona strikes me as funny. A small laugh escapes me. "Calm down. I took care of it."

"So, who's this guy?"

"Her boyfriend, Jeremy. He's a senior and captain of the football team."

Dante groans. "That's bad."

"Why is it bad? He's a nice, polite kid. He gets good grades and is super respectful."

"And you just found him in your daughter's room. Trust me. No high school kid is going to be good news where Fiona is concerned."

"Ugh. Point taken," I admit.

A moment of silence fills the line. Then Dante asks, "Be honest, Bridge. How are you handling things?"

I contemplate his question and how honest to be. I finally respond, "I'm nervous, don't want to go, and am unsure how to get out of it."

"All understandable."

I sit back in the chair and confess, "I'm not sure how to face them."

"Just hold your head high and be you, dolcezza. And I'll be next to you."

My heart stammers. I quietly question, "Why are you still on my side when you know what I've done?"

"I'll tell you again what I've said before. I don't know your reasons. I want you to tell me, but even in the dark, I know you and your heart. Something led you to make that decision, or you wouldn't have."

I don't speak, fighting with myself to tell him. But Niall and Shamus's threats ring in my ears.

"Dolcezza, can I see you tonight?"

Another fight erupts within me. All I've done when I'm not with Dante is want his arms around me. The more I crave him, the more I tell myself I need to stay away. Falling for him isn't an option. I clear my throat. "No. Not tonight."

"Why not?"

"I have kids," I reply.

"The kids are fine. Fiona will be in her room all night, and Sean is going to be in his. Stop using them as an excuse."

"I'm not," I insist, but it comes out weak.

"Jesus, Bridge. When are you going to stop running from us?"

"I keep telling you there is no us."

Dante sniffs hard. More uncomfortable silence fills the air before he says, "Tell you what. Why don't you gather all the reasons you're fighting us being together, and we'll talk about it?"

My chest tightens. The last thing I can do is say my complicated feelings about Sean and Dante out loud. I'm also not foolish enough to know my thoughts wouldn't hurt him. Plus, I'm afraid that if I ever did start to spill things, it would lead me to tell him what happened the night of Sean's murder. That would only add another layer of danger to my children, and it's already spiraling out of control.

My lack of an answer only angers Dante. I can't say I blame him. But his sharp tone goes straight to my heart. "Trying to push me away isn't going to stop what's happening between us. I'll see you tomorrow night." He hangs up.

I set the phone down and close my eyes, wishing things were simple and I was the carefree, optimistic, fearless woman I used to be before Sean's death. But how can I ever be her again? My children will always be in harm's way. Now that the O'Malleys are back in their lives, surely Niall and Shamus know.

For hours, my fears take over. Flashbacks of my real-life nightmare never stop. All I see are Sean and me and the mistakes I made that led to his death. I hear Niall and Shamus quietly telling me the new rules and consequences while my children play in the backyard. I feel the rain on my face as Sean's coffin gets lowered to the ground. And I see the grief in the O'Malleys' expressions when I saw them last, and they had no idea what I was about to do.

Then I feel Dante's protective embrace. I see the intensity in his eyes and get confused again about how I could have such strong feelings for another man when I had everything with Sean.

I finally cry myself to sleep. When I wake up the following day, dread digs into my bones. Somehow, I need to figure out how to protect my children, but I no longer know how.

16

Bridget

THE CAR STOPS IN FRONT OF THE MARINOS' HOME. SNOW covers the ground, and the lit-up mansion feels overwhelming, even though I can see the energy of the party through the windows.

Fiona and Sean have spent the day here, so it's only my father and me. My chest tightens, but it's becoming a normal state for me. I grasp my trembling hands together while taking deep breaths, trying to get fresh oxygen into my lungs.

Our driver opens the door. A cold burst of air hits my face. My father steps out then reaches in to help me on my feet. He guides me up the stairs, and my stomach twists.

Dad nods to the guards, and the door flies open. My nerves turn into shock.

Sean's oldest brother, Declan, has his hand around Jeremy's neck. The O'Malley look of death is plastered on Declan's face. He freezes, staring at me with pain, betrayal, and so many questions in his gaze, my heart instantly hurts.

All the guilt I've felt for so many years snowballs. My lips tremble, and I blink hard, fighting my tears. I instantly want to tell Declan everything, but my father pulls me back into reality.

"What the hell is going on, Declan?" he barks.

Declan's expression returns to anger, but he keeps his focus on me.

"Declan!" Dad exclaims.

He pins his glare on Dad, a new burst of rage erupting like a volcano spurting hot lava in the air. He keeps his hand on Jeremy's neck and seethes, "Have you met this punk?"

Horror and fear fill Jeremy's face. I've never seen him look scared. He's always confident and polite. I'm not sure what occurred that's making Declan act like this, but surely Jeremy wouldn't have done anything to deserve this.

My father cautiously answers, "Yes."

"Declan, let him go," I demand.

Declan scowls at me, creating a new wave of sharp pain in my heart. He declares, "You're not in a position to give orders."

"Watch it," Dad warns.

"Fuck off," Declan growls. "Not only did he have his hands on Fiona's ass, but he also lipped off to my brothers and me.

That was while he helped himself to a glass of Angelo's champagne."

My initial thought is to deny Jeremy would do such things, but I'm not naive. The things I did or saw in high school should have made me see past his innocent, polite nature. I kick myself for not being more vigilant and letting my guard down.

Dad's ice-cold gaze cuts into Jeremy. He winces. It hits me he's scared of my father but must have underestimated the O'Malleys.

Dad snarls, "Are you stupid, son?"

Jeremy's face turns white. He swallows hard and clears his throat. "Sir, it was only one glass."

Declan's face turns almost purple. He shoves him out the door. Jeremy stumbles to stay on his feet. Declan warns, "Get the fuck out. Don't go near my niece ever again, or I'm coming for you. I guarantee you whatever fear you have of Tully will be grossly outmatched when I get my hands on you."

"Declan!" I reprimand, understanding he's pissed—hell, I'm pissed—but not wanting to deal with a lawsuit from his parents or some other drama. He's still a kid, and Declan's an O'Malley. They protect their own. And it may have been five years, but I know him well. He's on the edge of tearing Jeremy to shreds.

Declan surprises me, spins, and grabs my elbow. "Finn needs to see you. Now."

"Get your hands—" Dad starts to threaten him but is cut off.

He releases me and turns to Dad. "You're both fucking up. We had to convince Sean not to emancipate himself from you. This all stops now, and shit gets cleared up, or you're going to lose your children. It won't be our fault."

Horror fills me. I cover my mouth, feeling sick. I know Sean's mad at me but emancipation?

Declan motions to Angelo's study. "Now, Bridget."

I hesitate, still processing that my son hates me so much he would try to get himself emancipated from me.

Declan leans closer to me. "We're doing everything we can to stop Sean from cutting you off. Every word we speak to him is about not hating you. I suggest you face up to what you've done and deal with us instead of what he will eventually do if this doesn't get worked out."

I blink hard then close my eyes. Everything seems to spin, and my knees almost give out.

My father steps forward and puts his palm on my back. He quietly orders, "Bridget, go into the study."

I inhale sharply, square my shoulders, and hold my head high, faking confidence. I avoid Declan as well as Nolan and Killian in my peripheral vision. Dad leads me past them as my stomach dives so fast, I think I'm going to get sick.

We step into Angelo's study. Dad shuts the door. "Don't let him get to you. I have your back."

I ignore him, staring at the wall, trying to pull my emotions together instead of lashing out at him. I'm now in this situation because of his promise to Killian. All I want to ask is how did he have my back when that deal was made?

Yet, I'm fully aware this entire problem is my fault. I'm the one who lied to the O'Malleys, told my kids they didn't want to see them, and created this pain we all now feel.

Dante's deep voice fills the air. "Bridget. Are you okay?"

I close my eyes, wanting him to wrap his arms around me and shield me from all that's to come. But it's pointless. There is no more hiding from the O'Malleys, so I stay frozen.

Like always, it's as if Dante has a sixth sense about my desires. He protectively puts his arm around me, pulling me into him. The scent of sandalwood and amber flare in my nostrils, helping to calm my insides a little bit. I sink into his warmth and safety, not able to resist it, even though my father is in the room.

He tilts my chin, forcing me to look at him. Worry fills his dark eyes. He says nothing, assessing me, which only makes my tears brew more.

"Sean wants to emancipate himself?" I barely get out.

"He's not," he sternly replies.

I shake my head, trying not to let the tears spill, but one drips down my cheek.

Dante wipes it. He leans down so only I can hear him. "I promise you he isn't doing anything of the sort. We'll talk later about it."

"I-I can't do this. I need to go," I state, attempting to turn.

Dante holds me to him. "You can't run, Bridge. All of them are outside the room, waiting to talk to you. It's time to deal with this."

No amount of breathing will help me. I wonder how I'll get through this without putting my children in even greater danger. The notion to come clean and divulge the entire truth appears, but I remind myself what's at stake. I don't even know how I would speak the horror of the night of Sean's murder or the days after. And if I did, my dad and the O'Malleys would be so driven by rage, they would surely tip off the Baileys and Rossis.

Before that night, I never thought the Baileys or Rossis could infiltrate into the O'Connor or O'Malley families. But I'm no longer a fool. No one is trustworthy. The years of my father discovering his top men were Baileys, or hearing Angelo tell my father he had a similar experience with the Rossis, keeps me from doing anything else to jeopardize my children's safety.

Angelo comes into the study. He kisses me on the cheek and offers a smile. "Good to see you, Bridget."

I nod, unable to speak.

Angelo and Dad talk off to the side.

Dante squeezes my waist. "No matter what happens, I'm going to be here, right by your side. Let me get you a drink."

It's a statement that I usually would refute, claiming I don't need him. Yet the only thing I feel is gratitude and the ache for him to stay. I study him pouring the glass of whiskey. He's soon at my side handing it to me when the door opens.

My heart stammers when the O'Malleys step inside. All of them, including his cousin Finn, are pieces of Sean. While it's only been five years, they've aged. And I hadn't seen Finn for longer since he was in prison. Every one of them have features that remind me of Sean. It tears at my heart as I wonder how Sean would have aged. And when Finn went to prison, he was barely a man. We had spent a lot of time together, along with his girlfriend, Brenna. We were all close. I want to reach out and hug all of them, but especially him. Then I see the hatred in his eyes. It's a replica of Sean's brothers, and I cringe inside.

"It's time you told us who is coming after you, Bridget," Killian blurts out.

I flinch, not expecting anyone to be nice, but the harsh tone hurts. It's a question I didn't expect, nor do I have a response ready. I'm not sure how I'm going to get through this. I reply, "I don't know what you're talking about."

Declan steps closer. "It's not threats against the O'Malleys you're scared of, is it?"

I grip the tumbler so tight, I think I might crack the crystal. "Of course it is."

Declan steps even closer and softens his tone. "Stop lying."

"I'm not."

"Bridget—"

"Does it have to do with Brenna?" Finn blurts out.

I gape at him, and my hand trembles harder.

Why would he think it has to do with Brenna?

My voice cracks as I ask, "Brenna?"

"Don't lie to me. I have the photo," Finn calmly states.

Photo? What is he talking about? Is this why he looks pissed? Is it not about the kids and my lies?

I step back, unsure how to decipher or answer him.

"Bridget?" Dad questions.

Finn takes a deep, calculated breath. "You can all discuss the kids later. Everyone except Bridget out."

My chest tightens. I feel like I'm about to get thrown from one hurricane to the next, and I'm unsure why. But Finn looks like he wants to throw me to the wolves.

What did I ever do that he would get this upset over?

Why does he say it has to do with Brenna?

Then it hits me. There's one thing I never told anyone except Sean. I assumed Finn knew, but maybe Sean never told him?

On a trip to New York to visit my father, after Finn got sentenced and Brenna disappeared, I ran into her in the park.

But why is he talking about a photo?

A chill runs down my spine. *Were one of the Rossis or Baileys following me?*

My father declares, "I'm not leaving my daughter—"

"I'll stay with her," Dante says.

Finn's voice hardens. "No. Everyone out. You, too."

"Tully, let's go find the kids," Angelo states.

Tully points to Finn. "If you harm my daughter—"

"Don't threaten any of us, Tully. Get back on the same side like we used to be. Remember those days? O'Malleys and O'Connors? An alliance so strong, you allowed your daughter to marry into our family? Or did you forget about the son-in-law you claimed to love who fathered your grandchildren and would have given his last breath for them and your daughter?" Liam bellows, walking into the room, his green eyes glowing with disdain.

I stare at Liam, remembering when I saw him last. He was in prison, too. It had to have been over a decade since I saw him. Something about him exudes power, confidence, and maturity. He's not the same kid he was when he got sentenced.

The same feeling I had when I saw Finn and Sean's brothers hits me. I want to hug him, but I can't. Before tonight, Liam had never looked at me with anger. I wince inside once more.

Angelo points to us all. "Everyone except Finn, Dante, and Bridget out. This is my house, and I make the rules. Now, out."

I pull my gaze from Liam's and refocus on Finn, trying not to fall into a victim mode. Once upon a time, I never thought the O'Malleys would hate me. Now, it's written all over their faces. And I knew this moment would be challenging, but I had no idea how hard it would be to feel their anger and know it's all directed at me.

Finn sniffs hard but doesn't object again. Declan pats him on the back, takes a few steps to leave, then stops.

My heart races.

Declan lunges at me, tugging me into him. He quietly states in my ear, "No matter what's happened, I've missed you. We all have."

No wall on Earth can hold up my emotions. I break down as my entire body convulses in sobs. He squeezes me tighter and shushes me, but I can't stop the train wreck that's taking place. It seems to go on and on until I finally pull it together. Declan releases me, and the room clears.

Dante hands me his handkerchief. I turn, wiping my eyes. When I finally spin back, Finn's orbs drill into mine. There's a mix of anger and sadness.

All the memories of my time with him and Brenna flash before me. I start, "Finn—"

"How could you keep this from me?" he asks.

I shake my head and decide he must know I saw her in the park. More tears fall. "She begged me not to tell anyone."

"You knew I was looking for her," he growls.

I nod. "I know. I-I told Sean."

More rage flares in his expression. "Don't lie to me, Bridget."

"I'm not. I told him everything. He said he'd handle it and to keep it between us," I insist.

"Sean would never have kept it from me. Never," he hurls.

I cover my face with my hands. I did tell Sean. He told me not to say a word to anyone, and he would handle it. I also tried to convince Brenna to come with me, but she ran away from me.

"Bridget! Look at me, dammit!" Finn demands.

Pain crushes me all over again. I insist, "I did. I told Sean as soon as I returned to Chicago."

Dante steps closer to me, calmly questioning, "Where did you see her?"

"In Central Park. I-I didn't think it was her at first. She was so thin. And she dyed her hair, but it was her."

"What did she say?" Dante prods.

The vision of Brenna, distraught, is something I've never forgotten. At times, I've dreamed about her, wondering where she is and what's become of her. And that encounter is another thing I feel guilty about in my life. I should have screamed for my father's men to chase after her. It just all happened so fast, and I was pregnant. I close my eyes, responding, "Not a lot. She told me to forget I saw her and not to tell anyone. She was crying. I don't think she had slept. Sh-she smelled like she hadn't showered in a long time."

Finn cringes. He loved her as hard as Sean loved me. It's still evident that after all these years, he still does. "Where was she living?"

"She didn't say, but she was dirty. I-I didn't get to ask her, but I think she was living on the streets."

He swallows hard, as if he's trying not to get sick. "Why didn't you bring her home?"

"Finn, I asked her why she hadn't come home. She started to respond, and it's like something spooked her. She made sure my father's bodyguards were with me before she left. I-I couldn't get her to stay, and I was pregnant, so I couldn't run after her."

"What spooked her?"

"I don't know."

"Stop lying to me!"

"I don't know!" I scream, losing my ability not to be emotional. "Don't you think I've tried to figure it out all these years?"

"I don't know. Have you? Do you even give a shit about the O'Malleys anymore?" he snaps.

"Finn," Dante quietly warns.

"Shut up, Dante. She took Sean's kids, *our blood*, away from us. We welcomed her into our family with open arms, and she acts like we don't even exist but won't tell us why."

A new river of tears falls. My voice shakes as I declare, "I love your family. I loved Sean more than life. I still do. But it's not safe for my kids, and I won't lose them, too."

"What isn't safe, Bridget? Don't tell me it's safer in New York with all the threats Tully receives."

I turn toward the window, not able to stop my tears and on the verge of completely losing it again.

"Who took this photo?" he demands, shaking it in front of me.

I barely see the picture. Brenna and I are younger. It's of that day, in the park. She looks exactly as I remember her. It feels like the last part of my heart remaining gets sliced to ribbons. My shoulders shake, and I claim, "I don't know."

"Of course you do," Finn insists.

I almost tell him my suspicion, that somehow, one of the Rossis or Baileys were following me and I didn't know it. How else would there be a picture of Brenna and me? But then I'd have to explain it all. So I stay quiet except for my sobs, with my fear spiraling all around me.

Finn reaches for me, but Dante steps between us, then shoves him back. "Enough. This conversation is over."

"It's over when I say it is," Finn seethes.

Dante shakes his head. "No. This is my house. She's told you what she knows, now lay off."

Finn scowls. "Fine. But this conversation isn't over, Bridget. I want answers."

"I told you all I know," I reply, but it's weak. Finn knows it, and I know it.

He gives me one final glare then leaves.

As soon as the door shuts, Dante wraps his arms around me. I sob into his chest, wishing I could stop. He murmurs, "Shh. It's all over."

I glance up, blurting out, "For now. I-I didn't know he was still looking for Brenna. You don't know Finn. He's not going to let this go. H-he loved her. Hard. You don't know what that's like until you lose it."

Dante's jaw clenches. He sniffs hard and studies me.

My gut drops. "Why are you looking at me like that?"

His fingers swipe my tears. "I know exactly what it's like to lose the one person you love."

I stop breathing then shake my head, realizing he's talking about me. But he doesn't love me. He can't. "No, you—"

"Don't stand here and act like you don't already know this. I've always loved you. I've always regretted losing you. And I would have done anything—*anything, dolcezza*—to get you back. If I hadn't seen how hard Sean loved you, and how happy you were with him, I would have destroyed him. So if anyone understands Finn's obsession, it's me."

My heart pounds hard against my chest. Dante's dark eyes pierce into mine, but it's too much. I tear my gaze from him, feeling the confusion that plagues me all the time lately.

How can I have feelings for Dante when I loved Sean so fiercely?

Once again, it's like Dante can read my mind. He reaches for my chin and forces me to look at him. He swallows hard. Several moments pass by as he gathers his thoughts while intensely staring at me. He lowers his voice and states, "I'm not him, Bridge. I'm never going to be him, nor am I trying to be. I'm also not naive enough to pretend I don't know what you two had. But I do love you. I always have. It's not going to change or disappear. And I'm not walking away just because you try to toss me aside."

"I-I haven't—"

He puts his finger over my lips. "Don't deny it. One thing I've never been is ignorant." He kisses me on the forehead then steps back. "You should clean the mascara off your face before you leave the room. Otherwise, there'll be rumors going around all night. I'll have Arianna bring you some things."

He moves toward the door, and I call out, "Dante."

He freezes then spins, arching his eyebrows.

"I...umm..." I blink, but more tears fall. *What am I even trying to convey?*

He sighs. "It's okay, Bridge. Take a breather. When you're ready to come out, I'll be waiting."

17

Dante

Several Days Later

"DID YOU TALK TO MY MOM YET?" SEAN ASKS.

"I will today."

"She's going to say no," he grumbles.

"Let's try some positivity. We talked about this," I remind him.

He snorts. "You try living with her."

"Hey! Watch your mouth," I warn. "We also discussed showing your mother respect."

The sound of a locker banging shut fills the line. Sean grumbles, "I have to go."

"Wait," I say.

"What?"

"I called to see if you did what we spoke about."

"Jesus. You're annoying," he moans.

"Did you?"

"Yeah. I said good morning to her. Are you happy?"

"I'd be happier if you cut the attitude regarding your mother."

"Is this lecture over?"

I bite my tongue, trying to keep the balance of supporting Bridget and not creating a situation where Sean no longer trusts me. "All good. I'll let you know what she says."

"Good luck," he mutters and hangs up.

I rub my hand over my face then pause. Gianni's behind me. I don't need to turn to know it. I can always feel my brother when he's within several feet. He senses me as well. I ask, "You eavesdropping?"

He grunts. "You're asking for trouble taking Sean under your wing."

I spin. "Didn't ask for your opinion."

He crosses his arms. Disapproval is written all over his face. "When you and Bridget coming clean?"

My chest tightens the same way it always does whenever I think about how Bridget still hasn't accepted us. I sniff hard. "Did you come into my office for a reason?"

He shakes his head, clenching his jaw.

"Fine. I'll see you later," I state, brushing past him.

"Wait!"

I turn, scowling. His ongoing stance I end it with Bridget is getting old.

His eyes darken. "I think we need to move forward with our plan at the docks."

My stomach dives. Papà still hasn't agreed to it, which is increasing Gianni's irritation. The more time that passes, the harder it gets for me not to go against my father's wishes. The Abruzzos are moving in the gray zone, getting closer to our territory. It's no longer just two men, either. They increased to six this week. I state the same thing I've been saying, "We need to get Papà on board."

The hatred in Gianni's eyes spirals into a dark tornado of fury. Whenever I see it, I know he's a few steps away from taking matters into his own hands. So I move closer and warn, "Don't do something without my agreement. If we do go against Papà, it's together, just like everything else we've ever done."

"I'm over your hesitation. That port is our livelihood. It's time to take the Abruzzos out. We've got Rossi weapons to plant to pin it on them. I've talked to the O'Malleys and Ivanovs. There's no reason not to move forward."

"Except Papà still isn't on board."

"He's delusional on this matter. We both know it."

Sighing, I shift on my feet. The inability of our father to give us the go-ahead is testing me in a way I've never experienced before. Patience isn't a trait I execute very often. Like Gianni,

I make a decision and act. But defying the orders of the head of any crime family, no matter if you're blood or not, is a severe offense. Once we enact our plan, Papà will know it was us. It won't be something we can hide. I reply, "There will be consequences if we move forward. You and I are both aware it could create a war between Papà trying to keep control and us taking reign of the Marinos. I don't want to test how Papà will react. Neither do you."

Gianni grinds his molars then lowers his voice. "If Papà can't keep control of our port, then we have no future. If he would rather go to war with us, then that's his decision."

A pain streaks through my heart. I put my hand on my brother's cheek and sternly warn, "You're speaking from emotion. Let's speak to Papà again, but you don't do something without me. Understand?"

"Is that what you'd risk?" Papà's voice booms behind us.

My stomach flips, and I turn. He pins his angry eyes on us, but I don't miss the betrayal in them.

I quickly reply, "No. We won't."

He clenches his jaw, studying us. His wrath and Gianni's twist in my nerves, almost making me dizzy. The silence only intensifies the tension.

I motion to the sitting area, trying to diffuse the situation. "Let's all sit down and talk."

Papà shakes his head then points at us. "My own blood? My firstborn sons are two people I need to worry about?"

"No," I reiterate, silently willing Gianni to agree, but his stubbornness won't allow him.

Papà crosses the room, not tearing his gaze off Gianni. When he gets in front of us, he asks, "You would be willing to start a war with me?"

Gianni finally caves. "No. That's not what I want. None of us do."

"That wasn't my question," Papà seethes.

"The port is our most important asset."

"And you don't believe I know this? You no longer have faith I'm waiting for the right moment to attack and having conversations with the right people?"

Gianni's expression softens. "What does that mean, Papà?"

Papà points in his face. "It means that you still don't know everything involved in making decisions for this family. You aren't aware of all the moving parts or things in the background that must be perfect for executing something like this. And it shows me that you haven't matured enough for me to hand over more control to you."

"That's not true!" Gianni blurts out.

Papà nods. "Ah, but it is."

Gianni scrubs his face. "Maybe if you informed us of how you're handling things, we wouldn't have to have these conversations."

More silence fills the room, thickening until oxygen feels nonexistent. I finally state, "Papà, we're only trying to protect the family. Please. Sit and let's discuss."

"I'm the one who decides how to do that!" he barks.

I hold my hands in the air. "Yes. We know. So let's discuss it."

His cheeks turn red. He stares us down, his eyes darting between both of us.

My heart beats harder against my chest cavity. I understand why he's upset. I wish he'd never heard our conversation and reprimand myself for not shutting the door while discussing this with Gianni.

Papà finally declares, "Tonight. We execute tonight. Vincent and Nico will go with the others and take them out."

The hairs on the back of my neck rise. "Why our new recruits?"

Papà crosses his arms and motions to us. "You two need to learn your place in this family. Just because you can do something doesn't mean you should. It's time you understood that you, along with Massimo and Tristano, need to start having others implement your orders. You've shown your hands enough for those in the family to understand your abilities. It is now time to test these new men you've brought into our family."

"Surely something this important needs to have us executing it," Gianni asserts.

A low growl rumbles in Papà's throat. "Your inability to recognize your love of violence influences how you see things. As the underboss, you're more valuable holding those in our family accountable."

"And there goes all our fun," Gianni mutters.

I cringe, wishing my brother would just shut his mouth for once.

"Exactly my point!" our father hurls.

To move things along, I interject, "He's just being sarcastic. Your orders are understood. Who else are we putting on this?"

Papà studies us a moment longer then responds, "You two decide. Let me know when it's complete." He moves toward the door then stops and spins. "By the way, if you ever cross me, I'll bring all of Italy down on you. And that's a promise." His gaze throws more daggers at us before he disappears.

I slap the back of Gianni's head when Papà is out of earshot.

"What the fuck!" Gianni shouts.

I fume, "No more talk about going against Papà. Do you understand?"

His nostrils flare, but he doesn't speak.

"Answer me," I demand.

"Fine. Let's put Amadeo and Manlio on this."

I nod, finding no reason our cousins won't execute the job to perfection. "Handle it and inform our brothers. I need to go." I leave him and head directly toward the garage, attempting to lose my unsettling feelings about what just happened between Papà and us.

When I get there, I assess my automobiles. A brief thought hits me that I wonder why I even have other vehicles. I almost always choose my Gemballa Porsche, and today is no different.

The moment the engine revs and I pull out, my anger dwindles. I turn out of the gate and shift, accelerating to fifty in no time. I hit the button on my phone and call my longtime assistant, Pina.

"Well, to what do I owe the pleasure?" she answers.

"Funny."

"Someone has to add humor to this relationship," she claims.

"I know how to add humor."

She snorts. "Sure you do. So what do you want me to do?"

"Cancel my meeting with Rubio today."

"Kind of last minute. He's going to be pissed."

"Don't care. Remind him who's boss."

"Oh, so you're having a *show everyone who Dante Marino is* day," she chirps.

I ignore her remark. "Tell him I'm saving him time. I want everything tripled."

"Tripled?" she asks in surprise.

"You heard right. Glad to see that you aren't losing your hearing in your upper thirties."

"At least I'm not nearing mid-forties," she stabs.

"I keep telling you to drop those younger guys and find a real man."

She asserts, "Not looking for a pill-popping daddy in the sheets."

"Please. Stop putting real men in the same category as your loser exes," I reply, taking a turn faster than I should. The wheels shriek on the pavement, and I shift to go faster.

"Don't forget my review with you tomorrow."

I groan. "Why don't we skip it? You're getting a ten percent raise, and your bonus is doubling."

"I want thirty percent."

I smile, knowing what her response would be before I spoke. I'll give her more, but Pina always negotiates. So I've learned to start low. I voice, "That's a lot. What have you done to earn it?"

"Please," she huffs.

"Go ahead. Tell me why you deserve it," I state, just to mess with her. She's worth thirty percent. It's tempting to hand it to her without a fight, but I don't like her getting used to always getting what she demands.

A long, dramatic sigh hits my ears. "Would you rather I find another boss?"

"Would you rather I find another assistant?"

She laughs. "No one else can put up with you. I dare you."

"Don't wish for things you'll regret," I threaten, but she's right.

"Dante, I want thirty percent," she sternly reiterates. "I'm worth every penny of it, and you know it."

The blaring of horns fills the air as I speed through the red light, weaving through the traffic. "Tell you what. I'll give you twenty percent and triple your bonus."

Silence fills the line for several moments. I wait it out, not giving in to the temptation to speak first.

"No," she asserts.

Shock fills me. "No? That's way more than what you're asking."

"Thirty percent and triple my bonus."

It's my turn to laugh. "You don't ask for more after you've already stated what you want."

"If I take your offer, I'm starting lower next year when I negotiate. And a bonus is risky," she adds.

Bridget's subdivision comes into view. I slow down, annoyed. "Since when have you not received your bonus? I always come through."

"Yeah, well, I'm not looking to tempt fate."

"Way to be a positive-thinking team player," I point out.

"Dante, don't test me on this."

"Don't threaten me, Pina."

"You couldn't survive a week without me," she claims.

I don't argue. It's pointless. "Final offer, Pina. Take it or leave it. Twenty-five percent raise and triple your bonus. It's still way more than what you were asking. Smile and say thank you, world's best boss."

She caves. "Fine."

"Don't sound so ungrateful."

"You know I'm worth the thirty percent."

"That you are. But when your safe is full with more hundred-dollar bills from that bonus, you're going to be happier I'm such an awesome boss. Call Rubio. And I'm not available the rest of the day." I hang up and pull up to the gate.

Tully's guards wave me through. I drive up to the entrance and get out at the same time Bridget and the kids are stepping out of their car.

Bridget's eyes widen in question. Fiona waves and goes inside the house. Sean nods then follows his sister.

I get out and open the passenger door, ordering, "Get in."

"Dante, what are you doing here?" she asks.

"I promised Sean I'd speak with you. Now, get in."

Her head jerks back. "About what?"

I motion to the passenger seat. "As soon as we get out of here, I'll tell you."

She hesitates then gets in. I shut the door and get in the driver's seat. Neither of us says anything. As soon as I get out of the gate and on the part of the road where no one is in view, I pull over. I lean over and kiss her then murmur between her lips, "Are you doing okay, dolcezza?" I slide my tongue back in her mouth before she can answer, holding her head firmly to mine.

For several moments, I forget why I picked her up. It's just Bridget and me.

She pulls back. Worry fills her expression. "Dante, what's going on?"

I caress her cheek. "Nothing to worry about, I promise. Let's go to dinner, and we'll talk."

"Just tell me now."

I start driving again. "Sean wants to box."

"Not happening," she replies.

I glance over at her. "Hear me out, Bridge."

"This isn't your business."

"I'll train him. I'll look out for him. You have my word," I vow.

"And are you going to guarantee he doesn't get hurt?" she asks.

"You know I can't do that."

"Exactly. It's not happening."

I turn out of the subdivision then accelerate. "You have to give him something. He needs his mind off emancipation and a way to release his rage."

Her voice turns angry. "How dare you use my fear of emancipation to try and convince me of this."

"I would never do that."

"You are right now."

I veer to the side of the road and put the car in park. I sternly state, "No. I'm stating the facts. And if you take a step back, you'd realize how wrong the statement you just made sounds."

"My statement?" she fires back.

"Yeah. As if I would ever do something manipulative and hurtful toward you."

She huffs.

"Seriously?" I quietly ask, hurt she could ever believe that and pissed she still doesn't trust in my love for her.

She squeezes her eyes shut, takes a few deep breaths, then slowly looks at me. "I've told you I don't want Sean boxing and why."

I reach for her cheek. "Listen to me, dolcezza. Fighting is in his blood. If you give him this, it's going to make things better between you two."

"How?"

"He needs to feel a win right now."

She blinks hard. "I'm not allowing my son to put himself in harm's way."

"He's an O'Malley. They box. And I will—"

"You'll do nothing to protect him because you just admitted you can't!" she cries out and pushes my hand off her cheek. "This conversation is over. Now, take me home."

I don't move, holding in my anger. One thing I know is that Sean needs this. He's an O'Malley. It's in their genes to fight.

Plus, he already got the bug from his father years ago. All I want to do is help Sean and Bridget, but she can't seem to let go of the notion I'm going to harm her.

"Bridge, if you just—"

"Stay out of my business, Dante! They're my kids—my blood! Not yours!" she yells.

Words don't usually affect me, but she might as well have punched me in the face. I seethe, "Yeah, I know whose kids they are. It doesn't diminish my role in their life or how much I care about them."

She laughs and points at me. "Your role? You aren't their father. So stay out of my business. Now, take me home." She turns toward the window and crosses her arms.

For several moments, I study her, drowning in the new sting she dealt me.

"Take me home," she repeats, not glancing at me.

"All right, Bridge. Have it your way. That's what this always is between us, right?"

Her head snaps toward me. Blue flames burn in her orbs. "What's that mean?"

"You know damn well what it means. Any chance you get to run from me or avoid my help, you take. All you do is try to shove me out of your life," I admit, hating how it sounds out loud.

"Don't be dramatic," she claims.

I make a U-turn, shift, then hit the accelerator. The rest of the ride is quiet until I pull through the gate. When I park, I warn, "One of these days, you're going to push me too far, Bridge."

She opens the door and finally meets my gaze. "And there it is. The real Dante who gets bored has now stepped forward."

"Jesus, Bridget! It has nothing to do with being bored, and you know it. Are you ever going to get past old shit?" I roar.

She lifts her chin, throwing green daggers my way. "Never. I'm never getting past anything because I'm always going to remember who you are, Dante. The last thing I'll do is be your fool twice." She jumps out of the car and runs up the steps.

I watch her disappear into the house while fighting the urge to follow her. Instead, I slam my hand on the wheel, debating my options, not sure how I'm ever going to convince her she's mine.

Pissed at myself, I replay the conversation, wishing I wouldn't have said anything until we were at dinner. I hate the reality of what she thinks of me, but I also let Sean down. And both things hurt equally.

18

Bridget

I SLAM THE DOOR, IRRITATED DANTE'S BEEN TALKING TO SEAN about boxing. He already knew how I felt about it. Everything about our conversation reminds me of how my father made a deal with Killian behind my back and upheaved my entire world.

It's another sign I shouldn't trust Dante. I curse myself for continuing to stay involved with him. I was starting to trust him again, even though I knew better.

At least he showed his true colors before I became even more invested.

Time to end whatever this is that's going on between us.

A sharp pain slices through my chest. I put my hand on the table, steadying myself and taking deep breaths.

Why does the thought of not being with Dante hurt so badly?

I need to get a grip. The only thing I should be focusing on is my kids.

When my anxiety relaxes, I pull my phone out of my purse, ready to text Dante that we can't continue seeing each other. Before I can, Sean turns the corner.

"Mom, did you talk to Dante?" Hope fills Sean's expression. I want to slap Dante for putting it there.

I straighten my shoulders, take a few steps forward, and place my hand on Sean's shoulder. I softly state, "The rules are the same. No boxing. I don't want you to get a concussion or get hurt so badly you have lifelong consequences."

Darkness fills Sean's green eyes. He shrugs out of my grasp, shakes his head, and seethes, "I told him it was pointless talking to you. Guess you made my decision for me."

New fear ignites in my belly. My attempt to keep my voice firm fails. It shakes as I question, "What are you talking about?"

Deep hatred shines in Sean's eyes. It's so painful to see, I swallow hard and have to force myself not to look away. He fumes, "I have the application to emancipate myself. I'm filing it with the court and moving to Chicago."

The room spins so fast that I fight through dizziness. "Sean—"

"No! I'm tired of listening to everyone telling me to be nice to you or not to do anything drastic. The only thing I had to hold me here until I graduated was the thought of training with Dante. He's just as talented as any O'Malley, but you couldn't give me that, could you? You took my family away, lied to me for years, and can't even let me try to be who I'm supposed to be," he hurls.

Tears stream down my face. I put both hands on Sean's cheeks. "Sean, please. Listen to me. I know you're angry and confused. I don't blame you. But you're my son. I will not let you do this."

"You can't stop me, *Mom*," he sarcastically asserts.

My hands tremble. "Sean—"

He grabs my hands and holds them between us. "Don't touch me ever again. From now on, you're nothing to me."

My stomach dives as my world crumbles around me. "Sean, please!"

He releases me and stomps to the door. I follow him. He throws it open, stepping out into the cold air.

"Sean!" I reach for him as he trots down the steps.

He spins, his eyes blazing green flames, yelling, "Don't touch me! I want nothing to do with you! Do you understand that? Nothing!"

"Sean! Don't talk to your mother like that," Dante's voice booms.

Sean turns toward the driveway.

I glance past him, surprised to see Dante still here.

Sean takes the steps two at a time and points in Dante's face. "I told you she wasn't going to change her mind."

"This isn't the way to deal with it," Dante states.

Sean starts to walk toward the end of the driveway, calling over his shoulder, "I'm over dealing with it."

Dante motions for me to stay and follows him. "Sean, where are you going?"

"Away from here."

"Sean!" he calls out then reaches for the back of his arm.

"Don't touch me!" Sean screams, his eyes glistening and his breath coming out in a cloud.

Dante holds his hands in the air. "All right. Get in my car."

Sean stares at him, saying nothing.

Dante firmly repeats, "Sean, get in my car. Stay at my place."

He hesitates.

Dante softens his voice. "You want to go to Chicago? I'll fly you on my plane tomorrow. But right now, you need to get in my car."

My insides somersault at the consequences of Sean going to Chicago, but I'm not sure what to do right now. He's as stubborn as any O'Malley. I don't put it past Sean to run away tonight.

Dante motions to his Porsche. "Get behind the wheel."

"I don't have a license," Sean states.

Dante shrugs. "So what. Get in the car, Sean."

I put my hand over my mouth as more tears fall. I feel paralyzed.

Several moments pass before Sean tears his eyes off Dante's and gets behind the wheel.

Dante takes a deep breath, watching Sean. When the door slams shut, he steps in front of me.

"He can't go to Chicago. Do not let him go," I demand through tears.

Dante scans my eyes, nodding. "Okay. I'll call you later."

"H-he has the paperwork to emancipate himself ready to be filed," I admit.

Dante tugs me into his body and holds my head to his chest, murmuring, "I need you to hold it together, Bridge. Call Killian and tell him what's going on. He seems the closest to Sean. Maybe he can talk some sense into him."

I sniffle, but my entire body is shaking.

Dante kisses me on the head. "Go inside, dolcezza. I'll call you as soon as I can."

I tilt my head up. For some crazy reason, I blurt out, "He's going to kill your gears."

Dante winces. "Probably. Now go inside."

Not sure what other options I have, I obey. I watch through the window as Dante's car stops and starts, moving several times before it disappears through the gates.

When all I see are the iron bars, I go into the library and pull up Killian's phone number. My stomach dives again, but I take a deep breath and call him.

"Bridget," he answers. "Everything okay?"

I cry out, "No. Sean's going to emancipate himself. He took off, but Dante made him go with him."

The line goes quiet.

"Killian? Are you there?" I ask.

He clears his throat. "Yeah. What happened?"

I sit down on the bench seat then admit, "Dante asked me to let Sean train with him. I said no. He...he says he's moving to Chicago."

Killian sighs. "We all told him not to do that. We insisted he finish high school in New York."

I close my eyes and lean my head against the wall. "I'm losing him. I don't know what to do."

"Let him box, Bridget."

I squeeze my eyelids tighter. Silence fills the line, and my heart pounds against my chest cavity.

"He's an O'Malley. It's what we do. It's in our blood. He needs an outlet. If Dante's working with him, he'll be fine," Killian states.

"He could get seriously injured."

Killian snorts. "Yep. And he can die in a car crash. Let him fight. You know if Sean were alive, this wouldn't be a conversation. Your son would be in a ring, and you'd be cheering him on."

More tears escape. My shoulders tremble, and I quietly say, "Yeah, but he's not, is he?"

Killian sniffs hard. "No. He's not. But we can't do anything about that, can we?"

"Sean would have protected him," I admit.

"So will Dante," Killian asserts.

I stay quiet, knowing in my heart that Dante would never intentionally let anything happen to my son, but it hits me that I feel like I'm somehow letting go of another piece of Sean.

"Bridget, hand him over to Dante and let him box," Killian orders.

I still don't speak. My heart seems to split further from the realization that part of this isn't about Sean getting hurt but about all the grief I can't seem to get over. I mumble, "Why does everything have to hurt so bad?"

Killian lowers his voice. "It's going to hurt worse if you don't keep Sean with you. Give him a win, Bridget. He needs it, and so do you."

I swallow more emotions and manage to get out, "Okay. Will you call him tonight? Convince him not to leave New York? Please?"

"Of course."

"Thank you. I-I know I don't deserve your help."

"Well, I'm sure we can spend hours dredging shit up, but I think at this point we have to move forward, don't you?"

My tears fall so fast, I can hardly speak. "Mmhmm."

"Okay then. But let's make our next conversation be about all the things you've missed about me," Killian states in his cocky voice.

I laugh through my tears. "Still arrogant, I see."

"Yep. Admit you missed me."

"I did," I confess, smiling.

"Good. I tell Arianna every day if she ever left me, she'd be miserable from missing me so much. When I see you next, I'll have you tell her."

I groan. "Poor Arianna."

He chuckles. "I'll call Sean and text you later. Just give him this one thing, Bridget. He's in good hands with Dante."

"I know," I admit.

"Okay, then. Tell him he can box, text me after you let him know, then I'll call him and reiterate Dante's rules."

"What are Dante's rules?" I ask.

"He didn't tell you?"

"No."

"Dante was clear with Sean that he has to be respectful toward you and Tully. He has to stick to the training schedule, finish high school in New York, and he can't register to fight until he's eighteen. I'm sure Dante will lift that last restriction if you allow it," Killian adds.

"So he isn't going to be fighting right away?" I ask.

"No. Not unless you let him. Dante's just taking him under his wing right now. Not sure why."

The growing emotions I can't seem to ignore surrounding Dante hit me hard. I close my eyes again, ashamed of how I lashed out at Dante earlier instead of listening to him. I admit, "It's very nice of him."

Killian grunts. "We were all shocked when he volunteered and, frankly, pretty damn relieved."

"Relieved?" I inquire.

Killian replies, "No one wants him uprooted. As much as we want to see the kids more, we want what's best for them. He needs to stay in school in New York. We've all reiterated it."

"Thank you."

A group of men's voices fills the line, and Killian states, "I have to go. Let me know when you've talked to Sean. But we always have your back, Bridget. Don't forget it."

I start to cry again. "Thank you."

"Sure. And I don't know what's going on between you and Dante, but he's a good dude."

I hold my breath, not sure what to say. I wasn't even aware the O'Malley's had any suspicion about us.

"It's okay, Bridget. To move on. You know this, right?"

My lips quiver. I can't see through the river of tears flowing out of my eyes.

"Bridget, Sean would want you to be happy," Killian claims.

I start to sob.

"Shit. Bridget, are you okay?"

"Yeah. Sorry. I have to go. Thank you for calling Sean," I voice.

"Anytime."

"Bye." I hang up and go directly to my room then sit on the bed and cry some more. Several months ago, I felt like my world was semi-safe. There was always the threat of the Baileys or Rossis coming after the kids and me, but I felt like I had some control over it as long as I obeyed the rules.

Now that Dante is in the picture, all the feelings about Sean and his death I've tried to keep hidden inside me have surfaced. I'm not sure what to do with them. I don't know what all of them mean. And I have zero clue how to let Sean go and be happy.

I go into the bathroom and wash my face, staring at my swollen, red eyes. I wonder how happiness could even be a reality for me again. My children are under a constant threat, and I can't tell anyone. Dante loves me, yet I don't deserve it or even know how to embrace it. All the things he did to me when we were in high school seem to pale in comparison to the toxicity I bring to his life right now.

My phone rings, and I answer. "Dante, I'm sorry. I—"

"Take a breather, Bridge."

I sit on the couch and stare out the window into the darkness of the night.

"Everything is going to be fine," Dante declares with such confidence, I think that maybe he's right and it will be.

"Sean can box with you."

The line turns quiet.

"If-if you're sure you are still good with it?" I ask, suddenly worried he'll retract his offer.

"Of course I am. Are you sure about this?"

"Yes," I answer, nodding.

"That's good. I'll tell Sean."

"Please don't let him go to Chicago," I plead, as my insecurities pop up again.

"I'm not. Don't worry. I got this, dolcezza."

The phone beeps, and I hit the video chat button. Dante's concerned face appears.

"I'm sorry," I repeat.

He sighs. "Don't apologize again."

I blink hard, trying not to return to my tears.

"Listen to me, okay?" he demands.

I nod.

Dante's expression turns to the serious, confident, take-charge look he usually wears. "Everything is going to be fine. I'm keeping Sean here for the night, and I'll make sure he gets to school tomorrow. Then I'll pick him up. After our session, I'll drop him off at home, okay?"

The dam breaks, and my cheeks are once again soaked. "Okay. Thank you."

"Sure." Dante stares at me for a moment then says, "I wish I could come over there right now."

I nod but say, "Don't leave him, okay? Please don't."

"I won't."

I blow out a breath of relief then force a smile. "Thank you."

"You don't have to keep thanking me."

"Yes, I do."

He shakes his head. "No."

"Ummm...do you think you can get Sean on the phone?"

Dante swallows hard. "I know this is hard, but give him a night to decompress. I'll tell him you'll let him box."

I scrunch my face then nod again. "Will you text Killian once you've told Sean? He said he'd call him after."

"Consider it done."

"Thank you."

"Bridge—"

"I'm sorry about what I said. I-I just don't know how to get through the past sometimes, you know?"

He nods. "Yeah. It doesn't help I was a dickhead—"

"I'm not talking about you," I blurt out, then feel my cheeks get hot.

His jaw clenches. "I'm not trying to replace anyone, Bridge. I just want you and me. I want *us*."

"I'm not really sure who I even am anymore. And I don't know why you'd want me," I admit.

A tiny smile forms on his lips. "You're the girl I've always wanted. The one I foolishly threw out and didn't know how to get over. And you're the one I'm going to hold on to this time."

I sniffle hard. "Am I still her? I don't feel like her anymore."

"Yeah, dolcezza. You're her. You've always been and will always be."

I stay quiet, unsure how that can be true but void of the energy to argue anymore tonight.

"Get some sleep. Tomorrow's a new day," he instructs.

"Okay. Thank you," I repeat for the hundredth time.

"Since you insist on thanking me, you can do it again in person." He winks.

I laugh.

"Go to sleep. There's nothing left for you to do tonight. I'll take care of this." His lips form a kiss, and he hangs up.

I rise, rewash my face, then put on a pair of pajamas. I go down the hall to Fiona's room and knock. She doesn't answer, so I open the door and stick my head inside.

She's on her bed, with homework all around her and her headphones in her ears.

I walk in. She looks up then removes her earphones. I sit on the edge of the mattress and ask, "Hey, sweetie. How was your day?"

She shrugs. In a neutral tone, she responds, "Fine. Nothing exciting."

I smile then glance at the books on her bed. "What are you studying?"

"History. I have an exam tomorrow. Is there something you need?"

I take a deep breath, wishing I could change things between us but still clueless about how I can. "No. I just wanted to see you."

She shifts on the mattress, blinks hard, then proclaims, "I should get back to studying."

I slowly rise. "Sure. Did you eat dinner?"

"Yep."

"What did you have?"

"Steak and a salad." She stares at me.

I take a few steps forward and lean down to kiss her forehead. "Don't study too hard."

She stays quiet.

I refrain from begging her to forgive me and leave her room. I go directly back to mine, take off my pajamas, and get into Sean's T-shirt. I slide into bed and text Dante.

Me: *Thank you again. I owe you.*

Dante: *No, you don't. I'm here to help you, Bridge. You don't have to do all this alone.*

I choke up again then turn on my side, hugging my pillow.

Dante: *Killian's talking to Sean now.*

Me: *Good. That's good.*

A few moments pass.

Me: *Did Sean grind your gears?*

Dante: *Let's not talk about it.*

Me: *I'm sorry.*

Dante: *Not your fault. The kid needs to learn to drive. I'm giving him lessons tomorrow.*

I smile.

Me: *Are you sure your Porsche can handle that?*

Dante: *I'm taking him out in Massimo's Ferrari.*

Me: *Massimo agreed to that?*

Dante: *Nope.*

I laugh, imagining how pissed Massimo will be when he finds out.

Dante: *Sean just finished talking to Killian. Are you in bed yet?*

Me: *Yes.*

Dante: *Good. Rest up. I'll see you tomorrow.*

Me: *Thanks. Night.*

Dante: *Night, dolcezza.*

I put my phone on the charger and curl into my pillow. As soon as I close my eyes, I drift to sleep.

All night, I feel happy in my dream. It isn't the past. It's the future, but we're in Chicago at the O'Malley's gym. Sean's a bit older, in the ring, surrounded by his uncles and Dante. He lands a punch on his opponent's cheek and knocks him out.

The gym erupts in cheers, and the feeling of adrenaline and happiness I used to get when his father boxed surges through me.

And then I see my dead husband's face and hear his voice. "He'll be okay, Bridge. And so will you. Just let me go."

I sit up in bed, covered in a cold sweat. I take several long breaths, glancing around the room, but he isn't there.

It's only me, my empty bedroom, and my blinking phone.

I pick it up and read the screen.

Dante: *I forgot to tell you that I still love you.*

19

MC

Dante

Several Weeks Later

"IT'S LIKE SOMEONE TIPPED THEM OFF," I STATE, CROSSING MY arms. It's been several weeks since the Abruzzos have gone into the gray zone. Our guys are ready, waiting every night, but the thugs never show up.

Papà arches his eyebrows. "How well did you vet the new guys?"

"They checked out. Why are you blaming them?" Tristano asks.

Papà studies each of my brothers and me as deafening silence fills the air. The hairs on the back of my neck rise, and the longer he gives us his knowing look, the more dread grows in me.

Gianni and I exchange a glance, and everything he's feeling intensifies the churning in my gut.

Papà finally declares, "The four of you need to use this as a lesson. Why do you think I assigned the new guys to this?"

Shit. How did I miss this? Of course my father would test their loyalty.

"You think they're working for the Abruzzos? They hate them," Massimo proclaims.

Papà's eyes turn to dark slits. He shakes his head at my brother.

The pit in my stomach grows. "You think both Vincent and Nico are rats?"

My father shifts on his feet, taking a deep breath. "I don't know. Are they?"

"We put them under a rigorous test," Gianni claims.

Papà's head snaps toward him. "What would be another reason the Abruzzos would back off? Can you think of anything besides not wanting to get into a shootout with their own men?"

Thick tension fills the air. No other reasons stick out. Bile rises in my throat the longer I contemplate what could be happening under our noses. If either Vincent, Nico, or both are Abruzzos, how did we miss it? And what about our other two recruits, Daniele and Toni?

Gianni sniffs hard. "What do you want us to do?"

Papà's voice is calm, but his face is red with anger. He points to Massimo and Tristano. "Reassign Vincent and Nico. Tell

269

them the threat is over. Dig into all four of the new guys' backgrounds again. Have them followed and their phones tapped. I don't want them to piss without knowing about it. Do you understand?"

"What about the port?" I ask.

He motions to Gianni and me. "My guess is the Abruzzos won't waste any time encroaching again. You two are on the night shift. Take those motherfuckers out."

"Consider it done," Gianni replies.

I don't need to look at him to know he's got the start of a smile on his face he can't stop or hide. Nothing makes Gianni happier than taking out our enemies.

"Where do you want Vincent and Nico reassigned?" Massimo asks.

My father walks to the window and glances out at the snow. "Split them up on truck duty. Vincent and Daniele guard the northern part. Nico and Toni take the southern. Tell them if the Abruzzos come within eyesight, to shoot them."

Stunned, I stare at my father. It's highly likely they'll see an Abruzzo if guarding the northern or southern point. I blurt out, "I thought you didn't want an all-out war?"

He spins, scowling. The darkness swirls in his eyes, darting into me. "We won't have one if they're rats."

"And if they aren't?"

"It's a risk we're going to need to take to keep our house clean."

"We could be putting all four of them in a war zone."

"Your point?" Papà questions.

"What if only one or two of them are Abruzzos and the others aren't? We're putting our men in the line of fire with no backup," Massimo interjects.

Papà snaps, "Of course there will be backup. You and Tristano will take our sharpshooters with you. Understand?"

Tristano cracks his knuckles. "Let the games begin."

"This isn't a joke!" my father fumes.

Tristano holds up his hands. "Easy!"

"You two need to grow up!"

Massimo groans. "Here we go again."

"Shut up!" I order.

Both my younger brothers glare at me.

A moment passes with pressure building in the air. My nerves hum with an uneasiness. War isn't something my father ever advocates. He's usually warning us not to make any moves that will start one.

"Anything else? Or are we done here?" Massimo asks.

Papà scrutinizes us further then finally replies, "Go do your jobs."

We all leave the room. Massimo and Tristano split. Gianni pulls me to the corner, grinding his molars, saying, "If we have traitors on our hands, it's our fault."

Guilt and disappointment fill me. I want to claim it's impossible, but there doesn't seem to be any other answers. This was Gianni's and my task to execute with one hundred percent precision. There was no room to mess up. If we let Abruzzos in our house, we put more targets on our family's back. I admit, "I don't think it's an if."

Gianni's eyes turn to black flames of rage. He glances toward the fading daylight. "Time isn't on our side right now. Let's get ready and go."

We part, each going to our wings of the house. I quickly replace my suit with black sweats, a matching hoodie, and sneakers. When I grab my leather gloves, my phone buzzes.

"Shit," I mutter, glancing at the alarm on my screen to pick up Sean. I swipe at the notification then call Bridget.

"Hey," she answers.

I smile, as I usually do whenever I hear her voice. "Hey, dolcezza. What are you doing?"

"Waiting outside school. If I went home, I'd have to turn around and come right back for Fiona. So I'm twiddling my thumbs in the car, debating about what to wear to dinner tonight."

My stomach flips. I hate that I'm going to let Sean down. I've not missed any of our sessions, and I genuinely look forward to them. I also had a date planned with Bridget. I haven't seen her for a few days. Ever since we got past the Sean boxing issue, I felt a wall come down. It's one of the few times I gave her a heads-up about taking her out and trusted she'd say yes. I take a deep breath and state, "Bridge, something has come up for work. It isn't something I can push off. I hate to do this, but I won't be able to pick Sean up or take you out tonight."

She tries to hide her disappointment, but I hear it and cringe. "Oh. Okay. No problem."

"Bridge—"

"It's okay. Will you be safe?"

My smile grows. Other women I dated who came from mafia families would ask about my safety at times, but I didn't care. Every time Bridget shows me any affection, it gives me hope she'll someday fully accept us as real. "Yeah. Can I make it up to you tomorrow night?"

"Sure."

"Can you tell Sean I'll pick him up tomorrow if he's free? Just have him text me."

"Okay. Will you text me when you get home? So I know you're okay?" she asks.

My heart stammers. "It's going to be late...you'll probably be sleeping."

"It's okay. Please?"

"Sure. I'll see you tomorrow, then?" I ask, hating that I even have doubts she'll let me take her out tomorrow.

She replies, "Yeah. Of course."

Relief hits me. "Okay. Tell Sean I'm sorry."

"I will. Be careful, Dante," she says with concern in her voice.

"Don't worry about me. I have to go. See you tomorrow." I hang up and meet Gianni in the garage.

One of my father's black SUVs is waiting next to the door. I hop in the backseat next to my brother.

He holds his hand up, motioning for me to be quiet. He seethes, "I've made myself clear, Cara."

I hold in a groan. Ever since Gianni found out Bridget went to the club with Cara, he's been hellbent on making sure she cuts off contact with Uberto. Cara and Gianni had an on-again, off-again, volatile relationship for years. While I don't know all the details, Gianni's never once denied his issues with Cara were his fault.

In high school, Cara put up with every sordid act Gianni did. He had her around his finger and got away with all his usual seedy bullshit. When they hit their thirties, Cara suddenly had enough of Gianni's games. She moved to Europe, which didn't stop him from trying to pursue her on our trips to Italy. But Cara wasn't the same naive, lovestruck young girl she was before. Her inability to resist Gianni's advances was gone. She made it clear she would never have anything to do with him again.

Gianni acted like it didn't bother him, but I know my brother well. His denial couldn't hide the truth of how he felt about Cara, even though he played her for years.

"I don't care if your upper-east-side family heritage is into what mine is or not! You're putting yourself in it by hanging out with that thug!" Gianni explodes.

The SUV pulls out of the garage. Snow comes down in a thick, white sheet. The car accelerates and creeps toward the gate.

Gianni throws me a look, shaking his head. "Jesus. This isn't about our past, Cara. You're playing with fire."

Part of me wonders if she's still hanging out with Uberto because she's that into him or if it's to piss off Gianni. Either way, Uberto is with the Abruzzos, making him the enemy, regardless of Gianni and Cara's history.

"If I come into the club and see you one more time—"

The faint sound of Cara raising her voice over Gianni's hits my ears.

"Do not hang up on me," Gianni growls then tosses his phone across the cab and into the opposite seat. "Fuck!"

I arch my eyebrows. "At what point do you accept she's on the other side now?"

"Shut up! She doesn't realize what she's doing," he claims.

"You sure about that?"

Gianni's eyes meet mine. "It's Cara."

I shrug. "Lots of people change. You don't know if she's working for him or just fucking him."

"Shut. Up," Gianni barks.

"Don't tell me you still have feelings for her? I thought you finished with her after she turned you down in Italy?" I ask, wishing for once he'd admit his feelings for her.

Gianni shifts in his seat, sniffing hard. "She didn't turn me down. We mutually agreed not to see each other anymore."

"Is that what you call it?" I taunt.

"Change the subject," he warns.

We ride in silence for a while until Gianni pulls a case out from under the seat. He opens it, picks up a Glock, then shoves a 33-round magazine in it.

I choose mine, do the same, then sit back. "Been a while since we took out an Abruzzo. This should be interesting."

Gianni grunts. "I'm surprised Papà's letting us have all the fun."

I take a few calculated breaths, trying to soften my delivery. "If we had gone behind Papà's back—"

"Don't start with me."

"I'm just pointing out that even when we don't understand why Papà is doing what he is, there's always a reason. We need to remember that," I state.

Gianni turns in his seat. "We should have taken the Abruzzos out and secured our territory as soon as they crossed the line. I maintain that Papà isn't acting as fast as he should these days."

I sigh, wishing Gianni would give Papà the trust he used to. Lately, for some reason, Gianni seems to believe he knows better. While I did think Papà was making a mistake, today's events restored my faith that he knows what he's doing, and we still have a lot to learn.

Gianni adds, "At some point, we have to do what we think is best to secure the Marino legacy."

His comment irritates me. I snap, "So you still want to go against Papà?"

"No. But if he isn't going to eliminate threats quick enough, then we have to."

"Jesus. You should listen to yourself."

Gianni points at me. "No. You should step into your role."

"What's that mean?"

"It means that you're scared of Papà."

I snort. "I am not scared of Papà. I respect Papà, and you should, too. Not only as our father but the head of this family."

"I do respect Papà. But if he's not going to act as the head, then we need to."

"For Christ's sake. Are you going to go against me down the road, too?" I hurl.

"No. If you're fucking up, I'll punch you until you see the light."

The air in my lungs turns stale. "Not funny."

Gianni's face falls. He lowers his voice. "You know it's you and me, brother. Till the end, like it's meant to be."

"Then stop trying to go against Papà. We're all on the same team. And someday, we're going to have to make all these decisions on our own. Let's not act like we know everything we need to because I can assure you, like today proved, we don't."

Gianni turns away from me and stares out the window. "You know I hate those cocksucker Abruzzos. Especially after what that thug did to Arianna."

A pain shoots through my chest, remembering how her ex-boyfriend kidnapped and almost raped her before Killian killed him with his bare hands. The thug was secretly working for the Abruzzos. I quietly agree, "You and me both, brother. But don't forget, if anyone might hate the Abruzzos more, it's Papà. His revenge started way before ours, and Arianna is his daughter."

Gianni nods. "That's true."

The SUV pulls into the port and parks in a dark corner. I tap Gianni's thigh. "Let's take care of this and go home."

He grabs our night vision goggles and hands me a pair. We get out and weave around the containers until we get to the last one before the gray zone. It's always there and designed to monitor the area. Gianni and I climb inside, positioning ourselves in front of the small holes to see the gray zone.

The air is so cold, our breath comes out in a fog. We silently watch the activity in our line of sight, but all night, the Abruzzos never enter the gray zone. When daylight comes, we're exhausted and frustrated.

We go home, and Papà orders us to return to the port when it turns dark. I crawl into bed, sleep through the day, and when I wake up, it's time to return.

I don't look at my phone until I'm in the SUV heading back toward the port. There are several missed calls and text messages, but I only care about a few of them.

Sean: *Where are you?*

Sean: *Thought I could count on you. I knew it was too good to be true.*

Bridget: *Are you home yet?*

Bridget: *Should I be worried?*

My heart sinks. "Shit," I mutter then try to call Sean, but he throws me into voicemail, so I text.

Me: *I'm sorry. Work got crazy. I promise you I'll make it up to you.*

Sean: *Nah. We're finished.*

Me: *No, we aren't. And stop being a victim. I've got a work issue, and that's life. As soon as this gets handled, we'll be back on schedule.*

He doesn't reply. The vehicle pulls up to the docks and parks. I text Bridget.

Me: *Sorry, dolcezza. I forgot to text you when I got home. I'm back out again. Hopefully, I'll get to take care of this issue tonight. Sorry to cancel dinner.*

I put my phone in my pocket then step out of the SUV. Gianni and I take our positions like the previous night. For several hours, nothing happens. Around nine, Gianni states, "Maybe Papà's instincts are wrong, our checks were accurate, and there's another reason the Abruzzos backed out of the zone."

"What would the—" I cut myself off as the hairs on my arms rise.

Six men appear in the gray zone. They walk toward us. My brother and I both hold our breaths and position our guns.

I glance through the binoculars. Even in the dark, through night vision googles, it's clear they're Abruzzos. Two of the men have the Abruzzo open-mouthed snake on their necks.

They get closer, and Gianni mutters, "Now."

We each fire three shots, barely audible due to our silencers. Each man gets a bullet between the eyes and goes down. Blood pools on the ground around them, spreading as we stare at it, waiting to see if more Abruzzos were with them.

We wait an hour, and when no one else appears, we get in the SUV and head home.

I pick up my phone and call Papà.

He answers, "Is it done?"

"Yes. Six of them. We waited an hour after, but no one else arrived."

"And you used the Rossi bullets just in case the port authorities decide to investigate?"

"Yes."

"Good. Get home and change. There's business at the club you need to attend to."

I close my eyes, irritated. It's early enough I could have still gone over to Bridget's and taken her out. Now, I'm going to be stuck at the club all evening. I haven't enjoyed stepping foot in it since the night I pulled Bridget off that thug. It's not a place I would ever take her, and now that we're together, I have no desire to go there. I sigh then reply, "Fine." I groan when I hang up.

"What's wrong?" Gianni asks.

"Papà has something he needs us to do at the club."

"So, what's the problem?"

"I wanted to see Bridget tonight," I confess. Gianni's the only one I've been straight up with about Bridget. He knows the entire situation. Even though he still believes it's reckless, he hasn't said anything to my family.

He sniffs hard and does something on his phone. He scowls then picks up the phone.

"Who are you calling?" I inquire.

He holds his finger up, his eyes in slits. He seethes, "Cara, I told you not to be anywhere in the vicinity of the club."

I shake my head at him, not sure why he's continuing to dwell on this. Cara is an intelligent woman. She can make her own decisions, and she's been clear Gianni isn't who she wants.

Several moments pass with Gianni going back and forth with her. He finally asserts, "Go ahead. Step foot in it. I'll take you right back out, and I'll make sure I make a scene."

"Jesus," I mumble, scrubbing my hands over my face. When Gianni gets in this kind of a mood, there's no predicting what he'll do. Drawing attention to yourself in the club isn't good for business. And Papà sure isn't going to approve.

"Don't cross me, Cara," he threatens and hangs up.

"You have to stop this," I warn.

He snarls, "Mind your own business. Her days of associating with Abruzzos are over."

20

MC

Bridget

I TAKE A BITE OF STEAK, ATTEMPTING NOT TO LISTEN TO Cara's phone call. I'm still trying to calm down from the anger I feel over Dante ignoring me all day, not to mention standing Sean up with no warning. Now he's back to sulking and snapping at me. This was after I got into it with Fiona. She decided to skip class and make out with her boyfriend in the janitor's closet. The principal caught them, and when we got home, she decided to scream at me. I grounded her and took her phone.

When Cara called to go to dinner, I needed to get out of the house and cool off. But the entire conversation has been about Dante and Gianni. It's not doing anything to help me forget about my problems.

"Ugh!" Cara exclaims and tosses her phone on the table.

"Who was that?" I ask but have a feeling I already know.

She huffs. "Who do you think?"

"Gianni?"

"Yep. Telling me that he warned me not to go near the club."

"We're a block away," I state.

She scoffs. "Yep. Which means that bastard has a tracker on me again."

I put my fork down. "Again?"

She rolls her eyes. "Yep. It doesn't matter how many phones I get. He always seems to know exactly where I am."

"Gianni's such a creeper." I pick up my wineglass and take a sip. A normal person would be appalled, but it's such a Gianni move that it doesn't shock me. He's always done whatever he wanted, just like Dante. Both of them stop at nothing to get what they want.

"Well, he must not have that good of a tracker on me because he thinks I'm at the club now. He and Dante are on their way." She puts a cherry tomato on her fork and plops it in her mouth.

My stomach flips, and my anger intensifies. "Dante is going to the club with him?"

She chews and swallows. "Sure. He's always there with him. You know how those two are. They're never separated, and even when they are, they still are joined at the hip."

I shift in my seat, staring out the window. All my insecurities about Dante not being faithful come racing back. Nothing good happens in that club. There's only one reason men go there. If Dante stood me up but has time to visit the club, it only means one thing.

Cara lowers her voice and puts her hand on mine. "Bridget? Sorry. I didn't mean to upset you."

I turn back toward her, locking eyes with hers. "Let's go."

She cocks an eyebrow. "You want to go to the club?"

I nod, rage building in my stomach. There's no better way to catch a cheater than by busting in on them during the act. And seeing Dante with another woman will hurt, but it'll be the visual I need to end things for good with him. The last thing I'm doing is staying with an unfaithful man. I raise my chin. "Yes."

She squints. "I thought you said you never wanted to go there again."

"I did. Now I want to. Let's go." I grab cash out of my evening bag, toss it on the table, and rise.

Cara gapes at me then finally asks, "You don't even want to finish dinner?"

"I'm no longer hungry. Are you?"

Her lips twitch until she's wearing a full-blown smile. "Not for food."

I force myself to laugh. I'd rather cry at the thought of Dante in that club with another woman, but this isn't the time to be weak.

We make our way to the car. I instruct my driver to go to the club. When he parks in front of the building, I order, "John, my father isn't to know about this. Pull down the block and wait for me. I won't be long."

He hesitates, pissing me off further. I'm not ignorant to the fact that the moment he's away, he's going to notify my father.

I'm a grown woman.

Dad's going to be livid.

I'm not a child, I tell myself, to find the courage to do what I need to finally cut the cord with Dante.

Cara and I step out of the vehicle, quickly making our way inside. I follow her as she weaves through the club. We go into the elevator and up to the VIP floor. I scour the premises the entire time, but I don't see either of the Marino twins anywhere.

"There's Uberto," Cara says, beelining toward his suite.

The hairs on my neck rise. I grab her arm. "Cara, wait."

She spins, her eyes widening.

I declare, "Uberto is an Abruzzo. I can't go in there."

She shakes her head. "He isn't. He swears he didn't know Michelotto was working for them."

"He's lying, and you shouldn't be hanging out with him."

She glares at me, snapping, "Not you, too."

"Cara—"

She steps closer and lowers her voice. "Uberto doesn't lie to me. I don't care what Gianni claims. Uberto's not an

Abruzzo. Gianni just wants to do the same crap he's done to me my entire life. Well, you know what? He's not pulling me back in. And honestly, your family wars have nothing to do with me."

"The Abruzzos are bad people, Cara. I know you think Uberto is innocent, but Michelotto—"

"Was just his acquaintance. That's it. Now, are you coming with me or not?" Cara puts her hand on her hip.

I glance at the suite. I don't see any Abruzzos, but that doesn't mean anything. I square my shoulders. "No. And you shouldn't go, either."

She sighs. "I'm not letting Gianni rule my life. I'll be in the suite when you're ready to join me." She spins and leaves.

I watch her through the glass. Uberto embraces her. I say a silent prayer that we're all wrong, and he's not with the Abruzzos, but my gut says he isn't innocent.

Find Dante then get out of here.

I glance around the club, attempting not to stare or look shocked about all the sexual acts going on. I roam the hallway, peeking in rooms to get a glimpse of Dante or Gianni, but they don't seem to be anywhere. When I get to the end of the hall, I go into the bathroom. I need a break from the atmosphere. Everything about the club makes my skin crawl, from the lewd acts to the fact that members of every crime family, both allies and enemies of my father, are here. It also includes the Rossis and Baileys.

I shudder at the thought as the scents of sweat, garlic, alcohol, and lavender flare in my nostrils.

I put my hand on my stomach and blink hard. The last stall is empty, so I go in it. I stand facing the door, counting to one hundred, trying to calm my insides and giving myself a pep talk to stay in the club until I catch Dante.

When I feel strong enough to continue, I open the door and gape.

Brenna, Finn's girlfriend from years ago, stares at me in shock. Her hand flies over her mouth, and we stare at each other. Unlike the last time I saw her in Central Park, she looks fabulous. She's wearing designer clothes that probably cost thousands and looks like she hasn't aged. Her naturally blonde hair is brown with highlights, and her makeup is flawless.

I tug her into the stall and shut the door. Throwing my arms around her, we both tear up. I exclaim, "Oh my God! Brenna!"

We both sob for a brief moment. I retreat and hold her cheeks. "Where have you been?"

She scrunches her face. "Here."

"Where?" I ask.

She squeezes her eyes shut, and more tears fall. I pull her back into an embrace, saying, "Please tell me what's going on? I never thought I'd see you again. And then Finn found a picture. Someone took a photo of us and—"

"Finn? What are you talking about?" she asks, as if surprised.

I swallow the lump in my throat, remembering how Finn thought I knew where she was and just wasn't telling him. I admit, "He's out of prison. He's been looking for you."

"W-what do you mean? Finn's dead. I-I saw the photos and his death certificate," she states.

I shake my head hard. "No. He's not. He was in New York at Thanksgiving."

Her lips tremble and the color drains from her face.

A new thought occurs to me. I question, "Is that why you never came home? You thought he was dead?"

"I-I didn't have money to get home. I was on the street, running from the Baileys. Th-they bought me. I killed another man!"

The Baileys. She's been running from them, too? How did she end up in that situation?

I blurt out, "Another? What do you mean?"

"Brad, of course."

My heart beats harder. Brad was her ex-boyfriend who wouldn't leave her alone. Finn went to jail for murdering him. Not once did he ever claim his innocence. I inquire, "Finn didn't kill him?"

Her voice cracks. "No. I did."

Too shocked, I stay silent, putting the pieces together.

"Did Finn not tell you the truth?" Brenna asks.

I nod. "No. But it makes sense now. He loved you."

She looks like she's about to break down, processing the information.

"He *still* loves you," I firmly state.

Her lips curve, but then the beginning of her smile falls. "Tell him I love him. I-I..." Her tears fall quickly, dripping off her chin. She pushes her chin out. "But tell him to stay away, or he'll get killed."

Confused, I pin my eyebrows together. "Brenna. No. He won't stop until he finds you. I have to tell him."

"Please. I already ruined his life. If he's...if he's alive, then I don't want him to die because of me. The man who owns me—"

"Owns you?" I interject.

She squeezes her eyes shut.

"Brenna, tell me who's hurting you," I demand.

She slowly opens her glistening eyes, whispering, "It's Giulio Abruzzo. H-he bought me from the Baileys the day I ran into you."

Every guilty feeling I could ever have fills me, along with horror. I should have had my father's bodyguards follow her that day. I've replayed that scenario so many times in my life, especially the last month since I saw the photo Finn showed me. I scold myself further. This is my fault. What has she been through all these years?

"Come with me. I'll call my father and we'll leave now," I claim, knowing if the Abruzzos are involved, and especially Giulio, who is one of their head men, then I need my father involved. In all reality, I have no idea how we'll get out of here.

She laughs, and it sounds so sad my heart hurts. "The moment I walk out this door, the bodyguards will follow me. Listen to me. There is no saving me. I'll never escape him."

"I'm not leaving you. Now that I know—"

"You aren't listening. And if you go tell Sean—"

"Sean's dead," I blurt out, feeling the sharp sting as a flashback of him tied to the car and screaming flashes in my mind.

She gapes at me then demands, "What are you talking about?"

I attempt to stop the emotions and sniffle. "The Baileys killed him. I moved back to New York years ago with the kids. We live with my father." I'm unsure why I don't also say the Rossis or why I chose to admit it to Brenna when I've never uttered the phrase before. Perhaps it's because she's been harmed by them, too?

She hugs me tightly, just like all those years ago on that bench in Central Park.

I tighten my arms around her, not wanting to let her go. We were close friends before she disappeared. It feels good to have a piece of my past that I assumed was gone forever right in front of me. "Brenna, I have to get you out of here."

"I can't. We'll both die. His guards are all over the place," she claims.

She's right. There's no way Giulio would not have her watched when she's not with him. I've never met him; I've only seen him in passing or in photos, but he's ruthless. I respond, "Okay. If not tonight, then there has to be some other way."

Defeat fills her expression. "There isn't. Trust me. If I could have done it, I would have."

We stare at each other for several moments. I try to figure out how to not let this be the last time I see her and how to help her. I finally remove my phone. "Give me your number."

"Bridget, I only have his and his daughter's numbers. There's no one else. He will have my phone traced."

I shuffle through my evening bag and pull out Fiona's cell. "Take this one. My daughter and I fought before we left, and I grounded her."

"Tough mom," Brenna teases.

I wink. "I'm a bitch. She and my son both hate me right now."

Her face falls. "I'm sorry. I'm sure you're a great mom."

"I don't know. Take the phone." I push it at her.

"I can't. He'll find it. I have zero privacy."

I scrub my face in frustration then stop. "What kind of phone do you have?"

Brenna glances at my hands. "The same one you do."

I nod then give her my phone and purse. "Hold this for a moment." I remove the SIM card from Fiona's phone. "Take this. You can switch it out on your phone, and I can text you."

She stays quiet, with fear written all over her face.

"Brenna, Finn's not going to stop searching for you. And I am telling him I saw you and where you're at."

She grabs my arm. "No. Listen to me. He will get killed. You don't understand the number of men Giulio has guarding his house and him."

"I won't hide this from him," I insist.

She takes the SIM card. "Don't tell him yet. Promise me. I'll check this once a week. Let me think about how it could even be possible to escape."

"I can't hide—"

"Please. Give me some time. I don't want anyone to get hurt," she begs.

I consider her proposition for several moments as she begs me with her eyes. If I tell Finn, he'll be at the Abruzzo compound shooting it up tonight. She's right. He could die, and so could she. As much as I hate to keep this from Finn, I nod. "Okay. Are you here a lot?"

"Few times a month. Now I have to fix my makeup and get back, or Giulio's guy will be busting in here. You go first," she orders.

I hesitate.

"Go, Bridget. You never saw me."

It takes every ounce of courage I have to leave her. When I get out of the bathroom, I see a man who I assume is her bodyguard. I force myself to keep moving, catching a glance of Giulio in a suite. After I pass it, I pretend to overlook the dance floor. Sure enough, when Brenna steps out of the restroom, the man steers her into his suite.

My stomach flips, and I swallow bile, wondering how I can leave her here when I already failed her once before. I stare out at the dance floor then catch a glimpse of Dante and Gianni entering the club.

My anger resurfaces. I watch them maneuver through the busy first level. Then I move to a corner so Dante doesn't see me. The twins get off the elevator and go directly to a suite.

I move closer and position myself so that I can see them through the glass. Instead of Dante or Gianni having girls around them, they're aggressively speaking with several men. Several moments pass, and they move toward the door.

I step back and watch Dante and Gianni get into a heated conversation. Dante shakes his head and the two part ways. Gianni walks in my direction. Dante disappears into the elevator. I turn to face the wall, with my back toward Gianni, my heart racing and praying that he doesn't see me.

But Gianni's on a mission. He storms past me just as my phone buzzes.

I pull it out of my purse.

Dante: *Dolcezza, is it too late to see you? I'm sorry about all the shit I've had to deal with the last two days. Can I come pick you up?*

I close my eyes briefly, feeling like an idiot for being in this club and not trusting that Dante's genuine with me. It hits me that he's done nothing but try and show me he's changed.

I take a deep breath, thinking I need to stop assuming the worst of him.

I text quickly.

Me: *I'm already out. Meet me at the Ritz?*

Dante: *I'll meet you in the lobby.*

Dante

"IDIOTS," I MUTTER, GETTING INTO THE SUV AND SLAMMING the door.

Two of our top guys, Frankie and Al, screwed up one of our deliveries. While they were partying at the club, over a million dollars' worth of jewels crossed the border into Vermont instead of Pennsylvania. It shouldn't have happened, and it's pissed off our buyers. When deliveries are late, everyone takes a hit, including us.

Gianni and I told Frankie and Al any monetary loss, including an extra two hundred percent, is coming out of their paycheck. The two hundred percent might be excessive, but they could cost us our distributor relationship. They aren't happy about it, but they need to learn a lesson. This isn't a minor mistake. It's something you'd have to be extremely careless about to screw up. It's a problem that should have never happened, so it only irritates me.

Adding to my annoyance is my brother's obsession with Cara. It's going to be his downfall. No matter what I say, he's not listening. Plus, knowing their history and how Cara loves to disobey Gianni only adds more fuel to the fire. I'm still unsure if she's involved with the Abruzzos or only with Uberto, but either way, it's something Gianni should get over. He needs to move on with his life. Nothing good will come from his determination to get Cara to do what he wants. He's proven this repeatedly, but something about her drives him to make decisions he otherwise wouldn't.

"Ritz," I tell my driver, and he pulls out of the parking garage. I take several deep breaths, trying to calm myself. The last thing I want is to be angry around Bridget.

I text my contact at the Ritz.

Me: *Have my suite ready. I'll be there in a few moments.*

Once I started seeing Bridget, I decided it was easier to keep my card on file and not have to deal with checking in. My guy hands me the key as I walk through the lobby, and it's a seamless process. I don't like that Bridget refuses to stay at my place, but it's a fight I'm not winning, so this is the next best thing.

I call Papà. He answers, and I relay, "It's taken care of."

"Those aren't mistakes senior men make," he states, which is only a repeat of what he said when Gianni and I went home to change.

My stomach twists. There's no denying it. It makes Frankie and Al look suspicious. I don't want to contemplate them crossing us, but it's such an elementary error, it's hard not to.

Papà's voice turns colder. "I'm putting Johnny and Charlie on them."

I stare out the window, watching a fresh wave of snow fall as my driver pulls up to the hotel. Johnny and Charlie can sniff out a traitor with hardly any evidence to go on. They'll do it discreetly, so Frankie and Al don't even know they're under the microscope. Yet, the thought of having our top guys cross us makes me feel sick. I sniff hard, stating, "Hopefully, they won't find anything. I'll see you tomorrow."

I step out of the vehicle and turn to see Bridget's driver pull up behind me. I quickly help her out of the car and lead her inside. My contact is waiting near the door and hands me the key. I steer us toward the elevator.

Once we're by ourselves in the tiny lift, I push her against the wall and slide my hands over her cheeks.

Her eyes blaze with green. "Hey."

I don't respond to her with words. I dip to her lips and slide my tongue in her mouth, pressing my body against her frame.

She weaves her hands through my hair, caressing the back of my ears with her thumbs. It sends a jolt of tingles down my spine as her tongue dives deeper into my mouth.

The elevator dings. I pull back, taking a moment to stare into her eyes, hating how long it's been since I last saw her. And I hate even more how I let her and Sean down. "I missed you. I'm sorry about the last few days."

A tiny curve forms at the corner of her lips. "It's okay."

"It's not," I insist, wanting to do better for her and her kids.

She straightens her shoulders, and the old Bridget I've always known appears. There's a fun mischief in her expression that I don't get to see very often. "Then show me how much you missed me."

I chuckle, peck her on the lips again, then guide her to our room. After I secure the dead bolt in place, I remove her coat, then reach around her to unzip her dress. It effortlessly falls to the floor, displaying her black see-through bra and panties. My dick hardens further. I reach into my pocket and remove the lube I shoved in there earlier tonight, hoping I would get to see her. I tug on her hair and wrap my hand around her neck, lightly squeezing.

She inhales sharply. Her eyes widen, swirling with blues and greens.

I press closer, and she unbuckles my pants. A faint clang fills the air when they hit the carpet. She begins unbuttoning my shirt as I study her for several moments, knowing I'm at the edge of cutting off her air supply.

Something about it turns me on. It's as if her life is in my hands. But I also know she craves the level of power I exert over her.

Several moments pass. I tighten my grip, feeling her heart pound faster against my chest. I toss the lube on the bed, then I lean closer to her ear, still watching her expression, murmuring, "I want to try something new tonight, dolcezza."

She blinks a few times, and I shove my tongue in her mouth, inhaling her breath as I loosen my grip just a tad. Her hands move my shirt over my shoulders, and she pins her fingertips on them.

I unlatch her bra with my other hand and clutch the string of her panties, grazing my knuckles on her hip.

She moans so quietly, I barely hear it. Her body shudders, and her fingertips dig into my muscles.

I move my lips to her chest, rolling my tongue around her nipple, pinching her other one as I suck.

"Jesus," she cries out.

I rotate her nipples and repeat it while grabbing her ass cheek. Her palms cup both sides of my head, keeping me close to her body.

I move her two steps backward then flip her. I order, "Time to be a good girl, dolcezza."

She turns her head and arches her eyebrows.

I reach down, remove my belt from my pants, and demand, "Lace your hands behind your head. Elbows out."

She doesn't argue, moves into the position, and waits.

I wrap the belt around her neck and wrists. I secure it, so there are only a few inches of tension, then ask, "You okay?"

She releases a shaky breath. "Yes."

I put my lips on her ear. "How much do you trust me?"

She turns her face until her mouth meets mine, murmuring, "I trust you to do whatever you want to my body."

My lips curve. "Whatever you do, don't fight the belt."

Nervous confusion fills her eyes, but she replies, "Okay."

I kiss her again then abruptly push on her spine until her cheek is on the bed. She gasps, and I drag my tongue over her shoulder, moving her feet wider. "I'm tired of not seeing you every day." I hover my face over hers.

She briefly closes her eyes then pins her orbs on mine.

"Tell me you don't want me when I'm not with you," I challenge, simultaneously tracing the bone in her forearm and curve of her ass.

She whimpers.

"Tell me," I repeat with more force.

"I miss you all the time. All day. Every minute," she confesses.

Satisfaction fills me. I've asked her this question several times before. It's something she never admitted before. I reach for her neck, grasp it under the belt, then slap her on the ass.

She swallows hard against my hand.

I pump two fingers into her. "Fuck, you're always so wet for me, dolcezza."

She pushes her lower body into me, whispering, "Oh God."

I slide my fingers out and thrust my cock into her, hitting my pelvis against her ass.

She lurches up, crying out, "Dante!"

I bend over her, my flesh against her warm back, and lean on my elbow. I keep my hand on her neck and curl my other around her fingers. Then I tug her hands so there's no more slack in the belt.

Her body quivers, eyes flare with heat, and my erection strains. I thrust slowly, watching her expression, loving every second of how she submits to me.

Her moans get louder, and her cheeks flush. Tiny spasms flex against my shaft, growing more intense.

"Please. Oh God! Please," she groans.

"You want to come?" I growl.

"Yes," she barely gets out.

I increase my speed, pounding into her, squeezing her neck tighter. Her muffled cries barely register in the room. The sharpness of her nails digs into my hands as her entire body erupts underneath me. The blue in her eyes swirls faster, growing smaller until all I see is white.

I hold myself back from releasing inside her. When she comes down, I let go of her hands and neck, then tug on the belt so her head is arched backward. I squirt lube on my finger, slide my cock out of her pussy, and inch a digit into her forbidden zone.

"Oh God!" She arches her body into the bed.

Staying still, I splay my hand on her spine. "Relax, dolcezza."

She obeys, and I spend a minute preparing her, then I enter her until she's taken all of my cock.

Her back arches and breath hitches. I lean down again so my lips hit her ear. "Okay?"

She nods. "Yeah."

I thrust a few times, groaning. "Fuck, you're tight." I continue sliding in and out of her, holding her neck back until she's whimpering. Tiny pellets of sweat cover her skin as I demand, "Tell me you love this, Bridge. Tell me my dick in your ass is just as good as in your pussy."

"Oh..."

"Tell me," I order, reaching around her body and circling her clit.

"Yes! Oh God!" she screams, and her body convulses again.

I thrust faster until I can't hold it any longer. "Fuck, Bridge!" I bark, going dizzy as I release into her. I let go of her neck and collapse over her back, breathing hard.

For several moments, neither of us moves except for our chests expanding as we suck air into our lungs.

When I can see straight again, I unbuckle the belt and release her arms. Then I roll over and tug her into my chest. I kiss her forehead, and she looks up. I ask, "You okay?"

She smiles. "Yeah. You?"

I tuck a strand of her hair behind her ear. "Good, now that I'm with you. I'm sorry about the last few days."

Something passes in her expression. I'm unsure what it means. She hesitates then replies, "It's okay. I'm aware how stuff comes up in your business." She reaches for my face and traces her thumb over my lips. "I'm glad you're safe."

"You don't ever have to worry about that," I firmly state.

Her face hardens. "Don't say things that aren't true."

"It is," I insist.

Her eyes darken, but she doesn't tear her gaze off mine. "That's what Sean always said. What's crazier is that I used to believe him when he said it. But even when I left him that night, I knew I shouldn't have. It's why—" Her eyes widen, then she squeezes them shut before turning away.

The hairs on my arms rise. I've always thought Bridget knew more about Sean's death than she let on. Nothing ever happened to him until the night he was killed. She has to be referring to that night.

Her heart beats harder against my body, and I turn her chin toward me. I softly question, "Bridget, where did you leave him?"

Her lips tremble. She shakes her head hard as her eyes fill with tears. "Nowhere. Forget I said that."

"No. Tell me what you know about his death."

"I don't know anything." She moves to get up, but I cage my body over hers, holding her down. "Dante, get off me," she demands.

"No. Tell me what you know."

She glares at me as a tear falls. Her voice shakes. "I don't know anything."

I stroke her cheek. "You can trust me, dolcezza."

She closes her eyes and begs, "Please drop this. I don't want to get into a fight with you."

Silence fills the air. I don't want to fight with her, either. Instead of pushing, I kiss her tears and then lie on my back with her in my arms. "Okay. How bad did I screw up with Sean?"

She outlines my pecs, not responding.

"Bad, huh?" I ask, pissed at myself again.

She glances up. "He's angry all the time. Try not to let it eat at you. I'm the one who made him this way."

I caress her hair. "I'll make it right with him tomorrow. I promise."

Sympathy fills her expression. "I'm not sure if Sean gets his stubbornness from the O'Connors or O'Malleys. Maybe it's the combination of both. Don't beat yourself up if he doesn't forgive you right away."

My chest tightens. I have no idea how I'll make things right with Sean, but I know I need to. Not because of Bridget but because of the relationship I've always had with him. I firmly state, "I'll handle Sean. How's Fiona treating you?"

Bridget scoffs. "She hates me. The principal caught her and her boyfriend making out."

My insides tense, thinking about her boyfriend. Declan insisted he was an asshole on Thanksgiving when he threw him out. I make a note to pay him a visit to have a little talk. I arch my eyebrows, remembering my high school days and the building. "Janitors' closet?"

Bridget nods. "Yep. The one and only."

I groan. "You think they'd learn to lock it up."

"Right?"

"Want me to talk to Fiona?" I ask.

"And say what?"

I shrug. "Not sure yet."

Bridget smiles. Her voice softens. "It's okay. Thanks for the offer, but I think it might make it worse."

"Maybe she'll just hate me instead of you?" I tease, but I would take that bullet to get Bridget off the hook.

She kisses me. "That's sweet, but I'll keep that in the back of my mind if I think it'll come in handy down the road."

"All right. Where were you when I called you tonight?" I ask.

She hesitates then says, "Just out."

Something about how she says it makes me suspicious. "Where?"

"To dinner."

"With who?"

She hesitates again.

I sit up. "Bridget, what aren't you telling me?"

She shakes her head. "Nothing. I was with Cara."

Rage fills me. "Cara was at the club."

Bridget shrugs. "We had dinner first."

MAGGIE COLE

"I told you not to ever step foot in there again."

She jumps off the bed. "I went to dinner. How do you know Cara was at the club? Were you there?"

"Yeah. I had a situation I needed to take care of."

"So it's okay for you to hang out there, but I'm not allowed? You're so hypocritical, Dante."

Blood pounds between my ears. I firmly claim, "I have family issues I need to take care of from time to time. You know this."

"Do I? Or do you just miss all the amenities?" she snaps.

"Don't flip this around. And stop insinuating I'm cheating on you. It's getting old, dolcezza," I state.

She huffs and moves into the bathroom. I follow her and grab her elbow, spinning her into me. "Is the club somewhere you want to be?"

"Of course not!"

I hold her head so she can't avoid looking at me. "Then tell me you weren't there, Bridget."

She waits a moment then says, "I wasn't there. I went to dinner with Cara. End of story."

Something feels off about her admission. A mix of relief and dread fills me. To double-check, I question, "So you have no desire to go there?"

"Of course not!"

"It's not safe for you. I only went in tonight for a few minutes because I had to. I've not done anything in there since the night we got together."

She sighs and puts her hands on my chest. "I know."

My panic dwindles. "So I don't need to worry about you being in the club?"

She shakes her head. "No."

I release an anxious breath then tug her into my arms and hold her head to my heart. "Good. I don't want anything happening to you. That place is full of bad men who don't follow any rules."

She shudders. I tighten my hold around her as she claims, "I know. I have no desire to go there."

I push the rest of my fear aside then kiss her head. I raise her chin so she's staring at me. "Okay. Just promise me you won't ever go there again."

She takes a deep breath, nods, then says, "I promise."

MC

Bridget

One Month Later

"HEY! DON'T YOU HAVE YOUR SESSION?" I ASK SEAN AS HE enters the living room. Dante made good on his word and somehow convinced Sean to forgive him. Not a day has passed without Dante training him. And while things aren't back to normal with Sean and me, it has gotten better.

Sean shrugs. "Dante texted that a work issue popped up. He might not be free for a few days."

The hairs on the back of my neck rise. Dante didn't text me anything was going on. No matter what he claims, I'll never not worry about his safety when he's handling business that keeps him away for days. Still, I force myself to smile big so Sean doesn't sense anything is wrong. "Do you want to go out for dinner tonight?"

"Nah. I already called Giselle. She's coming over and we're going to watch a movie," he states.

"In the theatre, not your room," I remind him. Lately, I've had to keep both him and Fiona in check. Too often, I've caught their significant others in their rooms. Since Dante's been training Sean, I haven't had any incidents with him, but I'm not going to turn a blind eye.

He rolls his eyes. "Yes, Mom." He leaves the room.

I follow him out, thinking I'll ask Fiona to go to dinner. She's still upset with me, too, but since Sean's attitude changed, hers has as well. I have to give Dante credit. He told me he would be strict with Sean about showing me respect, and whatever he's doing is working so far. I don't know if my children will ever fully forgive me, but at least I have hope again.

My phone buzzes. I pull it out of my pocket, expecting it to be Dante, but it's not. My heart races.

Brenna: *Friday. Club. Nine. Don't involve anyone else yet.*

I stare at the phone then snap out of it. I text back.

Me: *Bathroom.*

Brenna: 9:25

My mind races over whether I should tell Dante or even call Finn. I've wanted to disclose to both of them that I ran into Brenna at the club, but I promised her I wouldn't. I already failed her once. I don't want to do it again. And I know one wrong move could kill her and others I love.

He's already dealing with another work issue, I think, convincing myself to continue to keep this between Brenna and me for now.

Time drags over the next two days. My stomach is a never-ending cycle of knots. When evening rolls around, I take my time getting ready, but the hours seem to continue to slowly grind by. I choose a black cocktail dress and slip it on. My anxiety only grows when I get into the car. By the time I arrive at the club, I have to give myself a pep talk.

I've only been here twice, and Cara was with me both times. The flashbacks of Rossi and Bailey hands on me, along with Michelotto pinning me on the couch, almost paralyze me.

Don't do this now.

Brenna needs you.

Closing my eyes, I take deep breaths and push the visions and smells away. I open the back door. My driver usually does it for me, but I instructed him to stay in the vehicle like previous times. The freezing air and snow slap me in the face. I hurry into the club as quickly as possible, getting through security and avoiding any eye contact as I move through the bottom level.

I take the elevator to the top floor where Brenna should be. My heart almost stops when I see her sitting on Giulio Abruzzo's lap. We catch each other's eyes through the window, but she breaks our gaze and turns toward him.

I go down the hall, trying to figure out which suite will be safe to enter when I run into Rubio.

His smile fills his face. He leans in and kisses my cheek. "Hey, Bridget. Who are you here with?"

I square my shoulders and stick out my chin, trying to fake confidence while hoping to hide my nervousness. "No one. Is this your suite?" I point through the glass.

"Yeah. Do you want to come inside? Cara is in there."

"Oh?" I raise my eyebrows, surprised she's here again.

"Yep." He motions for me to go through the doorway.

I step inside, spot Cara with some other women, and go over to her. I tap her shoulder.

She spins, her eyes widening, and hugs me. "Hey! What are you doing here?"

I shrug.

"Thought you didn't like this place?"

"Needed to get out of the house," I lie, trying to keep an eye on the glass so I can see Brenna when she goes to the restroom.

Concern fills Cara's expression. "Are you okay? Are the kids still giving you a hard time?"

I shake my head. "No. Things are a lot better between us. Just need to blow off some steam, you know?"

She nods. "Yep. Well, I'm glad you're here."

"Thanks. It's good to—"

My mouth turns dry. Finn walks into the suite and locks eyes with me, scowling as if he wants to kill me. Goose bumps break out all over my arms and legs. I turn away from him and spot Dante and the rest of the Marinos, along with Killian. I cross my arms, cursing myself.

Why are they all here?

Surely, they don't know Brenna messaged me?

Dante isn't going to forgive me for being here.

My mind races but not for long. I feel and smell him before he puts his arm around my waist and murmurs in my ear, "Bridget. We need to talk."

I turn and face the music.

Dante's dark eyes are so cold, I shiver. He quickly escorts me to the corner of the room. My back is against the wall, and he steps so close to me, I can feel his body heat through his suit.

My insides quiver.

He lowers his mouth to my ear. "How long have you known about Brenna?"

I close my eyes, attempting to keep my tears from falling. It's bad enough I told my children lies about the O'Malleys not wanting to see them all these years. Finn already thought I was lying about Brenna before I even saw her at the club. He's never going to forgive me. And now Dante, the one person who has stuck beside me when no one else has, is going to think I lied about this, too.

"Bridget, start talking," he orders.

I swallow hard then place my hands on his warm chest to steady myself, even though I couldn't fall if I wanted. He's got me pinned between his hard frame and the wall. I admit, "I saw her a month ago...the night you were here and we met up at the Ritz."

His jaw clenches. I feel it contract against my cheek. "You were here? You lied to me?"

"I'm sorry. I-I couldn't tell you! She made me promise not to tell anyone. I gave her Fiona's phone chip so she could contact me and we could figure out how to rescue her."

"Keep talking. I want the entire story. Now," he calmly demands, but I feel the anger radiating off him.

"Giulio bought Brenna. The day I ran into her in Central Park, all those years ago. She saved his daughter and then he bought her. The Baileys were after her," I confess.

Dante moves his head slightly so I can see his eyes. "What were you planning for tonight?"

I shake my head, blinking hard. "I don't know. I was meeting her in the bathroom. I-I need to watch for her to pass the suite. She's supposed to go around 9:25." I move my hands to his cheeks. "I swear. I didn't know where she was all these years. It was a coincidence I ran into her. Please. You have to believe me."

He studies me briefly.

"Dante—"

"You're going to do exactly what I say, Bridget. Don't you dare question me or try to disobey me. Do you understand?" he snarls.

My entire body trembles. I nod and a tear falls. "Yes."

He wipes my tear. "Get ahold of yourself. You're going to go into the bathroom as planned and wait with Brenna for my instructions. Understand."

I sniffle and stand taller. "Okay."

"I mean it, Bridget. Whatever I say goes."

"Dante, what are you going to do?" I fret.

His face hardens. "What needs to happen. Let's go." He spins, but Finn moves toward us. Killian is standing in the doorway. His eyes meet mine, and it only makes my heart hurt more. When I break our gaze, Finn's cuts into mine like a razor.

I reach for Dante's arm, but he wraps it around my waist, pulling me close to him, as if to protect me. Emotion swells in my chest that he still wants to protect me, even though I don't deserve any of his affection or safeguarding.

Finn's hands clench into fists. His voice feels like nails drilling into my skin. "If you lie, Bridget, so help me God—"

"Brenna was bought and held captive by Giulio," Dante states.

Finn briefly closes his eyes.

Dante continues, "Bridget's going to the restroom in about five minutes. Brenna will join her. There's a bodyguard who follows her, but others will be watching. I'll send Tristano and Gianni to stay outside our suite and take them out. Killian and Massimo will stay here, clearing away whoever else comes out. There's a service elevator near the restrooms. It leads to a parking garage under the building. I'll take her guard out. You take Bridget and Brenna to the car. Don't stop. Don't look back. Go straight to my father's."

My stomach drops like I'm on the first hill of a high roller coaster. I grip Dante's thigh, feeling like I'm about to witness another tragic death of a man I love.

Then it hits me that I love him. As much as I've tried to fight it, I love Dante. If something happens to him, I'm not going to survive again.

I close my eyes, swallowing hard. I try not to argue and anger Dante further, but I'm scared about what's going to happen. Yet there isn't any other choice. I know there is no way the Marinos or O'Malleys will leave here without fighting for Brenna.

Finn looks at Dante. "I'll take the fall with Angelo."

Dante shakes his head as his nostrils flare. "No, you won't. This is my call. Now, go tell the others."

Finn obeys, and Dante moves me to the glass, keeping his arm around me. His breath hits my ear as he asserts, "I need you to stay strong, dolcezza. There's no room for a mistake, understand?"

I glance at him, nodding.

"Good." He moves his hand over my ass cheek, and his cold eyes warm slightly. "You go with Finn. Do what he says."

"I-I don't want to leave you," I admit, right as Brenna walks past the glass with her guard's arm around her. She sees Finn and the color drains from her face. Her knees give out. She stumbles, and I watch in horror as the man grabs her, pulling her up and shouting something at her while practically dragging her down the hall.

"Go now," Dante orders.

"Dante—"

"Now, Bridget!" He guides me toward the door and says, "I need you to do your part." His arm leaves my body.

The same feeling I had when I left Sean outside of the abandoned warehouse fills me. However, I do what Dante says, leaving the suite and going to the bathroom.

I enter only a few steps behind Brenna. As soon as the door closes, I hug her. "Are you—"

Two shots ring out almost simultaneously through the air.

Women scream in the restroom. Brenna's eyes go wide. I pull her closer to the door, keeping my arm around her, saying, "It's okay. Just follow—"

More gunfire fills the air, and the door opens. Dante's voice booms, "Now!"

We're both shaking, but I force myself to lead her out of the bathroom. Finn circles his arms around us both, and we get into the service elevator. I stare at Dante as the doors shut, trying not to lose it. Flashbacks of driving away from Sean hit me, and I try to step back out of the elevator, but Finn's grip around me is tight.

Gunfire continues to ring as the elevator lowers.

"Finn," Brenna barely whispers.

I try to face forward to give them privacy, but there's not a lot of space. When the elevator opens, Finn guides us to Angelo's SUV. We get in, but he doesn't.

He stands outside the SUV and cups her cheeks. "God, I've missed you, firefly."

She starts to sob, and he pulls her into his arms. "Shh. It's okay."

Then a gunshot rips through the garage. An SUV comes racing toward us, and a deep voice bellows out, "Brenna!"

Finn jumps in and slams the door, shouting, "Get down."

Trembling, I push my head to my knees. We speed through the garage, weaving through the different levels. More gunfire fills the air.

On a curve, Finn slides over Brenna and me, lowers the window, and starts firing his gun.

There's a crash, more shots, and Finn commands, "Stop."

"Are you crazy," the driver barks.

"No. Stop!" Finn insists and reaches for the door.

"Finn! What are you doing?" I yell.

"Finn! No!" Brenna clasps his biceps.

He shrugs her off, seething, "He's dying tonight. Take them home," he orders the driver as he jumps out.

Brenna and I scream for the driver to stop, but he keeps driving.

The next half hour to the Marino compound is chaotic. I spend most of my time trying to calm Brenna down and pushing my worries about Dante to the back of my mind. The driver's phone rings, and Brenna's and my bodies stiffen as we watch him answer, then say, "Yeah, I've got the women." He hangs up.

Afraid something terrible has happened, I ask, "Who was that?"

"Dante. He's in the car."

"Oh, thank God," I blurt out, feeling a sense of relief I've never felt before.

"Who is Dante?" Brenna asks.

"He's a Marino."

The blood drains from her face, and her lips tremble harder. I spend the rest of the time trying to convince her the Marinos aren't bad people, but Giulio seems to have brainwashed her. We pull up in front of the house, and she panics further. She has the notion that the Marinos are going to kidnap and hurt her worse than Giulio did.

Headlights fill the inside of the vehicle. Someone pulls the handle next to her, and she jumps, cowering against me, squeezing her eyes shut.

"Bridget," Dante booms, and more relief fills me.

Brenna shakes harder.

"It's safe," I tell her again. "That's Dante and—"

My door opens. "Brenna! What's wrong?" Finn frets.

I squeeze her one last time, release her shoulder, then get out into the freezing cold. Thick snow falls, and I can barely see. I tell Finn, "She didn't know who my father was and is worried about the Marinos."

Finn gives me another hate-filled look, and I cringe inside. He's never going to forgive me, but I can't linger on it. Dante's arm circles my waist, and he steers me into the Marino mansion, directly to a private corner of the hallway.

All I want to do is kiss him and tell him how relieved I am that he's safe. And I want to tell him that I love him—that I've been stupid not to allow myself to realize it until now. But when he looks at me, his dark eyes are full of too many things.

Pain.

Betrayal.

Rage.

An intense awareness hits me. This is the end for us. I've pushed him too far with my lies, and he's not going to be able to get past this one. My other sins didn't directly involve him. This one goes against a promise I made to him.

Dante Marino wormed his way back into my life. He dug into the depths of my heart without me realizing it. Now, I'm going to lose him. There's no way to gaze into his wounded eyes and not know my fate.

MC

Dante

ANYTHING I THOUGHT ABOUT BRIDGET'S AND MY relationship no longer is true. I assumed she only wanted me. Sure, she hasn't told me she loves me or that I'm the only man in her life. But I thought I had her exclusivity.

I don't.

She lied to me and went to the club.

Why was she there?

Who did she want to see?

Has she been sleeping with someone else this entire time?

Since learning from the O'Malleys that Bridget was going to the club, I've struggled to stay calm. Every bone in my body wanted to go to her house and confront her. Yet, I couldn't risk anything going wrong during Brenna's rescue.

Killing the Abruzzos felt good. But my satisfaction didn't last long. As soon as I left the club and the adrenaline started to die down, the ache in my heart expanded until it became hard to breathe. Oxygen felt stale. Pain seized my chest. Even the top-shelf scotch I drank in the SUV only succeeded in burning my insides further.

Seeing Bridget step out of the SUV gave me a sense of relief that she made it safely to our compound. It, too, is a moment of false emotion. Everything I'm raging over races back, dissolving my relief. I'm so angry, I ignore Papà's menacing scowl as he motions for me to go into his office.

There are going to be consequences for what I allowed to happen this evening. Papà ordered us not to shoot the club up, but in my eyes, there was no other way to get Brenna and Bridget out of there. Plus, Giulio and his men wouldn't have stopped searching for Brenna.

Papà may have reasons for wanting to keep the peace, but he wasn't there. I made the call we needed to make. I'll pay for it later, but for now, I whisk Bridget past him, my brothers, and Killian.

I'm so blinded by my emotions, I can't even make it to my wing of the house. As soon as we turn the corner, I push Bridget against the wall. Her lips are trembling, and her eyes are a brilliant shade of glistening green. "Dante—"

I plant my forearms on the wall, caging my body around hers. I warn, "Don't lie to me."

She reaches for my cheek. Tingles race down my neck. They're a brutal reminder of how much I love her touch. How much I love everything about her.

She lied. Snap out of it.

She shakes her head. "I'm not going to. I wanted to tell you, I did. But I tried to do the right thing."

"The right thing?" I bark.

A tear escapes, rolling down her cheek, which makes me feel like a bigger pussy. I hate seeing Bridget cry. This time is no exception. A sharp pain rips through my heart. Normally, I'll do anything to prevent or stop it. This time, I have to remind myself she owes me answers.

I sniff hard. "How often do you go there?"

Her eyes widen. "I don't!"

"Stop lying to me!"

She grips my face tighter. "Dante, please! I'm not lying."

I remove her hands from my cheeks. "You told me you'd stay away from all of it."

"I can explain," she pleads.

"You better," I threaten, trying to do the impossible and stop my insides from shaking.

She glances past me then re-pins her gaze on mine. "Can we go to your room?"

I sarcastically laugh, allowing the anger to control my words. "Now you're okay going to my room? All these months of not wanting to acknowledge us or stay with me here, and now you're suddenly okay with it?"

She squeezes her eyes shut. A river falls down her face and drips off her chin. She whispers, "I've been scared."

"Of what?" I snap.

She opens her eyes, choking out, "Of us."

I swallow hard, glaring at her more intensely. I sneer, "Yeah, I'm fully aware."

Hurt fills her expression. I loathe myself for causing it but remind myself she's been going to the club. She reaches for my cheeks again and rises on her tiptoes. In a louder voice, she chokes out, "I'll explain everything. And I'm sorry I've not been easy to deal with all these months. But I do love you."

I freeze, wanting to believe it's true. It's all I've ever wanted to hear her say. Yet, I don't want to be a fool. I finally fume, "Don't tell me more lies, dolcezza."

She squares her shoulders. "I'm not."

I stare at the wall above her head.

She tugs my face so I can't avoid her, enunciating, "I love you. I *will* explain everything. Nothing is what you think. Let's go to your room."

I study her for a moment then threaten, "If you're playing me—"

"I'm not. I wouldn't. There's not been anyone but you and won't ever be."

Slowly, I inhale another stale breath of oxygen. I finally step back and grab her hand, leading her through the house to my wing. I take her directly to my bedroom, shut the door, then guide her to the couch, ordering, "Sit."

She obeys, and I follow. Instead of staying seated, she straddles me, running her hands through my hair. She softly states, "I've been to the club three times, including tonight. The first time was the night you saved me. The second was a month ago. You were gone for several days, and I hadn't heard from you. I was at dinner with Cara. Gianni called. She told me you were going to the club, so I..." She deeply inhales.

Fresh anger pummels me. "You thought I was cheating on you?"

She winces then nods. "Yes. I'm sorry."

I stay silent, pissed she still can't get past what happened to us in high school.

"I'm sorry. I really am," she claims.

"I haven't looked at another woman since the night I found you in the club. Every woman I've ever been with and didn't commit to was because of you. And deep down, you already know this, don't you?" I arch my eyebrows, waiting for her to admit she believes in my obsession with her, tired of constantly trying to prove it.

She caresses the side of my head and leans closer so her lips are an inch from mine. "I know you love me. And I should have told you a long time ago that I feel the same. I love you, Dante. I do."

My heart soars again at those words. A part of me relaxes, yet I still have unanswered questions. "Why were you at the club, Bridget?"

She scrunches her forehead. "The night I went to find you, I ran into Brenna in the bathroom. I swear I hadn't seen her for years. Not since that day in Central Park."

"Why didn't you tell Finn or me? You knew he was looking for her."

"I told you. She made me promise. She was adamant Giulio's men would kill Finn. I was worried she might die, too! I didn't want anything to happen to either of them," Bridget proclaims.

I study her for a moment, trying to find any sign she may be lying.

She scoots her knees closer so they hit the back of the couch. The heat from her pussy penetrates my pants, and my dick hardens. I silently curse myself. Unable to resist, I palm her back, no longer able to be this close and not touch her. She's always been my weakness. I suppose she always will be. I couldn't stay mad at her if I tried.

I tug her hair and lean over her face. She gasps as I demand, "From now on, you trust me. You don't keep these types of things from me. Do you understand?"

Her eyes turn blue and fill with more remorse. "Yes. I'm sorry."

I search her face for a few seconds then state, "No more Ritz. You stay at my place, with me. Or I'll stay at yours. Are we clear?"

A sliver of panic fills her expression. She closes her eyes, but then opens them and nods. She whispers, "Okay."

"You hesitated."

"No. I-I just..."

"Just what, dolcezza? Hmm?"

She pauses.

My gut dives as I wait.

She cautiously replies, "Here. Can I just stay here? I-I don't know if it's a good idea for you to be at my place with the kids."

Hurt rises again. I release her hair and sniff hard. "Because you're never telling them about us?"

"No!" She laces her fingers around my neck. "I don't want to cause more issues. They'll see me as a hypocrite. I'm constantly fighting with them about not having their boyfriend or girlfriend in their rooms."

I consider what she's saying then respond, "Okay. I can agree with that decision. But from now on, you'll stay here. No more Ritz."

She smiles, lighting up my world. "Yes."

Satisfied, I tighten my arms around her. "Does this mean we can stop hiding from everyone?"

She turns her head and scrunches her face.

Angry again, I turn her chin back. "Are we ever telling anyone about us? Or are we going to hide our entire lives?"

"I don't care about the others. Your family. My father. They can all know. But I don't know how to tell my kids," she blurts out, a new worry filling her expression. "I-I want to. I do. But I just... I'm not sure how."

Tension leaves my body. I swipe my thumbs over her cheeks. "All right. Let's tell my family and your father. We'll start there and figure out how to talk to Fiona and Sean."

She sniffles. "You're okay with that?"

I slide my hand through her hair and hold her face in front of mine. "Yes, as long as we're moving forward. I want the kids to know, but I'm not going to pressure you about it. It's your call when and how we tell them."

"It is?"

"Yeah." I take my other hand and pull her dress over her hips. I unzip the back and shove it over her shoulders so it falls to her waist. Then I trace the outline of her panties. "Now show me how sorry you are."

Smirking, she reaches for my belt and unbuckles it. Then she releases my pants. My cock springs out of my boxers. Her eyes sparkle as she bats her eyes. "How dirty do you want me?"

The blood rushes through my veins, igniting heat through my entire being. I reach behind her, unclasping her strapless bra. "As dirty as you can get." I toss the bra to the floor and trace her nipples with my index fingers until they pucker.

She moves her panties to the side and slides over my cock, taking all of me in one move.

I groan, the heat of her wet pussy sheathing my shaft. I shove my tongue past her lips and grip her hip, but she's already riding me. "Fuck, you feel good, dolcezza."

She laughs in my ear, increasing her speed. "Don't come."

I tug her hair and look her in the eye. "Then you better get your hot pussy off my dick."

She rides me faster and pushes her lip out into a pout. "Aww. I thought you wanted me dirty."

"I do." I scrape my teeth down her neck then grip her hair, watching her expression.

She puts her lips on mine and says, "Then don't come, baby." She reaches behind her body and cups my balls, rolling them in her hand.

"Jesus." Somehow, she's taken me from one to ten in under a minute. I play tongue-tag with her for a few minutes until tiny tremors fill her body and her walls squeeze my erection. I hold myself back from releasing in her, muttering, "But I love coming in your pulsing cunt."

"Oh God," she moans.

I nip on her lobe then suck on it while rolling my thumb on her clit. I taunt, "Where's my dirty girl?"

Before I know what's happening, she slides off my lap, gets on her knees, and deep throats me.

"Fuuuuuck," I growl. I fist all of her hair then order, "Look at me."

She lifts her eyes to mine while continuing to suck me. The room disappears. It's only Bridget's eyes and her plump lips on my cock.

It's fucking perfection, and all the years of wanting her, I imagined it too many times. I lean closer to her, controlling her mouth, sliding on and off me. I ask, "You like how you taste?"

"Mmm," she hums, not flinching or taking me out of her mouth.

I let her take me to the point I'm going to explode then push her off me. Her dress slides to the floor. I demand, "Take off your panties."

Heat flares in her eyes. She pushes them down her legs.

I push my pants to my ankles and direct, "Stand behind the couch."

She does as I ask, giving me a moment to control my arousal.

I reach for her waist, pick her up, and pull her over me. Her thighs press against my shoulders, and her mouth is near my cock. She yelps as I demand, "Suck."

She takes all of me in her mouth again.

I return to controlling her movement then palm her ass cheeks with my other one. My cock twitches in her mouth as I inhale her arousal. Then I lick the length of her pussy.

She whimpers, sucking me harder.

I slap her ass then squeeze it, licking her faster. She moans louder, riding my face until her clit is pulsing against my lips.

Then I gently suck her, knowing it'll drive her crazy.

A muffled, "Please," fills the air.

I slap her ass harder and rotate between little licks and sucks, nibbling her from time to time.

Our sweat merges, dripping down our bodies. Adrenaline expands in every cell of my body, torturing me.

I suck her hard, and her back arches. My dick falls out of her mouth, and her body trembles like a violent earthquake. She cries out, "Dante! Oh God!"

Continuing to make her orgasm, I smack her ass, then rub out the sting.

She shakes harder. Her breath shortens, and her cries turn into incoherent sounds.

Pulling her over my shoulders, I move her body off me and position her so she's on her knees, facing the couch. I instruct, "Don't move."

Her cheeks are maroon from hanging upside down. Green and blue heat swirl in her orbs. Her breath is shaky. She grabs my head and kisses me.

I return her affection then pat her ass. "Stay here," I reiterate then go to my dresser, open a drawer, and scan the different items. I've been waiting for her to stay at my place. I bought every piece the night after we first got together.

Studying the toys with her in the room is overwhelming. There are too many things I've been craving to do with her. Too many ways I've wanted to unleash sensations in her she never knew she had.

I glance back at her, catching her eyes in the darkened room.

Her voice comes out raspy. "What are you doing?"

"Turn toward the wall," I demand. "And don't ask me questions."

She takes a deep breath and obeys.

Her obedience fills me with pride. There was a time when Bridget would have fought my orders, but she's submitted more and more to me over the last few months.

I assess the drawer again then select a collar with chains that have nipple clamps attached. I shut the drawer then position myself behind Bridget. Leaning into her ear, I move her hair over her other shoulder. I drag my finger over her collarbone and murmur, "You know why I wanted you here, in my room?"

She fills her lungs with air, turning her head, pinning her gaze on mine. "Because you love me, and I'm yours."

Her words take me by surprise. It's better than anything she could have said. After all these years, she finally gives me the only thing I've ever desired—her.

"Good answer, dolcezza." I kiss her deeply, sliding the collar over her neck and clasping it. I leave enough room for my fingers to slide beneath the leather. "Look around."

She furrows her eyebrows.

I hold her chin and point. "I designed this room. For every part of it, I envisioned you and the ways that design element would allow me to have you." I wait a moment, letting her study the space, holding in my chuckle.

To an outsider, the room looks like I invested in art. But it's not. There are numerous places to restrain her and different furniture to position her how I want. Over the years, the more time that passed that I didn't have her, the more things I added, like what I'm about to do now.

Sliding my fingers under the collar, I rise and guide her to her feet. So many questions flitter over her face as I move her to the wall.

I push a button. The ceiling opens and a set of metal restraints lower toward us then stop an arm's length above her head.

Bridget studies it. My hand is still in her collar. I can feel her pulse quickening. She meets my gaze, her eyes filled with heady, curious anticipation.

"Arms up," I instruct.

She hesitates, her eyes darting between mine and the restraint.

Worry fills me. I step closer and push a lock of hair off her forehead, tucking it behind her ear. I've never restrained her like this before. It's always been without warning with my tie or some other vanilla article. I suddenly wonder if she's not going to be into this. "What's wrong, dolcezza?"

She takes a deep breath and closes her eyes momentarily.

"If you don't want—"

"I trust you." Her eyes fly open, and she lifts her arms.

Part of me is elated, ready to do all the things I've wanted. But a tiny part of me questions if I'm about to do something I shouldn't. "Are you sure?"

She keeps her hands in the air and presses so close, her hard nipples graze my skin. Her voice strengthens, and she squares her shoulders. "I'm yours to do whatever you want to."

24

Bridget

MY HEART IS POUNDING AGAINST MY CHEST CAVITY. DANTE'S tied my hands behind my back or to headboards, but it's nothing Sean hadn't done to me before. Something about the metal-hinged handcuffs makes me nervous. I try to sound as confident as I can, but as soon as I tell Dante to do what he wants, another flashback of the night Sean died appears.

This is Dante.

This isn't them.

I close my eyes, pushing it away like I've learned to do over the years.

Get a grip.

Don't let your past ruin your future.

Dante's fingers caress my cheeks. "Dolcezza—"

"Fuck me how you want," I firmly state, keeping my arms over my head.

"Are you—"

"Dante, squeeze my throat when you kiss me."

His lips twitch and fire blazes in his eyes. "Is that what you think of? Me squeezing your throat, kissing you, with adrenaline surging through your body?"

"Yes," I admit, my breath hitching at the thought.

The night of Sean's murder, one of the Rossi men squeezed my throat so hard, I blacked out. It confused me when Dante did it. I enjoyed it. Sean never squeezed my throat. The first time any man did was the night of his murder. But something about Dante doing it turns me on. I spent hours analyzing it afterward. I finally came to the conclusion I trust Dante with every part of my body. He would never cut off my air supply and make me black out or kill me. And maybe that is why what he does makes me wet, even after that horrific night.

Dante's hands slide under the collar. He adds pressure to my neck.

I gasp, my pussy clenching, and I stare at him in anticipation.

His lips touch mine as he says, "Have you used nipple clamps before?"

"No," I barely get out. New flutters hit my belly, which surprises me. They aren't bad flutters but full of excited anticipation. Nipple clamps have always scared me, but everything Dante does reiterates he knows exactly how to make my body feel good.

Darkness fills his expression. It's a look that makes me shift on my feet. Every time I see it, I become a wet puddle, weak-kneed and pining for every deviant thing he'll do to me. He slides his hands up my arms, creating a buzz of electricity that races down my spine. He cuffs my wrists and curls his fingers around mine. His hot breath enters my mouth as he gazes down at me.

I wait for him to speak, my pulse racing, a drop of arousal dripping down my thigh and the scent of it flaring in my nostrils.

"So you're finally mine, after all these years." It's more of a statement than a question.

"Yes," I reaffirm, finally owning all the feelings I have for him, then adding, "And you're mine."

Something tender flickers in his eyes. He dips down and slides his tongue in my mouth, rolling it quickly, then deepening the kiss until I feel pressure on my nipple.

I inhale sharply.

He moves his hands to my other breast and secures the other clamp to it.

I move my head and gasp, freezing.

Dante drags his finger down my cheek, neck, then to my nipple. He circles the clamp. "Fuck, you're beautiful, Bridge."

I swallow hard, waiting for him to make the next move.

The more time that passes, the wetter I get. I finally whisper, "Please."

He cocks his eyebrow. "Please, what?"

"Please touch me."

The corners of his lips curve up. He takes a deep breath then steps back, hitting something on the wall. The tension in the chains gets tighter until I'm on the pads of my feet.

My butterflies spread their wings in a frenzy.

Dante slides behind me, his naked body warm against my back. His arm circles my waist, inciting more tingles in my cells. His other hand glides under the collar. He tugs my head back on his shoulder.

A ripple of pain and pleasure shoots through my nipples. I breathe, "Holy!"

His lips and hot breath on my ear send a rush of endorphins to my head, making me borderline dizzy. He traces the outside of my pussy. I squirm, but the tension from the restraints and his hold on me doesn't allow me to move much. His voice turns deeper. "I've changed my mind."

I turn my head to meet his gaze, activating the nipple clamps again. "Oh!"

He smirks then pecks me on the lips and steps back. I immediately miss his body heat. He drags a desk chair across the room, hits the button, and the chains loosen.

"Spread your legs."

I obey, and he slides the chair under me.

"Squat," he orders.

I do it, and he presses the button again. I'm about two inches off the seat when the chains stop moving.

"Good girl," he praises then moves me a step back, sits in the chair, then repositions me over him. "Grab the chains for leverage."

I wrap my hands around them.

He rubs his hands over my inner thighs, and I shudder. "So wet all the time for me," he mumbles, his lips against my cleavage.

"Yes. Always," I confess.

His eyes trail up my body. He grabs my hips and slams me over his cock.

"Oh fuck!" I cry out.

He wraps his hand under the collar, brings my mouth to his, and orders, "Ride me, dolcezza. Show me how much your pretty little pussy wants me in it." He slides his tongue in my mouth, squeezing harder.

I urgently kiss him back, using the chains as instructed, riding him and unable to stop the whimpers flying out of me. His body connecting with mine is a roller coaster of never-ending adrenaline seizing me. It's hit after hit of tension, making me jones for his high.

His deep groan ricochets in the air. He palms my spine, holding me tighter to him. My chest grazes his, sending more sensations through my nipples and straight to my core. But the pain is now barely there. It's a new type of pleasure I've not felt before. Between kisses, he mumbles, "I'm going to marry you, Bridge."

I freeze, staring at him, taking shallow breaths of the tiny amount of air I can inhale.

His face turns stern. "Don't freak out on me."

"I-I'm not. Just—"

"I'm not asking you right now. We're telling the kids before I do," he states.

Shock hits me again. There's relief he said that, but I'm also disappointed. It's a slap in the face that I want to marry him. I never thought I would get married again or feel anything like what I felt with Sean. Everything I feel for Dante mirrors it but is also different. What we have isn't like what Sean and I had. I can't describe it, but all the pieces of Dante and me together fit. And something about being his makes me feel indestructible.

I should run. I made that mistake in the past. But I can't hide from us anymore. Fate wants us together, and I don't want to keep fighting it.

"I'll say yes," I blurt out, blinking hard, but tears escape.

His lips twitch. He slides his hand out of the collar and cups my cheek, swiping his thumb at my tears. "Good girl."

I kiss him, putting everything I have into the kiss, circling my hips over his body.

TOXIC

He breaks our kiss, removing a clamp and dipping down to suck on my nipple.

An intense surge of adrenaline whips through me. My walls spasm on his cock, and an orgasm pummels me.

"Dante!" I cry out.

He grunts, does the same thing to my other nipple, and I think I might black out. I grip the chains tighter as he mumbles, "Fuuuuck." His hand slides back under the collar, and he squeezes my neck again while kissing me and moving my hips faster.

One orgasm after another annihilates me until his lips freeze against mine. He breathes in my exhale, and his cock pumps violently inside me.

The room becomes an echo chamber of our cries. His dark eyes penetrate mine until white stars fill my vision.

Full of tremors, I don't know how long I sit slumped against him. He finally reaches up and unlatches the cuffs. My arms fall over his shoulders. He rises with me around him and carries me to the bed.

He tugs me against his frame, spooning my backside, cocooning me, as if I'm a part of his body. He kisses the back of my ear and says, "Don't disappear like you always do."

I turn my head so I can't avoid him. "I won't."

He pecks me on the lips. "Good. There's something I want to give you before you leave."

I arch my eyebrow. "Oh? What is it?"

He kisses me again. "You'll see. What time do you have to be home tomorrow?"

I yawn. "It's Saturday. The kids will be sleeping until noon probably."

Approval fills his expression. "Good. Now, go to sleep."

I snuggle into him, closing my eyes. He's a blanket of safety, warmth, and I finally can admit it also includes love. For the first time in a long time, I don't have any nightmares. The entire night, I sleep in peace.

When I wake up, Dante is staring at me.

"Morning," I say and move my mouth to his.

He returns my affection then says, "Morning. I'm getting out of bed. I'll only be a minute. Don't leave."

"Noooo," I whine. "You're nice and warm."

He chuckles. "I'll bring my warmth back." He releases me, gets out of bed, then disappears through the door.

I wait for a few minutes, and he returns. He slides back under the covers, sitting up with his back against the headboard. I turn on my side and rest my head on his chest, caressing his pecs.

He kisses my forehead and says, "I've had this in my safe since I was twenty-five." He holds up a large, stunning crystal. Flecks of blue and green shimmer throughout it.

Gaping, I sit up, staring at the magnificent gem.

"The moment I saw it, I thought of your eyes. It's rare for Montana sapphires to be this many carats. In all the years

I've been dealing with them, I've never come across another one like this," he admits.

Still stunned, I reach out and run my finger over the smooth stone, gushing, "It's beautiful."

He circles the platinum chain around my neck and clasps it. Then he sits back, staring at me. "It looks better than I imagined."

A wave of emotion hits me. I blink, but tears escape. I get on my knees and straddle him, lacing my fingers behind his neck. "Thank you. It's amazing."

His grin widens. "I knew you'd love it."

"I do." I put everything I have into my kiss.

He tightens his arms around me and mumbles, "What time do you need to be home?"

I retreat, stroking the side of his head. "What time is it now?"

"Ten."

I groan. "I should probably go before the kids see me strolling in, in my dress from last night."

His eyes light up. He points at a bag on the couch. "Or, you could put on the outfit I got you."

I tilt my head. "When did you do that?"

"Ordered it last night when you fell asleep." He winks.

"Well, aren't you resourceful," I tease. "What is it?"

He beams. "Yoga pants, an oversized tunic, shoes, and undergarments. Perfect for looking like you went out to grab a coffee or something."

I peck him on the lips. "That was very thoughtful of you."

He pats my ass. "As much as I want you to stay here, go get dressed. We'll grab some coffee on the way to your father's. I need to speak with him, so I'll break the news to him about us."

My stomach flips, not because I want to keep hiding but because this is finally becoming real.

Dante's face falls. "You haven't changed your mind, have you?"

I shake my head. "No."

Relief replaces his worry. "Good."

"I can talk to my father though. You shouldn't have to."

Dante scoffs. "Nope. I will. Now, go jump in the shower. You smell like sex."

I laugh. "Are you joining me?"

"Yep."

We both rise, I throw my hair in a knot, and we shower. I put on my new outfit then wrap my arms around Dante. "I love this."

He gives me a chaste kiss. "I'm glad. Ready?"

"Yep."

He takes my hand, guiding me through the Marino mansion. We're close to the door when his father appears. His eyes dart between us, then he nods at me. "Bridget."

My face heats, but I smile.

He redirects his attention to Dante. "We need to discuss last night."

My stomach dives. Dante shot up the place. Angelo doesn't look too happy about it. I'm sure there will be consequences.

Dante circles his arm around my waist, tugging me close to him. "I'm taking Bridget home and need to speak with Tully. We'll talk when I return."

Angelo's dark eyes turn to slits. He scowls at Dante, but Dante seems unfazed. Angelo finally turns to me and kisses my cheek. "It's good to see you, Bridget."

"Thanks. You, too," I reply.

Dante whisks me past Angelo, and we step outside. His driver's waiting. We get into the back of the SUV.

As soon as the door shuts, I turn to him. "Your father is upset with you, isn't he?"

Dante snorts. "When isn't he?"

Surprised, I ask, "He usually is?"

Dante shrugs. "Lately."

"I'm sorry. Maybe if I had told you—"

"Don't, Bridget."

"But—"

He pulls me onto his lap, holding my head firmly. "One way or another, Giulio and all those other Abruzzo thugs were dying. Let's not rehash it."

His statement doesn't reduce my worry. Several moments of silence fill the air until he leans into my ear. "We've got ten minutes until we're at your place. Tell me again how much you love me."

25

Dante

A Month Later

PAPÀ POINTS HIS FINGER IN GIANNI'S FACE, SEETHING, "I'VE warned you to stay away from Cara at the club."

Gianni's face hardens. He grinds his molars, scowling at Papà. "I told you what I do at the club isn't your concern."

"Not my concern!" Papà shouts, his eyes widening in rage.

I cringe, wishing my brother wouldn't respond to Papà with defiance. If he would shut his mouth and not say anything, the lecture would go quicker. But it isn't in his wheelhouse. Hell, most of the time, it's not in mine.

Gianni knows he's disobeyed our father again. For some reason, he can't stay away from Cara. The more she insists on seeing Uberto, the worse decisions Gianni seems to make.

His latest stint of drinking too much, barreling through Abruzzo security, and attempting to make Cara leave with him wasn't the brightest of ideas.

Plus, the Abruzzos aren't the only ones pissed. The heads of all the families got together to discuss banning Gianni from the club.

I'm on Papà's side on this one. Gianni is acting recklessly. If he loses access to the club, we're going to have major issues. Still, I can't watch him take Papà's lashing and not interject. "I think what Gianni meant to say—"

"Don't you dare stick up for him!" Papà threatens, pinning his steely gaze on me.

I exhale through my nose, clenching my jaw, trying to exhibit self-control instead of speaking.

"Is there a point to this conversation?" Gianni spouts.

I cringe inside then glare at my brother, unsure why he can't see that riling up Papà isn't going to help the situation.

Our father's face turns almost purple. His fists curl at his sides as he snarls, "You two are going to be the death of our family."

"Us? I didn't do anything," I claim.

Papà's anger turns toward me. "You're the next in line. Every time you excuse his behavior, you're setting yourself up for a future filled with problems."

"And more confidence in the sons you raised," Gianni mutters.

"Shut up," I warn, pissed he can't seem to keep his comments to himself.

"Get out of my office—both of you," Papà orders.

Gianni and I shuffle out, heading toward the gym. Sean arrived right before Papà called us into his office. I instructed him to warm up with Massimo and Tristano. When Gianni and I are almost there and out of earshot, I push him against the wall.

"What the fuck are you doing?" he barks, pushing back at me.

I jab him in the chest. "Papà's right. You're out of control. If you lose access to the club, we're fucked. And for what? A woman who wants nothing to do with you?"

He scoffs. "Says the man who obsessed over a married woman for years."

"Shut up. Don't you ever talk about her," I warn.

He shrugs out of my hold. "Stay out of my business."

I spin him around. "This is my business. And you're putting it in jeopardy. We're already in the hot seat for shooting up the club. If we didn't destroy the video footage, we would be screwed."

"Yeah, well, Arianna marrying an O'Malley has its benefits. I'll remember to contact Declan to hack into the system the next time I do something against Papà's orders." He turns back and yanks open the door to the gym, signaling the end of our conversation. This isn't something I can speak of in front of Sean, nor would I.

For several moments, I don't go inside. My time with Sean is important to me. The last thing I want to do is bring my toxic shit with Gianni into our sessions. When I feel calmer, I go into the gym.

Massimo is holding pads while Sean punches them. I watch for several minutes, proud of how quickly he's adjusted his form. He's a quick learner and listens to what we tell him. I figured he'd do well, knowing how good of a fighter his father was, and his uncles, too. It's in his blood, but he's surpassed my expectations.

I clap hard several times and pat him on the shoulder when Massimo tells him to break. "You're killing it."

He grins, catching his breath. I tug his gloves off, and he pulls his shirt up and wipes his face on it. "Thanks. Did you talk to my mom about the fight?"

I shake my head. "Not yet. I'll discuss it with her later today."

"Why don't we skip asking her and just do it? She won't even know," he states.

I smack him on the head.

"What the fuck, Dante!" he cries out.

I cross my arms. "You know the rules. Remember what I'm about to make you do the next time disobeying or sneaking behind your mother's back crosses your mind."

He looks at me in question when I don't finish. "What are you making me do?"

"Go clean the gym toilet."

He snorts. "Funny."

"I'm not joking. Get your ass in the bathroom and clean the toilet. If it's not lickable when you finish, I'll find another one in the house for you to clean next," I tell him.

His eyes widen. "You're serious?"

"Yep. Go now. Cleaning products are under the sink." I nod toward the bathroom.

He doesn't move.

"You better start trotting, or I'm going to take a shit first," Tristano calls out.

"Assholes," Sean mutters, shoving past me.

I call after him, "You don't disrespect your mother. We've been through this too many times to count. Lying and hiding things from her is something a boy would do. Be a man in the future."

He slams the door.

Tristano chuckles. "He was doing so well."

"Yep," I agree.

Massimo steps forward. "He needs to be in that match. He's ready."

My chest tightens, knowing I've got a fight in front of me with Bridget. She's still scared he's going to get hurt. The truth is, a few weeks ago, I did approach it with her. But she wasn't open to it. I backed off, hoping I planted a seed and she would be more willing to discuss it at a later time. I reply, "He's ready when Bridget gives her permission."

Massimo groans. "I liked Sean's idea better."

I slap his head harder than I hit Sean's.

He elbows me. "I've told you not to do that!"

"Don't put ideas into Sean's head. If you do, I'll slit your throat in your sleep, little brother," I threaten. The last thing I need is any of my brothers influencing Sean in the wrong direction. I promised Bridget I'd take care of him and do things on her terms. I'm not breaking my word.

"Wow. So much for blood is thicker than pussy," Massimo loudly states.

Angry heat flares in my cheeks. I grab him by the collar, lowering my voice, pinning my gaze on his. "Shut up."

He holds his hands in the air. "Easy."

I glance toward the bathroom to make sure Sean's still out of earshot. "If I find out you told him about his mother and me, I won't ever forgive you."

"You need to tell him."

"Not your business," I proclaim, but he's right. It's a constant strain in Bridget's and my relationship. Everyone knows about us except the kids. The day I dropped her off and spoke with Tully, I already asked his permission to marry her.

Bridget's so worried about repairing her O'Malley issues with Fiona and Sean that she can't see that this has nothing to do with it. All she sees it as is another reason for them to get upset with her.

Lately, it's causing more tension between us. If we didn't have this issue, we wouldn't have any. I've tried to be patient and let her be comfortable with telling them, but I'm starting to feel like she never will be. As much as I don't want to take it personally, it's getting harder not to.

Massimo pushes out of my hold. "Suit yourself. I have to get ready."

"Where are you going?"

"He's going to make that librarian suck his cock again," Tristano taunts.

Massimo spins. "Shut up, cocksucker."

The hairs on my neck rise. I hope it's not who I think it is, but there's only one librarian I can think of who he knows. I firmly interrogate, "What, librarian?"

He shoots daggers at Tristano.

"Hey, man, I told you to come clean," he says.

"Come clean about what?" I ask, but I already know where this is heading.

Massimo sniffs hard, standing taller. "She's not with them."

I move closer. "You can get pussy anywhere. Tell me you aren't fucking a woman who helped the Abruzzos."

He shifts on his feet. "Donato forced her to help him."

"Bullshit," I snap.

Gianni steps next to me, shaking his head. "She helped that bastard hold Arianna hostage."

Blue flames burn in Massimo's eyes. "She only told him how to get underground. She didn't know what he was going to do. You know how those thugs threaten women. It's not her fault."

"Open your Goddamn eyes! Our sister was held captive, and this woman was a part of it," Gianni growls.

"Not true. She gave Donato access months before he kidnapped Arianna," Massimo claims.

"She was working for the Abruzzos!" I fire.

"No, Katiya did what Donato made her do," he firmly replies.

"Who's Donato?" Sean's voice interjects.

My stomach dives. The last thing I need is Sean knowing anything about any of our business. He already plans on joining the O'Malleys when he's old enough. Bridget is going to have a fit, but it's in his blood. There isn't any way to stop him, but I want him to stay away from mob business for as long as possible. I spin. "No one worth mentioning again. Is it clean?"

"Yeah. Do you want to get in the ring, and I can show you how much I loved doing that?"

I snort. "Don't disrespect your mother again, got it?"

"Yeah," he agrees then clenches his jaw.

I point toward the large bag. "Put your gloves on. I'll meet you there in a minute."

His eyes dart between my brothers and me. "I totally interrupted something good, didn't I?"

"No. I'll see you later," Massimo replies, slaps him on the back, and leaves the gym.

"Go," I reiterate to Sean, motioning toward the bag.

He obeys, and we spend the next hour training hard. When we finish, I shower and message Bridget.

Me: *I'm dropping Sean off. I need to talk to you about him.*

Bridget: *Is everything okay? Did something happen?*

Me: *Everything is fine, dolcezza—nothing to worry about. I'll see you soon.*

Bridget: *Okay. I'm in the library. Love you.*

My grin hurts my face. Every time she tells me she loves me, I still have to pinch myself. It's finally real between us.

Me: *Love you, too.*

Sean and I go into the garage. The roads have been clear for a few days. I open up the cabinet with the keys. "Pick anything but my Porsche," I state.

He rolls his eyes. "I hadn't driven a stick before. Are you ever going to get over me grinding your gears?"

"No. Now, pick."

He mutters something incoherent under his breath then takes the keys to Tristano's silver Lamborghini Veneno. It's a rare vehicle developed to celebrate Lamborghini's 50th anniversary. He's going to want to kill me when he finds out I let Sean drive it, but it's no different than the times I let him drive Massimo's or Gianni's vehicles.

I chuckle and walk toward the car. "You've been eyeing it for a while. Good choice."

Sean glances around. "I thought Tully had a lot of cars. Your garage makes his look sad."

I stop and cross my arms.

Sean arches his eyebrows. "What did I do now?"

"It's Daideó to you, not Tully. We've been through this."

Sean glances at the ceiling, his face hardening. While things have gotten a lot better between Bridget and him, he's kept a chip on his shoulder where Tully is concerned.

"What's your beef with your granddad?" I ask.

Sean's nostrils flare. He continues to avoid looking at me. "Nothing."

"Bullshit."

He meets my gaze. "For once, can you drop it?"

For several moments, I study him. He never flinches, matching my intense stare. I finally decide to let it be for now. "Okay. Don't kill Tristano's gears, or I'll have to pay to replace them."

He snorts. "You know I'm a better driver than that now."

While I have to agree with him, I'm not admitting it. But Sean can drive any car in the garage, including my Porsche, and he'd do it with ease. Just like boxing, he learned how to drive faster than I anticipated. He's got a natural skillset about him, and part of me believes it's the O'Malley in him. However, I can't disregard the O'Connor genes, either. All of Bridget's brothers seemed to learn things quickly when we were kids. They also drive sticks, and we used to have illegal races when we were in high school and all through our early twenties. It was always a crapshoot whether a Marino or O'Connor would win.

"Don't get cocky," I tell Sean and get in the passenger seat.

He slides in, revs the engine, then guns it as soon as we get outside the gate. Within no time, we're sitting in front of Tully's. We get out and go inside, parting ways.

I head toward the library, carefully shutting the door so I don't disturb Bridget. She's reading a book on the couch, curled up in a blanket. The warm feeling in my chest I always get whenever I see her ignites. I sneak up behind her and dip down so my lips touch her ear. "Reading anything hot?"

She slightly jumps, laughing, then turns her head. I steal her lips the moment I can and roll my tongue against hers. She reaches up and caresses the back of my neck, sending a buzz of energy down my spine.

My dick twitches, and I pull back, then walk around the couch and sit next to her. I tuck a lock of her hair behind her ear. "How are you doing, dolcezza?"

She shuts her book, smiling. She reaches for my cheek. "Okay. Did you have a good day?"

I push all the crap that went on in my day to the back of my head. "Better now that I'm with you." I give her another peck.

She glances at the door.

My stomach flips. "Don't worry. I shut it."

Relief fills her expression.

It only irritates me more. Yet, I push that away, too, focusing on Sean's situation. "I need to talk to you about something."

Her face falls. "You said everything is okay though?"

"Yeah, don't worry."

She smiles again, studying me. "Okay. What is it?"

All day, I debated about how to tell her. I still don't have a clear strategy, so I blurt out, "Sean wants to fight."

Her face hardens, and I realize I was wrong. Sean's stubbornness isn't from his father or any of the O'Malleys. It's from her. I almost chuckle at my realization but don't want to get off track. She declares, "We've discussed this. It's too dangerous. He isn't fighting."

"He's more than ready. If he were in Chicago, he would already be fighting," I add.

She blinks hard. Then anger and fear ignite in her eyes. Blue swirls against the green so fast, it's mesmerizing. She hurls, "But he's not in Chicago, is he? Nor is he to go there!"

"Calm down. I didn't say he was going to Chicago, but—"

"Why are you doing this?" she accuses.

A storm stirs inside me, but I keep my voice steady. "Doing what, exactly?"

"I've told you how I feel about this."

I nod. "Yes, you have. But it doesn't mean it's the right choice for Sean."

"I know what the right thing for my son is, don't insinuate I don't!" she snaps.

"Whoa! I never did anything of the sort. I'm asking you to reconsider. He has talent—a lot. He's worked hard, and he needs to do this, Bridge."

"He needs to go into a ring and have his head beat in?" she fumes.

I attempt to lighten the mood. "Or he can beat another kid's head in."

"*Not* funny," she enunciates through gritted teeth. I put my arm around her, but she slides out of it, jumping off the couch.

I rise as well. "No, it's not. He's a natural, and you can't protect him forever. He's almost an adult. At some point, he's going to do it. The experience he'll get now—"

"You promised me if I let him train with you that you wouldn't pressure me about this."

I sigh, scrubbing my hands over my face. I count to five in my head, attempting not to get emotional about this. "I'm not trying to pressure you."

She puts her hand on her hip. "You are. And you promised you wouldn't. Is that what you want our relationship to be? Broken promises?"

I jerk my head backward, no longer able to keep check of my thoughts. "Broken promises? You're one to talk."

"What does that mean?"

"When are we telling Fiona and Sean about us? Hmm?"

She looks toward the window, her eyebrows pinched. Tense silence fills the air.

The longer it exists, the more pissed I become. The fear inside me comes out. "You're never telling them, are you, Bridge?"

Her glistening eyes meet mine. She softly replies, "Of course I am. I just..."

"You just what?" I seethe.

Her lips tremble. "It's not straightforward, and you know it."

My months of patience wears out. All I want to do is move forward with our lives—together. I want to propose and marry her as soon as possible. I don't want to spend another night in my bed without her. Yet, none of that can happen until Fiona and Sean know about us. I fire, "What exactly isn't straightforward about it? I'm not some guy off the street. I'm a man who's always been in their life. I was there the day Fiona was born, for Christ's sake. Or did you forget that?"

Her eyes widen. "Of course I didn't!"

"But I'm still not good enough for you, am I?"

"Dante! That's not true!"

"Then let's tell the kids right now."

More deafening silence fills the air. Anxiety overpowers her face and the truth I didn't want to admit, I can no longer hide from. I can barely say the words, but I manage to state, "I can't live in a lie with you anymore."

A tear drips down her cheek. She reaches for my arm, shaking her head. "Dante, I just—"

"Then give me something, Bridget. Tell me why you kept the O'Malleys from the kids all these years."

She scrunches her face, squeezing her eyes shut. She whispers, "I can't."

"Then tell me what happened to Sean. What about his death aren't you telling anyone?"

A slight tremor courses through her body before she reaches for the wall to steady herself. She opens her eyes, pinning fear, guilt, and grief on me.

It's all I need to see. I quietly state, "You have so many secrets. You're never letting me in. Are you?"

She opens her mouth then shuts it.

I shrug out of her grasp. "I'm done." I leave the room, ignoring her plea not to go, and hightailing it through the mansion.

The cold wind whips my face when I step outside, but I barely feel it.

All I can think is there is no future. Everything I've wanted will never be. *She* will never let us be.

No truth has ever been more painful.

26

Bridget

SPRING IS AROUND THE CORNER, YET THE GROUND IS STILL frozen with traces of snow lingering. It's exactly like how I feel.

Cold.

Dead.

Unable to figure out how to ever get out of the web of lies I've weaved or dispel the fear that plagues me daily.

The crazy part is that over the last month, I felt it lessen. Fiona and Sean acted nicer toward me. Dante and I were in a good place. I convinced myself I could have a future with him, but now, the truth is evident.

He's never going to stop asking me why I made the choices I did or what I know about Sean's death. And I want to tell

Fiona and Sean about Dante and me, but I don't know how. They only started being nice to me again. I'm so scared to rock the boat, I can't see the path to do anything that moves my life forward.

All night, I couldn't sleep. Dante filled my thoughts. The sense of loss hit me harder than I ever expected. I tried to figure out how to win him back, but deep down, I know the only thing that will make things right is to tell the truth.

Every fear I've been living with expands. The dread of the Baileys and Rossis, as well as Niall and Shamus, coming after my children feels as sharp as the day they first threatened me.

And now Dante's under my skin. I want to tell him everything and no longer hold this in, but I can't.

Sean wanting to fight in matches doesn't surprise me. He's always wanted it, and I'm fully aware it's in his blood. But refusing to let him get in the ring is the only way I can keep him from the danger of physical harm. Maybe it's stupid, but it's all I have left.

The lack of sleep, too many years of secrets and lies, and the never-ending feeling that I'm going to crack take hold. Everything spins together. The ache in my heart over losing Dante swallows me until I'm struggling to get fresh oxygen in my lungs.

"Bridget, we need to talk," Finn's voice booms.

My pulse races, and I squeeze my eyes shut.

What did I do now?

It's no secret Finn still hates me. Years ago, I never would have thought it was possible. He was like a brother to me.

I find the last ounce of strength I have and spin. "Finn. Brenna. What are you doing here?"

Finn scowls. "I'm here for the truth."

"About what?" I ask, my heart racing so fast, I think I'm going to fall over.

"Everything."

I cross my arms. "What does that mean? I keep telling you I haven't lied to you." I glance at Brenna. My anger over the way my life has turned out and what my children and I have lost whips around me like a tornado. I turn on Brenna and accuse, "You begged me not to tell him we ran into each other, even though I said I wouldn't keep it from him. You made me promise not to say anything until we could figure out a plan so he didn't get killed. Did you not tell him?"

"Of course I did!" Brenna exclaims.

"Don't put this on Brenna," Finn warns.

More rage festers within me. I huff out an exasperated breath. "Just tell me what you want from me, Finn."

He steps closer. I almost step back, but I force myself to raise my chin and stand firm. He demands, "Why didn't you tell me Niall and Shamus were the ones who took the photo of you and Brenna?"

A claw scrapes at my gut. It's the first time I've heard their names stated since I left Chicago. I struggle to keep my voice steady, questioning, "Niall and Shamus?"

Finn's cheeks turn red. "Don't play stupid, Bridget."

"I'm not! I didn't know they were ever in New York when I was, and I didn't know they took our photo. Why don't you ask them if you don't believe me?"

"I can't."

"Why not?" I inquire.

"They're missing."

My insides shake harder. I'm confused why he would think I have anything to do with it if they're missing. But what does that even mean? I ask, "Missing?"

His cold eyes dart to mine.

My hands shake, and I cover my mouth when I realize what he's saying.

They can't be?

Can it be true?

What would it mean for me and the kids?

I finally question what I hope is true. "They're dead?"

Tense silence expands in the air, increasing my anxiety. An earthquake could be in my body right now. Every cell quivers as I stare at the floor, taking deep breaths that taste stale. I reach for the desk and grab it, but it barely gives me any security. I will myself not to cry, but my tears make my sight blurry.

Finn barks, "You're crying over those two? You never even liked them!"

I gape at him, unable to fully see him, trying to form a coherent sentence. I manage to choke out, "W-when did they die?"

Finn replies, "They went missing a few weeks before I got out of prison."

My knees give out, and I steady myself, then sit on the couch.

"Bridget, if you don't start talking—"

"Finn! Cool it!" Brenna scolds. She sits next to me and takes my hand, softly asking, "What do you know about them?"

Everything spins. Finn. Brenna. The room. Most of all, the truth I've been holding in for longer than I ever imagined I could. I turn toward Brenna, but she's blurry, too. I state, "I need to know they're dead first." I shake my head, squeezing my eyes shut. "I-I won't speak unless they are."

Brenna clasps my hand tighter, claiming, "They are. Tell her, Finn. And sit down. You're making me nervous."

Several moments pass before Finn lowers his voice. "It's not to be repeated, but they're dead."

Any discipline I have left disappears. Years of too many emotions spiral out of control. I wail, unable to stop my violent sobs.

Brenna puts her arm around me and holds my head to her chest. I don't know how much time passes until I'm able to quiet my outburst.

Finn's demeanor changes. He calmly repeats, "What do you know about them?"

Numb once more from shock, I glance up at him, not sure how to answer his question or how to even lie anymore. Several minutes pass until I say, "I swear to you, I told Sean about the day I ran into Brenna in Central Park. As soon as I returned to Chicago, I told him."

"He would have told someone," Finn insists, but he doesn't sound as hateful as before.

I don't break our gaze. It's important to me he believes me. He may hate me forever, but I told him the truth. I repeat, "I swear to you, I told Sean."

He lets out a long breath. "Okay. Say I believe you. What do you know about Niall and Shamus?"

My stomach flips then dives, then flips again. I put my hand on it, swallowing down bile. I can't even think anymore and admit, "Darragh had Sean, Niall, and Shamus working together."

"Doing what?"

It's a question I wish I knew how to answer. For too many years, I tried to figure out what, but I wasn't involved in the family business. Sean kept me away from it all. I reply, "I don't know everything. It had to do with the Rossis. I overheard them talking one night. I asked Sean about it, but he wouldn't tell me. He said it was clan business and to forget I heard anything."

Finn leans closer. "What did you hear?"

"Not a lot. Niall and Shamus were at the house. Fiona was struggling to sleep, and I just got her down. I went out to the kitchen, and I heard the name Rossi. Sean told me to go to bed." Another wave of nausea hits me, and I focus on the ground.

Brenna squeezes my hand, softly asking, "Then what happened?"

It's like Pandora's box opens. I can no longer hold in the truth. Everything is crashing around me, and I answer, "A few weeks passed. Sean was gone a lot at night, but it wasn't anything new. There were always times he'd be out late. H-he came home with a new dress and told me to put it on. Said he made a reservation and arranged for your mom to watch the kids for the night." Visions of Sean giving me the dress, getting ready, and dropping the kids off at Finn's mom's house fill my mind. I continue, "We were at dinner, and I kept asking him if everything was okay. He seemed...distant. He wasn't himself."

Finn and Brenna stay quiet as I struggle with my guilt.

I shift in my seat, staring at the floor. Somehow, words flow out of my mouth. "We were in the car on the way home. His beeper went off, and I got a horrible feeling. He turned it off and pulled the car over." I wipe my face, but it's pointless. The dam has broken, and I don't know how it'll ever stop. I look at Finn. "He told me if anything happened to him, I was to come to my father's with the kids. He said I wasn't to stay in Chicago."

Finn arches his eyebrows. Confusion fills his expression, mimicking how I've felt all these years about so many things regarding that night. He asks, "Why?"

I swallow my sobs. "He wouldn't tell me. I begged. He made me promise. Then he drove to an abandoned warehouse and said to pick up the kids and go straight home."

Finn's fists clench on the arms of the chair. "Who else was there?"

I nod from the memory of it all as if it were yesterday and years haven't passed. "No one. I didn't see anyone and tried to stop him. But he yelled at me to go. So I did, but I didn't get very far."

"Why? What happened?"

I twist my fingers in my lap, wishing for the millionth time I never left him and could redo that night. "I thought I was going to get sick. I-I knew I shouldn't be leaving him. So I turned around and went back. When I pulled in, Shamus and Niall were there. They had guns pointed at Sean, b-but they weren't alone."

The color drains from Finn's cheeks. "Who was with them?"

I swallow hard. "Three other men. I recognized Lorenzo Rossi."

"What did you do?" Finn questions.

My voice shakes, mimicking my insides. "One of the men shot my tire. They dragged me out of the car. Sean was screaming for them to let me go. They..." I turn away, and my body collapses in convulsions.

Brenna pulls me to her, trying to calm me, but I don't know if I'll ever feel sane again. It's been too many seconds of living in grief and lies.

I choke out words I've never spoken. Pain shoots through my heart as I admit, "They raped me—all of them—while they made Sean watch. They had him tied to the hood of a car. The lights were on and pointed at me. I-I still hear Sean screaming. I kept blacking out. Th-they kept asking me if I liked Bailey or Rossi dick better." I lose it again, unable to look at either of them. The scent of sweat, garlic, alcohol, and lavender flares in my nostrils. The sound of their voices and Sean screaming fills my ears. And I realize I'm never escaping it. No matter how much time passes, I'm never getting them out of my memories.

Suddenly, Finn's strong arms are around me. He softly says, "I'm so sorry."

I meet his gaze. "I don't know how long it lasted or how many hours I was out of it. At some point, I woke up, but I was in my house. Niall and Shamus were there. They said I was to get my kids from your mom's and not say a word to anyone about last night, or they would kill them."

Finn tightens his arms around me. "Do you know who else besides them and Lorenzo was there?"

I shake my head. "No. I kept asking for Sean, but they wouldn't tell me where he was. I-I already knew he was dead, but I didn't want to believe it."

Finn asks, "Then what happened?"

I sniffle, taking staggered breaths, hoping my heart doesn't explode from the intense pain racing through it. I confess, "They threw me in my shower. They tossed clothes at me and told me to get my kids or they would." I squeeze my eyes shut, wishing it would all just go away. Yet, I know it won't. It's impossible, so I divulge, "They followed me. When I got back home, they made the kids go into the backyard and play. They drank beer on my deck while they told me the new rules."

"The rules?" Finn questions.

"As soon as the funeral was over, I was to leave town. The kids and I were no longer to be O'Malleys. I was to have no contact with anyone. If I uttered a word before I left or after about what happened, the Baileys and Rossis wouldn't just come after me but the kids, too." I take a few broken breaths. "They said they would sell the kids in an auction. I would go to one of their whorehouses. And they warned me not to go to Darragh. There were more Baileys in the O'Malley clan than just them, they said."

Finn's eyebrows pin together. "Did you tell Tully?"

Dizziness hits me. All the nightmares I've had about how my father would handle this and what would happen to my children fill me. Over the years, whenever he found Bailey or Rossi members in his clan, it only proved I was right not to tell him. I panic, "No. And you can't tell him! Now you see why the kids can't go to Chicago to visit. It's still not safe for any of you to even be here."

"Niall, Shamus, and Lorenzo are all dead. Most of the Baileys and Rossis, too," Finn declares.

"You don't know that," I state, unable to believe everyone is dead and there would be no danger.

"I do. And I know it because we killed them."

Anxiety explodes throughout my body. I shake my head. "They told me there are Baileys in my father's clan. If I tell him, they'll find out."

Finn sternly orders, "Bridget, in the last year, your father eliminated over a dozen Baileys from his clan. Liam told me. You have to tell him."

"I-I can't. I don't want him to know what..." I turn, covering my face to hide from the shame. "My kids are all I have left. They hate me right now. I don't blame them. But please. Nothing can happen to them."

Several moments pass before Finn rises. "We will no longer let the Baileys or Rossis or any other family destroy our lives. This needs to end, Bridget. Your father needs to know."

"Finn, please. I can't... I can't look at my father and tell him..." I hide my face in my hands again.

"I'm sorry, but I promise you, it's the right thing to do. Both of you stay here," Finn orders then leaves the room before I can find the strength to get up and stop him.

Brenna slides her arm around my shoulders. We sit in silence, from time to time glancing at each other. I'm unable to move or stop the frantic thoughts in my head.

I just told the truth. There's no going back. I put my children in more danger. My father will be so livid he won't be able to stop himself from having all his men hunt for any Rossi or Bailey left. Who knows which of his men are traitors.

What have I done?

Me

Dante

"I'll kill him if you force my hand, Cara," Gianni threatens into the phone when I walk into the room. My brother has a tone in his voice that I know too well. It signals he's lost all his patience and is about to snap.

My gut twists. I don't need another incident with the Abruzzos. It's pointless to ask him who he's going to kill. In all reality, I'm surprised Uberto is still alive. The incident at the club was pretty ugly. And the longer Cara defies Gianni, the more unhinged he's becoming.

Gianni tugs on his hair. "You don't know what you're doing with him. End it, or I will." He tosses his phone on the desk and spins toward me, sneering. "Don't look at me like that."

I release a breath. It's a lost cause talking to him. Gianni is going to do what Gianni wants to do. I hold my hands in the air. "Not here to talk about your personal shit. Rubio just sent a message we have a shipment arriving tonight from Florida."

He sits behind the desk, scratches his cheek, then pauses for a moment. "Nothing is due from Florida for two weeks. He must be misinformed."

Goose bumps break out on my skin. Shipments from the southeast are Gianni's territory. When Rubio texted me, I checked our log. Nothing was on the schedule. I assumed Gianni arranged something last minute and didn't log it. I sit across from him. "You don't know anything about this?"

His eyes turn to slits. "No. Nothing comes in without me knowing about it. It has to be a mistake."

More bad feelings erupt in my cells. "I called Rubio. He says it's not. He spoke with the captain."

Gianni's eyes turn darker, locking on mine. He firmly states, "I didn't authorize any shipments."

Cold silence sits between us. Unspoken words increase my anxiety. Any shipment not authorized is a hazard. Different crime families have sent shipments to other's ports before. It usually resulted in an FBI raid, taking out the higher-ups in enemy families.

We both rise at the same time. "I'll tell Papà."

"No. I'll handle it," Gianni insists.

I lower my voice. "We need to tell him."

"I don't need another lecture right now. I said I'll handle it."

I cross my arms. "We're not ignoring protocol on this."

Gianni shakes his head. "Fine. Tell Papà. I'm still handling this my way."

I groan. "Jesus. What's gotten into you?"

Gianni clenches his jaw.

There's a loud knock, and the door opens. Papà steps inside.

"Are your ears burning?" I ask.

He grinds his molars, assessing both Gianni and me.

"I have an issue to deal with, so if you could speed this up," Gianni states.

Papà shoots daggers at him with his gaze. "I already took care of it."

Gianni's face falls. "How did you even know about it?"

Papà sniffs hard. "I know everything. It's my job."

"I was going to take care of it," Gianni claims.

Papà points to the chairs. "Sit."

My brother and I obey, and Papà sits next to me. Tension fills the air as he assesses us. I work hard not to squirm in my seat, aware he's about to drop some sort of bomb on us. He finally informs us, "Leo stopped the shipment."

Relief fills me. Leo roams the sea, several miles from the port. He has a crew of men and is there to intercept shipments when needed. I ask, "What was on it?"

Disgust fills my father's face. "Women."

The blood drains from my cheeks, running straight to my toes.

"Jesus," Gianni mutters.

Papà nods. "Yeah. Now we've got a bigger problem."

Gianni and I exchange a glance.

"Where are they?" he questions.

Papà taps his fingers on the wooden desk. "Leo's men took over the ship. They took care of the crew, and I instructed him to bring Sam here."

"Once again, we missed out on the fun," Gianni sneers.

Papà inhales slowly, not happy with Gianni's sarcasm. He points to him. "This is your territory. It has Abruzzo written all over it."

More silence hangs in the air. Papà's right. It's a direct attack on Gianni. He's pissed off the Abruzzos too many times.

Papà continues, "Our contacts confirm the FBI was raiding our dock tonight."

I close my eyes, wishing this would all go away. The Abruzzos are heavy into human trafficking. One surefire way to end up in a cell forever is to get caught in it. Death would be an easier option than living in prison for the rest of your life. I blurt out, "Where are the women going?"

Papà slowly shakes his head. "I don't know yet. Leo's waiting for orders in international waters, but we need to figure this out."

"I'll take care of it," Gianni claims.

"How?" Papà questions.

"I'm not sure yet, but I'll figure it out."

"We have limited time. The longer that ship sits out in open waters, the more risk we have of Leo being picked up," I declare.

Papà rises. "No one makes a move without my permission. Gianni, you've got thirty minutes to figure out some solutions. Meet me in my office and we'll discuss your thoughts on the matter. Massimo and Tristano will interrogate Sam in the dungeon when he arrives. Dante, you're to meet with Rubio. All shipments get double-checked two miles away from US territory before entering the port. Until I say otherwise, we're officially on heightened security."

"Got it." I stand, exchange another glance with Gianni, and walk with Papà out of his office. I go directly to the garage. It's snowing again, so I grab the keys to my Land Rover.

As soon as I get out of the gate, I tap the accelerator and hit the call button.

"Well, well, well. If it isn't my favorite boss," Pina answers.

I grunt. "I'm not giving you another raise. Save your suck-up talk for another day."

"And I see Mr. Grouchy is here. What can I do for you?"

"I want all our suppliers double-checked."

The line turns quiet.

"Pina? You there?"

She clears her throat. All teasing is gone from her voice. Pina doesn't get access to all our business, but she knows enough that if I'm double-checking our suppliers, I suspect a traitor in our house. I hope everyone is clean, but you can't take any chances when other families try to set you up with the FBI. The FBI is the enemy. It's a signal of full-on war, and the Abruzzos don't need to send any more messages. They'll stop at nothing to destroy us. There's no denying the reality of our situation. She replies, "Yeah. On it."

"I want all reports. Nothing gets overlooked."

"Done."

I hang up and head to the port. I turn, and my phone rings. I glance at the screen, answering, "Killian. What's up?"

"I'm sticking my nose where I shouldn't."

My gut dives. "What do you mean?"

"Liam just told me Finn and Brenna took the jet to New York."

More dread erupts. "Why are they coming here?"

"They're already there. They went to talk to Bridget."

I swerve between two vehicles, turn, and horns blare. I step on the gas. "Why?"

"I'm not entirely sure. Liam said Finn wasn't talking. It's not my business, but I'm not stupid. I know something is going on between you and Bridget."

I grind my molars, saying nothing. Until this issue came up at the port, I've forced myself not to contact her.

"Anyway, I thought you should know. I still don't know why she did what she did, and Finn has his reasons to be pissed, but when I spoke to her last, she was kind of a mess. I thought you'd want to know," Killian states.

I let out a breath. "I do. Thanks." I hang up and accelerate, weaving in and out of traffic, ignoring red lights and stop signs.

When I get through the O'Connor gate, I don't knock. I pass the guard and open the door, yelling, "Finn!"

The door to Tully's office opens. Finn pokes his head out and asks, "Why are you shouting?"

"Where's Bridget?"

"In the den with Brenna. Why?"

"What do you want with her?"

"Dante, come in and close the door," Tully's voice booms.

Finn opens the door more and steps back. His face turns solemn.

I've lost track of how many times I've had a bad feeling course through my bones today. But it's more intense than previously. I struggle not to shudder. I walk past Finn. He closes the door, and I stare at Tully. "What's going on?"

He and Finn exchange a glance. I'm not sure what it means, but I know it's not good.

"Tell me what the hell is going on," I demand.

Tully points to his chair. "Get a drink and sit. Both of you."

"I don't want a drink. Why are you here?" I direct to Finn.

Finn sits and motions to the seat.

I take it and tap my fingers on the arm.

It feels like forever, with Finn and Tully nervously looking at each other, before Tully takes a long drink of whiskey and clears his throat. Over the next fifteen minutes, I swallow bile too many times to count as he and Finn disclose what happened to Bridget.

When they finish speaking, I take a few moments, trying to gather my thoughts and forcing my emotions down my throat. My fists curl so tight, they go numb. I stare at the edge of Tully's desk, attempting to regulate my heartbeat. I finally seethe, "I'll kill every one of those bastards."

"We think they're all dead," Finn replies.

I snap my head toward him. "Think? Think is not good enough."

He nods. "Agreed. But Niall and Shamus, as well as Lorenzo, are dead. Bridget doesn't know who the other men were. We took out the majority of the Baileys who were in Chicago. I know there are still some here, but we hit them hard. Same for the Rossis."

"Not good enough," I snarl then jump out of my seat, heading toward the door.

"Dante," Tully calls out.

I spin. "I'll deal with this accordingly. This stays in this room, between us. Not one of your men is to know about this, do you understand me?"

Tully nods.

"I mean it, Tully. You don't speak about this to any of your advisors. I don't care if you trust your life with them."

"I'm not going to."

I grind my molars and take off down the hall. When I get to the den, I open the door and find Bridget staring into space. Her swollen eyes are red. Brenna has her arm around her and pins her gaze on mine.

"Finn's in Tully's office. I assume you know where it is?"

She nods and kisses Bridget's head. Brenna leaves the room.

Bridget meets my eyes and blinks, as if she's registering where she's at and that I'm standing here. Then her lips tremble and tears fall fast down her cheeks.

I pull her onto my lap and into my arms. She loses it, sobbing uncontrollably, at times choking out, "I'm sorry."

"Shh," I croon, stroking her hair and kissing her head. I hold her as tight as I can, vowing to find all the information I can about the men who raped her. If any of them are still alive, I'm hunting them down. My punishment for them is going to be ten times as gruesome as what they put her through.

A long time passes before Bridget stops crying. She glances up, but the pain is still all over her face. She takes a shaky breath. "How am I going to protect the kids now? My father...he'll...oh God!" Tears fall again.

I wipe at them, shaking my head. "No. He's not saying anything to anyone. You have my word. No one is touching the kids. No one will know you said anything."

"Do you understand why they can't go to Chicago?" she panics.

I hold both her cheeks. "Listen to me. The kids aren't going anywhere until I'm positive it's safe. I promise you."

"But Sean. He's always saying—"

"I will take care of it. Now, what can you tell me about these men? Until I know for certain they are all dead, I won't rest, dolcezza."

"I-I only recognized Lorenzo. It was dark. I-I only remember their smell. An-and one of them had a tattoo," she manages to reply.

I give her a chaste kiss on the lips, praising, "Good. That's good, Bridge. Tell me about the tattoo."

She squeezes her eyes shut. Her raspy voice is barely audible. "One guy's forearm had an animal. I-I think it was a wolf. There was a sword entering its mouth and fire coming out of it."

"Good, dolcezza. Do you remember anything about any of the others?"

She keeps her eyes closed, taking shallow breaths. I kiss her forehead, and she deeply exhales. "One man's neck has a scar. I-I think he got burned. It ran up half his face on his right...no...left side."

I continue telling myself to stay calm, but I'm so infuriated, my heart's pounding against my chest cavity. "What about the last man? Finn said there were six?" I inquire.

"I don't know."

I tighten my arms around her. "Okay. Is there anything you remember about him?"

"N—" She swallows hard.

"What is it?" I gently prod.

She shudders. "He had a gold chain necklace. It had a crucifix with an emerald-green center. It was longer. He..." Her face turns green, and she puts her hand over her eyes.

My gut churns. I quietly question, "What did he do with it?"

The ticking of the clock fills the air. I wait until she admits, "He put it around my neck twice then slid his hands under it until there was no slack. He kept telling me to pray, and I couldn't breathe. That's—" She takes several broken breaths. "That's when I blacked out the first time."

Potent rage like I've never known before annihilates me. I count to one hundred, holding Bridget as tight as possible, cursing myself for ever touching her neck or using the collar. I wonder what role I've played in hurting her further and how I'll ever make it right. The desire to inflict violence on these men—violence of a level I've never before reached— feels like it's suffocating me.

Bridget's the first to speak. She meets my eyes, and it shatters my heart further when she states, "I know I don't deserve your love. But will you promise to help me keep the kids safe? Please?" Tears fall so fast, they drip off her chin.

I slide my hands to her cheeks, holding her in front of me. "There's no one who deserves my love more than you. And that's *never* changing, dolcezza."

She sobs harder and I pull her into me, vowing to myself that from here on out, nothing is getting my attention except hunting her rapists down.

Dante

A Week Later

ALL WEEK, I'VE BEEN IN MEETINGS WITH PAPÀ, MY BROTHERS, Tully, and Bridget's brothers. As soon as Tully learned the truth, he called his sons back from Ireland. We've all agreed no one except our small circle, plus the O'Malleys and Ivanovs, are allowed to be part of this hunt.

I've tried to make sure Bridget is okay, but I'm struggling to figure out how that's even possible. What those monsters did to her is unfathomable. The fact she dealt with this all on her own for so many years makes me feel sicker.

I haven't pushed her to tell the kids about us. My focus is solely on her and hunting down these three remaining thugs. Finn returned to Chicago, relaying information to Liam and Maksim about the little we know about the men. Both families are searching records to try to figure out who they are and if they're dead or still alive.

Bridget's not saying much. It's like the truth was a bandage ripped off. The sore is open, oozing with agony and other emotions. I don't think I fully realize what those are yet. The hollow look on her face reminds me of the day I saw her when she first got to New York after Sean's death.

I've made sure I stay on track with Sean's training. My brothers have been giving him extra sessions. Nora flew in and arranged a slew of activities with Fiona. So far, our efforts to keep the kids occupied so Bridget can process things seem to be working.

Every night, I've stayed in her room, carefully coordinating with Tully when to arrive and leave. Most nights, we barely speak. I just hold her. A few times, she's had nightmares, and I could barely wake her up. Last night, she had another one. Each time it happens, the turmoil spinning in my gut creates nausea I can hardly keep down. Then I spend hours attempting to convince her the kids are safe and that nothing will happen to them.

And it'll be over my dead body before anyone gets to Fiona or Sean. Between my brothers and Bridget's, we've got extra security on the kids, both inside and outside their school. They don't go anywhere unnecessary, and we're controlling it right now by keeping them too busy to notice.

It's early in the morning. I've been studying Bridget for hours, wondering what I should be doing to help her deal with this. My entire life, I've solved problems. I'm trying to figure out how to be useful, but it feels like a losing battle.

This is out of my wheelhouse, and I'm scared that I'll lose her if I don't do something soon to help her.

Her eyes flutter open, and I stroke her hair. "Morning, dolcezza." I kiss her on the cheek.

She turns toward me. Her eyes are red from lack of sleep. Her face is gaunt, void of her usual color and fullness.

More worry fills me. I stroke her back, cringing inside. She's barely eaten the last week, and I can feel her bones. It's like watching her wilt away, but everything I do to try and make her eat hasn't worked.

"What time is it?" she asks.

"Early, but the kids already left for the day."

She furrows her eyebrows. "Why?"

I tighten my arms around her. "Fiona has a meeting for the yearbook. Massimo picked Sean up for a morning workout. Do you want me to have breakfast brought up, or should we go downstairs?"

She shakes her head. "I'm not hungry."

"You have to eat, dolcezza," I demand, trying to keep my voice soft but struggling.

She tries to turn away from me, but I hold her firmly to my body.

"You've lost too much weight. If you don't eat, I'm having the doctor come over with IVs."

Her eyes widen. She snaps, "You'll do no such thing!" She tries to roll away again.

I cage my body over hers so she can't escape me. "I'm not letting you do this."

She pushes my chest, but she's weak. I barely feel it. Tears well in her blue-green orbs. "Leave me alone."

I shake my head. "No, dolcezza. I'll never leave you alone, and you already know this. Now, choose where you want to eat, or I will."

"I can't," she whispers.

"Yes, you can," I insist.

The damn breaks, staining her cheeks. "Why are you doing this?"

"Because I love you. You're the most important person in the world to me."

She squeezes her eyes shut, choking out, "I can't be."

My heart sinks. Ever since she told me what happened, she thinks I can't love her and that I'm going to run. It's like the truth being out in the open gave her the impression I won't think she's worthy of my love, or I somehow won't want her.

I lower my face another inch so my lips are touching hers. "Open your eyes, Bridge."

She slowly obeys, sniffling.

"I'm going to tell you this a thousand times if I need to. You're my everything. Nothing that happened will ever change my feelings for you. Get it out of your head."

Her face crumbles, and her chest heaves. "I-I can't."

I sigh, wishing I knew how to take away the pain. I slide my arms under her, roll on my back, and hold her head to my chest. "I can and always will." When she calms, I add, "I made an appointment with a therapist for you. She's coming to the house at ten."

Bridget's head snaps up. Fear fills her expression. "W-what are you talking about?"

My chest constricts. I knew this was going to be a fight, so I adamantly order, "You will eat and meet with the therapist. If you want me with you, I'll be by your side."

"I'm not seeing a therapist!"

"You are. I don't know how to help you with this."

"Then stay out of it," she hurls, trying to sit up.

I don't release her. "Fighting me will get you nowhere. If I have to tie you to a chair, I will."

"I'm not your child," she spouts.

"No. You're my heart. My future wife. And I'm not sitting back and letting you deal with this all on your own anymore."

She turns her head and closes her eyes. Her voice lowers. "We aren't engaged. I'm not marrying you."

I ignore the pain shooting through my heart. I grab my phone off the nightstand then call her brother Aidan.

"Dante," he answers.

"Bridget and I are coming down for breakfast. Alert the doctor we might need him."

"Dante," Bridget snaps.

"Done." Aidan hangs up.

I rise and scoop Bridget up off the bed.

"Let me down!" she screams.

I don't respond, move her into the bathroom, then turn on the shower.

"Dante!" she cries out, pushing me with barely any strength.

I test the water then set her in the shower, even though she's wearing my T-shirt. She shrieks, and I step next to her. The warm water soaks my boxers. I slide my hands on her cheeks, forcing her to look at me. "You are mine, dolcezza. I'm sorry I don't have all the answers, but you will do what I say. Do you understand me?"

She loses it again, and I pull her into my chest. She wails, "I can't do this."

"You can. You're the strongest woman I know."

She keeps crying. Eventually, she stops. I dry her off, comb her hair, and help her put on yoga pants and a sweatshirt.

I give her a chaste kiss on the lips. "Time to eat." I lead her through the house and into the dining room.

Her brothers Aidan and Brody are sitting at the table. They glance at us. The same helplessness I feel is reflected in their expressions. They try to cover it, but it's obvious.

I pull a chair out and motion for Bridget to sit. I ask her, "What sounds good?"

She stays silent, pleading with her eyes for me to drop it.

I'm not going to. She's eating, or I'm calling the doctor, and she knows it. I pick up a plate and put some eggs, toast, and fruit on it. "Here, dolcezza. Try some."

Silence fills the air. I stroke her back, softly pleading, "Take a bite."

She caves, picks up her fork, and eats a bite of scrambled egg.

"Good girl." I kiss her on the side of her head. Aidan slides a plate at me, full of bacon, eggs, and toast.

"The O'Malleys and Ivanovs will be here soon," Brody states.

I hold Bridget's toast to her lips. She takes a bite. Satisfied she's eating, I shove a forkful of eggs in my mouth. I exchange a tense gaze with Aidan and Brody. Liam called the night before. He stated they found something, and they were flying in this morning.

"Why are they coming here? Did they find something out?" Bridget asks, and all the anxiety she always exhibits when she worries about the kids' safety reignites on her face.

I slide my arm around her shoulder. "I'm not sure what they discovered. As soon as I find out, I'll let you know."

"It'll be nice to see the O'Malleys again. How long has it been?" Brody questions.

Bridget tilts her head, pinning her gaze on him. "Sean's funeral."

Silence fills the air until Aidan's phone vibrates. He glances at it then rises. "They're here."

Nora walks into the room. She chirps, "Morning. Everyone's here."

Relief fills me. "Morning. So we hear. Can you give me a moment with Bridget?"

She smiles. "Sure."

Bridget's brothers and Nora leave the room. I turn Bridget's chin toward me. "The therapist comes at ten. I'll make sure I'm free."

She exhales and rolls her eyes. "I don't need a therapist."

"We aren't fighting about this. If you want me there with you—"

"No." She shakes her head.

I study her and finally ask, "Are you sure you don't want me there?"

She closes her eyes and takes a few deep breaths before drilling her gaze into mine. "I'm sure."

Reluctantly, I reply, "Okay. If you change your mind—"

"I won't."

Another few minutes pass.

She motions toward the door. "You should go."

I stroke her cheek. "Keep eating. I'm making Nora give me a full report."

She gives me a defiant stare.

I chuckle, rise, and bend down to kiss her on the lips. "Glad to see you're still stubborn."

For the first time in days, her lips crack into a smile. She sings, "Not as much as you."

My grin widens. "But you love it." I wink, kiss her again, then leave the room. I tell Nora to make sure she eats then go to Tully's office.

Liam and Declan O'Malley and Maksim and Obrecht Ivanov exchange hellos with me. Everyone gathers around Tully's conference table, then Obrecht pulls a stack of photographs out of his bag. He says in his thick Russian accent, "I think I found two of them."

My pulse races. As I glance at the photos, the rage I can't seem to escape beats into me so hard, I hold my breath. There are several photos of a man with a tattoo on his forearm. It's just as Bridget described—a wolf with a sword entering its mouth and fire coming out of it.

I sniff hard, clenching my fists at my side. "That has to be him. Who is he?"

"Anthony Rossi."

"Where is he?"

Obrecht's cold blue eyes match his voice. "Dead."

"You're sure?"

"We killed him in Gary, Indiana, at the strip club when we killed Lorenzo Rossi," Maksim seethes, his Russian accent thicker than normal and filled with hatred.

Obrecht stacks the photos in a pile. He puts three more down then points. "Here's your other guy."

My blood boils, staring at the man who's also a perfect match based on what Bridget described. He's got a scar on his neck running halfway up the left side of his face. I ask the same question, "Who and where is he?"

"Dead," Liam states.

I question, "How do you know?"

"His name was Tadgh Bailey. Nolan killed him the night we took most of them out."

"You're sure?"

"Yep. Look at this," Declan states, pounding his fingers on his laptop then turning the screen.

Surveillance footage of the city, with a body lying on the street, is on the screen. Declan hits a button, and it zooms in. There's no doubt it's the guy in Obrecht's photo.

Aidan steps next to me, peering closer. "Five down, one left. Any info on the last one?"

Obrecht tosses a photo on the table. "This guy. Liam found this photo in Niall's safe after he raided it yesterday."

My gut spins so fast, I clench the side of the table.

No.

It can't be.

I pick up the photo and study it closer. Two men are smoking cigars together. One is wearing a necklace. It has a crucifix with an emerald in the center of it.

"Dante, why do you look like you've seen a ghost?" Aidan asks.

I don't answer. I can't see past the anger snowballing in my gut.

Jesus. We let another traitor in our house.

I pick up my phone and swipe at the screen, my heart beating so hard, I think it's going to break my chest cavity.

Gianni answers, "Dante."

"Pick up Daniele. Strip him and chain him upside down."

The phone goes silent.

"Did you hear what I said?" I bark, my insides shaking over the fact that another one of our recruits is a traitor and how close he could have been to harming Bridget and the kids.

"Yeah. Want to tell me why?" Gianni asks, but I'm sure goose bumps are popping out on his arms just like mine.

"He's one of the six."

Dante

THERE ARE FOURTEEN MEN AND ONE PATHETIC, NAKED, bleeding, pissing-himself, begging-for-his-life piece of shit.

Bridget's four brothers, Tully, Liam and Declan, Obrecht and Maksim, along with me, my three brothers, and Papà, are all in the dungeon below my house. Before we left, I made Bridget confirm the three men, assuring her that two were dead and we already had custody of the third. I felt horrible leaving her after making her look at those photos. Nora was with her, but I still hesitated.

Bridget saw it then squared her shoulders. Fresh tears dripped down her cheeks, but she ordered, "Go. You kill him, Dante, or I will."

Papà and Tully have been drinking scotch and smoking cigars. It's a rare occasion Papà comes into the dungeon anymore. Yet, there was no question in my mind he would be joining us.

When we got here, Tully made the first move, slicing a line down the length of Daniele's dick then spitting on him. His screams filled the cell, but it was only the beginning. Papà made the second mark, cutting across his ass cheeks.

My brothers and the Ivanovs took a backseat, only assisting or handing more tools to Bridget's brothers or Liam when needed. Declan and I have stayed back. Images of his necklace asphyxiating my dolcezza burn in my mind. I'm wise enough to know, once I touch him, there's no holding back. His last breath will come from my hand.

But Declan has his own war raging in him. This piece of shit raped his sister-in-law but was also a part of his brother Sean's murder. The number of times we've assessed each other is too many to count.

From time to time, Maksim or Obrecht advise the O'Connors to change the angle of their knife or to use a different device. I knew the Ivanovs were skilled in torture, but even I've picked up some pointers.

Hours pass. Sweat covers our skin. The smoke from too many cigars and little ventilation stains the air. I hand Declan a tumbler of Jameson, and I take one of McCallan, nodding to him. We down the alcohol then step forward.

"Playtime's over," I declare.

Daniele screams as Aidan digs his eyeball out. When he has it in his hand, he spins and tosses it to Brody. "Keep that. I'm putting it in a jar."

"Well, that's not fair. Give me the other."

"Get it yourself," Aidan taunts.

Declan pats Brody on the back. "Sorry, lad. Time's up. Get it when he's dead."

"No fun," Brody claims and tosses the rest of his drink back.

I watch Declan study Daniele's bloody cock. He sniffs hard, and we exchange a glance. He states, "You know what I'm doing."

I pull out the gold chain Tristano found in Daniele's car. I wrap it around my hand and step in front of him. I dangle the crucifix in front of his remaining eye. My insides shake, but my voice is calm. "Remember how you used this on her?"

He winces.

"Ah. You do," I assert, my stomach diving from the thought. I lean forward, murmuring, "I'll see you with the devil. Until then, burn." I nod at Gianni, stepping back.

He takes a can of gas and pours it over Daniele's head.

Daniele shrieks louder than before as the liquid runs into all his cuts.

I wrap the necklace around his neck, looking at Declan.

He steps forward. Locking eyes, we both do our part. I remove all slack from the chain until Daniele is choking. Declan grabs his cock and, right before he blacks out, slices his dick in half.

In the few remaining moments, we all stay silent until there's no more struggle from Daniele. When only his corpse remains, I hang his necklace around him and order Massimo, "Take a picture."

He obeys and sends it to me.

Slowly, we all file out of the dungeon and shower.

On the way back to Tully's, Declan states, "Somehow doesn't feel like we gave him enough."

I meet his blue eyes. "Nothing would have ever been enough."

And it's not. I know in the depths of my soul, no matter what, nothing could ever make right what happened that night—not for Sean, and not for my dolcezza.

Bridget

Three Weeks Later

KILLIAN EMBRACES ME, SQUEEZING ME TIGHT, THEN KISSING me on the cheek. He locks his green eyes with mine. "How are you doing?"

While I'm relieved I no longer need to live in fear of Sean's murderers, who raped me, a part of me wishes I could go back to when no one knew what happened. My therapist is helping me, and I'm glad Dante made me get counseling. I'm working through the shame of my attack and guilt of dropping Sean off that night, but I still have a long way to go. I force a smile. "Better."

Killian hugs me again. "Good. Now, tell me how much you missed me."

I laugh, relieved to have the topic turned away from my well-being. "I missed you more than you'll ever know."

He wiggles his eyebrows. "Good answer."

"Killian." Dante's voice hits my ear. He puts a hand on my back and, with the other, shakes Killian's. "Flight okay?"

"Yep. It's hard traveling in a private jet, you know?"

I smile bigger, shaking my head. "Glad to see you haven't changed."

He shrugs then discloses, "Arianna gets irritated when I make comments about the private jet."

"How is my sister? Am I ever going to see her again, now that her business is up and running?" Dante asks.

Pride fills Killian's face. "She *is* busy, but she's here. She hired an assistant, and I convinced her to come. She's visiting with your papà."

"Ah. Good. I'm glad I'll get to see her."

Killian nods, then his smile falls. "So, are the kids here?"

My stomach dives. Killian and Dante convinced me to sit the kids down and talk to them about why I lied to them for years. I don't want to tell them the details of what happened to their father or me, but Killian and Dante think a bit of truth with their support would solve many issues.

Dante and I are also going to tell them about our relationship. I'm ready to stop hiding it from them, but I'm still unsure how they'll take it. They've only known me with their father. This is uncharted waters for them, and I don't want anything else to come between us. However, I can no longer keep my love for Dante a secret.

Every day, my future with Dante becomes clearer. I can't imagine moving forward without him. The love we have for each other only grows, and he's been my rock while I've been dealing with emotions I tried to bury for too many years.

Dante pulls me closer to him. "The kids are in the den with Tully."

My stomach flips, but I hold my chin higher.

Killian assesses me, cautiously asking, "Are you ready?"

I exhale. "Yes."

Dante gives me a peck on the lips. "Let me know when you're ready for me." He squeezes my hand.

"Okay." I square my shoulders and walk down the hall with Killian.

As soon as we step through the door, Fiona and Sean jump up.

"Uncle Killian! What are you doing here?" Fiona asks, tossing her arms around him.

He embraces her, chuckling. "Came to see if I need to knock any of your boyfriends around."

She pulls back, her face falling. "Not funny."

"I'm joking. Sean," Killian replies and hugs him.

"So? Why are you here?" Sean asks.

Killian points to the couches. "Let's sit down. Your mom, daideó, and I want to talk to you about some things."

Sean tilts his head, squinting his eyes. His voice turns firm. "Like what?"

"Sit," Killian orders, motioning again to the furniture.

Fiona and Sean sit on one couch. My dad and Killian sit on either side of me, on the larger sofa, across from the kids. They anxiously wait for us to speak.

I clear my throat then state, "I want to tell you why I lied to you for all those years."

Tense silence fills the air. Anger and surprise appear in both of their expressions. It makes my gut flip again.

Killian grabs my hand. "While we didn't know or understand why your mother made the choices she did, we now do. There's not one O'Malley upset with her. She did everything to protect you both, and it was courageous of her."

The kids both stare at Killian, avoiding my gaze. I wonder if I tell them what Killian, Dad, and I agreed on if it'll even make a difference.

"It has to do with your father's death," Dad blurts out.

Fiona blinks hard. Sean's jaw clenches. It's always been difficult for them to hear anyone mention their father's death. I suppose it will never get easier. Sean inquires, "What about it?"

I confess, "I was there."

The color drains from his face. Fiona's eyes widen.

My chest tightens, but I continue, afraid I'll not be able to go on if I don't. Killian squeezes my hand again, and I declare, "I won't go into all the details. Don't ever ask me to. But I was there. Your uncles Niall and Shamus were in bed with the Rossis and Baileys. There were six of them, including your uncles. They..." I stop, swallowing hard, closing my eyes to try and pull it together.

My father softly interjects, "They made your mother watch. Then they threatened to kill both of you and her, should she not leave Chicago. None of you were to ever return or see the O'Malleys again."

Sean sniffs hard, his eyes glistening. Fiona's tears freely fall.

I wipe my face. "I didn't want to do it. I... I felt like I had no choice."

Sean's voice cracks. "Why didn't you tell someone? Any of the O'Malleys could have helped, or Daideó."

Killian releases my hand and firmly replies, "No. We've all had traitors in our clans—men high up who we would have trusted to hunt down your father's killers. Your mother did the right thing. Over the years, numerous men we would have relied upon to help us seek revenge would have possibly gotten you all killed."

Moments of silence pass. My heart hurts as I watch emotions pass over my children's faces. Fiona finally meets her tear-filled eyes with mine. Fear fills her expression. She sniffles and asks, "So who is coming after us?"

I rise off the couch, sit between my kids, and pull her into my arms. "No one. They're all dead now."

"How do you know?" Sean asks.

I keep my arm locked around Fiona and circle my other around him. "Your uncles and Dante killed them all."

No one speaks for several more minutes. Sean sniffs hard, turning to me. Rage fills his voice. He speaks slowly, with his fists curling in his lap. "What did they do to Dad?"

I struggle to find my voice.

Killian answers for me. "We aren't going into details. What we do want you to know is that your mother did the right thing. She saved all of your lives. This resentment and anger you have toward her needs to end."

Sean's face turns red. His breathing picks up, and he looks at me again. "What did they do to you? While they made you watch?"

I blink fast, willing myself harder than ever before, not to cry.

"Mom?" Fiona whispers.

"They held me down and made me watch," I manage to get out, vowing that this will be the last time I don't fully tell my kids the truth.

Sean stares at me as if he doesn't fully believe me. Fiona takes a deep breath, and I'm not sure if she's buying it, either.

"Can we all agree to let the past be the past and move forward?" Killian asks.

The silence resumes as my pulse quickens. Maybe I was right, and my kids never will forgive me. I finally choke out,

"I'm sorry. I truly am. Please. You have to forgive me." My tears finally fall.

"You're lucky you have a mother who loves you so much she'll do anything to protect you," Killian declares. "Stop being stubborn."

Fiona throws her arms around me, sobbing. "I'm sorry, Mom. I-I wish I would have known what you went through."

I embrace her, relieved she's hugging me for the first time in what feels like forever. "It's okay, baby. I just want us to move forward."

She tightens her arms around me. "I know. Me, too."

I hug her for a long time until she pulls back. Anxiety reappears when I turn toward Sean. There's so much anger on his face. I'm scared it doesn't matter what he knows. He's never letting me back into his life. I beg, "Please, don't keep hating me."

He grinds his molars, reminding me of when his father used to do it. His fists stay clenched in his lap. He turns toward Dad and Killian, seething, "You should have let me kill them."

Dread fills me. I don't want my son to become a killer. I know Sean was, and the O'Malleys, my father, and Dante all are. I know it's in his blood to go into the clan, but it doesn't mean I want to accept it.

"You have everything going for you. Our world is not one any of us want you getting involved in," Killian declares, filling me with gratitude he's on the same page as me.

Sean's body stiffens. He straightens and sarcastically laughs. "I'm an O'Malley and O'Connor. No matter what name I legally have, both make it clear what my path is for my life."

"Not true. You have choices we didn't," Dad states.

"This isn't the time or place to discuss this, either. You're in high school and smart enough for college. The future of our clans isn't in the ways of the past. It's in using our brains, not fists. If you want to dedicate yourself to either clan, you should keep that in mind at all times," Killian reprimands.

Sean stares at him for a moment then turns back to me, asking again, "What did they do to you, Mom?"

I put my hand on his cheek. He's always been a protector, just like his father. But if he learns the truth, it's only going to destroy him. I lie again. "Nothing except what I told you. Now, please. Can we move forward?"

He takes several deep breaths then asks, "Can I change my name back to O'Malley?"

I nod and get up. I go to the bookshelf and pull a novel off of it. I take an envelope out of the book where I stashed it. I open it then hand a piece of paper to Sean and one to Fiona. "I already did."

Fiona cries some more, her tears dripping onto the paper. Sean reads it several times then finally throws his arms around me.

I laugh, hugging him. "Does this mean we're okay?"

"Yes. Thank you, Mom."

"You're welcome. I'm sorry, again."

He retreats. "Does this mean I can go to Chicago?"

"No! You're finishing school in New York!"

He holds his hands in the air. "I mean to visit."

I sigh. "Oh. Yes. Of course. We can plan a trip."

Killian rises. "Okay. Any more questions? Or can I send Dante in?"

"Dante is still here?" Sean asks.

My butterflies spread their wings again. "Yes. We have something to tell you."

Sean and Fiona exchange a glance.

"Why are you looking at your sister like that?" I ask.

"I'll get Dante," Dad says and moves toward the door.

"Is this where you tell us you're madly in love with him?" Fiona questions.

I gape at her.

"We aren't stupid, Mom," Sean asserts.

I refocus on him. "You-you both know we're dating?"

He shrugs. "It's kind of obvious."

"Why didn't you say anything?"

"So you could lie to us some more?" He arches his eyebrows.

Heat flares in my cheeks. I'm not sure what I would have done if they had asked me about Dante.

Sean rises, addressing Killian. "Can we skip the confession and get in the gym? Oh, and convince my mom to let me fight."

I stand and turn his cheek toward me. "You can fight. Thank Dante and Killian for that win."

Sean grins. "I can?"

I sigh, still worried. "Yes. But, please be careful."

He hugs me again. "Awesome. Thank you, Mom."

Killian tugs on Sean's shoulder. "Let's go. Show me your new skills."

"Wait!" I exclaim.

"What?" Killian asks.

My eyes dart between Sean and Fiona. "So you don't care I'm seeing Dante?"

"Why would we? We love Dante," Fiona responds.

"Nope. But if he doesn't treat you well, I'm going to kick his ass," Sean states then winks.

"You won't need to kick my ass." Dante's voice booms from the doorway.

"Hope not," Sean cockily states.

Killian steers him toward the door, asking Dante, "You joining us?"

"I'll be there in a minute."

"Fiona. You come, too. You can tell me about this new boy you're seeing."

She obeys, leaving the room with them.

Dante smirks, walking toward me. "Sounds like things went well?"

I smile, happy with the outcome, hoping things will someday be back to normal. "They did."

He slides his hands on my cheeks and holds his face above mine, his dark eyes studying me.

My flutters take off. No matter how much time passes, Dante still makes me weak-kneed.

"So, we're moving forward then?"

I nod. "Yeah."

"Focusing on the future?"

"Yes."

He kisses me then arrogantly smiles. "Does this mean I can stay the night and not hide?"

I reach up and lace my fingers around his neck. "I wouldn't have it any other way."

Dante

The Next Day

CARA STEPS OUT OF HER CAR AS I'M LEAVING BRIDGET'S. FIRE blazes from her eyes. She meets me halfway, seething, "Tell your brother to get out of my life."

I cringe inside. Still, I'll always have my brother's back where others are concerned. I sniff hard. "What's going on?"

"Uberto thinks I'm cheating on him with Gianni."

I cross my arms. Cara and Gianni have had such an on-again, off-again past that I wouldn't put it past them to hate fuck then deny it to whoever they're dating. "Why would he think that?"

Her eyes turn to slits. She tilts her head and jabs me in the pecs. "Stop playing dumb, Dante! You know everything Gianni does."

"No. I don't."

She huffs. "Like you two piss without the other one knowing."

"Cara, I don't know what's going on, so either get it off your chest or go inside. Bridget's waiting for you, and I've got shit to do today." I shift on my feet, trying to still be polite, but I'm not a fan of anyone poking me.

More rage fills her expression. "He went to Uberto's work."

The hairs on my arms rise. My brother has no business getting into any confrontations with an Abruzzo over a woman—especially one who has made it clear she wants nothing to do with him. I stay neutral, putting on a good face. Gianni and I are having words when I get home. I arch my eyebrows. "And?"

"And?" she snaps. "And he held a gun to his head, telling him I was his and if he saw me with him, he was going to shoot him."

My stomach dives. Gianni has officially lost it. I step closer to her and lower my voice. "I'll talk to him. But, Cara, what are you doing with an Abruzzo?"

"He's not an Abruzzo," she declares.

"You're wrong. He is," I insist.

"No. He's not. But if he were, I have nothing to do with your family wars."

"Don't be naive, Cara."

"I'm not an idiot. I know who I'm dating."

"Okay. Tell me what he does for a living," I demand.

"He's in the import business."

"Of what?" I question.

"Goods."

I snort. "You don't know. And you won't because he's into shit he'll never tell you. Be careful, Cara. I don't want to see you become a victim of the Abruzzos."

She groans, annoyed. "Talk to your brother. He needs to stop coming in and out of my life whenever he pleases." She pushes past me and stomps up the steps.

I close my eyes, take a few breaths, then get into my Porsche. I drive as fast as I can, getting to my house in record time. As soon as I storm through the door, I yell, "Gianni!"

He walks out of Papà's office. "What?"

I grab his shirt and drag him to the corner. "What the fuck are you doing?"

"What are you talking about?"

"Cara just told me you pulled a gun on Uberto?"

Gianni's lip curls. His eyes darken like they do right before he tortures or kills a man. "Damn straight, I did."

I move him farther down the hall, glancing behind me to make sure Papà doesn't hear, and lower my voice. "Are you crazy?"

"Stay out of my business," he warns.

"When you pull a gun on an Abruzzo, it's my business. It's all of our business," I declare.

"She isn't listening."

"She isn't yours to protect," I roar. If Cara doesn't want him, he needs to let her do what she wants. If she won't listen, that's her fault.

"She'll always be mine to protect," he snarls. "Now, stay out of my business, brother. I didn't interfere with you and Bridget. No matter what you've done, I've always had your back. Do me the same favor." He spins and walks away.

I lean my head back against the wall and close my eyes. If Papà finds out what Gianni did, he's going to go apeshit. And my brother keeps doing things that put the family at risk. He needs to let it go with Cara.

I go up to my suite, take a shower, and put my suit on. Then I get back in my car and drive to Ettore's shop. It's in Little Italy. I get there before it opens.

He lets me in and locks the door behind me. "Dante. It's all ready." He goes behind the counter, pulls out a ring box, and sets it down.

I open the lid and smile. It's perfect. The platinum, five-carat, flawless, round halo engagement ring sparkles in the light. Several rows of tiny diamonds circle it. I hold it up, saying, "You did good, Ettore."

He beams. "You picked a good gem."

I put the ring back in the box then shake his hand.

"Good luck," he offers.

"Yeah. Thanks." I leave the jewelers then spend the day trying not to think about my date with Bridget tonight, while I work.

At four, I take another shower, put on my tux, and have my driver take me to her house. When I walk up to the door, the nerves in my stomach escalate. I curse, ordering myself to pull it together, then double-check the ring is in my pocket. Since the guards know me well and I have clearance, I step inside just as Bridget walks down the staircase.

My breath hitches and my heart soars. She's stunning, as always, but tonight she's radiating happiness. Ever since yesterday, when she spoke with the kids, a weight has lifted off her shoulders. I can feel it, and the light I longed to see again is back in her eyes.

When she gets to the bottom of the stairs, I kiss her, then hold her hand in the air and twirl her. She's wearing an emerald-green, form-fitting, silk designer dress. It hits the middle of her calf. Her matching stilettos put her lips a few inches below mine. And she's wearing the sapphire necklace I gave her. My dick twitches, and I say, "You look gorgeous, my dolcezza."

She puts her hand on my shoulder, straightens my tie, and cocks her head. "You always did wear a tux well."

My grin grows. "Glad you approve. Are you wearing a coat?"

"No. It's getting warmer. I'll be okay."

I slide my arm around her waist and lead her toward the door, asking, "Did you tell the kids you won't be back tonight?"

"Yeah."

"Good." I guide her to the car, and once we're inside, she leans into my chest. I kiss the top of her head. "How many of these events have you been in charge of?"

She shrugs. "Enough."

"Well, I'm ready to see you in action." It's true. Bridget's the head of the fundraising committee for a human trafficking nonprofit. It's also something my family stays out of, which isn't typical for organized crime families. It's one of the few things we refuse to touch based on our morals. I've watched her from afar raise money, but this event has grown over the years, and it's because of Bridget's efforts. Now, I finally get to go with her.

She laughs. "I'm sure you'll be bored."

"Watching you run the show? Nope!"

She laughs. "At least there will be good scotch for you."

I trace her kneecap then palm it, turning my face so it's in front of hers. "This dress looks good on you."

"Thanks."

"It'll look even better sliding off you later tonight."

She wiggles her eyebrows then leans closer. "Maybe we should skip the event and go straight to your place?"

"Don't tempt me, dolcezza." I tug her onto my lap, fisting her hair and tugging her neck back.

Her breath hitches and her eyes widen with heat.

I study her face, taking in every feature while my stomach somersaults. I graze her lips with mine, and when she tries to slide her tongue into my mouth, I retreat, holding her an inch from my lips so she can't. "I think it's time you became my wife."

She inhales sharply, her lips curling. "Yeah?"

I slide my hand in my pocket and take out the ring. "Every day I spent without you has been torture. Not waking up with you in my arms is Hell on Earth. If you marry me, I promise I'll cherish and protect you until the day I die. When you become mine, every part of me will become yours to do what you want with—to love or destroy. I'm giving all the power to you, Bridge, because I'm a desperate man. Without you, I have no life, no happiness, no soul. And I need you. I always have. All these years, I've needed you more than you ever needed me. I still do. So, will you give me the only thing I've ever wanted, and marry me?"

A tear drips down her cheek. She nods. "Yes."

"You will?" I ask, in shock I'm finally getting what I've wanted all these years.

"Yes."

"Say it again," I order, not able to contain my grin.

"Yes," she says on a laugh.

I kiss her. Slow at first to savor every part of her then deeper and deeper, unable to control my desire for her.

That's the thing about Bridget O'Connor. She got into my heart without me knowing it. No matter how many years passed or how hard I tried to shake her, I never could.

Our road may not have been easy up to this point, but we made it. And I'll be damned if anyone or anything comes between us ever again.

I hold her face. "I always knew that you were the one meant to be beside me. Are you ready to be Queen of the Marinos?"

She strokes my cheek, the light I love glowing brighter in her blueish-green eyes. "I'm ready to be wherever you are and whatever you need."

"The only thing I'll ever need is you by my side, dolcezza." It's the biggest admission I've ever spoken, and I'll die with it still ringing true.

EPILOGUE

Dante

A Month Later

"You look beautiful, Bridget," Papà declares, embracing my dolcezza and kissing her on the cheek.

She hugs him back, glowing with happiness. Pride fills me, knowing she's only a few months away from being Mrs. Dante Marino. She replies, "Thank you, Angelo."

The house is bustling with last-minute preparations. Papà is throwing another one of his huge parties, but this time, it's to celebrate our engagement. All the O'Malleys and Ivanovs, along with the O'Connors, will be here. Arianna planned the entire party, just like she still plans Papà's monthly ones, but Fiona helped her. They decided to make the theme of the party an Irish and Italian mix.

I glide my hand across the silk of Bridget's royal-blue dress, covering her ass. She leans closer to me, and I don't miss the soft inhale of her breath.

It makes me hard as nails, which isn't new. The intensity of how much I want my dolcezza never seems to fade. It only grows more potent, driving me crazy even when I'm not around her.

She tilts her head, glancing up at me. In a low voice, she murmurs, "Did you get me what I requested?"

My butterflies spread their wings in anticipation and a bit of nerves. Ever since I learned what those thugs did to her, I haven't restrained her or put anything around her neck, including my hand.

Last week, we talked about it, and Bridget told me she not only wanted it but needed me to do it again. While I've been dying to repeat it, I expressed my concerns. I'd rather kill myself than ever hurt her. Yet, no matter what I disclosed to her about my fears, she kept pushing me to do it.

Bridget confessed she spoke to her therapist about why she loved it so much with me when she experienced such a traumatic incident. We met with the therapist a few days ago and discussed this in depth. While I'm still a bit hesitant, Bridget wouldn't keep insisting if she didn't want it.

I brush my lips to her ear, taking a quick lick of her lobe, and she shudders. Softly chuckling, I state, "I got it. And when I use it on you, that sweet pussy of yours is going to attempt to break my cock."

"Oh God," she whispers, grabbing my thigh.

My dick hardens further. I fist her hair and tug her head then kiss her like she's my possession.

But she is.

I'm hers, and she's mine.

Nothing has ever felt more right in my life.

"Dante!" Massimo barks behind me.

I sigh and release Bridget. "Don't go anywhere."

"We could ditch the party...?" She raises her eyebrows.

"Dante!" Massimo growls again.

"Don't tempt me, dolcezza." I kiss her on the lips and spin to face my brother. My face falls, and my gut churns. "What's wrong?"

"Not here." He storms into the hallway and doesn't stop until we're in the library.

I shut the door. "This better be good. If you haven't noticed, this is my—"

More rage darkens his blue orbs. "Are you oblivious to the fact Gianni isn't here?"

Every nerve in my body turns cold. "No. Where is he?"

Massimo sniffs hard, his nostrils flaring. "That bastard, Uberto, put Cara up in his auction."

The blood drains from my head down to my toes. Through clenched teeth, I repeat, "Where is Gianni?"

Massimo's face hardens. "He went to buy her."

418

I hope you loved Toxic! Want to read one last steamy scene with Dante and Bridget? Click here for your freebie chapter!

If freebie chapters aren't your cup of tea, then go right into IMMORAL - BOOK TWO OF MAFIA WARS New York!

TOXIC - FREEBIE STEAMY SCENE

Can't get enough of Dante and Bridget? Want to see one last super steamy scene? Download this bonus scene for one more hot read! Click here!

If you're on a paperback go to: https://dl. bookfunnel.com/xzvy970e4u

If you have any issues downloading this, please contact pa4maggie@gmail.com.

Come back when you're done to find out what's happening with Gianni and Cara in Immoral, book two in Mafia Wars New York!

My ex bought me at an auction and forced me to marry him.

He said it was for my protection.

All I can think is he had it all planned.

Because what Gianni Marino wants, he gets—everything, except for me.

I won't forget how his broken promises left me scarred.

So this time, I'm determined not to give in to the temptation, no matter what he vows.

I only wish my skin wouldn't sizzle under his touch, or my heart wouldn't pound out of my chest from his irresistible grin.

Most of all, I long to believe in him…in us, again.

Each time our enemy tries to hurt me, Gianni saves me, making his promises more believable.

If only I could trust him.

READ IMMORAL - BOOK TWO OF MAFIA WARS New York!

CARA SERRANO
IMMORAL PROLOGUE

M C

Cara Serrano

HAMMERS POUND INTO MY SKULL. MY THROAT FEELS RAW, almost as if it has cracks in it from a lack of water. I attempt to open my eyes, but my head spins.

I squeeze my lids, trying to make it stop.

What happened?

Where am I?

Slowly, the last thing I remember flashes through my mind in pieces.

Uberto was screaming at me about Gianni. I insisted nothing was going on between us, but Uberto wouldn't believe me. I couldn't blame him. Gianni wouldn't stay away, and he not only warned me to break up with Uberto but threatened him, too.

Gianni's face pops into my thoughts. My pulse increases, and I curse myself for the millionth time. No matter how much I try to convince myself I'm no longer attracted to him, I fail. Time has only made him sexier, which I never thought would be possible. He's taken excellent care of himself, maintaining a ripped physique any male on Earth would envy. It complements the gray streaks in his hair and tiny lines around his eyes that only serve to enhance his dominant aura.

Stop thinking of him. Focus!

I lick my lips, wondering why my mouth is so dry and my head hurts so badly. I reprimand myself again and concentrate on my foggy memories, but all I remember is Uberto and how scared he made me. I'd never seen him so angry. I tried to leave, but he wouldn't let me. And then I remember him forcing me to the kitchen and jabbing something sharp into my leg. After that, everything turned black.

Rage fills me as I realize he must have drugged me. Then hurt replaces the rage, followed by horror. I squeeze my eyes tighter, holding in tears. Was Gianni right all this time? Is it possible he wasn't just jealous and trying to ruin my love life?

That would be a first.

Several moments pass before I can push my emotions away. I need to figure out where I am and get out of here. Slowly, I open my eyes. Gray darkness surrounds me. As my vision adjusts, sounds hit my ears. I shudder as other women, all naked and lying on the concrete floor, become visible. I look down at my unclothed body, and a new fear shoots through me.

A shrill sound pierces through the air. The faint outline of three men appears as they step through a metal door. I sit up and hug my knees, trying to cover and protect myself.

One of the men stomps toward me. I recoil, looking at the ground, praying he isn't coming for me, shaking from the sudden cold air and fear. But then I see his shoes—shiny, designer Italian loafers. I smell the musk of his cologne, and I know who it is.

Uberto.

How could I not have seen he was evil?

Why did I not listen to Gianni's warnings?

What is he going to do to me?

He crouches in front of me and grabs my chin, yanking it so I'm facing him. My lips tremble, and tears escape my orbs, sliding quickly down my cheeks. He digs his fingers into my skin. His stale breath reminds me of someone who's been drinking for hours. The red in his eyes confirms my theory. His voice is an angry calm. "You were doing so well, Cara."

I stare at him, unsure what he means.

He leans closer. I attempt to retreat, but he holds me firm. His lips hit my ear, and I tremble harder as he states, "Since you're a whore, you get to live the rest of your days as one."

Words get stuck in my throat. I don't know all the details of what he means. Something tells me I don't want to find out.

He lodges his fingers deeper into my chin. I wince, and he grunts. "You should have thought twice before betraying me with a Marino." He releases me and stands.

I grab his leg. "Uberto! Please! I never—"

"Shut up!" he screams then tugs his leg back and leaves.

"Uberto!" I call after him, but my voice is weak from whatever drug he gave me.

Another man comes over and yanks me off the ground. My mind says to fight, but my body still lacks the strength. He leads me to a wall where other women are huddled together. Before I can figure out what is happening, cold water forcefully gushes over me.

I shriek, along with the other women.

Everything becomes a blur. I'm ordered to shampoo and condition my hair, wash my body, and dry off. The men lead us to a changing room where another group of women is waiting.

These women aren't naked. I beg them to help me, but they avoid making eye contact. One of them blow dries and styles my hair. She puts more makeup on me than I'm used to wearing. One of the men orders me to put on a pair of stilettos. He fastens a collar with a leash around my neck and shoves me out of the room.

I go through the same door Uberto went through. The man forces me up the stairs and down a long hallway. The sound of men talking and laughing fills my ears. Cigar smoke wafts in my nostrils. We stop in front of a curtain. He fists my hair and tugs it so harshly, pain flares through my neck.

"Ow!" I blurt out.

He points a gun at my head and snarls, "Go on stage. When you're ordered to turn, you obey. Whatever you're told to do, you do. Understand?"

My pulse races so fast I get dizzy. I don't reply.

"Answer me," he barks.

I jump. "Y-yes."

He separates the curtain and pushes me forward.

The lights are bright. I stop, blinking to focus my vision.

He growls, "Move to the X!"

I take a few steps and stand on the taped X. When I look up, I'm horrified. The room is full of men sitting around, drinking alcohol, and smoking. Some of the men have naked women on their laps. Scared expressions stare back at me. The same type of collar I have on wraps around their necks.

I cover my breasts and lower body, but there's no hiding. A man in an expensive-looking suit stands several feet from me. He holds a microphone and orders, "Raise your arms to the side."

I freeze.

He steps closer and reiterates the same thing, only this time, there's a warning in his voice. "Raise your arms to the side."

His demeanor scares me, so I do what he says. Tears fall fast and drip on the floor.

"Cara Serrano. Forty-one. Educated in New York. Spent quite a while in Europe. Speaks several languages," he rattles off.

My heart beats harder against my chest cavity. My knees wobble, but my situation only gets worse.

"Starting bid, $100,000," he proclaims then demands, "Spin."

Unsure what to do, still foggy from whatever Uberto drugged me with, and not wanting to get killed, I turn around.

Men start shouting out numbers. I squeeze my eyes shut, wanting all of this to be over, wishing I had listened to Gianni and stayed away from Uberto when I had the chance.

The announcer slaps my ass, and I jump. He orders, "Bend over and grab your ankles."

Humiliated, I obey.

More numbers get shouted into the air until someone yells, "Ten million."

The room turns silent. Blood pounds so hard against my ears, I wonder if they can all hear it.

"Going once. Going twice. Sold."

The room erupts in applause. A dark-haired man with a scar across his cheek comes on stage, grabs me by the shoulder, and steers me through the curtain. I'm still weak from the drugs, but I try to push away from him.

"Stop fighting me, or you'll make it worse for yourself," he warns.

"Please," I plead, but he doesn't even acknowledge it.

He takes off his suit coat, puts it around me, then opens a door.

Cold air rushes inside, slapping my nearly naked self. Everything is dark, minus the outline of an SUV. I try to fight again, but the man pushes me toward it then opens the back door. Before I can process anything, another man inside tugs me in and over his lap.

I scream, but it falls on deaf ears. The slamming of doors ricochets through the air before the car starts moving. I try to sit up, but whoever has me over his lap won't release me.

Then I hear his voice and freeze. The fight in me changes into a new one.

I'm no longer fighting for my life.

This is a fight for my heart.

READ IMMORAL - BOOK TWO OF MAFIA WARS New York!

READY TO BINGE THE ORIGINAL
MAFIA WARS SERIES? GET TO KNOW
THE IVANOVS AND O'MALLEYS!

He's a Ruthless Stranger. One I can't see, only feel, thanks to my friends who make a deal with him on my behalf.

No names. No personal details. No face to etch into my mind.

Just him, me, and an expensive silk tie.

What happens in Vegas is supposed to stay in Vegas.

He warns me he's full of danger.

I never see that side of him. All I experience is his Russian accent, delicious scent, and touch that lights me on fire.

One incredible night turns into two. Then we go our separate ways.

But fate doesn't keep us apart. When I run into my stranger back in Chicago, I know it's him, even if I've never seen his icy blue eyes before.

Our craving is hotter than Vegas. But he never lied.

He's a ruthless man...

"Ruthless Stranger" is the jaw-dropping first installment of the "Mafia Wars" series. It's an interconnecting, stand-alone Dark Mafia Romance, guaranteed to have an HEA.

Ready for Maksim's story? Click here for Ruthless Stranger, book one of the jaw dropping spinoff series, Mafia Wars!

ALL IN BOXSET

Three page-turning, interconnected stand-alone romance novels with HEA's!! Get ready to fall in love with the characters. Billionaires. Professional athletes. New York City. Twist, turns, and danger lurking everywhere. The only option for these couples is to go ALL IN...with a little help from their friends. EXTRA STEAM INCLUDED!

Grab it now! READ FREE IN KINDLE UNLIMITED!

CAN I ASK YOU A HUGE FAVOR?

Would you be willing to leave me a review?

I would be forever grateful as one positive review on Amazon is like buying the book a hundred times! Reader support is the lifeblood for Indie authors and provides us the feedback we need to give readers what they want in future stories!

Your positive review means the world to me! So thank you from the bottom of my heart!

CLICK TO REVIEW

MORE BY MAGGIE COLE

Mafia Wars New York - A Dark Mafia Series (Series Six)

Toxic (Dante's Story) - Book One

Immoral (Gianni's Story) - Book Two

Crazed (Massimo's Story) - Book Three

Lethal (Tristano's Story) - Book Four

Mafia Wars - A Dark Mafia Series (Series Five)

Ruthless Stranger (Maksim's Story) - Book One

Broken Fighter (Boris's Story) - Book Two

Cruel Enforcer (Sergey's Story) - Book Three

Vicious Protector (Adrian's Story) - Book Four

Savage Tracker (Obrecht's Story) - Book Five

Unchosen Ruler (Liam's Story) - Book Six

Perfect Sinner (Nolan's Story) - Book Seven

Brutal Defender (Killian's Story) - Book Eight

Deviant Hacker (Declan's Story) - Book Nine

Relentless Hunter (Finn's Story) - Book Ten

Behind Closed Doors (Series Four - Former Military Now International Rescue Alpha Studs)

Depths of Destruction - Book One

Marks of Rebellion - Book Two

Haze of Obedience - Book Three

Cavern of Silence - Book Four

Stains of Desire - Book Five

Risks of Temptation - Book Six

Together We Stand Series (Series Three - Family Saga)

Kiss of Redemption- Book One

Sins of Justice - Book Two

Acts of Manipulation - Book Three

Web of Betrayal - Book Four

Masks of Devotion - Book Five

Roots of Vengeance - Book Six

It's Complicated Series (Series Two - Chicago Billionaires)

Crossing the Line - Book One

Don't Forget Me - Book Two

Committed to You - Book Three

More Than Paper - Book Four

Sins of the Father - Book Five

Wrapped In Perfection - Book Six

All In Series (Series One - New York Billionaires)

The Rule - Book One

The Secret - Book Two

The Crime - Book Three

The Lie - Book Four

The Trap - Book Five

The Gamble - Book Six

STAND ALONE NOVELLA

JUDGE ME NOT - A Billionaire Single Mom Christmas Novella

Made in the USA
Middletown, DE
28 April 2022